Black Bats 2:

It's all gone tits up

By

Ochil Kinnaird

Published by: OK 62 Publishing January 2017

Copyright © Ochil Kinnaird 2017

Second Edition

The author asserts the moral right under the Copyright, Designs and Patents Act 1988 to be identified as the author of this work.

All Rights reserved. No part of this publication may be reproduced, stored in a retrieval system or transmitted, in any form or by any means without the prior consent of the author, nor be otherwise circulated in any form of binding or cover other than that which it is published and without a similar condition being imposed on the subsequent purchaser.

ISBN: 978-0-9934469-9-3

Cover& Layout Designed by OK62 Publishing

Also available from the same Author:
Black Bats: 1% / 13
Black Bats 3: Is it really over?
Black Bats 4: Freed but not Free!
Born Racer … It's a way of Life!
There & Back
A Deadly Hobby (Taken too far!)
A Secret No More

Visit WWW.OCHILKINNAIRD.ORG
for more information and where to buy.
-www.OK62Publishing.co.uk-
Self-publishing packages available

Preface

The contents of this book are loosely based on actual events, therefore the names and places have had to be changed (yet again) to protect not only the 'guilty' but others, who for some reason, managed to get themselves involved in the lives of the Bats through association!

Chapter 1

The door banged and banged and I could hear Rooster shouting my name through the letterbox, but I just lay in bed staring at the ceiling and, eventually, the banging stopped. I think that must have been about the twentieth time someone had been at the door. I knew that I'd need to open it eventually, but right now I just wished that they would all fuck off and leave me alone. I had no idea what I'd say to anyone and I had no interest in hearing what anybody wanted to say to me, so my plan was to hide away until I decided what I was going to do.

I'd been in the flat on my own for nearly 3 days, but it felt like it had only been 3 hours. I knew that I needed to give myself a bit of a shake and that the police would want to talk to me about the accident, but I felt I still needed time to get my head around it all.

I got up, wandered through to the kitchen, opened the fridge and realised that today would be the day I needed to go out as I had absolutely nothing to eat or drink left in the flat.

I poured myself a glass of water and sat on the sofa. I picked up my cigarettes, opened the packet and looked at it, shit, it was empty. I crushed the packet in my hand and threw it against the wall. I could hear myself shouting: "Fuck, fuck, fuck", but then I remembered Malky had always kept a packet in his drawer in the bedroom.

I went and checked. Yep, good old Malk! He always said that he hated running out of fags because it always happened when the shops were closed. I lifted them out of the drawer, smiling away to myself. I opened the packet and saw there were about 6 left. I lit one up, headed back into the living room and slumped down onto the sofa.

I heard the door being knocked again, but this time it was much more of a soft knocking sound rather than the loud banging I'd been getting used to. I then heard the letterbox being opened and something being pushed through.

Then a voice said: "I hope you're okay, Ochil. I've left you a note about Malcolm's funeral. If you want to talk: you know where we are." Fuck, it was Malky's mum. I swear my heart missed a beat. I couldn't believe she would have taken the time to come and see how I was, especially when it was me who'd got Malky killed. If it wasn't for me getting him involved with the bikes, he'd still be here.

I could feel myself welling up and the tears started rolling down my cheeks yet again. I waited until she'd left then picked up the envelope and opened it. There was a note inside written by Malky's mum:

Dear Ochil,

I know you will be blaming yourself for what happened to Malcolm, but please don't. Malcolm was always at his happiest when you were both together. When you bought him his first motorbike for his birthday it was the most excited we had ever seen him. I know he's gone now and we all miss him very much, but we always need to remember the good times we had with him.

Please don't waste your life feeling sad because I know that would really upset him. You now have to live your life to the fullest, not only for yourself, but for the both of you. Please remember, anytime you need us, we will always be here for you. The funeral is on Friday and I hope you can make it. The family car will be leaving from our house at 10am and we would all like you to travel with us.

Hopefully, we'll see you then.
Beth

I read the note about 3 times, tears still rolling down my cheeks, but I didn't really know how I felt about it. On one hand, I was relieved that they didn't blame me. But on the other, I knew that if I hadn't got him involved then he'd still be here. I decided at that point that I needed to give myself a shake. I thought that if Malky's mum could take the time to visit me then the least I could do is get a grip of myself.

The first thing I did was write a note, thanking Malky's mum for coming to see me and to tell her I would be at the funeral. I decided I needed to go out to the shop and thought I could slip it through her letterbox on the way back home. I stuffed it into my leather jacket then had a bath, cleaned myself up and headed out to get some provisions. After getting what I needed, I went to Malky's and slipped the note through the letterbox without being noticed, then quickly headed home.

I bumped into Mark on the landing and he told me he was sorry about Malk and asked how I was. I just told him I was fine and thanked him for his kind words then went straight into the flat. I closed the door and locked it behind me. By now I was breathing really heavily, and felt like I was having some kind of palpitations. I quickly dumped the shopping in the kitchen then sat on the sofa. I started breathing through my nose, slowly inhaling large breaths and then slowly exhaling until my lungs were empty. I could feel the palpitations starting to ease and I started to relax a bit.

Bumping into Mark had made me fearful of speaking to anyone else. I hadn't thought that I was ready to face anyone yet and seeing Mark just confirmed it to me. After I got my breathing back to normal, I got up and put away my shopping then stuck the kettle on and lit up a fag. While I waited on the kettle boiling, I stared out the window and watched the people outside just going about their business, all oblivious to the pain other people, like myself, were feeling.

It's one of those things you never ever think about, you just always think everyone's doing okay. It's only when something happens to you that you wonder if anyone else is feeling as miserable as you are. Just as the kettle clicked, I heard a sound like the front door getting smashed in. I immediately ran through to the hall, just in time to see Rooster, Provo and Stiff standing there and the door hanging off its hinges.

"What the fuck are you doing!" I screamed at them. "Look what you've done to my door, ya bunch of fuckin nut-jobs. I can't fuckin believe you just fuckin did that! What the fuck is wrong with you?" Rooster came towards me, grabbed a hold of me and started telling me to calm the fuck down. But, for some crazy reason, I punched him right in the mouth then grabbed a hold of him with the intention of giving him a proper kicking.

The next thing I know, I'm flat on my arse in the living room with the three of them on top of me and Rooster, again, telling me to calm down. However, this time he had his hand around my throat and the blood from his mouth was dripping on my face. "Shug, we're going to let you go now and you're going to get up and sit on the couch, aren't you!" he told me. I just nodded. "You're not going to try anything else now, are you?" he asked. I just shook my head. He then released his hand from my throat and they all got up. Rooster put his hand out to help me up and I took it. I stood up, gave Rooster a hug, apologised for hitting him and said sorry to Provo and Stiff. They all just nodded and sat down.

Rooster sat beside me and asked me how I was doing and I told him I had no idea. Stiff then interrupted, "We were worried about you, ya little cunt. Rooster's been to see you about 20 times and with you not answering, we thought you might have done something fuckin stupid." I thought I was hearing things when Stiff said they were worried about me. In all the time I'd known them that was the one thing I'd never heard any of them say to anyone.

"Did you think I'd topped myself or something?" I asked him. "Who knows what the fuck I thought. I know how tight you and Malky were and with what happened to him I wouldn't have put it past you to do something that fuckin stupid," he told me. "Anyway, now I know you're okay I can forget all about that shit."

"What's happening about the funeral?" Provo asked. I told him what Malky's mum had told me and he then asked me if I would go and speak to Malky's family and tell them that the Bats would organise the headstone. "Hang on a minute, Provo," I interrupted, "there's no way I'm going to tell Malky's dad that someone else is doing anything for Malky's funeral, especially not the Bats. He'll go fuckin mental." Provo then said something to me that took the feet from me.

"Okay, that's cool. I'll just pop round there and tell them myself. I just thought it would be better coming from you." "Whoa, whoa, hang on a fuckin minute, Provo. You can't just knock someone's door you've never met before and tell them you're going to buy the fuckin headstone for their son's grave! Fuck me, man, that's way out of order," I told him.

"Listen, you, ya little shit, Malky was a prospect for the Bats and that made him a brother, just like you, and he WILL be getting a Bats funeral and headstone whether you, his family or any other cunt likes it or not. It's what we do, without exception. So you can decide how you want this to play out, but just remember that it's happening, end of."

I had heard enough. I got up from the sofa, walked to the front door (which was hanging by half a hinge), opened it as best I could and asked them all to leave. None of them moved, they just continued talking amongst themselves. "Eh, what part of leave don't you fuckin understand?" I shouted at them. Rooster looked at me, told me to close the door over, stop being a dick and made it clear that no one was going anywhere.

I pushed the door into the space as best I could and went back into the living room. They were all sitting looking at me. I stood in the middle of the room, raging. "What is it that you fuckin want?" I asked them. "Just fuckin tell me what it is then please fuck off and leave me alone."

Rooster stood up, came over to where I was standing, looked straight at me and put his arms around me. He started whispering in my ear, "Shug, man, you're a Bat now and we're your family, that's why we're here. We know you're hurting. Fuck, we've all been there, you know that. So, come on, let us fuckin support you." He then cuddled me, gave me a few pats on the back then sat down.

I sat down as well. "Guys, I need to tell you something," I heard myself saying. The minute I said it, I wished I hadn't. I was looking at the three of them and they were all staring straight back at me. I could feel the sweat starting to run down the shuch of my arse. "Come on, Shug, spit it out," Provo said, still staring straight at me.

I coughed a bit, cleared my throat and started. "Well, it's like this: The day Malky died, I set fire to my originals, my steelies and my cut-off. I decided there and then that I was finished with the Bats and all the shit that goes with it. The lifestyle I was living died along with Malky, it just couldn't be the same doing it without him. So, for me, it's now a done deal." I didn't realise that while I was talking I'd been staring at the floor. It was only when I finished and looked up at them that I was conscious of it.

No one said anything for what seemed like an age. Provo and Stiff looked at each other then looked at me, then back again at each other. Rooster never took his eyes off me. I just looked around at everyone then sat back in the chair and closed my eyes. I had no idea what would happen next, but, if truth be told, I didn't really give a monkey's fuck, or so I thought. "Shug, listen to me, man." I heard Provo saying, so opened my eyes. Fuck, I nearly had a fuckin heart attack. He was standing over me, staring straight at me. He was such a fuckin intimidating sight at the best of times, but standing over you as your eyes open - Jeez, it makes you glad you've got a sphincter muscle!

"Listen, Shug, don't worry a fuck about the patch, we'll sort you out with another one. Everybody does crazy things when shit happens, we've all been there, man. Come on, let's get you back to the farm and get you sorted out," he told me, then stretched out his hand to lift me up.

"Didn't you hear me, Provo?" I could hear myself talking to him, but had no idea where the fuck it was coming from. "Provo, I've just told you, I'm finished with all this shit. There's no way back for me, man. It's over, everything's fuckin over for me now. I just can't fuckin do it so please go and leave me the fuck alone." "Shug, I hear you, man, but now it's your turn to listen to me and I suggest that you listen fuckin good. I know you're hurting, fuck, we all are, man. This isn't the first time we've lost a brother and I'm sure it won't be the last. It's the worst thing that can happen to a chapter and it affects us all in different ways, you don't have to be close to a brother for it to hurt. Remember, we've all lost a member of our family too, so stop wallowing like a prick in a pool of self-pity and get a fuckin grip of yourself. I'm going back to the farm with Stiff now, and you and Rooster are going to follow us. I'll sort you out with another patch when you get there. Right, now you and Rooster get the rest of your shit sorted out. Tonight you're going to party like a fuckin lunatic, along with the rest of us, in the name of our lost brother Malky."

With that, the two of them headed out. They moved my front door which was now flapping about in front of the space it used to cover. As I watched them leave I wanted to say something, but had no idea what. Stiff went across the hall and knocked at Mark's door. Provo turned around and shouted, "Oh, by the way, Shug, Mark will be fixing your front door. Remember, I'm expecting to see you later tonight; just make sure it's at the farm and not here!"

Chapter 2

They both disappeared out the close and I could hear them firing their bikes into life before blasting away. Just then, Mark appeared with his toolbox and got cracking on the door. Before he started, he just said: "Hi, guys, I'll close the hall door and let you two get on with your shit, this'll only take me 5 minutes."

Straightaway, I was on Rooster's case. "Why the fuck does Provo not listen to a word I'm fuckin telling him? I'm going fuckin nowhere tonight and he can do what the fuck he likes. I've told him twice already, I'm fuckin out. What the fuck's wrong with his ears? Are the fuckers painted on or something? I don't know why you're still here, Rooster. You can get your fuckin arse back to the farm and let him know I'm not coming and remind him I've already told him more than once the reasons why."

While I was ranting away, Rooster had lit up a couple of fags and handed me one. I didn't realise that I'd been pacing the floor, pointing and gesticulating throughout my rant. It was only when I started to choke, after inhaling too deeply, that I realised I was smoking. It stopped me in my tracks. I went into the kitchen, grabbed a glass of water and drank it until the coughing subsided. I cleared my throat and went back into the living room, just in time to see Rooster and Mark shaking hands and Rooster closing my newly repaired front door.

Rooster came back in and slumped on the couch. "Feeling any better after your fuckin rant then?" he asked. "How the fuck can I?" I told him. "Provo never listened to a fuckin word I said and now he expects me to go to a fuckin party! A party for a lost brother, a lost fuckin brother! It might only be a lost fuckin brother to him, one he didn't even fuckin like, by the way, but for me, he was my best mate." Rooster jumped up from the couch and interrupted me, he was almost in my face, and let rip, "Whoa, Shug, now you're well out of fuckin order. You better get a fuckin grip of yourself. I'm not listening to any more of this fuckin pish. All this self-pitying bullshit from you is getting right on my tits. You're not the only one fuckin hurting here and best you fuckin remember that. You WILL be going to the farm tonight, even if I have to knock you out and strap you to my fuckin bike - you'll be there." "Fuck you, Rooster," I roared at him. Then, for reasons I've yet to understand, I head-butted him flush in the nose, bursting it all over his face.

Much to my surprise, Rooster fell onto his knees, I think it was much more the shock that I'd done it rather than the power of the head-butt that dropped him. "I'm going fuckin nowhere and you can tell him that from me!" I screamed at him. He then quickly jumped up and punched me in the mouth, knocking one of my teeth out. As I started to fall, he followed it up with a few rapid to my face before I hit the ground. By the time I realised what was happening, I was kneeling on the floor holding my face, with blood running through my hands.

Rooster was standing over me and started roaring at me "Shug, you WILL be going tonight and you WILL fuckin enjoy yourself. We'll toast the memory of Malky and you WILL do it as a Bat. After that, as far as I'm concerned, you can do what the fuck you like cause I'm now past caring."

I made a beeline for him and caught him with a right hook which knocked him over. I then jumped on top of him and started laying into him. Rooster caught me with his elbow on my jaw, which stunned me a bit and totally stopped me in my tracks. The next thing I know, I'm lying on the floor with him on top of me and all I can taste is blood. Rooster went mental and set about me for what seemed like an eternity, calling me an arsehole and all sorts. He kept punching me and telling me I didn't know when I was well off. He eventually got off of me and sat on the floor with his back against the chair.

I was pretty dazed, not able to say anything or move too much, and I was hurting like hell. In my frenzy, I'd totally forgotten how tough Rooster actually was and, fuck, was I paying for it now. I was lying there, staring at the ceiling, thinking what a tit I was to hit him in the first place. I started dragging myself up from the floor, doing my best to lean my back against the couch.

I finally managed to get up and started wiping the blood from my face with my t-shirt. I looked over at Rooster and saw his face was pretty messed up as well. He lit up two fags then threw one over to me, which I gratefully accepted. "You punch like a fuckin pussy," he told me. "Well, I wish to fuck you did too," I replied, which made us both burst out laughing.

"Jeez oh, man, I should've remembered you used to fuckin box. I think you've broken some ribs, my nose and my fuckin jaw." "Well, my nose isn't too fuckin clever either with your stupid fuckin head-butting pish. Man, what the fuck's going on inside that crazy fuckin nut of yours?" Rooster demanded to know.

"Hey, man, I just can't get my head around the fact Malky's not here anymore," I told him, "and then that fuckin Provo telling me I had to party! That was the last straw. I just fuckin flipped and it just happened to be you that got it. I'm sorry, man, I was well out of order." "Hey, Shug, it's cool, you're fine. I'm just glad you decided to pick me to let it out on and not the other two. I don't think they would've been just so understanding."

"Understanding?" I said. "Tell you what, if that's you being understanding then thank fuck you weren't being serious!"

We both started laughing again, but straightaway, I stopped. I could hardly move my mouth, it was fuckin agony, and of course, this made Rooster laugh even more. Because he kept laughing, he was making me laugh with him. That's the worst kind of laughter, the one you don't want to do, but can't control. This was one of those times for me, I so wanted to stop because of the fuckin pain, but I couldn't.

We eventually stopped laughing, picked ourselves up and did the manly hug bit. I apologised again for being a dick, but Rooster told me to forget it. We both then decided that we'd better get ourselves cleaned up a bit. Rooster headed for the kitchen and I hit the bathroom. I washed my face with some warm water - fuck, even the water was hurting it. I cursed myself for being so stupid and for forgetting that Rooster couldn't half pack a punch or two. Standing there, staring in the mirror, it looked like I'd been run over by a truck: Black eyes, my nose all over my face and my jaw hanging every way, but the right way (and not for the first time either). I looked more closely at my jaw and it appeared to be a bit out of place. When I tried to open my mouth it was clicking a bit and very painful. It was so swollen that I wasn't sure if it was the swelling making it click or if it was actually bust.

I thought the best thing to do would be to leave it tonight and get it checked in the morning if it was still the same. I pulled off my t-shirt and threw it straight into the bin; there was no way it would clean up, considering the amount of blood that was on it. I grabbed another one from the bedroom and headed back through. Rooster had just finished cleaning himself up and was dabbing his face with a towel. "I think you've broken my nose, ya little cunt," he said, as he moved it around with his hand. "Aw well, I guess I'm the lucky one then. As you can see, I came out without a scratch," I reminded him. We both laughed again and I held onto my jaw.

We sat back down in the living room and lit up another fag. "You do know that you'll have to go to the farm tonight, don't you?" Rooster reminded me. I agreed with him "Yes, I know I do. I just wish I could find a way to get out of it; I really don't want to face anybody just yet. I'm not actually sure that I really want to see any of the guys ever again. I feel like that part of me, you know the one that loved it so much, isn't there now; it was always a joint thing. If truth be told, I just don't know if I'll ever get back into it."

Rooster then decided that he had a plan. "Here's what we'll do, Shug, we'll go and show face. I'll hang with you, fending off any shit that comes your way, and if you're not cool with what's going on you can make yourself throw up and I'll bring you home. What do you think of that?"

"Rooster, that's one of the dumbest fuckin plans I've ever heard, but I don't have anything better so I guess we best go with it. I don't plan to be there any more than an hour, though. I just want to be there long enough to satisfy Provo and Stiff then get the fuck out of there. Agreed?" "Agreed. Come on, let's get going, times moving on," he reminded me. "The quicker we get you there, the quicker we get you back." I just nodded, got up and headed into the bedroom to get my originals and steelies.

Then it dawned on me that I'd burned them all, along with my cut-off.

"Fuck, fuck, fuck," I heard myself shouting. Rooster came rushing into the bedroom thinking I'd hurt myself or something. "What's up, man?" he was asking as he entered. "I've just remembered that I burned all my gear and have fuck all to wear to the farm." Rooster then reminded me that Provo was getting me another patch. "All you need to do is shove on a pair of jeans and your leather jacket and we'll stop by my place and I'll get you a pair of my steelies, okay?" he asked. I just nodded in agreement, not really caring about it. "Great. That's it sorted then. Come on, let's go," he told me.

I just thought 'What the fuck' and did what I was told. We both headed downstairs to the bikes. I tried to put my helmet on without hurting my face and jaw, but it was impossible, there was no way I could tighten the chin strap so just let it hang.

Rooster pointed towards his bike, but I told him I would take mine. "Like fuck you will," he told me. "Remember the plan! How the fuck can I take you home if you've got your own bike? Duh!" As much as I wanted to, I never said anything else. I just jumped on the back and we headed for the farm, via his house. The closer we got, the more nervous and uncomfortable I became. My thoughts were all over the place: 'Fuck knows what everyone will be expecting of me', 'Should I put a brave face on things and do the party bit or should I be sombre and respect Malky's memory'.

I had no idea what to do, but I knew exactly how Malky would have dealt with it. He would have partied like fuck, shagged everything that walked and got fully loaded. He'd have taken everything he could get his hands on, passed out then started again the next day.

We turned off the main road and into the lane. Just as Rooster's headlight lit up the road, we saw Provo's and Stiff's bikes lying in the middle of the lane. Near the bikes, but just off the road, I could also see two bodies lying slumped together.

Straightaway, Rooster killed the engine and we jumped off the bike and ran over. It was Provo and Stiff! They were both unconscious and it looked like they'd both been stabbed a hundred times. Rooster told me to go to the farm and call an ambulance, saying he'd stay with the guys and try to bring them around. I blasted up the lane as fast as I could and almost crashed into the back door. I dropped Rooster's bike on the ground and burst into the kitchen screaming: "Somebody phone a fuckin ambulance! Provo and Stiff are fucked!"

There was no one in the kitchen and the music was blaring from both the conservatory and the big room so loudly that nobody could hear me. I kept running and burst into the conservatory, repeating my screams. Somebody immediately killed the music and within seconds there appeared to be about fifty people circled around me, demanding to know what the fuck was going on. "Has anybody phoned the fuckin ambulance yet!" I screamed.

"It's done. They're on their way," I heard Scooter shouting in the background, still with the phone in his hand. I started explaining what had happened and within seconds everybody was racing out the door, jumping on bikes and blasting up the lane. I ran out, picked up Rooster's bike and headed back up the lane too. By the time I got back to Rooster, some of the other guys were helping him with Provo and Stiff. Thankfully, someone was clever enough to grab a couple of blankets.

Stiff was mumbling away, but his speech was almost incoherent. Provo, on the other hand, was still unconscious and Rooster was applying pressure to one of his stomach wounds, which seemed to be almost spurting out blood. I could hear the ambulance sirens in the distance becoming louder and louder, this always gave me a feeling of relief and also of hope.

Looking around at everyone else, I could see lots of different emotions on people's faces, ranging from worry and sadness to rage and real, deep anger.

The ambulance and the police turned into the lane almost at the same time. Immediately, the medics jumped out and started working on Provo and Stiff. At the same time, the cops were trying to establish what had happened, but as usual, no one was saying a word, our eyes were on Provo and Stiff, and the work the medics were doing to them. Within ten minutes of them arriving, they had the guys in the ambulance and were on their way to the hospital. Rooster and Indie went in the ambulance with them and the rest of us followed behind on the bikes.

The police car led the way with its siren blaring. It was only when we were about halfway to the hospital that I realised that none of us had helmets on. When we arrived at the hospital, the ambulance was greeted at the door of the casualty unit by a couple of doctors, some nurses and a couple of porters. It was only then that it hit home just how serious they're condition must have been. By the time we parked up the bikes and got into casualty, Provo and Stiff had already been taken straight into operating theatres.

The police then decided it would be best for everyone if we were all removed ourselves from the casualty waiting room. They put us into a room which is normally used for pregnant women doing some sort of exercising shit or something. There were pictures all over the walls of pregnant people and loads of bean bags scattered over the floor. As they ushered us all in, I noticed there was already another couple of policemen in the room. One of the policemen who'd been with the ambulance tried to get everyone's attention and proceeded to inform us of what he expected would happen next.

Nobody really paid much attention to anything he said. The minute he finished talking, Rooster was in his face, asking him why the fuck we were forced into the room and why the fuck were they not out looking for the cunts that had done it. He then demanded to know what was happening with the guys. At the same time, Indie was having a bit of a pow-wow in one of the corners with half a dozen of the guys then they went to leave.

"Eh, where do you think you're going?" the policeman at the door asked them as they went to head out. "What the fuck's it got to do with you?" Scooter asked him. The policeman, who was young and just a bit naïve, then told Scooter and the guys to get a grip of themselves, sit the fuck down, shut the fuck up and wait until they were told they could leave. Without saying anything, Scooter butted him flush on the nose and dropped him like a stone.

The other officers then tried to grab him, but Indie told them to back off, which they did without protest. Indie explained to the pigs that the guys were heading back to the farm and that they should just be left to do that as tensions were running high, in light of what had happened earlier. The guys then left and the officers tended to their colleague with the broken nose. The four of us that were left then slumped onto the floor and lit up a smoke.

I asked Indie what was going on with the guys who'd left and he told me they were going to scout around and see if they could find out what had happened to Provo and Stiff.

Just then, a doctor came in and told us that Provo was pretty bashed up, but out of danger. However, Stiff was going to need an operation as one of his lungs had collapsed and was heading straight to surgery as he spoke. He told us we should all just go as no one would be able to see them until the next day. Indie thanked him then went to leave.

As we were about to go out the door, one of the policemen came over to us and said that he was willing to overlook the earlier incident with the officer as long as we promised to let them do their job and find the culprits without any interference. Indie just growled at him and said: "You're lucky we don't charge the bastard for threatening behaviour and harassment. Now fuck off and let me past!" With that, he brushed past him and we all left. At the door, Rooster turned to the officer with the busted nose and said: "Hey, big man, red's your colour, it really suits you," blew him a kiss and laughed.

As we left, the door was slammed shut behind us. We moved out to the car park, fired up the bikes and headed back to the farm. When we arrived, some of the guys' bikes were sitting outside. Indie skidded his bike to a halt and almost jumped from it, running straight into the farm. We all followed as quickly as we could, wondering why he was racing. I just got in as I heard him roaring, "You lot better have some fuckin news for me or a fuckin good excuse why you're not out looking for the bastards that done Provo and Stiff!"

Flick then told Indie that he got some info from a guy he knew who'd heard that some blokes had been boasting in the pub about wasting a couple of greasy bikers.

He then said: "I don't have much more detail, but when the blokes left the pub, my mate noticed that they fucked off in a gold Ford Escort with a mural on the bonnet. We've just this minute found out where that car is." Indie seemed to smile for a minute then asked if anyone knew the fucker who owned the car. Most of the guys agreed that they'd seen it around, but no one had any idea who owned it. Cowboy then piped up: "Hey, Indie, I've seen it a couple of times at Alfie Stone's bike shop. I remember going over to it and looking at the paint job."

"When was the last time you seen it there?" Indie demanded to know. "Not sure, but I think it was about a week or so before the fire," he told him.

Just then, another dozen or so guys came in. The only news they had was that someone had seen four cars sitting at the top of the lane with their lights out, about 15 minutes before Provo and Stiff got wasted. By now, most of the guys were back and everyone was looking to Indie, waiting for him to decide what would happen next. He told everyone that they would do nothing tonight. He would visit the hospital in the morning and see if the guys could remember anything about what happened, then they would sort out the bastards good and proper. With that, the discussion was over and most guys grabbed a beer and sat around chatting. I asked Rooster if he would take me back home, which he agreed to do.

We were walking through the kitchen, heading for the door, and Indie was getting a beer from the fridge. He turned and looked at us. "Where the fuck are you two going?" he asked. Rooster told him he was taking me home and would be back shortly. "Like fuck you are, the prospect stays. We've some serious shit to sort out here tomorrow and everyone stays, end of." Stupidly, I then tried to explain that I wasn't really involved anymore and that I needed to get back home.

Indie stared at me and said: "I'll pretend I didn't hear that. Now get the fuck into the conservatory and put on the patch Provo left for you. As for you ..." he said, looking at Rooster, "You should fuckin know better," he told him, looking straight at him, then shook his head as he walked out of the kitchen. Rooster then looked at me and said: "Thanks a fuckin lot, Shug.

Well done." "What!" I asked him, standing with my hands stretched out in front of me.

"What?" he said. "What the fuck do you think? Thanks a fuckin bunch. You made me look like a right dick there." "What the fuck did I do?" I asked him. "Oh, nothing, Shug, it's never you, always some other fucker to blame." "Hey, man, I'm really sorry you got grief from Indie, but how the fuck was I meant to know I wasn't allowed to leave?" "Surely you should've known that leaving wasn't on the cards, for fuck's sake." "I'm no fuckin mind reader," I told him, then reminded him that he had agreed to take me, which only got me a grunt in reply

Indie then gathered everyone in the conservatory and closed the doors. "Right, here's the plan: When I'm at the hospital tomorrow, I want everyone out and about. If that car moves, I want it followed. If you find out where the cunt that owns it lives, I want the house watched. If he meets anyone, if he goes to a shop, if he bumps into anyone - I want to know. I want us to meet back here at midday and have enough info to destroy every single part of his life. We're going to fucking waste him, his mates, his family and every fucker associated with him. When we're done with him, he'll wish he'd never heard of the Bats."

Indie got up to leave, picked up my patch and threw it at me. He then gave me a bit of a cold stare and left the conservatory. Everyone stood up. Most guys were growling and roaring. They were all looking forward to what the next day would bring. A few shook my hand and nodded, some gave me a playful punch. The guys closest to me gave me a bit of a hug.

Cowboy was last and was giving me a bit of a man hug when he whispered in my ear: "Don't fuck this up, Shug. Just go with the flow until this shit is sorted, then think about what next," he suggested, as he patted me on the back. I walked out and headed into the kitchen where Rooster was standing. As I approached him, he told me it was only the second time in his life that he felt he actually wanted to kill someone. I watched him as he opened the fridge and lifted a couple of beers out, the look in his eyes made me feel that he really actually did want to kill someone.

It brought a shiver down my spine, it made me see him in a different light. I think, for the first time, I saw a side of Rooster that was really scary, a side that made me think 'I know now why you're a Bat'. It seemed to be a common trait amongst all of the guys, that thing, whatever it was, that made them much scarier than your normal regular guy. He handed me a beer and asked me if I was okay. "Yeh, I'm fine, just thinking of Provo and Stiff," I lied through my teeth. "Come on, Shug, let's get fuckin wasted. Tomorrow's going to be a good one," he declared. We then raised our cans towards each other as a toast. Then Rooster said he was going to see Indie and that he'd be back in a minute.

I decided I needed a minute or so to myself so went outside and sat on the step and lit up a fag. I looked around and noticed there were bikes scattered all over the place. I could hear bikes being revved up in the barn and also some muffled sounds of laughter and shouting, it seemed most people were determined to enjoy the night and take tomorrow as it comes. For me, I couldn't get the thought out of my head of Provo and Stiff in hospital, and the real possibility that one or even both of them could die.

I worried about what the guys were going to do when they found the culprit and his cronies. I feared for what my role in the proceedings would need to be. I didn't want to be involved in such a heavy situation, but I knew I had no way of avoiding it. I looked out into the cool night air. I was reminding myself that I'd woken up that morning not as a Bat, but as a sad lonely guy, mourning the death of his best mate. I'd been feeling really sorry for myself before Beth's letter landed on the mat, but I'd quickly decided it was the catalyst I needed to give myself a shake.

12 hours later, here I was, back with the Bats. My door had been kicked in, my head busted by my mate, interviewed by the cops, Provo and Stiff critical in hospital and a bunch of fuckin nutters plotting their revenge! Oh, and me stuck right in the fuckin middle of it, just two days before my best mate's

funeral. I wondered, if I hadn't been moping about for the last few days, would this whole sorry set of events have been avoided, but I just shrugged my shoulders and decided that it would've happened anyway.

I was still daydreaming when a taxi arrived. The way it screeched to a halt brought me back to reality as I was hit with the stones, dirt and dust sprayed from its wheels. When the door opened, I couldn't believe it. Angel and Fiona half stepped, half fell out. The driver jumped out, helping Fiona out his side and I got hold of Angel. They were covered in blood and Angel's nose and eye looked like they were totally burst. I had to almost hold her up to prevent her from collapsing. "Holy shit, Angel! What the fuck happened to you?" I asked her. "Just get us the fuck inside and I'll tell you," she demanded, in a whispered voice that sounded like she was struggling even to speak.

We helped her and Fiona into the kitchen. I screamed for Indie to come. He casually walked in, wanting to know what all the fuckin screaming was about, until he saw Angel.

His demeanour changed instantly, he looked shocked and stunned. He knelt down beside her and she immediately cuddled him and started crying. I thanked the taxi driver for bringing them home. I asked him how much we owed him, but he wouldn't take anything, he just said: "I hope the girls are okay," then left. I shouted after him that we now owed him one, but he just raised his hand in a wave like manner, then disappeared out the door.

I turned back to Angel and saw Indie continuing to comfort her. He was telling her everything would be okay, that they would get her cleaned up and that he would look after her. She just continued holding him and sobbing loudly. I was trying my best to comfort Fiona as she was sobbing just as hard as Angel. Some of the girls who were at the farm got some water and towels and shit to clean them up. After about ten minutes, Fiona was able to talk. She started telling us that they were grabbed outside the pub and forced into a car by some blokes.

"We started telling them to fuck off and were screaming at them while we tried to kick and punch them, but they just started hitting us and pushed us into a car. They drove us to the lane and parked just opposite the entrance. They put tape around our wrists and over our mouths and told us to get ready to see a show. There were four cars and about ten guys altogether. When we stopped, six or seven of them got out, armed with bats, chains, knives and stuff. About twenty minutes later, Provo and Stiff came up the road and turned into the lane. That's when they knocked them off their bikes and started laying into them.

The guys pushed our heads against the window, making us watch, and kept telling us: 'that's what the bastards deserved' and 'that this was only the start. Soon the Bats would be no more'. After about ten minutes of them beating Provo and Stiff, they jumped back in the cars and raced away, taking us with them. A gold car stayed behind."

During the time Fiona was telling us what had happened, Angel was still sobbing uncontrollably into Indie's chest.

He asked Fiona what happened next and she told us that they'd driven them to the outskirts of the village and stopped the cars. They'd pulled them out and started touching them up, telling them they were going to have a gangbang and fuck the life out of them. They'd said they knew we were well used to being treated like scum, being 'black biker's slags'. One of the guys pulled Angel's knickers down and got his cock out while two others held on to her. Just before he could do anything to her, two police cars, with their sirens blaring, had come roaring up the road. When the guys saw this, they threw us to the ground, jumped in their cars and raced away. One of the guys had stuck his head out the car window and shouted: 'This is just the start, bitches, you're all fucked!' and as they drove away, all we could hear was him laughing loudly. Within a minute of them clearing off, the police cars were almost on us so we stepped onto the road to try and wave them down, but the bastards just flew past. Luckily, another car at the back of them, with a young bloke and a couple of girls in it, stopped and asked us if they could help. They gave us a lift back into the village and from there we got a taxi to bring us back to the farm.

Chapter 3

I looked at Indie cuddling Angel. He was shaking and staring like a madman; I thought he was going to explode. He asked the other girls to take Angel and Fiona up to one of the rooms. Before she went, he kissed Angel on the forehead and told her not to worry as he would sort everything. He stood up and calmly turned to head towards the conservatory and quietly told us all to follow. He sat down without saying a word and waited until everyone was in and the door was closed. He then got up and told us to go and get every brother in the chapter, without exception, and get them back here immediately. He said that any brother who didn't come had better be dead or dying and to make sure we were back within the hour. He then left the conservatory and headed into the office.

I looked at Rooster and he just nodded to me. I still hadn't put my colours back on so he lifted them from the table and threw them at me and watched me until I did. Again, we both nodded as we made our way out to the bike. The guys were all chatting outside, deciding who was going to see who. Rooster had five guys he was going to get. We blasted off up the lane, about sixteen bikes in total with around twenty guys on them. Even in such a serious situation I still couldn't help smiling, thinking that this was the most awesome feeling in the world.

As usual, my thoughts then came back to me and I considered my situation. 'What the fuck am I doing? Malky's getting buried in less than 48 hours and I'm heading out to round up brothers for what I'm guessing will be the biggest war the Bats have been involved in since I joined them.' I started to wrestle with my conscience and, not for the first time, a mixture of dilemmas raced through my mind: 'Should I be doing this? Should I make the break and disappear? Should I commit fully to the Bats?'

I could hear myself screaming inside my head. Just then, we came to a shuddering halt. I decided it best to forget my shit for now and go with the flow. Cowboy was right: Play this out then worry about it later. I got off the bike and asked Rooster who lived here. He told me it was a guy called Jelly. He said he was a Bat for ten years before his wife died of cancer and he'd had to dip out and look after his three kids. "Why are we here then?" I asked him. "Indie wants everyone, and you know the motto," he reminded me. "I've got five members, who are currently not active, to chase up, Jelly's the first."

Rooster knocked on the door and this small skinny guy answered the door. "Rooster," he said. "Jelly," replied Rooster. "Need you at the farm, man. Right now," he finished. "Give me half an hour, man," he said, then closed the door. Fuck, I didn't really understand that. Jelly never even asked why he had to come. I guessed he knew he had no choice or perhaps he totally was a 'Bat for life'. We jumped back on the bike and headed off. I was thinking about Jelly. I don't know why, but I had pictured someone called Jelly to be a huge fat guy covered in hair, not the small, frail person we'd just seen at the door.

Within five minutes, we were at another house and Rooster was knocking the door. A woman about forty answered it. The minute she saw Rooster, she said: "No, Rooster. Please, not now." "No choice, Mag. Need him out," he told her. "Please, Rooster, he's been clean for nine months, don't do this to us," she almost begged him. The next thing, a guy came to the door, behind the woman. He was much more what I'd expected Jelly to look like: a big bruiser of a bloke, short hair and a face full of fungus.

"Rooster," he said, nodding his head. "Hotwire, good to see you, man," Rooster replied. "Need you now, man, back at the farm," he told him. "Okay, be there shortly," he said, ushering the woman in and closing the door. As we got back on the bike, I asked Rooster what Hotwire's story was. He told me that he'd almost died three times of drug overdoses, spent about six months in the loony-bin, three months in rehab and had been out and clean for nine months. "Did he try to kill himself?" I asked. "No, did he fuck. He's just one of those guys that doesn't do anything by half and took way too much stuff, way too often. His old lady is trying to keep him on a short leash to keep him alive so he's been taking some time out from the Bats, but not tonight, he's needed."

'Fuck!' I thought to myself, 'Everyone's got a story to tell. You think you're the only one then you start to see the bigger picture. Sometimes it makes you feel a bit of a prick that you wallow in your own pish.' We knocked at another couple of doors and the response was the same, both guys telling us they would be at the farm within half an hour or so. At the final door we knocked, there was no reply. Rooster went around the back and I followed. In the back garden, there was a huge shed with no windows.

You could see from the bottom of the double doors there was a light on inside. Rooster rapped at the single door at the other side and walked in, with me following. "Hi, man, long time no see," Rooster said. The bloke he spoke to was crouched behind a bike, spannering away. "What's up, Rooster?" was all he said while he continued focusing on the bike. Rooster gave him the quick version of what was going on and at that point, he stood up, looked at me and nodded. I nodded back.

He was quite a small guy, around thirty, he had a silver tooth in the front of his mouth, something I'd never seen before. "You'll need to give me an hour or so and I'll be there. Okay?" he told Rooster. Rooster just nodded then turned and we both headed out of the shed. As I walked out, I saw his cut-off hanging up at the side of the door. It was a leather one and I clocked the name on it which I thought was very bizarre: 'The Reaper'. We jumped back on Rooster's bike and headed back to the farm. By the time we arrived back, there were over forty bikes scattered around. The barn door was open and the light was shining out into the cold night air.

After Rooster killed the engine, we could hear lots of noise from the barn. When we got off, I asked Rooster how the last guy we'd visited got his name. He just smiled and said: "It's a long story, remind me to tell it to you some time. Come on, let's hit the barn and see who's all here."

When we entered, I was completely taken aback. There must have been about 60 to 70 guys, all chatting, drinking, shaking hands and generally just catching up with each other.

But there was also a strange mood in the air, with a real eerie feel to it - all these guys in the one place, no laughing, shouting or carrying on - you just knew that something big was going to go down.

Rooster clocked someone he hadn't seen for ages and told me he was going to catch up with him. Before he did, he whispered in my ear, "I don't give a fuck what you do tonight, buddy, just make sure you stay here." I told him I was going nowhere and with that, he said: "Great," patted me on the back and headed across to the other side of the barn.

Cowboy must've seen me looking a bit lost and came over with a beer and a fag for me. "How you holding up, Bro?" he asked. "If I'm honest, I've no fuckin idea. With all this shit about Provo, Stiff and the girls, who knows where the fuck this is going to take me."

We sat together, almost in silence, watching all these people who were strangers to us coming into the barn. Almost all of them seemed to be getting a hero's welcome from one or other group of guys, with lots of back slapping and hugs going on.

After what seemed like an age for me, Indie arrived. He gestured to me and Cowboy and we went over to him. "You two, get outside. I want to know if the fuckin wind blows and don't move a fuckin inch from the door until I come out." He gestured for us to lift a baseball bat each and then ushered us out before pushing the large barn doors together. I looked at Cowboy and asked him why he thought we'd been pumped outside. He just shrugged his shoulders and suggested it was because I was a dick and that he needed to look after me, to which we both laughed.

I lit two fags up and handed one to Cowboy. We both then slumped to the ground with our backs against the barn doors. I asked Cowboy what he thought was coming next. He said he wasn't sure, but reckoned whatever was going to go down would be the biggest thing the Bats had ever done since he'd heard of them.

After about half an hour or so of us freezing our bollocks off outside, people started to pour out. Some headed to their bikes and the rest made their way into the farm. As Rooster came out, I asked him what the deal was and he said he would fill me in later.

Aaaggghhhh, fuck, he always says that to me. I'm sure he does it deliberately because he knows it always gets right on my tits. Just behind Rooster was Indie. He was talking to a couple of the guys that we'd visited earlier. They all shook hands before the guys headed towards their bikes. Indie then made a beeline for us.

"Anything stirring out here?" he asked. "Not a thing," Cowboy told him. "Thank fuck for that. I couldn't be arsed with any more shit tonight. I've told everyone to be here at Noon tomorrow: tooled up and ready to go. You two, make sure you're the same and don't be planning anything for the next couple of days."

"Indie, what about Malky's funeral, man? It's in two days time and I need to be there," I reminded him. "We'll all be there if we can, but right now there's much more at stake than attending a brother's funeral. Some bastard is trying to bring down the Bats and tomorrow they'll wish they'd never been fuckin born. Remember: here, Noon tomorrow, no excuses. With that we watched him almost run into the farm (something I had never seen Indie do). We guessed he was heading in to see how Angel was.

I asked Cowboy what he was doing tonight and he told me he was just planning to hang about at the farm. I told him I was doing the same, but that I wanted to go and check on Fiona. We both then headed into the farm and Cowboy grabbed a beer from the fridge. I went straight upstairs to see how Fiona was. I went into the room and there were a couple of girls in with her. She was sleeping so I just slumped on a chair. The girls decided to leave when I arrived and told me to give them a shout when she woke up. As they were leaving I told them quietly I would let them know when she came too.

I must've dozed off and woke with a start when I heard Fiona screaming. I jumped up, not knowing where I was or who I was with, but very quickly came to my senses when I saw Fiona wrestling around in the bed. I moved over to the bed to try to comfort her, but she was lashing out and screaming all sorts of shit. I grabbed hold of her and told her everything would be okay.

She then opened her eyes and realised who was with her and where she was. She cuddled me and began to cry. As she was sobbing, she was trying to apologise to me. I tried to reassure her that everything was cool. I lay on the bed beside her and eventually we both drifted off to sleep.

The next thing I know, there's screaming and shouting from downstairs, it sounded like there was a fuckin war going on beneath me. I jumped out of bed and ran down. The place was like a war zone. There was about twenty guys, all with baseball bats, running around, hitting everything that moved. I got to the bottom of the stairs and jumped on a guy's back. He was swinging a bat, but I still managed to knock him to the floor and hit him a few in the face. That seemed to do for him so I took his bat, hit him across the head with it then started swinging it about like a lunatic.

It actually felt really good to be hitting people. I had no idea why, but I guessed it was the bit of stress relief I'd needed. Normally, in that situation, I would feel really bad about hitting people, but on this occasion, I felt really good. I actually felt like I needed someone to hit me, but it seemed that no one could. Within about ten minutes of me coming downstairs, the Bats had taken control of the situation.

All the attackers had baseball bats, but the Bats had chains, knives, a couple of swords and a lot more fuckin bottle. Some of the attackers had tried to flee but, fortunately for us, about ten of our guys had just returned and had wasted everyone who'd ventured back outside. Within the next five minutes or so, we had rounded up the ones who were still standing and ignored the ones who were wriggling about in agony.

Indie grabbed one of the guys who was still standing and pushed him to the floor. He opened his flicknife and said: "You have five seconds to tell me what the fuck this is all about! If you don't, I'll slit your fuckin throat." The guy just said: "Fuck you, ya black bastard." Right there in front of me, Indie grabbed him by the throat, took his knife and slashed him from his ear to the corner of his mouth. As the guy screamed in agony, he did the same on the other side of his face. Fuck, I couldn't believe what I'd just seen, I'd heard of 'a Glesga smile' but never actually seen one and the blood was spewing everywhere.

I was still trying to come to terms with what he'd just done when he grabbed another guy. He started the same routine with him. He threw him onto the floor, stuck the knife to his throat and said: "Well, cunt? Are you going to talk or do you want a Glesga smile to go with your bum chum's?" The guy, to his credit, said: "Fuck you, dick. You'll do me anyway, so go fuck yourself!" Indie never even said a word. He just slit the guy's face the same way as before. He then grabbed another guy, wrestled him to the floor and told him he also had five seconds to talk. This dude was well up for talking. He asked Indie what the script was if he spilled the beans. Indie said that if he told him the score that he and the rest of his cronies could go.

The guy started to explain that Alfie Stone's brother had paid everybody fifty quid each. "We were all told that it was easy money," he said. "We had just to come in here, waste everybody then split. And it would be an easy earner. None of us knew it was a bike gang he was after. I reckon if we'd known that then half of us wouldn't be here."

Indie asked him where Stone's brother lived and how he could afford to pay that kind of money out. The bloke told him that the brother had got the insurance payout for the shop and that he lived locally somewhere - he also told him he drove a Gold Ford Escort.

Indie then told him he hated a grass and cut the tip of his tongue off. I was dying inside; I'd just watched three people get slashed and was looking at another thirty or so who were either totally beat up or being held by Bats. Indie stood up, covered in the blood of three people. He looked around the room then roared, "You can all fuck off, but make sure you tell that prick, Stone's brother, that we're coming after him tomorrow and there'll be no mercy shown. If any of you fannies go to the pigs … I'm sure you can guess what'll happen." One of the guys then told Indie: "Dinnae worry, if I see Stone's brother again, I'll fucking kill him myself."

Indie went right up to him and told him that if anybody killed him before he got to him then he'd make sure that their mother would be buying them a coffin. The guy just nodded then lowered his head, without saying anything else. Indie then told the Bats to chuck everybody out, which they did in a somewhat ungracious fashion. Some of the guys needed to be dragged out because they were unconscious. Finally, the three who were ripped were thrown into one of the cars. As the cars headed up the lane, Indie ordered us all into the conservatory. Once we were all in and the door was closed he told us what his plan was:

"Right, I want everybody cleaned up and ready to go in fifteen minutes. We're going to get this cunt tonight and end this fuckin shit right now. I know where he lives and I want him dead tonight. We'll take him from his house and do the bastard in a dark lane, the same way he did Provo and Stiff." He then pointed out a few guys and told them to go get everyone who'd left back to the farm immediately. When Indie finished talking, everyone split and I headed back up to see how Fiona was.

I quietly opened the door, in case she was sleeping, but to my surprise, she was sitting up in bed drinking a cup of tea. I asked her how she was, but she was more concerned about what had happened downstairs. I gave her a soft version of events, without mentioning anything about Indie slashing the guys. I also told her that we'd found out who was behind the attacks and that we were going to sort it out in the next fifteen minutes or so. I told her I just wanted to make sure she was okay before I left.

As I went to go, she burst out crying, so I gave her a bit of a cuddle for a minute then left, without either of us saying anything. When I went downstairs, everyone was tooling up. I had no idea what the fuck I should take as I'd never done anything like this before. There was a massive array of weapons lying on the floor: baseball bats, small swords, bike chains, knives and a couple of sawn-off shotguns. I stood for what seemed like an age just looking at it all, again thinking 'How in God's name did I end up here?'. It was only when Rooster gave me a jolt that I realised I'd been dreaming.

"Come on, man, get tooled up, we'll be going in five. You'll be riding with me. We're all going two's up, in case there's a welcome party." I grabbed the two things which were closest to me, which were a baseball bat and a knife. The knife was in a sheath so I attached it to my belt and carried the bat in my hand. When we went outside, it seemed like everyone and their granny was there, all jostling about, deciding who was riding with who, etc. Indie came out of the farm and told everyone to shut up. At that point, you could've heard a pin drop.

"I'm taking the van with Jelly and Hotwire. Everyone else, go twos up. We'll go to Stone's house in the van and get the bastard. Everyone else should kill their engines at the end of the street. I want the first half dozen to arrive to come in with us."

Normally, when all the guys are together, there's racing, wheelies and lots of carrying on. But not tonight. Tonight was so different; everyone was in a serious mood and the only talking was done by Indie. The night was cold and it was already pitch black. As we came towards the end of the lane, we could see the streetlights, they had an orange glow against the dark night and were surrounded by a cold mist. We all followed Indie onto the main road, everyone making sure they never over-revved. They just tickled their throttles, making the bikes roll along to the sound of a quiet purr.

Within five minutes, we were at Stone's street and, as agreed, we all killed our engines. We weren't part of the first group so we hung about at the end of the street. Indie drove the van into the street with Jelly and Hotwire; half a dozen of the guys walked along behind the van. We watched the brake lights shine as the van then came to a halt. There was no one else about and most of the houses were in darkness. Indie pointed to the house and they all headed up the path.

Jelly was carrying a sledgehammer and didn't even try the door, he just smashed it open and the nine of them charged in. Within five minutes, they were back out and chucked two half-naked guys into the back of the van. Four or five of our guys jumped in with them. Indie and Jelly were last out. They casually walked back to the van, jumped in, reversed it out and headed towards us. He flashed the lights and drove past us - our cue to follow him - which we all did.

As we passed the opening to the street, we could see some guys and girls staggering about, looking the worse for wear. The next thing that happened was something I reckon very few of us expected.

There was the sound of a gun being fired, BANG BANG, as clear as a bell, two shots, even over the sound of our bikes you knew exactly what it was. It's one of those sounds, once you've heard it there's no mistaking it.

We were already following the van so we had no idea if someone was shooting at us or if one of the guys had let rip, but we weren't hanging around to see. I never heard any bikes crashing to the ground so my guess was that the shots were fired by one of us.

We got back onto the main road and headed out the village. Indie then indicated and turned right. Fuck me, I couldn't believe it! He turned up the same lane that Malky and I had lured Alfie Stone up! It looked like his brother was going to get his comeuppance in exactly the same place.

When he turned in, he stopped the van, got two 'Road Closed' signs out and handed them to a couple of the guys. One placed the sign at the entrance once everybody was in, and two guys on a bike headed in the opposite direction to close off the other end. Indie jumped back into the van and drove a couple of hundred yards further up the road before stopping. He opened the back doors, grabbed Stone's brother and threw him to the ground. All he had on was a pair of jeans and nothing else. The guys had tied his hands and taped his mouth up, just as he'd done with Fiona and Angel earlier.

He already looked busted up and now the top half of his body was all cuts and scratches from being thrown out of the van as he'd been unable to protect himself from the fall. Cowboy was one of the guys in the back of the van and was holding the other guy, who was also gagged and bound. He had no top on either, but did have trousers and shoes on.

Indie went straight to the guy being held by Cowboy and asked him if he had anything to do with the planned rape of the girls. He shook his head trying to speak. Indie cut the tape from his mouth to let him talk. The guy told him he knew nothing about anything, that he was only Stone's next door neighbour and was invited to the party with his girlfriend about an hour before we'd arrived. Indie looked straight at him, staring into his eyes. I swear you could almost smell the fear off the guy as he tried to convince Indie that he wouldn't tell a living soul about this if he let him go. He was begging and pleading with Indie not to harm him, but Indie just ignored him and re-taped his mouth up before throwing him back in the van.

I reckoned the guy genuinely was just someone who was in the wrong place at the wrong time and wondered what Indie would do with him after he'd dealt with Stone's brother.

Indie then turned his attention to Stone, who by this time was trying to scream, but his sounds were muffled by the tape covering his mouth.

He actually pissed himself when Indie produced his flicknife, looking at his eyes I knew he was now totally petrified. Indie was on his hunkers with his head over Stone's. "You're a fuckin dead man, Stone, but not before I make you suffer," he told him. Then ran the point of his blade, coated in blood, all over Stone's chest. As he spoke, he was making little incisions as he went.

"Two of my brothers are in hospital because of you. My girl and her pal would've been raped if it hadn't been for the passing cop cars and my farmhouse is wrecked. So how do you think I'm feeling right now?" he asked him, knowing there was no way he could get a reply. "You probably don't give a fuck about my feelings, but I'm going to tell you anyway. I'm feeling pretty sad for my brothers, but pretty fuckin happy to be here with you. You thought you could pay some cunts to take us out, but you way underestimated the strength of our club. The first thing I'm going to do is cut off your fingers, one by one, then your ears and who knows what else." Indie then stopped moving the blade around Stone's chest and cut off part of the thumb on his right hand. He lifted it up and had a look at it before dabbing the blood-soaked end over Stone's forehead.

Stone was screaming and wriggling about, but again, it was muffled.

I watched Indie at this point and he looked like he was in a catatonic state, he kept staring at Stone and watched him wriggle in agony. I swear I thought he was enjoying this way too much. I was hoping that he would just kill him and get it over with, but I certainly wasn't going to be the one to mention it. Thankfully, Hotwire gave him a nudge and said: "Come on, Indie, man, the place will be swarming with pigs soon, let's just do him and get to fuck." He never even turned around. He just cut off Stone's other four fingers and slashed his throat. He stood up, spat on him then turned to Hotwire and said: "Guess you're right, big fella. Burn the bastard."

Indie got in the passenger side of the van as Jelly jumped into the driver's seat and they both sped away. Most of the guys headed off behind them, but half a dozen of us were told to stay behind and clean up. We threw Stone's body into the trees. One of the guys had the petrol container from the back of the van and poured it all over him. He then lit a rag and chucked it on him and, quick as a flash, Stone was up in smoke.

I jumped on the back of Cowboy's bike and we headed back to the farm. All the way back, all I could think about was how the fuck can I get away from all this fuckin madness - not for one minute did I think I was signing up for murder. I also wondered what the fuck Indie was going to do with the guy in the back of the van. I presumed he wasn't going to kill him or he would have been dead already, but I also knew he wouldn't leave him unharmed.

I'd just witnessed a murder and some serious shit dished out to a rake of people. I reckoned we were bound to get caught and when we did, my life would be fucked - a hundred years in jail and no parole. I was imagining what that would be like when we came to a shuddering halt. I jumped off and we headed into the farm.

Everyone was rushing around like mad people. The girls had cleaned up from earlier and the guys were getting rid of the weapons and cleaning the blood and stuff from their clothes and faces. I was looking around for Indie, but couldn't see him,

I guessed he was upstairs with Angel. I decided to nip up and see Fiona, but when I stuck my head round the door, I saw she was sleeping. I headed back downstairs and before I even got into the room I could hear that the guys had a party in full swing. I didn't have the stomach for partying, I was feeling sick and really screwed up from what had just gone down.

That was the bit I just couldn't understand. I never actually did anything, but I was still riddled with guilt. Yet the others, who were heavily involved, were chilling and laughing like what we'd done was as normal as eating your dinner. All I could think about at this point was that the police would be arriving soon. We would all be thrown in jail, Stiff or Provo would die and we'd all miss Malky's funeral - talk about the 'Prophet of Doom'!

I was feeling really ill by this point and had to go outside for some air. I hardly got the door closed when I started to throw up. I felt like I was dying. I could hardly get a breath between bouts of vomiting; at one point, I was sure I was going to stop breathing altogether. I eventually stopped throwing up after about ten minutes and calmed myself down. I went into the kitchen, got myself a large drink of water then headed back outside.

I sat on the steps, lit up a fag and blew the smoke out into the cold night air. I sipped at the water and closed my eyes, trying to make some sense of the last 12 hours. As I drifted away, embroiled in my thoughts, I felt a kick on my side. I opened my eyes and saw Rooster slumping down beside me. "What a fuckin day that was, man," he reminded me. "Don't I fuckin know it," I told him. "I can't believe the pigs haven't arrived yet," I said. "Me either, but you can bet your arse they're on their way," he assured me.

I asked him what happened to the guy in the back of the van and he told me that Indie had let him go. Well, what he actually said was that he threw him out after threatening to kill his whole family if he ever said anything. "Yep, Shug, I reckon we'll be back in jail within the hour," he suggested, and with that, we both nodded and took a long, lingering draw on our cigarettes.

At that point, we both decided to head back inside, agreeing it was fuckin freezing and thought we should get a few beers down us before the inevitable happened. Within an hour or so of going back in, the party fizzled out and everyone started heading to the rooms or crashing out where they lay. I headed up to see Fiona and, as she was still sleeping, I snuggled up beside her and drifted off to sleep.

I was awoken by the sound of some bikes firing up and jumped out of bed to see what was going on. I opened the curtains just in time to see Indie and another couple of the guys heading off. Fiona woke up and asked me what was going on. I told her I didn't know, but to go back to sleep and I would go and find out. I ran down the stairs, two at a time, still feeling disorientated. I didn't know what was up, if anything, or even what time it was.

When I got downstairs, I ran into the conservatory. People were still lying all over the place, sleeping. I went into the big room and it was the same there. I headed into the kitchen and Cowboy was sitting drinking tea and eating toast with a couple of guys. I asked him what had happened and he looked at me like I had horns. "What do you mean 'what happened'?" he asked. "I just saw Indie and a couple of guys shooting off. Has anything happened with Stiff and Provo?" I almost demanded him to tell me.

"Fuck's sake, Shug. Calm your jets, man. They're just off to hospital to see them and find out what the script is. Indie told us last night that was the plan, remember?" I nodded, suddenly recalling the conversation. "What about the pigs? Didn't they come last night?" I asked Cowboy. He told me nobody had shown, but most of the guys were still expecting a visit, sooner rather than later.

I checked the clock, it was nine in the morning. I remembered Indie saying that everyone had to meet at the farm for eleven. I asked Cowboy if that was still the case and he reckoned it was as Indie didn't want anyone going to the hospital and appearing to make us mob handed.

After a bit of toast and a fag, I told Rooster I had to go back to my flat to get dressed as I was going to Malky's house to see his mum and dad before the funeral. I removed my cut-off, handed it to Rooster and asked him if he would take it to the funeral as I wanted to bury it with Malky. He took it from me, but I could see from the way he looked at me that he had no idea why I wanted to do it.

"He loved his cut-off, Rooster. Fuck knows what happened to his, so I want to give him mine, okay?" I told him. I could see the change in his face when I told him, like the penny had just dropped. We sort of smiled at each other and then I left.

I went into my flat and for the first time, it seemed empty. For some reason, it didn't really feel like mine anymore. I felt like I wanted to grab my stuff and split. I started getting changed and was wondering what I was going to do after the funeral, assuming I wasn't heading to jail.

All I could think about was getting the fuck away from there and starting again somewhere else, but I gave myself a shake and decided to focus on the funeral and pick up the rest tomorrow.

Chapter 4

Malky's funeral came and went, the saddest day in my short life so far. In just over an hour it was all over, one scabbie, poxy, fuckin hour and he was gone for good. I travelled to the funeral with Malky's folks. I decided that I should do it as his mum had asked me to go with them in the family car. I went to the house (standing on their front step, I was shitting myself wondering what we would say to each other). I knocked the door and it was Malky's dad that opened it. The minute I saw him I thought, 'Fuck, this is a big mistake'. I looked at him and could instantly feel my eyes welling up. I just said: "Sorry," about turned and headed off.

"Ochil, where are you going?" I heard him shouting. I turned, looked at him and said: "I'm really sorry, Mr Campbell, I shouldn't have come." "Hey, don't be silly, we're delighted you came. You know Malcolm would have wanted you here and so do we." He then put his arm around me and ushered me into the house, closing the door behind us.

We were standing in the hall and he told me the living room was full of relatives and just wanted to prepare me. "Ochil, I need to tell you something before we go in," he explained. "You have to stop blaming yourself for this. After today, get on with your life. We miss Malcolm, and we always will, but you have to remember the last couple of years; he had a glint in his eye and loved every minute of his life. As much as we didn't approve, we knew he was doing exactly what he wanted to do. Not many people get that chance in life, but you gave it to him and we will always remember that."

By this time, the tears were streaming down my face and I wanted to talk, but I had no voice. It was probably a good thing because I had no idea what the fuck I would have said anyway.

Malky's dad then gave me a bit of a hug and told me he hoped I'd keep in touch with them after the funeral. I just mumbled that I would, but I wasn't sure how coherent my reply was. Just then, Malky's mum appeared and joined in the hugging, telling me she was so glad I had decided to come and that Malcolm would have been so disappointed if I hadn't made it.

This set the waterworks off again, but this time it was much more uncontrollable. My body was jerking up and down and I could feel myself shaking like a leaf. I think the fact that both of Malky's parents were so understanding and supportive towards me made me feel even more guilty. I expected things to be the exact opposite; where his mum didn't speak to me and his dad wanted to rip my head off. If truth be told, I think I would have preferred that. Then, at least, I would have got what I felt I deserved.

As we were about to go into the living room, there was a knock at the door. It was the undertaker, ready to take us to the church. Malky's dad told him to give us five minutes and we would be ready to go. He then announced to everyone that it was time to go. Everyone started to make their way out to their cars, except Malky's mum and dad, Julie, Spud and myself. Malky's dad then hugged Mrs Campbell and said: "Come on, love, time to do this." He then opened the door and ushered us to the car.

The minute we got out, we could see the hearse and it set us all off. I thought Malky's mum was going to collapse so I helped Malky's dad get her to the car, it was as if seeing the coffin had turned her legs to jelly. We all got in the car and no one said a word all the way to the church. I just kept staring at the floor, avoiding all eye contact, with the tears continually dripping from my eyes.

When we got to the church, there were about 40 bikes scattered all over the place and, as with Max's funeral, the guys were drinking, smoking and laughing. The minute they saw the coffin arriving, they all stopped what they were doing and bowed their heads. We got out the car and as we headed to the church Malky's dad acknowledged the Bats silence with a nod in Indie's direction. Then we all went inside.

The church was full to overflowing; lots of people were standing all the way around the outside of the pews and people were sitting on each other's knees.

The coffin was then wheeled into the church by the undertakers. When it reached the front of the church, I saw that there was a floral tribute placed on it which was exactly the same as the one that had been on Max's coffin.

Once the coffin was placed in position in front of the minister, the undertakers bowed in unison then made their way out of the church. All the Bats then came in and stood halfway down the Aisle. The service was very traditional; with hymns, prayers and readings. It was really sad and most people cried all the way through it. I kept a close eye on the Bats, fearing the worst, but to a man they were immaculately behaved and respected the wishes of Malky's parents (much to my surprise).

After the service, myself and Malky's family were escorted into the cars. We were then driven, behind the hearse, to the cemetery. Behind us, the Bats were in formation and did the same thing they had at Max's funeral. They controlled the traffic, closing off all the roads ahead to allow the full procession to stay together. At the cemetery, the Bats stayed away from the graveside until the minister was finished and everyone was starting to leave.

Malky's mum, sister and Spud got into the car and Malky's dad headed over to Indie. He shook his hand, thanked him for being there and for letting the family embrace the service. Indie nodded and thanked him for his words. He then returned to the car and asked me if I was going back to the hotel or staying with the Bats. At that point, I hadn't even thought about it, but guessed it would be best if I stayed with the Bats.

I told him I was going to stay and make sure Malky got a good send off. He smiled, gave me a hug and told me to look after myself. Again, I just mumbled incoherently, with tears running down my cheeks. I hugged him back then headed back to the graveside.

Just as I got to the grave, Indie was saying a few words. He then laid down the wreath. Cowboy and Flick produced bottles of spirits, opened them, threw the lids on top of the coffin, took a swig from each of the bottles and passed them around. Everyone did the same, as the bottles circled the group. Indie then produced Malky's cut-off, handed it to me and gestured for me to throw it in, on top of Malky's coffin. I took it from him, but I didn't want to throw it in, I wanted to keep it.

"Where did you get his cut-off?" I asked him. "Got it from the pigs. We do have some mates in there as well, you know," he told me. I thought to myself 'Well, why am I surprised about that. They seem to have a finger in every fuckin pie around'. I gestured to Rooster to give me my cut-off, which he did. I then turned back to Indie and asked, "Can I keep Malky's cut-off?" "Of course you can, but you need to tell me what you're going to do with it." "I'm going to wear it and give Malky mine," I told him.

"Excellent. That's what I hoped you'd say. Okay, give it to him," he said, pointing to the hole in the ground. I had a good look at the coffin for a minute and then threw it in on top, telling him I'd miss him like fuck. I then put Malky's on over my suit jacket, much to the amusement of everyone else. I felt weird putting it on, but I also felt strangely comforted as well.

After the bottles did another round they were thrown into the hole, on top of the coffin. Rooster threw the last one in and shouted "Hey, Malk, I hope you can see this prick with your cut-off on. Only Shug would wear it over a fuckin suit!" All the guys burst out laughing and I joined them, smiling away with the tears still rolling down my cheeks. It certainly raised everybody's mood as we said our goodbyes. The guys then made their way to the bikes and started heading off.

Rooster and I were the last to leave. He looked down at the coffin and said: "Hey, Malk, sorry there wasn't more people here today. But between the jail and the hospital there were a lot of brothers that couldn't make it, you know the score." With that, he patted me on the back and told me he would meet me at his bike. I just looked down at the coffin and kept asking myself 'Why the fuck it had happened?' and 'Why the fuck it was him and not me?' I started going over all the same shit I had done in the flat for three days.

I gave myself a shake then told Malky about the shit that had gone down in the last few days and how we were all lucky to even make the funeral. As I spoke to him, I even managed a bit of a laugh. I couldn't help thinking how much Malky loved that part of it. He was always waiting for the next disaster - or adventure (as he called it) - to happen.

I said my goodbyes, headed out the cemetery and jumped onto Rooster's bike.

He just gave me a pat on the leg and then we blasted up the road. Neither of us had helmets on and I was in a suit. The police watched us as we headed out of town, but never tried to stop us. They obviously respected the 'no helmet' tradition which was kind of nice I guess as they would usually try to 'do' us for anything they could.

Chapter 5

We arrived at the farm about 15 minutes after the rest of the guys. By then there was a fair scattering of bikes spread between the house and the barn.

We both headed into the kitchen, which surprisingly was empty, and even more strange, there was no sound of music and no roaring; it was like there was no one there.

I looked at Rooster and he looked at me, both shrugging our shoulders. We went into the hall and Rooster walked towards the conservatory and pointed me in the direction of the big room.

I opened the door and, again, the room was empty. I turned to see Rooster opening the conservatory door and walking in. I could see that lots of the guys were in there, but there was a real eerie hush. Indie was speaking very quietly and appeared really upset.

We both sat down on the floor just as Indie was explaining that the doctors had arranged for Provo to be taken into surgery just before Malky's funeral because they needed to remove a blood clot from his brain.

I had no idea what that meant and asked Indie if he could explain it to me.

He just looked in my direction and said: "If the doctor can't remove it then he's fucked, okay?" Rooster asked how Stiff was and Indie told him the doc thought he would eventually be fine, but that he could be in hospital for a lengthy spell. He then got up, told us he was going to the hospital alone and would be back after he got information on how the operation had gone.

A few of the guys said they would go with him, but he made it very clear to all of us he was doing it on his own.

Indie then got up and left, leaving us all looking around at each other, not knowing what to say or think. I decided to head to my favourite place - outside the back door. I sat on the steps and lit up a fag.

Within seconds of lighting up, both Rooster and Cowboy had joined me. Rooster gave me a gentle pat on the back. "How you holding up, man?" he asked. "Fuckin shite, the whole thing's fucked. I can't do it anymore, man. As soon as I hear how Provo gets on with his operation, I'm done. I've no idea what's next, but I can't stay around here. Fuck, I'm dying inside. I need to find some kind of fuckin normality, whatever the fuck THAT is."

Rooster put his arm around me and gave me a bit of a hug. "No arguments from me this time, mate, I almost feel the same myself. What's happened to us in the last couple of weeks shouldn't happen to anybody in a whole fuckin lifetime."

For the next 5 minutes or so the three of us stared out into the clear blue sky with our own thoughts, not talking or even realising there was anyone else there.

I drifted into a 'what's next for me mode' while pondering on Rooster's words.

That was the first time he had ever offered his support to me about moving on. Every other time, he'd tried to ensure that I cleared my head and stayed put.

I think the thing that struck me the most was the feeling I was getting that he was almost endorsing my decision, and the few words he'd said were the ones that sealed it for me.

Cowboy interrupted the silence by asking if we could hear a bike coming and we both nodded in agreement.

From that point on, our eyes were fixed on the lane and as the bike drew closer we realised it was Indie returning. "Holy shit, I don't like this, something must be up. He's hardly been away an hour," I blurted out.

Rooster agreed, but suggested we shouldn't think the worst until we heard what he had to say. Indie parked his bike and killed the engine.

"How's Provo?" Rooster asked. Indie never even lifted his head "Conservatory," was all he said.

We looked at each other and shrugged before following him in, all thinking the worst. By the time we walked from the kitchen behind Indie, everyone in the building was cramming themselves inside the conservatory, waiting for him to speak.

Indie never looked at anyone and the way he spoke next was unnerving.

"Provo's fuckin dead, didn't even make it to the fuckin operating table. He crashed before the surgery, a couple of hours ago. He died alone and no cunt thought to let us know. That's why I fuckin hate society, and the bastards that run it, so fuckin much, pretentious bastards, the fuckin lot of them …. Right, Meeting …. Tonight at 8pm in the barn …. Everyone …. and I mean every fucker, got it!" With that, he walked out and headed up to Angel's room.

I was numb, probably like most of the guys, and found the information really hard to process. I headed outside again for a bit of air and was joined by Cowboy.

"Fuck me, man, it just goes from bad to fuckin worse," Cowboy commented. "Exactly what I was thinking," was my reply.

"Hey, Cowboy, can you give me a run back to the flat so I can get this suit off and pick up my bike?" I asked him. "Yeh, no probs. I could do with a blast anyway," he told me. He got up, went inside, picked up a couple of helmets then came back out. He threw me one over and we headed off.

As we rode, I could feel the cold air biting into me through my cheap suit and thin shirt. All of a sudden, I could feel myself shivering and was wishing the trip would end.

Within 15 minutes, Cowboy had dropped me off and I was standing in my flat, looking around the place. This was the second time that I'd come in and felt that it was empty, hollow, void of life and really depressing.

However, for some reason, it began to give me a comforting feeling, like a kind of confirmation that my life no longer needed to be here and that moving on was the way to go.

I got changed, grabbed some juice from the fridge, plunked myself on the sofa and lit up a fag. I began to feel a bit more at ease so stretched my feet out onto the coffee table, flipped my head back and started planning my exit.

My first problem was the Bats: How can I get out without looking over my shoulder every day of my life? Then it struck me.

I didn't actually need to get out, I just needed to get a job far enough away that I couldn't be around all the time and as long as I did the odd weekend with them then I'd be fine.

I started to think about some of the other guys who I'd seen every now and then, like the dudes we gathered to deal with Stone's brother, who were in a similar position. How they operated seemed to work okay for them.

I decided to walk to the shop and get a couple of newspapers and check out some job adverts to see if there was anything that suited me.

I came out the shop armed with a local paper and two nationals that had job pages in them. As I left, I heard a shout: "You not speaking, Shug?"

I turned around and saw Julie waving. She'd come out of a car and was heading into the shop. Instead of going in, she ran over and gave me a big cuddle.

"Hi, Julie, great to see you," I told her. "Haven't seen you for ages, where have you been hiding?"

She told me that after her and Rooster had fallen out, for the umpteenth time, she'd decided she needed some time away from him to see if her feelings for him were the same when they were apart.

I asked her where she was working and she told me she was working in a psychiatric hospital, about 45 miles away, doing her psychiatric nurse training for a year.

She then said she had to run as she was heading back to work and was running late. Julie then got a pen and a bit of paper out and wrote down her address and phone number.

"Come and see me if you can, Shug. I'm working 9 to 5, Monday to Friday, and I'm off every weekend for the next couple of weeks, it would be great to catch up."

I told her I would do that as soon as I could and she then told me she looked forward to seeing me. As she went to get back in the car, she turned and said: "Oh, remember, not a word to Rooster!" And with that, she was off.

I walked back to the flat thinking how bizarre that had been. I hadn't seen Julie for months and Rooster had never said a thing about them splitting up. I thought they were still going out and were planning to settle down together.

I suppose, with all the shit going on, I never really gave them much of a thought. However, I was fascinated with the fact she was working in a psychiatric hospital and that it was a fair bit away from here.

My mind was racing, wondering if she could get me some kind of job there. It would be perfect: just too far to commute every day, but close enough to come back for a visit.

I decided that I would take up Julie's offer and go visit her at the weekend, suss out the place and see if there was anything she could do for me.

I started looking through the papers, but, very quickly, chucked it - I had already decided to focus on my job prospects through Julie and the hospital.

I must have drifted off to sleep and was awakened by a knock at the door. It was Mark. "Hey, man, come in," I told him, as I walked back into the living room.

"Is it true about Provo?" he asked. I told him it was and gave him a short version of what had happened. He was gobsmacked and told me he'd heard a couple of people standing outside the shop talking about it and couldn't believe it.

He then got up to leave. As he was walking to the door, he turned and said: "Shug, what the fuck are you thinking about, man? This shite's not for you. Get the fuck out while you still can." He never said anything else and I never replied. I looked up and saw him shake his head, just as he closed the door.

I sat back down and thought about what he'd said. I felt he was right: another person who knew me, thinking the same way. I started to think that the events of the day were no coincidence and confirmed to me it was definitely time to move on.

I decided to head back to the farm and see what was happening. I imagined that there would be lots of guys there after the news about Provo.

I put on my jacket and cut-off, grabbed my helmet, headed downstairs and jumped on my bike. I made my way to the farm, with all sorts of shit running through my head, but for some reason, my main focus was on the chop I got from Max.

The guys had finished it months ago, but I'd never been given it, even though Provo and Stiff had both told me it was mine. I had thought about it most days, but never seemed to find the right time to ask about it.

I'd been in the barn a few times and fired it up, sat on it and dreamed about riding it on a run. However, that's as far as it had gone and I guessed today was another one of those days when I couldn't mention it.

As I turned into the lane, there were another 3 bikes coming from the other direction. I recognised two of the bikes: one was Hotwire and another was Jelly, I hadn't seen the third one before. We just nodded to each other, then carried on until we arrived at the farm.

There were lots of bikes scattered around and the lights were on in the barn. Cowboy was sitting out on the step having a smoke and got up as we arrived. I killed the engine and made my way towards him. "Hi, man, how's things inside?" I asked.

"Very flat, lots of underlying anger. Everybody's looking for someone to blame, even though that bastard Stone's already dead. It feels like most of the guys want to kick off, just to get a release."

I asked him if anybody was in the barn and he told me there were about the same amount of guys in the barn that there were in the house.

"What do you think Indie wants us all here for?" I quizzed him. "Not sure, but some of the guys reckon he'll be organising a run somewhere, to get away for a couple of days before organising Provo's funeral," he told me.

Almost growling under my breath, I started barking away at Cowboy.

"Fuck's sake, man, it's Baltic! A fuckin run! Surely he's havin a fuckin laugh? That's all we fuckin need, a poxy run when everybody's emotions are all over the place, it'll be a fuckin disaster!"

Cowboy interrupted me in mid-flow, telling me to 'Shut the fuck up and keep my voice down'. "Jeezus, Shug, get a fuckin grip, man. I'm only telling you what the guys are thinking. Why are you freaking out like a fuckin lunatic?" he demanded to know.

I wasn't really sure why I'd reacted like I had. I guess it was more the thought of being forced to go to yet another thing before I split and also the fear that it would interfere with my plans to go and see Julie.

"Sorry, man, I just think it's a recipe for disaster and I'm worried we'll get caught up in something else, especially with this Stone thing hanging over us. None of us are thinking straight, well, at least, I'm not anyway," I told him, and I don't know why, but I gave him a bit of a hug and suggested we go in.

We hit the kitchen and Cowboy grabbed a couple of beers from the fridge. We then spent the next 15 minutes mulling around, catching up with people. I then decided to go upstairs to see Fiona, but she wasn't in her room.

I went back down and found Rooster. I asked him where Fiona was and he told me Indie had taken her and Angel to Fiona's pad. I asked him why and he responded by telling me he had no idea and didn't give a fuck.

"Whoa, man, take it easy. I only asked, for fuck's sake. There's no need to bite my fuckin head off. What the fuck's eating you?" I asked him.

He stared at me for a second and then told me to go outside with him, which I did. He lit up a couple of smokes, handed me one then started talking.

"Have you heard what Indie's planning?" he asked, I just nodded. "A fuckin run! He's planning a fuckin run! What a fuckin nightmare that'll be, some other cunt's going to end up dead. Everybody is as agitated as fuck and he wants us to go on a drink and drug-fuelled bender to some shithole place where every cunt will want a fuckin piece of us. I'm telling you, Shug, I think he's lost the fuckin plot."

I tried to calm him down and told him he wasn't the only one feeling that way, as I felt exactly the same. "Right, we need to talk to him, make him see sense, tell him it's a fuckin stupid idea," he declared.

"Hang on, Rooster," I reminded him. "Indie has just lost his best friend and his other closest mate is in hospital for fuck knows how long. Can you remember what I was like when Malky went? I was all over the fuckin place, man, and definitely not thinking straight. Give him a bit of time, he'll see sense."

"How much time can we give him? Once he's told everybody, that's it, game fuckin on, you know the drill, at that point nobody has a say. Fuck it, I'm going to see him now." And with that, he got up and headed to the conservatory.

Another set of fuckin dilemmas for me: Do I go with him and support him? Do I try to stop him or leave him to go alone? I decided to follow him in and play it by ear.

Thankfully, when we got to the conservatory, Indie still hadn't arrived back and there was only a small bunch of guys mulling around.

We turned and walked back out. I tried to talk to him and get him to calm down, but he wasn't taking incoming calls.

"Fuck's sake, Rooster, stop a minute, man, we need to talk," I told him, grabbing his arm. He stopped, stared at me, then stared at my hand holding his arm.

"Let me go, Shug. I'm going outside to wait on him. I need to see him before he starts." He then pulled his arm away and headed for the door.

I stood in the kitchen and took a minute to think about what Rooster was going to do and what the consequences of his actions might be. I decided that I would speak to Indie with him. Maybe even Cowboy would join in? Indie would surely take notice if three of us had a go at him.

When I got outside, Rooster was sitting with Cowboy on the steps. I stood in front of them and told Rooster he was right and I was with him, he just nodded. I then told Cowboy what we were up to and he said he was in as well.

I asked Rooster what his plan was and he asked me what the fuck I was talking about. "How are you going to tell him? Are you going to take him aside and make him see sense or are you going to do it another way?" I asked.

"Shug, you're a fuckin lunatic. You overthink every-fuckin-thing. I'm just going to wait until he stops, then ask him if he's planning a run. If he is then I'll tell him it's a shite idea and take it from there."

Before I got time to answer, Indie arrived back in the van and went to head into the barn. Rooster jumped up. "Indie, need a word before you go in, man," he said, as he walked towards him.

Indie, in turn, started walking toward Rooster. "What is it, man?" he asked. At that point, both Cowboy and I headed over to listen in.

Rooster then started talking. "Indie, I'm hearing you're planning a run tomorrow. Just wondered if that was right?"

"I'm thinking about it, why?" he told him.

"I think it would be a bad idea, man, the way everyone is feeling. I reckon it's bound to be a disaster or at best a riot, no matter where we go. The last thing the Bats need right now is members getting jailed, or worse."

When Rooster stopped speaking, Indie looked at us and said: "Well, do you two cunts feel the same?" We both nodded. He looked back at Rooster. "Has anybody else told you they feel the same?" he demanded to know.

Rooster replied with an honest answer. "Not sure, man, haven't really spoke to anybody else about it, just wanted to run it past you first."

Indie thanked Rooster for the heads up then told me and Cowboy to go over to the farm and get everybody to go to the barn, which we did.

As we were walking to the barn, Cowboy asked me if I thought Indie had taken Rooster's thoughts on board and I told him I reckoned he had.

"Indie trusts Rooster," I told him. "They've known each other a long time. I'm pretty confident he'll see Rooster is making sense. And if he thinks others are feeling the same way, he won't want to rock the boat with all the shit that's going on at the minute."

Cowboy nodded in agreement. "Yep, that's what I reckon too," he told me. We got to the barn and, other than a couple of stragglers, we were last in. Indie pointed to us to close the door, which we did.

"Right, guys, everybody knows about Provo and I've heard the pigs are starting to compile a case against us for the Stone shit. They have people watching the farm and I'm being followed everywhere I go. I took the girls away tonight, on my own, just to see if they would stay put or if they would follow me. They followed me, so I guess they're waiting for me to do something. We'll be doing nothing until after Provo's funeral. We won't get him back for at least a week so we can't make any arrangements just now, which leaves us in limbo. I've arranged with the Devils to spend a few days with them, so we leave at 9am tomorrow and everybody is going, no exceptions. I want them, and everybody else, to know we are as strong as ever. Some people might think the Bats will crumble now, well we'll let them know how fuckin wrong they are, we'll never be beaten. Whatever happens, this chapter will never die. Provo's gone, but by fuck, his legacy will continue, we'll all make sure of that. Come on, let's party for the big man."

Then everybody let out a roar, I could even feel myself wanting to cheer, but I kept it under wraps. I looked at Cowboy and he nodded in approval and I did the same in return.

I'd gone in there wondering how the fuck we could stop this, then a one-minute speech from Indie and I'm back on board.

As everybody started to filter out, I got hold of Rooster and asked him how he was doing. He told me he was now actually looking forward to the trip and felt a bit of a fud for trying to put a damper on it. I agreed, telling him I felt the same.

We did the manly hug bit and just as we stood apart, Indie approached us. "Well?" was all he said, Rooster then said: "Sorry, man, should never have doubted you. I was just a bit freaked about a run, but you're right, it's the best thing for us all."

Indie then looked at me and again made a one-word statement, which to me felt like both a question and a demand.

All he said was "And ..." I responded in a similar vain to Rooster, agreeing that it was the best thing for everyone and that I was looking forward to it.

He then said something that threw me a bit and made me as excited as I've ever been in my life.

"Hey, Rooster, best you help that little cunt check out his chop. We wouldn't want it to break down on the run and hold us back, now would we!" And with that, he left the barn.

I looked at Rooster and a stupid grin came over my face. "Fuck, Rooster, did you hear that? I've finally got my chop! Come on, man, let's fire it up." I almost sprinted over to the bikes. I lifted the dust sheet off and immediately sat on it.

I could see some of the guys who were still in the barn, laughing away. I guessed they were all remembering when they got their first proper bike. Either way, it meant nothing to me, all I was interested in was firing it up and driving up the lane.

I tried to kick it into life, but it was dead; I thought I was going to have a heart attack trying to start it. 'Fuck.' I thought to myself 'I finally get my bike, we're heading for a run tomorrow and it's as dead as a fucking dodo!'

'Fuckin typical' I thought, 'I never get a fuckin break'. It was only then I saw Rooster walking towards me with a battery in his hand, laughing his head off - along with everybody else in the barn.

"Bet it works better with this fucker attached!" I heard him say, amidst the shrieks of laughter. Even though everybody was laughing at me, and I felt like a right dick, the feeling of knowing I would be riding my chop out the barn, any minute now, far outweighed any feeling of stupidity I was experiencing.

By the time Rooster had fitted the battery there was hardly anybody in the barn and he gestured to me to get on and fire it up, which I did.

I switched on the ignition and Rooster got another dig in, explaining that it's amazing what a bit of electricity can do. "Oh look, it's even got lights on now," he said, then again burst into a roar of laughter, followed by the others who'd heard him.

But this time, I hardly even heard it - I was so focused on my bike. With the first kick, it fired into life, smashing a cloud of thick black smoke from both exhausts around the barn.

Rooster stared at me for a second and I smiled and nodded. As I sat tickling the throttle and could feel the engine purr throughout my whole body. I was lost in the moment until Rooster whistled at me and brought me back to reality.

He'd opened the door a bit wider to let me out and was summoning me towards him. I clicked my bike into gear and felt it jumping forward like it was straining to go.

I gently let the clutch out and slowly rolled out the barn onto the lane. It was absolutely freezing, but in the moment I never gave it a thought.

I rode up the lane, listening to the engine continuing to purr underneath me, looking straight ahead, watching the headlight pierce the dark night sky.

I was at the end of the lane before I realised it and as I turned back towards the farm, I could feel tears in my eyes as I remembered Max, Malky and Provo, and all the shit that had brought me to this point.

I thought about Julie and moving on. I thought about Fiona and the bond we'd built up between us. I wondered about the run and how it was going to pan out. Then my thoughts came back to me and my bike. As I drove back into the barn, I still had the widest grin on my face you could ever imagine.

Rooster and most of the guys had headed back into the farm and there were only a couple of guys still in there, messing around with a bike. I killed the engine and dragged it back into line with the rest of the bikes, stepped off, stuck the keys in my pocket and headed into the farm.

I went into the kitchen, grabbed a beer from the fridge and sat down at the table. I opened the beer and had a long drink. It was only then I realised I was fuckin freezing and started shivering a bit.

Even, as cold as I was, I could still appreciate the short run and the feeling of satisfaction of finally having the bike I'd been dreaming of riding for over two years.

Cowboy came in for a beer and mentioned he'd seen me on the chop and commented on how cool it was, which again left me with a stupid grin on my face. We both then headed into the big room where the party was in full swing.

The next morning, I woke up lying on the floor next to the radiator, not remembering anything about what went on the night before. I wondered if I'd only dreamt about Indie giving me the chop, but then I felt the key in my pocket and smiled to myself yet again.

Chapter 6

I got up and headed outside to see what kind of day it was. The minute I opened the door, I felt the cold air biting into me. The sight of frost everywhere suggested it was at least zero degrees. I zipped up my jacket and thought about the run and how cold it would be on the bikes.

I wondered if we would be going to the place we'd met the Devil Angels before and hoped it would be somewhere else. This was the first run I'd be going on without Malky, and I sure as fuck didn't want to go on the same road that he'd died on.

I watched as some of the guys were arriving, they had their sleeping bags tied to their bikes. As they drove into the barn, my mind raced back to the times I had enviously watched Max head off on a Friday, exactly the same way. I laughed to myself, remembering all the things I thought he was up to and here I was, doing the same shit.

I headed back inside and picked up my sleeping bag, grabbed a couple of bungees and went over to the barn to tie it onto my bike. The noise inside was almost deafening, most of the guys were checking out their bikes, revving them up while listening to the engines and screaming at each other about them.

Just then, another two bikes arrived. It was Hotwire and Jelly. They'd left the night before and were back for the run, which really surprised me. I thought they'd only come back for the 'Stone' thing, but I guess Indie really did mean EVERYONE was going on the run.

When Hotwire got off his bike, he made a beeline for me. "What the fuck are you doing with Max's bike?" he demanded to know. "It's not Max's bike, it's mine," I told him. "Provo gave it to me. Go ask Indie, he'll tell you the script." I tried really hard to be cool with my response and let him think I was relaxed, even though I was shitting myself.

"You better not be fucking with me or I'll be back to see you," he told me, as he walked towards the door. Then I said one of the stupidest things I've ever said: "I look forward to it, and I expect you to be back with a fuckin apology. Don't fuckin speak to me again until you do, prick."

I have no idea where it came from, but the minute I said it, I knew I was in a shitload of trouble. Hotwire stopped in his tracks turned around, gave me a right stare then started heading towards me. I stepped away from my bike, expecting the worst.

"What's your name, cunt?" he demanded to know. "Shug," I told him, staring straight at him. "I'll tell you what, 'Shug', you've got fuckin balls, I'll give you that, but you're way, way out of your depth and you've just crossed the fuckin line." Before he even stopped talking, he punched me in the mouth, knocking me to the ground.

He then leaned over me and said: "Let that be a fuckin lesson to you, ya little fucker. And if you ever talk to me like that again, I'll rip your fuckin head off. Got it?" then he turned to head out. That was when I said the second stupidest thing ever.

"Is that all you've got, old boy? I'll tell you what, for a big man you hit like a fuckin pussy!" I could hear myself saying it, but for some reason, I couldn't stop myself.

As he turned around again, I jumped up and wrestled him to the floor, but within seconds he was kicking the absolute shit out of me. It was all over within a couple of minutes and, again, I was feeling the worse for wear. I'm not even sure I managed to hit him, but by fuck, I knew he'd hit me.

As I lay licking my wounds, he left without saying anything to me, just muttering under his breath about thick young bucks not knowing their place. Within seconds of him leaving, the guys got back to their bikes and carried on like nothing had happened.

I dragged myself over to the wall and leaned myself against it. I started wiping the blood from my face with my jumper, a thing I seemed to have done a hundred times before. Fuck, I thought Rooster could dish it out! Well, I don't remember ever being hit as hard as Hotwire had just hit me.

A couple of the guys came over and suggested I head to the farm and get cleaned up as we would be leaving in an hour or so and helped me onto my feet.

As I was walking out the barn, Rooster was coming in. "Holy fuck, Shug, what now?" he asked. "It's nothing, man, just a misunderstanding, and it was all my fault," I told him.

"Misunderstanding? You look fucked! Was your misunderstanding with a roughcast fuckin wall?" he sarcastically asked. "Very funny, Rooster, ha ha. You're such a fuckin comedian. Let me tell you, I wish it had been - it would probably have been less painful," I replied.

"So come on then, who have you pissed off now?" he wanted to know. "Hotwire," I told him. "What? You challenged Hotwire! Are you fuckin mental? You're a crazy fucker sometimes, Shug. There's not a single cunt in the whole chapter who would challenge Hotwire unless they had to, and you go and piss him off. You're lucky he was in a good mood or you wouldn't be standing here, and that's a fact," he told me.

"I don't feel very lucky," I suggested. "Well, let me assure you, you are. And best you get your arse in there and apologise before he decides to waste you properly."

"Whoa, hang on a fuckin minute. You want me to go in and fuckin apologise to him after what he did to me? Are you fuckin mad? There's no fuckin way I'm doing that," I told him.

"Listen, Shug, trust me, you need to. If you don't, then down the road, you'll get much worse. Remember, he likes his stuff. When he's out of it - he always remembers situations like this and there's no controlling him when he goes off on one. Trust me, I know. I've seen it a few times and you don't want to be on the receiving end."

"Aw, fuck's sake, man, how the fuck do I get myself into this shit? Talk about lucky white heather. Why can't I keep my big fuckin mouth shut?" I asked him.

"Hey, man, listen, we all do stupid things. It's just that you seem to do really, really stupid things," he said, laughing away. After we had a bit of a chat, I eventually agreed I would go in and apologise. So I headed to the farm, licking my wounds as I walked.

When I walked in, Cowboy was demanding to know what had happened, thinking I'd been jumped or something. I told him it was cool and headed in, looking for Hotwire.

I found him with Jelly and Indie in the conservatory. When Indie saw me, he jumped up, demanding to know what had happened. I told him it was okay and what had happened was all my fault. I then went over to Hotwire and apologised for being a dick and offered him my hand.

He stood up and stared at me for a minute and said: "You're a little fuckwit, Shug, but I like fuckwits. Don't worry, we're cool." He then gave me a hug, which almost crushed the life out of me, reminding me of all the sore bits I had - thanks to him.

Indie demanded to know what the fuck had happened. Hotwire told him to take it easy and said it was just a playful romp in the barn with a brother, to get in the mood for the run. Indie then looked at me and shook his head.

"Fuck, Shug, I don't think you'll ever learn, will you?" he remarked. I just shrugged my shoulders, thanked Hotwire then left. I thought to myself what a prick I was: I'd just thanked someone for kicking the shit out of me. What a crazy fuckin world I live in. It's not even breakfast time and I've already been kicked up and down the barn by a drug crazed nutter, and now I'm waiting to go on a run, in the freezing cold, to fuck knows where, with another 50 or so lunatics, all with the same attitude. 'What does that make me?' I wondered.

I sat on the steps outside, lit up a fag and thought 'How the fuck am I going to be able to drive my bike? I can hardly fuckin stand up'.

My thoughts were interrupted by Cowboy, who sat down beside me and asked me what had happened, so I filled him in. We both agreed I wasn't right in the fuckin head and burst into uncontrolled laughter.

Our laughter was cut short by the roar of a cluster bikes coming down the lane. Between us, we counted around twenty-five or so. At the same time that they arrived at the farm, lots of the guys were bringing their bikes out of the barn.

We both decided to do the same and headed to the barn. As we went to get the bikes out, most of the guys in the farm joined us, with the exception of Indie, Hotwire and Jelly.

I reckon, by the time we all congregated outside, there must have been over fifty bikes, which I thought was a massive turn out, considering all the shit going on and the time of year. But, as Indie approached the barn, he didn't seem too impressed.

He jumped on his bike and summoned us all to follow him. He was leading the pack, with Rooster, Jelly, Hotwire and The Reaper directly behind him. As I looked on, I remembered that Rooster still hadn't told me how The Reaper got his name, so I made a mental note to ask him during the run.

Lots of the guys have strange club names, but none of them has 'The' in front of it, for some reason, it really intrigued me.

I sidled up beside Cowboy, towards the back of the pack, but in front of the two prospects. I pointed to the prospects as we started moving and asked Cowboy if he remembered the last time we went on a run and how it had been us that were stuck at the back. He just laughed and said: "Yep, changed days."

It felt really great riding my new bike, surrounded by all the guys. However, I couldn't help feeling a tinge of sadness for Malky. This was all he wanted from life, and while his was cut short, here I was, fulfilling his dream, not even sure if I liked the lifestyle anymore. Yes, I loved the bikes. And being part of the Bats was amazing. But the shit they got up to - it just didn't fit with me. The stuff most guys revelled in were the bits that made me sick to the core. I almost felt like I was two people, trying to decide which one I should become. I decided I needed to forget all the shit in my head until the run was over, then I would take it from there.

As we turned onto the main road, I could feel the aches and pains start to become very uncomfortable, and along with the biting wind and low temperatures, I knew I had a lot of suffering to endure on the road ahead.

We headed through the village and onto the dual carriageway. When we approached the first roundabout, I heaved a huge sigh of relief. We turned left onto the west coast route which meant we weren't going back to the Devil's patch, but meeting them somewhere else. What a relief it was for me to know I wouldn't need to be on the road where Malky died.

We travelled for about half an hour then stopped 'en masse' at a petrol station. When we were filling up our bikes, a prospect came and asked us for a tenner each. At that point, I remember looking at Cowboy and we both burst out laughing.

"What's so fuckin funny?" he demanded to know. We then laughed even louder so he just took our money and left, shaking his head and muttering under his breath.

We all fired up our bikes; the roar underneath the canopy was absolutely deafening. I could even see the ladies in the kiosk holding their ears.

I loved it and revved up my bike up as loud as I could. I was joined by almost everyone as we started to leave. I reckon, to this day, I've never heard a louder sound. As we all poured onto the road, I honestly felt like I'd gone deaf. It took a few miles to get my hearing back to normal.

Even though the sun was shining really bright, it was fuckin freezing. The frost on the road was glistening like cut glass and it was really hard to see any distance in front. What made it even worse was the reflection coming from the chrome on our bikes. Occasionally, it almost felt like you were being stabbed in the eyes.

I remember telling Cowboy before we left, that I was sure there would be a few casualties on the trip because of the weather and with the way a lot of the guys rode, but I couldn't believe how careful everybody was being.

We drove for around another hour or so before coming to a stop. We had arrived at a small town around lunchtime and Indie led us up an alleyway behind what looked like a very small pub. Both Cowboy and I looked at each other, wondering what the fuck he was up to, but we just shrugged and followed on. Behind the pub, there was a large parking area which appeared to be just some 'hard core' or 'type1' dumped on a disused field and flattened out.

Indie was already parked up and had made his way to a door at the back of the pub before we'd even got into the car park. By the time we found a spot, most of the guys were already in and I wondered where they were going to put us all.

I couldn't believe it when I went in; it was like a fuckin Tardis, the room was huge inside. I would never have believed, looking from the outside, that even half of us would have fitted in. Indie was at the bar talking to a bloke, who I guess was in charge. There were already three barmaids pouring drinks like their lives depended on it.

I could feel myself shivering and would've loved to ask for a cup of tea or a bowl of soup, but looking around, seeing everyone filling their bellies with beer, I thought it best not to.

Indie handed the bloke at the bar a wedge of dough so I guessed we would be here for a while. I got my beer and sat down beside Cowboy and Rooster. I raised my glass to them and started drinking. Fuck, it was freezing. I could feel it chill me all the way down.

They both started laughing, knowing that what was happening to me had happened to them a minute before. They had both experienced exactly the same sensation and were laughing as they watched me drink. The room was very warm and we all had that tingling feeling coming on, the one you get when you're thawing out. I think everybody was glad to be stopped and inside for a while.

I asked Rooster if he knew where we were going and he told me that Indie was meeting the Devil's President here and he was going to let us know where to go next. "I hope to fuck he takes his time coming and lets us all thaw out before we move on," I suggested. Rooster replied, as I expected him to, by calling me a fuckin pussy, to which we all raised our glasses and laughed.

Just then, one of the prospects came to the table asking for a tenner. Cowboy decided to take the piss and we sat back, watching.

"What the fuck do you want another tenner for, ya little prick? You've already had a tenner off me," he told him, almost staring straight through him. "Fuck off, you're getting fuck all."

The prospect then told Cowboy that Indie had told him to collect a tenner from everybody. "You tell him he's a prick and that I'm paying fuck all. Now fuck off, before I give you a good slap." We then turned away from him and started talking amongst ourselves.

The prospect just stood there, staring at us. Cowboy looked up at him and growled a bit. "Why the fuck are you still here? Fuck off!" he growled at him.

To say his reply shocked us was an understatement. "Listen, Indie wants a tenner from everybody and that includes you. If you think he's a prick then that's up to you, but I won't be telling him anything, it's not my business. Now, are you giving me the tenner or not?"

Rooster then burst out laughing and handed him thirty quid. "Take it easy, man, he's only fucking with you. By the way, I like the way you stood your ground, well done, I'm sure you'll get plenty of that shit on this run."

We all raised our glasses to him and laughed. You could see the relief all over his face when he realised he was being wound up.

We were still laughing away when we heard the roar of bikes passing down the alley at the side of the pub. Fuck, we could feel the whole place shaking. Everybody let out a roar and a few of the guys headed out to greet them.

Within minutes, between thirty and forty guys had piled in and the place immediately became jam packed. Just like the last time we met up: there were a lot of man hugs, back slapping and laughing as everybody greeted each other.

I watched from my seat as the President and SAA headed straight to Indie. They both appeared to be offering their condolences to him. He then gave them both a hug, handed them a pint before the three of them raised their glasses to Provo.

As I looked around, I noticed that there weren't any females from either chapter and thought that it was a bit strange. I asked Cowboy if he'd noticed and he told me he had. "Why do you think that is then?" I asked him.

"I'm guessing it's either too cold for them or we're going to have a rumble, don't think it could be anything else, do you?" he quizzed.

"Fuck, not sure. Now you've planted the seed, I'm guessing we're going to be boxing," I told him. "Ha ha, me too," he replied. "So best we get a few beers down our neck before it all kicks off," and with that, he headed to the bar.

I went looking for Rooster to see if he knew what was going down and eventually caught up with him in the loo. I asked him if he knew where we were going next and why there were no old ladies with us.

"Fuck's sake, Shug, we're out on the randan. Can't you just fuckin relax and enjoy yourself for once? There are no old ladies here because it's fuckin Baltic. Would you want to subject your Mrs to this fuckin weather? Come on, man, stop stressing and chill." With that, he rubbed my head then fucked off.

I stood for a minute, looking in the mirror. Fuck, I looked pretty well battered and bruised. I'd forgotten about my spat with Hotwire, but looking at myself brought it back and, all of a sudden, all my aches and pains seemed to magnify.

I went back into the hall and everybody seemed to be in good spirits. I clocked Indie, Jelly, Hotwire and three of the Devil Angels huddled around a table in the corner, obviously planning something - or so I thought.

I decided to take Rooster's advice and chill out a bit. Cowboy was sitting with a couple of guys at a table and introduced me to them.

"Shug, this is Kaneo and Bullet. They were saying they remember us from the last meet, watching us running around like pricks after everybody." I shook hands with them and smiled.

As I sat down, Bullet asked me how the other dude, who was prospecting then, was doing. I guessed he was talking about Malky and I told him he'd died on the way home. "Oh fuck, sorry, man, I didn't know. What happened to him?" he asked

I told him the story and he repeated how sorry he was. "The reason I asked was because I remember tattooing him, and him going fuckin mental in the morning when he realised what had happened." "Yeh, he was pretty pissed about it, but did see the funny side eventually," I told him.

Cowboy then raised his glass, "To Malky" he said, and we all followed suit. Kaneo then commented about the shit time we'd been having with Malky, the 'Stone' thing and then Provo. "Hey, guys, don't worry. You get times like that, but we always come out the other end much stronger," he reminded us.

We then raised our glasses again and thankfully, Cowboy changed the subject, as I could feel myself welling up a bit and didn't want to start blubbering in front of them.

We'd been in the pub for a few hours and I was pretty well on when the Devil's President announced that we'd be leaving in half an hour. "Any idea where we're going?" I asked Bullit.

"Yeh, we have about half an hour's drive from here. We're going to a shutdown nightclub which the owner has kindly allowed us to use for a couple of days. It's been closed for about six months, we've used it before and it's a great place for us, it's out of the way and there's plenty parking. It's now been sold, but the new owners aren't moving in for another couple of months or so." I laughed at the thought of getting a loan of a fuckin nightclub.

"How the fuck can you just get a loan of a fuckin nightclub! Is that even possible?" I asked him. Kaneo leaned over and said: "Hey, Shug, I'm sure you've got shit on people you use for favours? Well, we're no different." He then went into a hearty laugh and told us he would get the beers in before we left.

Within about fifteen minutes, everybody was out in the car park firing up their bikes, wrapping up as warm as they could. The sun had disappeared and the sky was dark, the biting wind and the chill in the air seemed much colder than when we'd arrived.

There must've been around eighty bikes, all driving out of the lane and onto the main road. Indie and the Devil's President led the pack. By the time I drove out the lane, they were out of sight.

I reckon that the half hour I spent on the run to the nightclub was the coldest I've ever been on a bike. By the time we arrived, I couldn't feel my feet or my fingers, my face was numb and I was shivering like mad.

When I got off, I noticed that everybody was exactly the same, I wondered if anyone had frostbite or hypothermia; it was that fuckin cold.

Once off my bike, I even struggled to get the key out of the ignition. A bike pulled in next to me and as the guy who was riding pillion stood up on the footpegs to get off, he lifted his leg over the cissy bar then fell to the ground. He was unconscious. As usual, I thought the worst, convincing myself he was dying of some cold-related illness. We carried him inside and immediately, when we entered, we could feel the heat consuming us.

We laid the bloke down on the floor and one of the other Devil's came over to check on him. He instantly declared that he was pished, put him in the recovery position and left him to sleep it off. I could feel the tingling thing happening again and decided to grab a seat until it passed.

I looked about the place and I still couldn't get my head around how they'd pulled this off. The place was lit up, the music was booming, there was drink in the optics and cases upon cases of beer piled up behind the bar. There were a right few females here too; a combination of Mamas and a healthy sprinkling of others with no patches.

Cowboy came over and handed me a beer. I gestured for him to put it on the table, which he did. "How the fuck can you drink beer, man?" I asked him. "I'm fuckin freezing, I can hardly feel my feet or hands, you must be the fuckin same?"

"Shug, I'm fine. We all are, except you of course, and we all know why you're not fine: it's because you're a fuckin pussy," he said, then raised his glass and disappeared, laughing loudly.

I turned my attention to the dance floor where there were about half a dozen girls strutting their stuff. Some of the guys were already in there, jumping about with them, pouring drink down their necks and rubbing themselves up and down against them.

I could now feel myself thawing out and allowed myself a wry smile, thinking this was going to be a good run after all. We were miles away from anywhere, and everything, so far, had been well natured. I picked up my beer, had a good long drink of it and for the first time today, I felt myself relaxing.

I was sitting, chilling when Rooster summoned me to the bar. I headed over to see what was up. "How you doin, Shug?" he asked.

"Actually, Rooster, for the first time in a while, I'm good. Why'd you ask?" "Just clocked you sitting by yourself over there and wondered if anything was up." "Not a thing, man, I'm good, just taking it easy. Hey, man, you told me to remind you about 'The Reaper', you promised to tell me the script about how he got his name." "Oh, yes, I forgot about that. C'mon, let's grab a pew and I'll fill you in."

We headed back to where I'd been sitting and Rooster began: "It's really no big deal, Shug. It was stuff that happened to him when he was young and it stuck with him. When he was 11, he was in a car accident with his parents, they both died, but he survived. After that, he went to live with his grandparents. When he was 14, his grandfather took him to a football match, but his grandfather had a heart attack on the way home and died and he was the only one with him at the time. Then his gran died in her sleep, about 2 months later, apparently of a broken heart. Again, he was the only one there and found her when he went to wake her in the morning."

I interrupted at that point, "Holy shit, talk about shit luck. Fuck, I thought I had it tough!"

Rooster then told me, "I know, but that's not all …" "Holy Fuck, there can't be any more!" I interrupted. "He was then put into care and placed with foster parents until he was sixteen. He got his first bike just after his birthday. He'd only had it a week when he hit a kerb. He went flying across the road and the bike bounced up onto the pavement and smacked into an old lady who was walking her dog. She died in hospital a few days later. Apparently, he'd hit a pot-hole in the road and that's what caused him to hit the kerb. The police called it an accidental death and he was freed of any wrong-doing. The family of the old lady got compensation from the council because of the pothole. He went off the rails at that point and started drinking heavily, taking drugs and stealing to feed his habit. This went on for around nine months until he got caught stealing and tried to beat up a couple of police officers. He ended up getting twelve months in a young offenders' institution. While inside, he met Provo, who was also in for the first time. Provo was already a Bat by then and during their time inside they became mates. When he told Provo his story, he convinced him to join the Bats and declared him 'The Reaper'. So there you have it. They both got out within a month of each other and 'The Reaper' joined up. He's been involved in one more death since, though. He was riding pillion with his mate and they crashed into an oncoming car. The Reaper was thrown free, but his mate died. Since then, he's always ridden solo."

"Fuck me, Rooster, how does he stay sane with all that shit in his head? He must have some fuckin nightmares!"

"Who knows, Shug, I think he takes a lot of drink and drugs when he's low, I guess that helps. Anyway, enough of the depressive shit, I'm going to get myself a shag," he told me.

"Hey, what about you and Julie? What's the story there?" I asked. "Julie and I are finished. Still mates, but she's fucked off, told me she can't cope with my lifestyle anymore. So, hey, fuck it. Shug, remember, we're not here forever - so live for the day, man." He then laughed, got up from his seat, rubbed my hair with his hand then headed to the dance floor.

I thought for a minute about our chat, trying to absorb the stuff about The Reaper and then I started contextualising my own shit. Fuck, I was actually doing okay.

It's amazing how hearing other people's stories can help you make sense of your own shit. Rooster's parting words also perked me up. I thought 'Fuck it, he's right. Live for the day. It's about time I started doing that'.

I headed to the bar, fired a few rapid back my throat and started mingling with everyone. I eventually found a chick who wasn't particularly good looking, but was well up for it.

We were snogging and fondling away at each other in one of the booths when a prospect came over and asked me for a fiver for the drink fund. I looked at him, standing awkwardly in front of us, and whispered to the chick, asking her if she was up for a threesome, to which she nodded.

"What's your name, prospect?" I growled, in as manly a voice as I could muster. "Zander," he said. "Well, Zander, before I give you a fiver, you're going to get a blowjob."

I lifted the chick onto her knees and dropped her knickers to her ankles. I then pulled my jeans down and took her from behind. I told the prospect to stick it in her mouth, which he did in a flash, and I started riding her like there was no tomorrow.

The prospect got her tits out and started rubbing away at her nipples. She was making all sorts of grunting noises and backing into me with a vengeance. The next minute, the prospect slumped on the chair, smiling, so I knew he'd shot his load.

The chick kept sucking away at him, but he removed his dick from her mouth - I think he was concerned she'd bite it off as she was a bit frenzied.

He got up, I then handed him the fiver, we shook hands, he thanked me and walked away. Fuck, what a weird couple of minutes that was: I was still shagging this chick (I hadn't even bothered to ask her name), she's giving it big licks, and I'm chatting to a cunt I didn't even know.

I laughed away to myself, then focused on emptying my sack. She turned around, sat me down then straddled me. She proceeded to bounce up and down on top of me. Fuck, she was like a pogo-stick on heat.

I eventually realised that I wasn't going to come. My dick was on fire with her mad bouncing so I stopped her in mid-flight and told her I needed a pish.

She got off me, looking a bit pissed, but I kissed her on the cheek and told her I'd be back shortly. I headed to the loo and had no intention of going back to her as my dick was throbbing, I didn't want anybody bouncing up and down on it for a good few hours.

I headed back to the bar, got a beer then spent the next few minutes just looking around. I noticed the chick had managed to get a more willing participant to jump up and down on and I offered myself a huge sigh of relief.

This was what I thought I'd signed up for: loads of guys having a great time and plenty shagging. I wondered why it couldn't always be like this.

There were guys having arm wrestling competitions, some were having drinking challenges and some were shagging. The rest were catching up with each other, laughing and joking and generally having a good time.

There were a few chicks doing a striptease on the dance floor and the music was booming away. Fuck, this really was what it was all about.

After catching up with a few guys, and drinking way too much, I headed out to get my sleeping bag off my bike. It was fuckin freezing and my bag was covered in frost, but I grabbed it anyway and headed back inside.

I decided to find myself a spot in a corner and crash. I reckon I must've zonked out the minute I lay down. I never heard a thing after that and had no idea how long the party lasted.

Chapter 7

I woke just after 7am and the place looked like a bomb site. No one was awake and heading to the toilet was like attempting an assault course challenge.

There were bodies everywhere, some in sleeping bags, some just crashed with drinks in their hands and others on chairs, even a couple lying on the bar. I made my way to the loo, gave myself a bit of a wash and freshen up then headed outside for some fresh air.

Even though the sun was shining high in the sky it was absolutely freezing. All the bikes were covered in a light coating of frost and the car park was glistening like a sheet of ice.

I lit up a fag and sat down on a crumpled old cardboard box. I looked around, noticing how peaceful and quiet it was. When we'd arrived the day before, I hadn't paid any attention to our surroundings, but looking at them now, the place seemed pretty affluent.

I wondered how come they had a nightclub in such a posh area. I was thinking the residents would have petitioned against something like that, especially now someone else had bought it and was planning to reopen it.

"Hi, man, how come you're out here on your own?" Fuck me, I was miles away, I about shat myself, I never thought anybody else would be up so early. I turned around to see the Devil's prospect standing beside me.

"Jeezus, Zander, you nearly gave me a fuckin heart attack!" I told him. "What the fuck are you doing creeping about at this time?"

"Sorry, man, I saw you coming out earlier and just wanted to come and say thanks for last night." I told him I wasn't sure what he meant, then he reminded me about the blowjob which made me laugh. "Hey, no probs," I told him. "We all have to start somewhere."

He came and sat down beside me and I offered him a fag, which he took. I gave him a light and watched him inhale deeply and blow the smoke out into the cold morning air.

"First time was it?" I asked. "Yep, sure was," he replied. "I told everybody I'd done it loads, as you do, but other than the odd fumble and touch up, I've never actually had a blowjob or a ride."

"Hey, we've all told everybody that shit at some time, but at least you're halfway there now," I suggested.

"Well, actually, I'm fully there. I had two rides with two different chicks last night," he told me. I patted him on the back and started laughing again.

"Good for you, bud, well done, sounds a bit like my first time," I told him. He then started laughing as well and had the biggest smile I'd seen on anybody's face for a while.

Zander told me that he'd only been prospecting for a couple of months and that this was his first run. We were having a bit of a chat about prospecting and being in our respective chapters, sussing out the differences, when about twenty cop cars and vans came screeching to a halt in front of us.

"Fuckin hell! Get inside!" I told him, and with that, we both jumped up and ran in. Zander went in shouting that the pigs were outside and I bolted the door.

Instantly, people started jumping up and racing around, looking for the clothes they had casually discarded during the frivolities of the previous evening.

I headed to Indie, who was standing with the Devil's President, and listened as they tried to determine the reason for the visit.

Their President told Indie that he reckoned it was to do with a bit of bother they'd had the previous week when a couple of policemen had been stabbed whilst trying to stop a scrap with some Mods.

"Fuck me, you might've given us a heads up about that. Fuck's sake, man, I told YOU about our shit with Stone!" Indie reminded him. "Yeh, sorry, man, I should've, but I didn't think for a minute it would follow us here."

He then told Indie he would go and see what the fuck they wanted. Indie then said: "Will you fuck, bro. We'll do this together. Come on, let's both see what the fuckers want."

As they were heading towards the door, the police were already banging on it and telling us all to come out.

When they opened the door, I couldn't believe what I saw, there seemed to be hundreds of them and most of them had guns.

'Fuckin hell!' I thought to myself, 'There must be some proper shit going down here.' I'd never seen the cops with so many guns. Everybody inside seemed to freeze.

The policeman at the door then said to everybody not to move and some of the other armed officers came in and grabbed the Devil's President, the VP and a handful of other guys.

They put all of them in one of the vans, except the Prez and VP. The officer in charge then stood in front of both of them. "James McCallum and Brian Wilson: I am arresting you for the murder of P.C. Calum McGregor ..." then continued to read both of them their rights.

Some of the Devils then went to make a move on the police. Almost in unison, the officers raised their guns.

There was a loud clicking sound as they all let off their safety catches at the same time, this stopped the guys in their tracks and they took a step back.

They then put the President and the VP in the back of one of the other vans as all the rest of the cops moved slowly back to their vehicles, never taking their eyes off us for a second. They never lowered their guns until they were all in the vans.

The police then headed away and Indie called for everyone to get back inside, which we did.

Indie then got what was left of the Devils officers together, along with ours, and they all huddled in the corner of the room. The rest of us just milled around, waiting to see what came next.

I caught up with Cowboy and asked him his view on what he thought would happen next. "I guess we'll be making our way home now. I reckon the Devils will also head off to regroup and get their lawyer onto the case," he told me.

I agreed that made sense, but reminded him we weren't in the game of doing sensible things. We both nodded to each other and smiled.

Just then, Indie shouted for everybody to shut up and listen, which we did. "We're heading back down the road. Sorry we're leaving so early, but we think it's best you guys sort out your shit with the pigs. Remember, if we can do anything, we're only a phone call away." After speaking, he turned to the Devil Angels Sergeant at Arms and they hugged.

Then the SAA addressed the remaining Angels: "Right, guys, get your shit together and let's get back up the road. Once we sort this mess out we'll meet up with the Bats again and have a proper fuckin blast."

Then he and Indie hugged again, shook hands and headed to the door. Everybody started piling out behind them, shaking hands as they went. When we all got outside, everybody started attaching their stuff to their bikes and firing them up.

I looked at Cowboy. "Good shout, man, you got it spot on," I told him. He just nodded and finished tying his bag to the front of his bike.

Indie rode out the car park and we all followed. For the first few miles, we noticed that there was a police car on nearly every fuckin corner. Most of the guys were giving them the finger or the tongs and laughing as they passed.

I was hoping that the trip home would pass without incident and it pretty much did. The weather was okay for most of the trip, apart from the biting wind. You could feel it chilling you to the very bone; the further we rode, the more my face and hands became numb.

I was so glad when we stopped for fuel. Just before we drew into the garage, I felt like I was going to pass out as I was that cold. As everybody drew in, I looked around and could see that I wasn't the only one feeling the cold.

While we waited for the pumps to free up, I watched a lot of the older guys lying over their tanks and placing their hands on their hot engines. Some were then placing their hands on their faces for a bit before putting them back on the engine.

I got back on my bike and did the same. I found it was a great way to warm up; as you lay across the tank, you got the heat rising from the engine which warmed the whole of your body. Then, by placing my warm hands on my face, I almost instantly made myself feel alive again.

By the time I'd fuelled up and was ready to leave, I was reasonably warm and ready to face the final part of the ride home.

We blasted out of the garage, making as much noise as we could. Looking around, I felt the mood of everyone seemed to have lifted a bit after the morning's escapades.

Some of the guys started messing around on their bikes, pulling wheelies and sitting the wrong way round and stuff. One of the guys riding pillion even swapped bikes without stopping.

Everything was going great until we were about fifteen miles from the farm and some of the guys started heading home. They all drove up to the front of the pack, nodded to Indie, then went their separate ways. There must've been about ten of us left as we approached the town. A bloke in a Volvo cut in on us and almost made a couple of the guys crash. He then sped away without acknowledging his error.

The whole group took up chase. As we crossed the bridge, we saw him sitting at the traffic lights. Jelly drew up alongside his car with everyone else drawing in behind.

He rapped at the driver's window and the guy rolled it down. Jelly then hit him flush in the face and as the lights changed, he shot away, laughing.

We all started overtaking the car as it sat at the lights while the driver tried to come to terms with what had just happened.

We all gave the car a bit of a boot on the way past and headed into town. The two prospects were 'two's up' at the back of the car and stalled their bike as they went to pull away.

The driver, by this time, had got his bearings and was coming up behind us. The prospects raced up beside the car and just as they went to pass him, he turned his car to the right and hit the bike, pushing it onto the other side of the road and into an oncoming car.

None of us really saw what actually happened. But later, eyewitness accounts explained in detail about how the prospects went head-on into the oncoming car. Both of them were thrown over the top of it; one of the guys landed on the bonnet of the car behind and the other hit the road and the kerb at the same time.

We all heard the thud and the screeches of cars trying to stop quickly. We all slammed on our brakes and turned around as quickly as we could and headed back to the crash.

By then, people were out of their cars and tending to the prospects. Buzz had hit the kerb and was unconscious while Duffy, the other prospect, had slipped off the car and onto the road. He was conscious and moaning really loudly.

I was looking around for the cunt in the Volvo, but he'd disappeared. Cowboy pointed to a side street and we saw the car had stopped halfway down it.

I got back on my bike and Cowboy jumped on the back. We headed down the road and stopped behind it. Cowboy jumped off and ran to the driver's side and saw the driver wasn't there. He then ran around the other side and saw there was a woman in the passenger seat.

Cowboy tried the door, but it was locked. He started banging on the window, demanding her to tell him where the driver was, but she just pointed to the building behind Cowboy.

He turned around and realised it was a police station. By this time, I had joined him and was trying to tell him to stay calm. I suggested we go inside to see where the cunt was and that he should let me do the talking, but he wasn't taking incoming calls.

The worst thing that could have possibly happened, happened. The driver came out of the police station with two cops behind him and Cowboy made a beeline for him.

The police told him to back off, but Cowboy grabbed him, pulled him to the ground and started punching fuck out of him (before the police had even realised what was going on). The police then started setting about Cowboy and that was my cue to join in.

The driver was on the ground, Cowboy was on top of him and the cops were trying to get him off. I jumped on the top of them all and started punching wildly at anything that moved.

Within minutes, it was only the two policemen and us scrapping. Somehow, the driver had managed to get away and when we heard the car screeching away it brought us to our senses.

The cops told us to get a fucking grip of ourselves and let them go to the crash scene to help our mates. That struck a chord with both of us as we'd almost forgot about them, in the midst of trying to get revenge on the driver.

We stood back and the cops ran toward the main road. "This isn't finished, by the way, we'll pick this up later," one of them shouted at us as they left.

I got back on my bike and Cowboy, again, jumped on the back. We arrived at the same time as the cops. By then, there were a couple of ambulances, a cop car and loads of people milling around. The police who were there had the other eight guys huddled together at the side of the road, trying to keep them away from everyone else.

We got off the bike and Indie was screaming at us, demanding to know where the fuck we'd been, so we quickly filled him in. At that point, the ambulance, with both prospects in it, shot off with the sirens wailing, heading to the hospital with a police escort leading the way.

Indie told the cops we were done talking and were heading to the hospital to see how the guys were.

Surprisingly, the cops agreed and told us that they would catch up with us later for more statements and moved out of the way.

A couple of the guys picked up what was left of the prospect's bike and pushed it off the road. Cowboy and I, with the help of some of the people standing around, picked up some of the bits that were scattered over the road and laid them beside the bike.

We then all headed to the hospital, followed by one of the cop cars. When we arrived, we were told that the prospects were in the treatment rooms with the doctors and nurses. It was also suggested that we have a seat in the casualty waiting room until there was more news.

We'd barely sat down when one of the officers came and asked us to follow him, which we all did. He took us to exactly the same room we were in before, with all the pregnancy shit in it, and I was getting a strange feeling of déjà vu.

The cop ushered us in and said: "You'll all be better off in here. I'll go and find out what's going on with your mates and get back to you as soon as I find anything out." He then closed the door and left.

I thought Indie would go ape shit about being shoved into the room out of the way, but he just slumped down on the floor and lit up a fag. Rooster, Hotwire and Jelly did the same. Cowboy lit two and handed me one and we joined in.

Jelly and Indie started trying to piece together what had happened then asked Cowboy to repeat what went on with us after the crash.

Cowboy gave him the full version and Indie asked him if he would recognise the driver again and he told him he would.

Indie then told us that we would do nothing today, but would pick it up again first thing tomorrow.

The room then fell silent and we all seemed to drift off into our own little worlds. All I could think of was 'Fuck's sake, nothing's simple with the Bats! It doesn't matter what the fuck we do, there always seems to be a consequence and a shitload of hassle to go with it'.

I started to wonder if the police would do anything about me and Cowboy scrapping with them? And If the cunt in the Volvo would try and press charges against Cowboy? AND if the bastard would get done for causing the crash in the first place?

I must have drifted off as the next thing I knew, a policeman and a doctor were standing chatting with Indie and Rooster.

I jumped up, still pretty incoherent, and tried to make sense of what the doctor was saying.

He was telling Indie that Buzz had to have 3 toes removed from one foot and two from the other as the steel toe cap in his boots had sliced into his feet causing irreparable damage. He also told him he had a broken arm, a broken leg and head trauma, which resulted in him having to have an operation and said and he would require a few more over the coming weeks.

Indie then enquired about Duffy and the doctor explained that he was worse. I couldn't believe it when he said Duffy was worse, I thought to myself 'How the fuck could he be worse than that?'.

He began to explain that the impact of the crash had broken most of his ribs and that one had punctured a lung, another had been embedded in his intestine; both of which were causing major concern.

He then said that he also had 2 broken legs and a broken ankle, along with lots of cuts and bruises which required a massive amount of stitching. He explained that both patients would remain in intensive care over the next few days as they required 24hour observation. He then asked if we had any questions.

Indie asked him if any of them could die. All the doctor said was that they were doing all they could and they would receive the best possible care. He then excused himself and left.

The officer who was with him stayed back and suggested to Indie that we should all go home as there was nothing we could do until the guys were out of intensive care.

Indie thanked him, asked him to give us a minute then told him we would head off after a quick chat. The officer nodded then left. Indie punched the wall, drawing blood from his knuckles, and growled under his breath. When he turned around, he started talking.

"Right, fuck waiting until tomorrow! The lot of you: find out who the fucker in the Volvo is. Find out everything about him, then get back to the farm. I'll head back there just now and round up the troops. I want you all back within two hours," he explained before leaving.

Hotwire then told us we should all go back to the crash scene and follow his lead from there. We all headed back through the hospital, stopping at casualty to ask if there was any change with the prospects. We were told they were still the same so made our way out to our bikes.

Riding back to where the crash happened, all I could think about was Malky and the day he died, it still niggled away at me. Never a day had gone by that I didn't feel guilty about it. Most days, I could keep it at the back of my mind. But at times like this, it was always my first thought.

We arrived much quicker than I expected, I couldn't believe how quickly the road was back to normal. The only way you would have known there had been a crash there earlier was the blood stains and the skid marks on the road.

Hotwire was already off his bike and ushering us towards him. He told us we should all head up the road, the same way the Volvo had been heading. Each of us should then take a turning, follow the road for a bit and see if we find it. And if not, should head back onto the road and keep doing the same until it turned up.

We got back on the bikes and followed his lead. At each turning, he would point towards the road and someone would turn off. I was last to turn off and headed into quite a posh estate with some really big houses.

I drove around it slowly for about 10 minutes, checking all the drives. I even had a look in some of the garages. At one of them, a guy came out and asked me what I was doing. I told him I was looking for an orange Volvo, described it and told him it was involved in a hit and run.

To my surprise, he told me he thought he knew the car and reckoned that it belonged to a local businessman's son, a guy called Tim Thatcher. He said he didn't know where he lived, but knew where his father's two shops were and gave me directions.

I thanked him, jumped back on my bike and sped off. I rode around for a bit, trying to find the others, but the only one I saw was Jelly.

When I passed on what the guy had told me, he suggested I head straight back to the farm and tell Indie and that he would rake around for the others.

I turned around and shot off in the direction of the farm then realised I needed fuel. I headed on a slight detour towards the garage. When I got there, I saw Cowboy filling up. I drew up beside him, told him my story and he decided to come back to the farm with me. We both got our fuel and within fifteen minutes, were back at the farm.

When we arrived, we knew a lot of the guys were inside due to the number of bikes scattered around. I guessed Indie had summoned them because of the crash.

We went in and I noticed the clock. I reckoned the rest of the guys would soon be back because the two-hour limit Indie had given us was almost up.

I went straight into the conservatory and told Indie and the guys who were there what I'd found out. When I finished, he smacked his hands together and said: "Fuckin brilliant, now we can decide how to take the fucker down. Right, let's wait until everybody gets back then we'll plan our next move. Well done, Shug, grab yourself a beer, man, and we'll talk later."

I headed to the kitchen with Cowboy. Just as we were grabbing a beer from the fridge the rest of the guys started piling in, within ten minutes everybody had returned. Rooster grabbed a beer and sat with us, asking me what Indie had said about it and I repeated what he'd told us.

Rooster said he knew the shops and had been in both of them a few times buying tools. He thought he remembered the guy boasting to one of his mates about how he was going to be taking over the business soon as his father was ready to retire.

We chatted for a while about what we thought Indie would do, but none of us were even close to what he had actually decided. He called us all into the conservatory and began to tell us his plans.

"Okay, listen up," he told us. "Tomorrow, I want everybody out and about in two's or three's. I want you to check out the two shops: find out who works there, where they all live and if they're related to the owner. I want to find out where this 'Tim Thatcher' lives: if he has a family and if he's married. Then I want to know all about his wife's family. I want to know if there's any dirt about them. I want to know about the father: find out if he's legit or if we can dig up anything that'll fuck him up. Nobody touches anyone, we just collect the info. Afterwards, we'll fuck the lot of them and their fuckin grannies too. Tomorrow night at seven, everybody back here for a meet, any questions?"

Nobody said anything and Indie headed to the office. We all spread around the house into our favourite corners. I headed to the back step with Cowboy, taking a couple of beers and some smokes with me.

"What do you reckon he'll do once we get the info?" I asked Cowboy. "Not sure, Shug, but my guess is he'll waste the businesses and probably hospitalise or kill the Thatcher guy." "Yep, I agree," I told him. "That would be my guess as well. Don't you ever worry about all this shit, Cowboy? Do you ever think it's just not worth it?" I asked. "Shug, if I worried about it all, I reckon that would be the time I'd need to chuck it. I did worry about it a lot at first, but now I just go with the flow. My philosophy is: no cunt will remember what you did when you're dead anyway, so 'fuck it' when you're living." He looked at me, raised his beer bottle towards me then put it to his mouth and proceeded to finish it in a oner.

He then stood up. "You for another?" he asked, I just nodded to him as he disappeared inside. I looked around the place for a minute, bikes scattered everywhere, music booming in the background, the night sky closing in and a real chill in the air. I inhaled deeply on my cigarette and began to think about what tomorrow might bring.

Just then, some of the guys came outside and jumped on their bikes. Jelly and Hotwire were both in the group and shouted to me that they would see me bright and early the next day. I just raised my bottle towards them and nodded. They both nodded back then sped off up the lane.

Cowboy then came back out with some more beer and Rooster also joined us. "Hey, Shug, you, me and Cowboy will be heading out together in the morning. Indie has just told me we're going to do a bit of nosing around in the shop at the other side of the town so it looks like the three amigos will be spending the day together. I hope you're not going to have your boring head on?"

Rooster and Cowboy then smiled, touched their bottles together and started laughing. "Very funny, Rooster, you're killing me with your pish patter," I told him, which made them laugh even louder.

We ended up going back inside as the night was getting colder and we all agreed that we needed a bit of warmth. More than three-quarters of the guys decided to stay over and we ended up having a bit of a party which went on until the early hours.

I ended up going to bed with Fiona, but we just cuddled in and went to sleep, much to my disappointment.

Everybody was up early in the morning. By the time I got downstairs, some of the girls who'd stayed over were making breakfast. I'd just grabbed a roll when Indie shouted me through to the conservatory.

When I went through, he handed me a large bag of dope and told me he wanted me to take it to a guy he knew in the next town. He handed me a piece of paper with the address on it and told me that the guy should have £300 for him and that I had to get the money and count it before I gave him the bag.

"Shug, remember, no dosh - no dope. Tell Cowboy to go with you." Before I got a chance to say anything, he shouted for Rooster and ushered me out.

'Fuck's sake!' I thought to myself, 'All this shit going on and he wants me to deliver drugs to some fucker I've never met!'. I raked about, looking for Cowboy, and found him crashed on one of the couches. I woke him up, told him the script and suggested he move his arse a bit sharpish.

I headed back to the kitchen to see if my roll was still there, but someone else must have scoffed it and I had to do with a bit of cold burnt toast.

Cowboy came into the kitchen, picked up a couple of bits of toast and we headed out to the bikes. I stuffed the bag into my jacket which made me look like I had a beer belly. I jumped on my bike, fired it into life then slowly headed up the lane.

I stopped at the main road and waited until Cowboy caught up. When he arrived, I handed him the piece of paper with the address on it and asked him if he knew where it was and he told me he did. I then gestured for him to take the lead and I tucked in behind him as we moved onto the main road.

It was fuckin freezing, the wind felt like it would cut you in half and Cowboy wasn't messing around. I had to push my bike a bit faster than I wanted just to keep up. The roads were pretty empty and it took us less than 20 minutes to get into the next town, then another five or so to find the address.

When we drew up outside the house, I was really surprised. It was a large detached bungalow with a brick wall around it and a huge garage at the side. There were two metal gates with a sizable drive and a brand new car sitting in front of the house.

We killed the engines and I got off my bike. I asked Cowboy to check we had the correct address and he told me we had. I said I would go in myself and that he should keep an eye out. He nodded in agreement.

I walked up the drive and rang the bell. The door opened and a well-dressed man in his fifties opened the door. He asked if he could help me in one of the poshest accents I'd ever heard. "I have a package from Indie," I could hear myself say. "Excellent, please come in, young man," he replied, opening the door wider and stepping out of the way.

I walked in and he closed the door. "Can I see the merchandise, please?" he requested. "Certainly. Can I see the money?" I replied. "No problem. One moment, please excuse me, I'll be back in a minute," he told me then disappeared into another room.

I looked around, the place dripped of money. I couldn't help wondering what the fuck I was doing here and why the fuck this old dude would need to be dealing in drugs? And especially, why the fuck would he be doing it with the Bats?

He came back through with a wad of notes and handed them to me. I counted the money and there was £320 in the bundle so I handed him twenty back. He then said: "Oh no, my good man, the extra is for you - for your trouble. Thank you for delivering it to me. Now can I please see it?"

I opened my jacket and handed him the bag. He took it then excused himself again and asked if I could wait another minute or so, to which I just nodded. He came back within a minute and handed me an envelope for Indie. He then opened the door, thanked me again, ushered me out then closed the door.

As I walked back down the drive, I thought that had been one of the weirdest things I'd ever done. When I got to the gate, I must have looked a bit off as Cowboy asked me if I'd seen a ghost or something. I just shook my head and told him I would fill him in when we got back.

I stuffed the envelope into my jacket, jumped back on my bike and we both headed back to the farm. On the way back, it started raining, which made it even colder, and I was glad when we arrived. I headed straight into the conservatory and caught up with Indie. He asked me if everything had gone okay and I told him it had, then gave him the money and the envelope.

I told him there was an extra £20 there as the guy insisted I take it as a tip. I then asked Indie who the dude was and he told me he was a top lawyer and the hash was for him and his cronies and that we did a monthly drop for him.

I then took it too far by asking how he got involved with the Bats so Indie told me it was none of my business, but to be assured it was a great thing to have them in our back pocket even though they didn't realise it.

I headed back to the kitchen to try and dry off and get a bit of heat. Cowboy was already standing in the front of the range warming himself and I muscled in beside him. I was just starting to feel like I was thawing out when Rooster came in and told us it was time to go.

"Rooster, give us a fuckin break, man. We're just back in, and it's fuckin freezing! At least let us thaw out, for fuck's sake!"

"Hey, listen, move your arses or go through and tell the big man you're not coming. Either way, I don't give a fuck, I'm heading now," he told us as he left. I looked at Cowboy and he suggested we head out after him.

I went out and straight over to Rooster, who had already started up his bike, and asked him what was eating him and why he was being a pain in the arse. He just told me to shut the fuck up and get a move on.

We all headed up the lane and straight into the town. Rooster was riding like a madman, taking all sorts of chances and spending most of the journey on the wrong side of the road.

When we arrived at the shop, he parked his bike and was in the shop before we even stopped.

Cowboy and I parked our bikes beside Rooster's. Before we went in, we chatted about Rooster and agreed that before we left we would find out what was eating him. When we went in, we saw Rooster at the counter talking to a young girl who was serving so we joined him.

He was asking for prices of stuff and she was looking up books and writing them down for him. Cowboy started talking to him like he'd just bumped into him and started asking him all sorts of silly shit like how he was doing and what he was in the shop for. I just shook my head and went for a rake about.

I was walking up one of the aisles and noticed a staff room/come office. I saw the Thatcher guy in there, on the phone. He was laughing away and smiling like he didn't have a care in the world, I could feel my blood boiling.

I headed back to the counter and grabbed Cowboy. I ushered him out the door and told him the guy was in a back room. I told him I wanted to waste him there and then and felt we should ignore Indie's instruction and do him right now.

He started telling me to calm the fuck down and not to do anything stupid. We were having a bit of an argument about it when Rooster came out. "What the fuck are you two arguing about?" he demanded to know. Cowboy filled him in and his reaction was to hurl a verbal volley in my direction, which I just took on the chin.

I asked him what the fuck was wrong with him as he'd been acting like a dick all day anyway. He just told me to shut the fuck up as it was none of my business and then we ended up getting into an argument which Cowboy had to defuse.

The three of us then jumped on our bikes and headed straight back to the farm. When we got back, Rooster went straight into the conservatory and Cowboy and I headed back to the range to heat up.

"What was the fuckin point of that?" I asked Cowboy. "Fuck, Shug, we were just checking where it was, how many people worked there and what the layout was. Why the fuck are you starting to moan like Rooster?" he demanded to know.

"Sorry, man, I just didn't see the value in it. I'm probably just being a pain in the arse coz I'm pissed with Rooster."

Cowboy then told me not to worry about it and said that if we got a chance later we could maybe have a go at trying to see what was going on with him.

Just then, Rooster came through to the kitchen. "Rooster, can I have a word?" I asked him. All he said was "Not now." then headed out the door. I went to go out after him, but Cowboy grabbed me and told me to leave it and let him go.

I told Cowboy I couldn't and headed out after him. When I got out, Rooster was standing beside his bike, putting his helmet on. I hit the kill switch on his bike and told him I needed to talk to him, again, he told me he didn't want to talk.

"Is it something to do with Julie?" I enquired. "It's fuck all to do with anybody, so butt the fuck out and don't fuckin ask me again, got it!" he raged at me. He then started his bike up and screeched away.

By this time, Cowboy was standing at the door. I looked at him and asked him what he thought was going on. He told me he had no idea, but that I should butt out as Rooster wasn't interested in sharing anything right now and suggested I should cut him a bit of slack.

"I'm worried about him, man," I said. "He's always been there for me and I'm only trying to do the same, I can't stand seeing a mate like this."

"Shug, if he wants to share it, he will. He'll tell you when he's good and ready, so let it go, man." "Yeh, guess you're right, I won't ask him again. If he wants to let me know what's up then he'll do it in his own time," I agreed.

Chapter 8

I decided to head back to my flat for a bit of a clean-up and a bit of 'me' time, so I told Cowboy I had a couple of things to do and headed off. I arrived back at the flat and headed inside. When I went in, I could feel the air even colder inside than it was outside so put the fire on full blast.

I ran a bath, deciding that would be the best way of warming up and also a good way to relieve my aches and pains. I turned the water off, got stripped and tried to get in the bath.

It took me a full 5 minutes to eventually get in because I was so cold. I felt the warm water was scalding hot, even though I'd topped it up with some cold. When I did get my body under the water, I then had to drain some water out and fill it with more hot. I closed my eyes and started drifting away, feeling warm and relaxed for the first time in a good few days ... Mmmmmm.

Next thing, there was a loud banging on the door which I decided to ignore. I stayed still, hoping whoever it was would think no one was in and fuck off. However, they wouldn't take no for an answer and kept banging away.

"Shug! Open the fuckin door, we need to talk." It was Rooster. I jumped up, grabbed a towel and almost ran to the door. I opened it and invited him in. "What's up, man?" I asked. He never said a word, he just walked straight through to the living room. I closed the door and followed him in.

He took off his jacket and threw it on the floor on top of his helmet. "Fuck, Shug, it's roasting in here. You fuckin ill or something?" he asked. I said I was fine and got straight to the point with him. "Why are you here, Rooster? What's going on with you, man, you're not really yourself this weather," I told him.

"Hey, Shug, I know that, man, that's why I'm here. I just wanted to apologise for being a dick. It's nothing to do with you, it's the shit Indie told me about Stiff, I just can't get it out my fuckin mind."

I told him not to worry about us and reassured him we were cool. I then asked him what had happened with Stiff.

"He's fucked, man. The doc told Indie that he has brain damage and although he'll recover physically, he'll never be the same up top. Indie said the doc told him he should be prepared for the worst as it is highly unlikely that he'll ever recover from the vegetative state he is currently in. Indie has told us not to say anything as he reckons we can't afford for anyone to know we've lost both our Prez and VP. That's why I've been such a dick recently, so now you know."

I looked at Rooster for a minute, not really sure what to say, then began, "Holy shit, man, no wonder you've been so agitated. That's fuckin unbelievable, you couldn't make this shit up, no cunt would ever believe it."

I then asked him what he thought was going to happen now and started to ask him all sort of shit about the Bats: about Indie and his view on whether or not he thought the Bats would survive this double disaster, and if so, who he thought would take over?

"Whoa, Shug, fuck's sake, man, settle yourself down. You're going off on one again, you need to slow it up a bit, one thing at a time. Why don't you get shifted and I'll put the kettle on, then I'll tell you what I know."

I almost sprinted into the bedroom, quickly drying myself as I went. I ditched the towel on the bed and frantically dressed in record time. My mind was racing. As usual, I'd managed to turn around the big picture into how it could affect me and wondered if, at this point, anyone would even notice if I left?

I headed back into the living room almost at the same time as Rooster was dumping a couple of mugs of tea on the table. He sat on the couch and I grabbed the chair. I picked up my tea and stared at Rooster in anticipation.

"What?" he asked.

"What! What the fuck do you mean what! Come on tae fuck, Rooster, spill the fuckin beans. For fuck's sake, man, the suspense is killing me," I told him.

"Okay, Shug, here's the deal: Indie spoke to me, Jelly and Hotwire. He told us what the doc had said then swore us to secrecy. He doesn't want word to get out amongst the guys, in case it starts a rake of rumours about the Bats demise or some other shit like that."

I asked him if they discussed who would take over and I also enquired about how Angel was? And if she knew yet?

"Indie has already told Angel. As you can imagine, she's totally devastated, but has agreed to stay away from the farm just now and not tell anyone. Fiona and her have gone to Fiona's sister's in the south for a week or so, to give him time to try and sort out all the shit here."

"Will Indie just take over as President now?" I asked Rooster.

"That's not how it works, Shug. It needs to be voted on by the officers. The big complication here is that there are two positions available! If Indie gets one then there's another one available and so on. All the positions have to be filled separately: you pick the Prez then he nominates his VP and the officers vote or nominate on that. Then the Prez and VP propose a Sergeant at Arms and so on. So it's not as straightforward as it seems and certainly can't be done overnight."

"What about you? Will you be made an officer or get one of the senior gigs? Surely you must be in the running, you've been doing it for months anyway," I suggested.

"I'm not sure about that. And anyway, I don't know if I'd want it after all the shite I've had to deal with over the past few months. It seems like one big hassle after another, I'm more than happy being a foot soldier with a little responsibility. I joined the Bats for the same reason as everybody else: I just want to ride, party and have the odd punch up. Now it seems that sometimes that's the last thing any of us ever do anymore."

For some reason, I decided that now was a good time to tell Rooster about my plans and dropped what he seemed to think was a bombshell.

"Rooster, I've decided I'm not going to chuck the Bats," I began, "But I am going to move away from the area. I plan to get a job in the same psychiatric hospital as Julie and I've arranged to visit her there this weekend to check it out and hopefully sort …"

"Whoa, Shug, hold it a fuckin minute here. Rewind that last bit about you moving, arranging, and visiting Julie! How the fuck do you even know where she is? How the fuck did this come about? Are you seeing her behind my back or something?" he demanded to know.

"Hey, man, you can get that shite out of your fuckin head right now. There's no way on this fuckin earth I'd shite on you," I roared at him.

"I met her at the fuckin shop the other morning and had a 10-minute conversation with her, that was all. I told her I was looking for a job away from here and she invited me to check out the hospital as they were looking for nursing assistants and trainee nurses. I agreed to go and check it out so she gave me her address and fucked off, that was it."

"So how come I'm only hearing about it now?" he screamed back at me.

"Eh, hello! I've been trying to talk to you for two fuckin days. You kept telling me 'not now', remember that? So this is the first chance I've fuckin had," I screamed back.

"Anyway, since we're talking about telling each other things, why the fuck didn't you tell me you and her were finished? I thought you might've shared that little bit of info with me!" I then challenged him.

"It was none of your fuckin business, Shug, that's why I never told you!" he roared. "If it concerned you then you would've been the first cunt I would've told. Anyway, we're not finished. She just needed to go and do some extra shit for her job and wanted a bit of space to do it. Okay? So now you know."

"Okay, I get the message," I told him. I thought at that point it was best to defuse the situation and change the subject. I could see Rooster was getting well agitated and the last thing I wanted right now was to be rolling around the floor, and me getting pummelled when he was clearly raging with me.

"I'm sorry. Can we just drop this shit and start again, man?" I suggested, to which he nodded back in agreement.

Reverting back to the original conversation, I asked him, "So what will you do if they vote you in, will you refuse it?" I enquired.

Rooster then stood up and started walking about the room, inhaling deeply on every draw of his cigarette.

"Fuck knows what I'll do, man. I feel I want to stay as I am. But I don't know how I can say 'no'. You've been there, you know what I mean. Anybody who's asked would see it as an honour and would jump at the chance. To refuse it would make you look like a right fuckin dickhead."

Rooster sat back down then turned his attention back to me. "So tell me about this grand plan of yours then, Shug: You fuck off and still stay in the Bats! How's that going to work?" he asked me. I took a deep breath and started my explanation.

"Well, you know how I've been trying to get out since Malky died, but just couldn't find the right way or the right time to do it? I think right now is perfect. Over the next few months, there'll be so much turmoil going on in the club that all the attention will be focused on making sure we get back to normal, and finding some kind of stability to allow everyone to put this shit behind us. No one will really be focusing on any particular individual. I'll tell Indie that I have a job and will be moving away, but that I'll be back every weekend. I'll do that for a short period then gradually come back less and less due to the work commitments."

"Sounds like you've got it all worked out, Shug," he told me. "Just one thing I think you haven't taken into account, though, What if Indie tells you 'no deal', then what?"

I was a bit shocked at his response. "What do you mean 'If' Indie says no'? It's fuck all to do with him, I'm not trying to quit, I'm only moving 45 miles away. Why in fuck's name would he say no!" I demanded him to tell me.

"Shug, settle, man, I'm only asking the question. I just think you should prepare for it, that's all. I remember when Fixer wanted to move up north, there was a massive debate about it and they only agreed to allow it because he was prepared to join the Devils, which forged our alliance with them.

"Fuck's sake, man, how can they do that! It's worse than the fuckin army. I only want to move somewhere else, not kill any cunt. Surely they have to see it from my perspective?" I screamed.

"Whoa, Shug, get a fuckin grip of yourself, man. You know the script. I don't need to remind you that the most important thing is always the club. That's what it's all about and it will always be like that. Fuck, that's why we all joined up in the first place, you need to remember that."

I knew he was right and nodded my head in agreement then changed the subject back to Stiff by firing some questions at him. "What happens first? How will this play out? Do you know when Indie will tell everyone?"

"Not sure," he told me. "Tomorrow, Indie is going to speak to the officers and fill them in. Then I guess they'll decide what comes next." "Will you be at the meet?" I enquired. "Yes. Indie has asked me to be there, but I think it's one of those meetings no one really wants to be anywhere near."

"Certainly puts your own shit into perspective," I suggested. "Sure does, Shug, makes you wonder if it's all worth it when shit like this goes down." Rooster then slumped back on the couch and took a long draw on his fag.

I looked at him and tried to remember if I'd ever seen him so low. Normally, he was always the positive one, but over the last couple of weeks, he'd become increasingly low in mood and much more aggressive than normal.

"Hey, big man, don't worry, we'll get through this," I told him, "it's just a blip. We'll come out the other side much stronger, we always do."

"Not so sure this time, Shug. This is the worst it's ever been. I can't recall any club having all this shit attached to it at the one time. Think about it, look what the fuck's going on here," he reminded me. "The Prez is dead, the VP is a fuckin vegetable, we have two prospects lying fucked in the hospital, we've a funeral to organise, a court case pending and a cunt strutting about who needs to get wiped out. The club is in complete disarray, most of the guys don't have a clue what the fuck's going on. Oh, and just to top it off, my best mate has decided he's getting ready to fuck off. I'd say that's not just your run of the mill normal shit, what do you reckon?"

"Fuck, Rooster, when you lay it out like that I guess you're right, man. Maybe we're all fucked!" I suggested.

I looked at him again and noticed he seemed totally shell-shocked. I tried to reassure him, telling him that if anyone could sort this shit out, it would be Indie. I reminded him of how well he'd done so far and suggested there was no one better to sort it out than him.

This seemed to strike a bit of a chord and he agreed that Indie was the man and we should stop wallowing in our own pish and make sure we backed him 100%.

I agreed and suggested a beer to lighten the mood so headed to the kitchen. We then started chatting, more about how we thought everything would pan out and ended up getting pretty pished.

For some reason, I stupidly asked Rooster if he fancied coming to see Julie with me at the weekend. He gave me a right mouthful of abuse, telling me what a fuckin stupid idea that would be.

It was one of those times that you say something and the minute it comes out your mouth you could bite your tongue off.

In my head, it had seemed a good idea at the time. I thought that if I asked him to come along then he would see there was no ulterior motive for me going, that it was purely a way to get a bit of distance from the Bats. Fuck, how stupid was I!

I tried to apologise to him, telling him I hadn't thought it through and realised it may put him in an awkward position. Rooster then told me that Julie had ditched him and that was the reason she'd fucked off.

He then said he was really missing her, but couldn't bring himself to tell her. I could see his eyes starting to well up a bit and I'm sure I saw some tears as well.

Fuck, I had no idea what to say next, I'd never seen him like this before. I jumped up and went to the kitchen for another couple of beers. I decided the best thing was another change of conversation and racked my brains for something to say.

I went back in and handed Rooster another beer. "Get that down your neck, big fella." I then changed the conversation completely. "Hey, man, is there any word on Provo's funeral yet?"

Rooster opened his beer, took a large drink then told me there was no word yet, but that Indie reckoned it would be the start of the following week. I then asked him what kind of turnout he thought he would get.

"I reckon it'll be the biggest we've ever had. Every single Bat will be there and the acting President of the Devils has said that there'll be brothers coming from their chapter and others from up north who knew him too. I reckon there'll be well over a hundred bikes and probably double that amount of people. Indie reckons we'll need to find somewhere big to party afterwards that can hold at least two hundred people. He's told me to source it. So guess what I'll be doing this weekend when you're living it up with my ex?"

Fuck, he'd spent ten minutes talking then brought it right back to Julie.

"Come on, man, for fuck's sake, can't you just fuckin drop it? I've told you the script already, surely you fuckin trust me? Fuck, you of all people should know I would never do anything to fuck up our friendship, it means too much to me. I thought you fuckin knew that?" I ranted at him. "Hey, Shug, you're right. I'm sorry, man, it's just that sometimes, well…. you know."

I did know. I knew exactly what he was going through. I was the very same with Lorraine. As long as I was busy, I never really thought about her too much, but when I was alone, she always came back into my head. I continually wondered what might have happened if we'd gotten into a proper relationship and how it would have panned out?

"Hey, Shug, I'm fucked. If you're cool with it, I'll just crash here. I've got a busy day tomorrow and can't be arsed going back to the farm." "Hey, no probs, I need to hit the sack myself," I told him.

I got up, shook his hand and told him to take it easy. "You too, man, sorry for being a bit of a prick tonight." "Hey,

Rooster, don't be daft, man, you'll never be a prick in my eyes," I told him. "Cheers, Shug, you're a good cunt. Man, don't ever fuckin change," he told me as he closed his eyes.

I went through to my room and lay on the top of my bed, trying to make sense of what the fuck had just happened, but very quickly gave up and drifted off to sleep.

When I awoke the next morning, Rooster had already split. I couldn't believe I hadn't heard his bike firing up. I had a look out the kitchen window to check he hadn't just gone to the shop or something, but his bike was away. I guessed I must've been sleeping sounder than I thought.

I looked around the flat, it was like a pigsty. I thought about tidying up, but then thought, 'Fuck it, I'm heading off tomorrow, it'll do until I come back'.

I decided I should go to the phone box and call Julie. After a couple of rings, someone answered and I asked if I could speak to Julie. She told me to give her my number and she would go and get her and asked if I knew her room number, which I didn't. She then said she'd need to find that out from the warden and it might take a bit of time.

I gave her my number and thanked her for taking the time to do it. She said: "No problem," and hung up.

I wondered why Julie hadn't answered, then the penny dropped. I realised it must be a payphone number that she'd given me.

I stepped out of the phone box and sat on the ground, resting my back against the door. I lit up a fag and started to think about going to see Julie and wondered if it really was a good idea.

When the phone rang and I spoke to her, all my fears were dispelled; Julie sounded like she was delighted to hear from me.

I told her I was planning to visit the next day and she seemed really enthusiastic about it. I told her I would leave early doors and hoped to be with her by lunchtime.

She gave me her room number and some directions and told me she would be waiting at the nurses home for me then finished by telling me she couldn't wait to catch up. I told her I was looking forward to seeing her as well then put the phone down.

I headed back up to the flat, my mind racing with the height of Julie's enthusiasm. I started to wonder why she was so 'up' for my visit and if maybe she was looking for a bit more than just a visit from a friend.

I told myself to stop being a dick and had a bit of a laugh at what I was doing. I always managed to grow arms and legs to everything I thought about.

I went back in and hit the bed, thinking I needed another bit of a kip. I must've been sleeping for a few hours when I thought I heard the door being banged.

I got up and sat on my bed for a minute, not sure if I was dreaming or not, then heard the banging again and made my way to the door. I opened it and Rooster was standing there with an envelope in his hand. "Hi, man, what's up?" I asked him and gestured for him to come in.

"Nothing's up, Shug. Everything's cool. Just wanted to let you know Provo's funeral has been arranged for Tuesday at half-three. Wasn't sure how long you'd be away and I knew you wouldn't want to miss it. Also, I was hoping you would do me a favour, man?" he requested.

"Of course, man, anything," I told him, gesturing again for him to come in. Rooster stayed at the door and so I asked him if he was coming in or not. He told me couldn't, that he just wanted to give me something then he'd need to split. I looked at him curiously and asked him what it was.

He then handed the envelope to me and asked if I would give it to Julie, which I agreed to do. I then asked him why he couldn't just come with me and give it to her himself.

He told me he couldn't and said that it was complicated and maybe he would tell me about it another time. He then thanked me for doing it, told me to have a good time, then left.

I closed the door and stared at the envelope for a minute, wondering what the fuck that was all about. All that was written on the front of it was 'Julie' but the envelope was really thick, suggesting there were quite a few pages inside. I placed it on the couch, beside my bag, then headed back to the bedroom.

I grabbed a couple of t-shirts, two pairs of scants, some socks and a jumper and fired them into my bag. I made myself something to eat and sat down on the couch. I started to think about the letter, wondering when I should give it to her.

If she saw it as bad news, and I gave it to her straight away, then that might fuck up my weekend. However, if I waited until I was leaving and it was good news, she might be well pissed. I decided that the best thing to do would be to just play it by ear, see how the weekend goes and decide from there.

I finished eating and got dressed. I decided to go for a spin, fill up the tank, check the tyres for air and give my bike a bit of a clean before having an early night.

I had just filled up my bike with fuel and was putting air in the tyres when a car drew up beside me. I couldn't see who was in it for the sun. When I stood up, I nearly shat myself.

"Lorraine! What the fuck do you want?" I stupidly blurted out. I was well taken aback. She was the last person I expected to see; I thought she would be away at Uni.

"Nice to see you too, Shug," she replied. "Sorry, Lorraine, I was just surprised to see you. I didn't mean to be rude," I told her. I then knelt back down and carried on putting air in my tyres.

"Shug, can we talk for a minute?" she asked. "Course we can, fire away. Say what you have to, but be quick, I'm in a hurry." I don't know why I was being so aggressive with her as I was delighted to see her, but I just felt I couldn't let her see it.

She crouched down beside me and started to speak. The first thing I noticed was how gorgeous she looked and how brilliant she smelled. She had the same perfume on that she wore when we first met and I loved it.

"Look, Shug, I know you're not happy with me and I understand that. But I hate this. I've been to your flat a hundred times and never got a reply. I'm really sorry how things turned out, but I still really like you. And I really, really want us to remain friends."

I interrupted her. "Whoa there, just hang on a minute, Lorraine. The last time we talked, you set me up and told me you'd chosen your father over me. At the time I was well hurt about it, but I've got over it now. If you remember, you said you weren't going to see me anymore and I had to accept that. Now, you tell me how we can be friends after all that shit? Oh, and have you forgotten that your precious dad said he would disown you if you ever saw me again?"

"I know all that, Shug, and you're right about everything, but you have to understand at the time everything was crazy, I don't think any of us were thinking clearly."

Again, I interrupted her. "Eh, well, I was thinking clearly enough. I told you I loved you and wanted to be with you, but you chose to stay with your dad and that was that."

"I know I did, but that's why I've been trying to see you. I've missed you so much and I've told my dad that if you'd take me back then I'd be with you in a minute."

"And what was his reaction to that?" I asked. "I bet he went mental!" "Well, actually, he didn't go mental. As you can imagine, he wasn't best pleased. But after a discussion with both him and my mum, he started to come round. He said he didn't want to see you in his house right now, but if it was what I really wanted then he wouldn't stand in my way. I've been trying to catch up with you ever since to tell you."

I had no idea what to say at that point. One minute I'm thinking of heading off for a fun weekend then this fuckin bombshell! I decided I needed to give myself a bit of thinking time.

"Lorraine, this is a lot to take in and I need to think about it. I thought we were history so I was just getting on with my life. You know I loved you, but I don't know if I feel the same anymore. I'm going away for the weekend and I'll catch up with you when I get back. We'll have a proper chat then, okay?"

"That's all I'm asking, Shug. I'm at Uni all next week, but I'll be back on Thursday night and will be home 'til Tuesday. So if you want, maybe we could meet up sometime then?"

I agreed to see her and told her I would get in touch when I got back. She then leaned over and kissed me on the lips, smiled, said thanks and told me she couldn't wait. She then got up, jumped in her car and left.

As I watched her drive out of the garage, I thought to myself 'Fuck, Shug, you couldn't make it up!'. I then finished putting air in my tyres and headed back to the flat.

All the way back, instead of enjoying the ride in the sun, I was tormenting myself with thoughts of Lorraine, her father and what the fuck next weekend would bring.

'Fuck, I'm already on to next weekend and I haven't even had this one yet, get a grip, Shug!' I told myself and tried to put it to the back of my mind.

I drew up at the close, determined only to think about this weekend and nothing else. I headed upstairs and into the flat. There was a note on the mat that had been shoved through the letterbox. I picked it up and all it said on it was 'Farm'.

'Fuck, fuck, fuck,' I thought to myself. That's all I needed tonight, so much for a quiet night in! I about turned, headed back downstairs, jumped back on my bike, but this time with much more of a purpose.

When you get a 'note', it means something is up and you have to get to the farm as quickly as possible. I drew up, ready to turn off the main road when I saw a rake of bikes coming towards me so stayed where I was and let the guys out before joining the pack. I bumped up beside Cowboy and Flick.

"What's up, man?" I asked Cowboy. "Four of the guys have just got a kicking in town from a bunch of fuckin football fans who were here for the game tonight – we're going to sort it." "Where are they?" I asked. "They're in the pub where Malky got his cut-off pulled," Flick shouted back.

"What's the plan then?" I shouted. "No plan. Straight in, burst everybody, steal what we can, then out," Cowboy told me. "So just the usual then?" I replied. "Correct!" Cowboy shouted back, laughing.

We arrived at the pub and drew into the car park at the back. I counted about twenty-five of us and wondered if that would be enough for a bus load of football fans.

I needn't have worried. When I saw what the guys had with them, I knew it was going to be a walk over. Everyone, except me, was tooled up with baseball bats, pieces of wood, metal bars and bike chains.

Rooster threw me a baseball bat and nodded to me. Indie directed us to the front and we piled in. We caught everyone by surprise and by the time people realised what was going on, they were either on the floor or running for cover.

I think, because of how all the guys were feeling about the other shit we were dealing with, they were using this fight as a release. They were venting all their anger here and the football fans were taking one hell of a beating.

There was very little resistance, but the ones who were prepared to fight got absolutely leathered. I smacked a few with my bat, but I really wished I was anywhere else but there.

After about fifteen minutes of complete lunacy, Indie eventually shouted for us all to get out. As I was making my way to the door, I looking around and it looked like a fuckin blood bath.

I was stepping over bodies with broken limbs, people who were unconscious and others who were screaming. I ran out the door trying not to think about what just happened. I then jumped on my bike, along with everyone else, and headed back to the farm.

We put all the bikes in the barn, closed the door and headed into the farm. Everybody was laughing, talking about the injured and slapping each other on the back.

I just felt a bit numb about the whole thing. Indie shouted to everyone to remember that we'd been here all day and to get the party started, which received a massive cheer.

The other two prospects, who'd only joined up a few weeks before with Buzz and Duffy, started running around with beer and were looking very pleased with themselves now that they had their first scrap with the Bats under their belt.

One of them handed me two cans of beer, smiled at me and said: "If this is what it's all about, man, I can't wait to get my colours," then continued passing out beers to the guys.

I sat at the kitchen table, opened one of the cans and took a long drink before opening the other one, knowing another mouthful would finish the first. I thought about what the prospect had said and remembered Malky saying the exact same thing, right here in the kitchen, and it made me think again about what the fuck I was doing here.

Just then, Rooster came through and asked how I was doing and it snapped me out of my wallowing. "I'm okay, man," I told him, "but I've had the strangest fuckin day ever. By the way, where did you fuck off to this morning?" I asked him. "Had a letter to write, remember?"

"Awe, right, sorry. I thought you'd done that a while ago."

"Nah, I've been wanting to do it for a while, just didn't know what to write. I'm still not sure if it'll make any sense to her. Anyway, that's for another day, come on, let's get fuckin wasted."

We grabbed another couple of beers and headed into the big room. I'd just got settled with Rooster and Cowboy when Indie came in and told me he wanted to see me in the conservatory.

I looked at Rooster, wondering if he knew what he wanted, but he just shrugged his shoulders. 'Fuck, what now?' was all I could think. I started trying to recall if I'd done something wrong, but couldn't think of anything.

I followed him into the conservatory and he told me to close the doors. My heart started racing; there was no one else in the room and I had no fuckin idea what the fuck he wanted with me.

"What's up, Indie?" I asked him, in the manliest voice I could muster. "Nothing's up, Shug, just wanted to ask you a couple of things." "Yeh, sure, what about?"

"Heard some rumours that you're planning to move away. Just wondered if they were true." Fuck, I didn't know what to say. Who the fuck would have told him? Only Cowboy and Rooster knew. I couldn't believe any of them would've said anything, but some cunt must have.

"Who told you that?" I asked him. "It doesn't matter who told me, I just need to know if it's true, is it?" he demanded to know.

"Well, it's not strictly true," I told him. "I may have a chance of a job at the psychiatric hospital in the city so I'm going this weekend to suss it out. If I get it, I'll still be here every time I get a day off, it's only about forty-five minutes away. The reason I haven't said anything is because, right now, there's nothing to tell. I haven't even spoken to anybody at the hospital."

"Right, so it is true. You are looking to move away. You want to tell me why?" he asked.

I decided to tell him the truth. Well, most of it anyway, and started to explain how I was feeling about all the shit that was going on and how it was affecting me. But he interrupted me and started lecturing me about my commitment to the patch and reminded me that it was my choice to join the Bats and that there should be nothing more important to me than my brothers.

I then interrupted him and told him getting a job somewhere else had fuck all to do with my commitment to the Bats and that I would always honour the patch. I then told him that if I did move that it would make no difference to my life as a Bat.

"Well, that's where your wrong," he told me. "If you're planning to fuck off somewhere else then how the fuck are you going to be here when I want you? Eh, answer me that?"

"Indie, it'll make no difference. I'll be here in half an hour or so, surely that's quick enough. Fuck, I've seen brothers who live five minutes from the farm take longer than that to get here."

"I hear what you're saying, Shug, but I've just got a nagging feeling that you still want out. If that's the case, you better tell me now." I could feel my stomach taking somersaults, I knew he could sense my plan and I knew I would need to convince him with what I said next or I was fucked.

"Look, Indie, I've had a really shit time recently. In fact, we all have, but since Malky died I just feel I want to have a bit of space from the village. I've been thinking of moving for ages. My flat has too many memories and I can't get a swap from the council so thought something like this would be good for me, it's got nothing to do with the Bats. Fuck, it took me so long to get my colours - the last thing I want is to give them up. When I got them, Provo told me 'When you become a Bat: You're a Bat for life' and I hope to fuck I am."

I stopped talking and looked straight at him, hoping I'd said what he wanted to hear and waited for his reply.

"Okay, Shug, I hear what you're saying, I hope to fuck you're telling me the truth. I understand the shit with the flat and the need for a job, but you have to understand that I need to know all brothers are committed to the chapter because it's the only way it can be."

"Indie, I'm only going to see the place and find out if I fancy it. It might be a lot of shit. And, fuck, realistically, what are the chances of them giving me a job anyway? Fuck, I've not exactly got a great track record with work."

He seemed to buy it and I felt my stomach starting to settle a bit, I was starting to feel less worried.

"Fine, Shug, you do understand that I had to ask the question? I just needed to be sure you were still with us."

"Sure am, and always will be," I reassured him "I love the Bats, it's the only real family I've had, and long may it continue," I told him.

He then got up from his chair and hugged me, I hugged him back. "Enjoy your weekend, Bro, I'll see you back here on Tuesday for Provo's funeral, okay?"

"I'll be here, don't worry about that. He was a top man, even though he gave me all sorts of shit, I fuckin loved him to bits." And with that, I left and went to head back to the party.

Indie then shouted to me, "Hey, Shug!" Fuck, my heart sank, I wondered if he'd sussed me out. I turned around and looked at him, he then said: "I'm glad you're still tight with the Bats. You're a good brother and we're glad to have you, take it easy, man."

"I will, Indie, thanks, man. I won't let you down," I told him. "I know you won't," he said, then nodded before heading into the office.

Fuck, I felt so relieved when he left, but then the guilt started to overwhelm me. I started to think too much again. Fuck, why do I always feel like this, every time I fuckin lie? I get so consumed with guilt and it fucks me up for ages afterwards.

Aaagghh! I decided to join the party and try and forget about it. I headed back through to the big room, grabbed a beer from the table and re-joined Rooster and Cowboy.

"What was that about, Shug?" Cowboy asked. "Some cunt told Indie I was thinking about moving and he dug me up about it. The only cunts who knew about it were you two, so who fuckin told him?" I asked them both.

Cowboy was first to speak, "Certainly wasn't me, I haven't spoken to Indie for ages," he told me. I then looked at Rooster "Well? Did you fuckin tell him?" I asked him.

"Look, Shug," he started, "I never actually meant to tell him. He told me he wanted you and me to do something this weekend and I told him you wouldn't be here. When he asked me where the fuck you'd be, I told him. And when he asked me why, it was out before I realised. He never said anything else about it and told me to pick someone else. I never thought any more about it. I'm sorry, man, I never thought it would come up again," he told me, quite apologetically.

I wanted to be mad at him, but he genuinely looked upset and I guess I never had the energy to argue. "Forget it, man, what's done is done, I know you wouldn't deliberately stick me in it," I told him. I cracked open my beer and told them it was time to get pished, raised my can in the air then started drinking.

Rooster then apologised for a second time and reassured me it wouldn't happen again and I knew he meant it.

The party was in full swing and I fancied getting a bit of skirt to end my evening on a high note. I told the guys I was going sniffing, to which they nodded before returning to their original conversation.

I stood up, checked out the chicks in the room and found my target. I chatted for a bit with some of the guys as I walked around the room, working my way towards my prey.

She was standing with another couple of girls and one guy. She was dressed in tight jeans and high-heeled boots. On her top half, she only had a leather waistcoat (her tits were almost bursting out of it). Her hair was black and really long, it almost touched her arse. She was a big girl, but not overweight, I reckoned she looked around 20ish. I approached the group, gave them a nod, then turned to the girl and smiled at her until she smiled back.

"Hi, I'm Shug," I told her and she replied, telling me her name was Kelly. I said to her that I hadn't seen her before and asked if this was the first time she'd been at the farm. To my delight, she told me that it wasn't and that she'd been a few times before.

I then thought that if she'd been before then she would know the drill and be well up for it. "Fancy a chat?" I asked her, pointing to the chair in the corner." "Yeh, okay, but I'd rather have a fuck," she told me. "That'll do for me," I agreed. "Fuck the chat, let's head upstairs," I suggested. She then blew me away with what she said next.

"Nah, don't fancy going upstairs, I'd rather fuck in here and see if we can maybe start an orgy or something." Fuck, I didn't know what to say, so I just pointed to the chair and suggested we start there.

She handed her drink to one of the other girls and walked towards the chair with me behind her, staring at her well-rounded arse.

She stood in front of the chair and turned around to face me. She knelt down and started unzipping my fly. "Let me look at what I'm getting and see if it's going to be worth it," she said, looking straight at me.

Well, if you ever wanted your hard-on to be at its rampant best then this would definitely be one of those times.

I was thinking to myself, at that point, 'What if she pulls it out and thinks it's not up to par? What a fucking beamer! I'll have every cunt in the room having a laugh at my expense'.

Thankfully, she pulled it out, had a look, never said a word then stuck it straight into her mouth. To say I was relieved was a fucking understatement if ever there was one.

She started sucking and biting for all she was worth, taking my full shaft and sucking it from top to bottom while massaging my balls with both her hands.

I had one hand on her head and a can of beer in the other, feeling fuckin great. I decided to stop her so I could get my hands on her tits. I pushed her head back and she looked up at me and asked what was wrong, she wanted to know if I wasn't enjoying it.

I told her it was great, but that I wanted to fuck her. I pulled her up, gave her a kiss, dropped my jeans to the floor and sat on the chair.

She responded by doing a bit of a striptease in front of me, much to the delight of the onlookers.

She put her foot on the arm of the chair, unzipped her boot, pulled it off, then did the same with her other one. She then unbuttoned her jeans, revealing a small pair of red panties, and pulled and tugged at them before wriggling out of them, shaking her arse about in the process.

She unbuttoned her waistcoat, revealing as perfect a pair of tits as you're ever likely to see. I motioned to her to come and sit on my now raging hard-on, but she had other ideas. She stood on the chair, grabbed my head and forced it into her pussy. Man, I was putty in her hands, it was fuckin magic.

I started to lick her out and tease her clit with my fingers, forgetting all about everyone else in the room and getting lost in the moment. Then I felt a hand on my dick and the next thing, a mouth.

I couldn't see who it was, but hoped to fuck it was a chick. The next thing, Kelly starts grunting and moaning and pushing my face into her minge much more forcefully than before. I guessed she was about to shoot her load until I realised the person sucking my dick had just rammed some fingers up her arse. I was trying to get my face out of her minge, to see who was on my dick, but she was having none of it and made sure I stayed where I was until she came.

Finally, she screamed to orgasm and slumped down on me, telling me she wanted my dick inside her. Naturally, I wanted the same, but my immediate concern was moving her out the way to see who was giving me the blowjob.

As I moved her to the side, I let out a major sigh of relief when I saw it was one of the girls who'd been standing with her earlier.

With my worries now dispelled, I grabbed Kelly and sat her on my knee, while moving the other chicks head out of the way to allow me to get my dick into Kelly's moist pussy.

As I slid into her, I could feel myself smiling. Kelly then wrapped her arms around me and slowly moved up and down on my shaft. I have always really enjoyed the feeling of closeness I get when someone is wrapped around me, naked.

However, the next thing that happened really put me off. We were cuddling and kissing and Kelly was continuing with her slow moving hips on top of me when the girl who was giving me a blowjob earlier started shoving her fingers up Kelly's arse again. Kelly leaned back and let out a groan of pleasure, the girl then removed her fingers and stuck them into Kelly's mouth; who started sucking and licking them for all she was worth.

Well, that was it for me, I just sat watching and could feel myself going limp. When the girl removed her fingers, Kelly then moved back to kiss me, but I just couldn't respond.

Now, I'm no prude, but all I could think about was how many times she'd done that before then kissed people?

I just couldn't bring myself to kiss her, knowing she'd just licked her own shite from someone else's fingers. As pretty as she was and as horny as I was, it was over for me. I lifted her up, got out of the chair and pulled up my trousers.

"What's up, Shug?" she asked. "Sorry, Kelly," I told her "I just remembered, I need to be somewhere else, thanks for the fun." I kissed her on the forehead then headed straight out the room and into the kitchen.

Rooster, who'd seen me leaving, followed me into the kitchen. "What's up, man? Everything okay?" he enquired. "Yeh, fine, mate, I'm just going to split. Busy day tomorrow and I want to get some zeds, I'm feeling knackered," I told him.

"That's cool, man, I just thought something was up," he enquired.

"Okay, bud, see you when I get back." I then held my hand out to shake his, but he hugged me instead and once again apologised for earlier. "Hey, we're cool, forget all about it, I have," I told him. I headed out and fired up my bike. As I was putting my helmet on, I realised I felt a bit drunk and decided I should take my time on the way home.

As I drove up the lane and turned onto the main road, I saw in my mirror that half a dozen cop cars were heading down the lane and thought 'Thank Fuck! If I hadn't left when I did then there would've been no weekend with Julie for me. It would more than likely have been a couple of nights, courtesy of her Majesty'.

I got home safely and parked up the bike, feeling pretty lucky. I walked up the stairs, wondering what was happening at the farm, and guessed that the guys would all end up getting lifted.

I went in, grabbed a beer and planted myself on the couch. 'Fuck' I thought to myself, 'What another strange day, Shug - how many more of these can you take?' It was still another two months until my eighteenth birthday and I felt like I'd been living for a hundred years.

I finished my beer and decided bed was my best option. As I walked through to the room, I laughed to myself, thinking about Kelly and what an idiot I'd been.

Then I remembered, if she hadn't licked her pal's shitty fingers, I would still have been at the farm when the pigs came, which made me laugh again.

I got into bed, but within minutes I started to toss and turn. Again, as usual, I was thinking way too much. The guys getting a visit from the pigs worried me. I just hoped that whatever was going on would be resolved before the big man's funeral.

I then started to wonder what Rooster meant about it being 'complicated' and why the fuck he wanted to give Julie a letter. I started to think about what might be in it and what effect it might have on Julie. I wondered how she would feel about me giving her a letter from him. Eventually, I must have drifted off.

Chapter 9

I woke up with a blinding headache and put it down to the lack of sleep and all the shit I was thinking about. I grabbed a couple of Aspirin and a drink of water and stared out of the window. The sun was out and I could feel the heat on my body through the glass. I stood for a few minutes, just soaking it up, and looking at my chop.

With the sun shining on it, the chrome was reflecting the sunlight all over the place and it looked awesome. I was really excited about my weekend away and was especially looking forward to going on my own. I just needed to be away from all the shite for a bit and this was the perfect way to do it.

I had a quick bath, a bite to eat and I was ready to head. I grabbed my bag and stuffed Julie's letter in the side pocket. I put on my jacket and cut-off then wondered if I should maybe leave the cut-off behind.

I wrestled a bit with the pros and cons of wearing it for a bit then decided 'Fuck it, I'm a Bat and it stays on'. I locked the door and headed downstairs, tied the bag onto my bike then fired it into life.

What a rip it gave, it always made me smile. Every time I started it up, I always felt that everything was great with the world, just knowing it was mine made me feel cool as fuck.

As I got on, I thought to myself 'Anyone who wasn't awake certainly will be now' then laughed to myself as I blasted off.

The sun was really warm, but the wind had a real chill to it. I always found that to be a strange sensation: when you struggled to see because the sun was so bright, but the wind was making you freeze your bollocks off!

I headed out of town and onto the motorway. It was pretty quiet and I decided just to cruise in the inside lane. I sat around fifty, enjoying the sights and smells I was taking in. I loved the feeling of being on my bike, not having a care in the world and not thinking about anything.

It took me about an hour and a half to eventually arrive in the town. I spotted a café and decided to grab myself a roll and a hot drink. I was pretty cold, but that 'good' cold, the one where you have a bit of a tingle going on, but you can still feel all your bits.

I ordered a coffee and a bacon roll and asked the woman for directions to the hospital before sitting myself down in the corner at the window. I was watching the world go by and smiling at the amount of people who were stopping to admire my bike.

Lots of people think bikers are black smelly criminals who should probably be locked up, but I reckon, deep down, most of them wish they had the balls to be one.

I finished my roll and headed out. I approached my bike and there were three young lads, around twelve or thirteen years of age, standing staring at it. I put the key in and fired it up, revving it really loudly. I swear they almost shit themselves, which made me laugh.

One of them said: "That's a cool bike, Mister, where did you get it?" "I made it," I told him, then blasted off, smiling to myself. I looked in my mirror as I left and saw the three of them standing with their mouths wide open, not taking their eyes off me until I disappeared out of sight.

'Fuck!' I had a thought to myself, 'He just called me Mr, I bet I'm only about five years older than he is!' I smiled again and started thinking back to my time with Max and how I thought he was well old too.

I arrived at the hospital and turned into the main entrance, it looked a really nice setting driving in. As you entered, you passed through a tree-lined road with lots of rhododendron bushes scattered around. I stopped at the first corner to read the sign, but there was no mention of the nurses home on it. There were lots of ward names, signs for the laundry, the pharmacy and the reception, but nothing I needed.

I decided to head to the reception, in the hope of getting directions there, but was stopped in my tracks by two elderly men who stood in front of my bike. One of them asked me to switch off the engine to allow him to be heard, which I did.

I got off my bike and asked them what they wanted. The taller of the two explained to me that motorcycles were not allowed on the hospital grounds and that I should remove myself and my bike to the other side of the entrance.

I asked him why this was the case and who he was. He stated that he was the senior consultant psychiatrist and that the reason motorcycles were banned was because, in the past, people had been using the grounds as a racetrack and a patient had been killed.

I apologised, and told him I hadn't seen any signs at the gate regarding this, however, I would head out and find somewhere else to park. He then thanked me for being so courteous.

I asked him if he could tell me where the nurses home was. As he started to give me directions, the other person asked if he could bum a fag off me, which I thought was a bit strange, until the consultant explained that he was a patient.

I took my cigarette packet out. When I opened it and saw there were only half a dozen or so left, I just gave him the packet.

Honestly, you'd have thought I'd given him a million quid, he took it from me then started hugging me, telling me God would watch over me, that no harm would ever come to me and that I was a saint amongst saints. I just nodded and wondered what the fuck he was all about.

Next thing, two nurses approached me, one male and one female. The female smiled at me and asked if I was okay, to which I just nodded.

She then got a hold of the guy who told me he was a consultant and asked him why he was annoying me. He then started screaming at her, telling her to fuck off, and started pointing at me, roaring that I wasn't allowed in the hospital with a fuckin motorbike and that I should be condemned to hell.

I was totally bamboozled with all this and had no idea what the fuck was going on. The male nurse then restrained the guy and headed off to fuck knows where with him.

While this was going on, the other guy was continually asking me for a light. I looked at the nurse, waiting for her approval before I gave him one. I lit his fag then she told him to head back to the ward, which he did. He shook my hand and said to me, "God bless you and keep you, my son," then headed off.

The nurse started laughing and said: "I take it this is your first time in a psychiatric hospital?" I just nodded. "I thought he was a fuckin doctor!" I told her. "Yes, so does he!" she said, still laughing.

"I'm Anna, I'm a staff nurse here," she said, holding her hand out. "I'm Shug," I replied, shaking her hand. "So how do I know if you really are a nurse?" I asked, smiling back. "Maybe I'll take your temperature later and you can decide from there," she suggested.

I told her I was well up for that and anytime she was available was good for me, she just laughed again.

She asked me what I was doing there, I told her I was trying to find the nurses home. "Anyone in particular?" she asked. "Yes, I'm looking for my mate's girlfriend, her name's Julie Richards, she's a student nurse and lives in the nurses home."

She told me she didn't recognise the name and that she was sorry, but she had to go as I'd made her late for her backshift.

She said she would take me to the nurses home and show me where it was if I dropped her off at her ward on my bike, to which I agreed. She then quickly jumped on the back and pointed for me to go straight ahead.

It was the first time I'd had anyone on the back of my chop (except the 10 second ride with Cowboy, chasing after the Volvo guy, Thatcher) and because it was a small seat, I could feel her pressing really closely against me.

She directed me through the hospital and pointed to the last building on the right, telling me that was the nurses home, then urged me to turn around. She then directed me towards her ward.

I drew up outside the front door and she got off. She said that if I was still around when she finished at ten, I could join her for a drink. I told her that I was staying for the weekend and wasn't sure what I'd be doing tonight, but that I was well up for that.

She handed me back my helmet, leaned over, kissed me on the cheek, and told me she was staying at the nurses home too.

She said she was going to a party after her work then ran into the ward.

As I headed away, I could see a few people watching me from the office and wondered what they would be saying to Anna when she went it. 'Fuck me, I guess it's true what they say about nurses' I thought to myself.

On the way back to the nurses home, I saw a fair amount of people walking around. I had no idea whether they were staff or patients, but I would certainly be on my guard after my last encounter.

I arrived at the nurses home and parked up. I stood back, taking a minute to look at the building. It was a huge building, like a fancy old hotel, there was a wide set of stairs, five in total, with stone bannisters at either side, supported by small round stone pillars. At the top of the stairs, there was both a revolving door and a normal one.

The bottom floor had two large bay windows on either side of the door, but from the first floor up it was just standard sash and case. I counted seven floors and an attic, which had six dormer windows.

I went inside and looked around. The entrance hall was massive and had a large wooden staircase on the left-hand side and a lengthy corridor straight in front of me. There was a small room next to the corridor with a sign on the door which said: 'Warden's Office' on it. I gave it a knock, but never got a reply.

There were two rooms off the reception, one on either side of the doors. I stuck my head into both and guessed they must be some kind of common rooms. One had a pool table, a dart board and a TV, the other was more like a library, with shelves of books all along one wall and some sofas and chairs scattered around.

The bay windows I'd seen from the outside had bench seats with cushions on them, which looked like an ideal place to relax and watch the world go by.

I went back out to the reception area. Looking around again, I couldn't believe there was not a single person about. I got the piece of paper out my pocket with the room number on it, to double check where I was going, and just as I was stuffing it back in my pocket, I heard Julie's voice from the top of the stairs.

"Shug, how you doing? I heard the bike as I was just getting dressed, hope you've not been hanging about too long, did you find it okay?" Julie was asking me a million things as she ran down the stairs, but I never answered her yet.

She gave me a big hug and told me it was great to see me. Then she noticed my cut-off. "I see you've got your colours, you must be well chuffed?" I told her I was and asked her how she was doing.

"I'm great, come on upstairs, I'll show you my room and introduce you to my friends." And with that, she grabbed my hand and almost pulled me up the stairs.

We got to her room and she pushed open the door and ushered me in. I'm not sure what I was expecting, but a box room with a single bed and a sink wasn't exactly what I'd imagined. I walked over to the window as Julie shut the door.

I saw we were facing the front which I was glad about as I could see my chop, which gave me a bit of comfort. The overall view was really good: there was a football pitch next to the road and I could see the hills beyond, a spreading of fields with no obstructions and a scattering of farm buildings and cottages.

"Nice view, Julie," I told her. "I know, Shug, pity about the room, though," was her reply. "Yes, it's pretty basic, and a bit smaller than I thought it would be," I suggested. She nodded in agreement then told me that it suited her needs as she hardly spent any time there and she was happy enough with it.

I decided I would give her the letter straight away and get it over with. "Julie, Rooster gave me a letter for you," I told her, as I raked about in my bag for it.

"Keep it Shug, and give it back to him, tell him I don't want it. And please, let's not talk about him this weekend, okay?" At that point, I wasn't really sure what to do, this wasn't one of the reactions I'd envisaged.

"Julie, he told me to give you it and I don't want to take it back. Just let me leave it here and we'll say no more about it, you can do what you want with it when I leave." I then looked at her and nodded, while putting it down on her desk. She nodded back then completely changed the subject.

She jumped on the bed and motioned for me to join her, which I did "So, Shug, tell me what's been happening with you over the past few months?" "Fuck, Julie, where do I start? What was the last thing you heard?" I asked her.

"Well, the last thing Rooster told me was about you and Lorraine, and her father catching you shagging her in his bed." "Yes, well, that wasn't one of my finest moments, as you can imagine," I told her before we both burst out laughing.

"Oh, Shug, do you fancy a beer? I've got some in my fridge." Before I could answer, she jumped up and grabbed two, handed me one then sat back down. "So, come on then, share the gossip," she demanded.

I asked her if she'd heard about Provo and Stiff or the prospects. She told me she hadn't so I gave her a short version of the events and told her about me leaving the farm last night before the pigs got there, and that seemed to satisfy her.

"Now it's your turn," I told her and asked her to fill me in with her gossip. "Nothing much to tell, really," she said. "Came here, working away, enjoying my course, met some nice people and getting on with my life. That's about it."

"Any boyfriends on the horizon?" I asked her, which got me an evil stare. "No, no way. I've had my fucking fill of them, there'll be no fucking more of them!" she said angrily.

'Fuck, had I touched a nerve or what? What the fuck had happened between her and Rooster?' I wondered. I don't think I'd ever heard Julie swear and she did it twice in the one sentence.

"Sorry, Julie, I didn't mean to upset you," I told her, "I was only making conversation, I didn't mean to offend you." "Hey, Shug, you're fine. It's me that needs to apologise. I didn't mean to go off on one. It's just that Rooster and I didn't finish on good terms and well, hey, …" then stopped herself and, again, changed the subject.

"We said we weren't going to mention him and here we are, within five minutes, we're at it already. Come on, I want you to meet a few people. I told them you were coming and we all agreed that a trip to the pub was in order."

With that, she jumped up and told me she would be back in a minute. I got up, finished my beer then went back to the window.

'Fuck, what went down with them?' I wondered. I started to try and think of anything that would make Julie act like this about Rooster. The best I could come up with was that she caught him fucking about.

I looked again at the hills and thought 'Yep, I could do this. I could get well used to seeing that view every morning I woke up'. Julie then burst into the room with three girls and two guys. She introduced me to them all, telling me their names (which I instantly forgot - except for one of the guys who was called Calum). I thought straight away that he was a fuckin poof. When he shook hands with me, he had one of those fuckin limpy handshakes that I fuckin hate.

He looked well-built and was a fair bit bigger than me, but had a fuckin squeaky voice. That, along with the fuckin handshake, made me know I wasn't going to like him.

"Come on, let's go and get pissed," Julie announced and ushered us all out the door. As we headed downstairs, they were all yapping away, mostly about work stuff. I just listened while I tried to suss everybody out.

When we got outside, one of the girls ran over to my bike and commented on how awesome she thought it was. "Shug, will you take me a run on it?" she asked. "Yeh, no probs," I told her. "Not now, Becky," Julie shouted to her, "maybe tomorrow. Right now, it's drink time, come on, let's get to the pub," she told her, grabbing her arm.

I made a mental note of her name and thought 'Two down, three to go. Fuck, I'm hopeless with names when I'm told a bunch of them at the same time.

We walked through the hospital for a bit and out a different gate than I'd come in. We walked up what they called the 'back road', which took us to the main road I'd driven up earlier. We crossed it, walked up a hill beside a garage then down the other side before arriving at the pub.

We went in and straight to the bar. I decided to get the round in and asked everyone what they wanted.

The girls ordered vodkas and the other bloke, who seemed okay, wanted a pint. The poof asked for a G&T! I ordered up and Calum stayed to give me a hand with them. The rest went to grab a table.

The barman said he'd not seen me before and asked if I'd started working in the hospital, I just said no and paid for the drinks. When he came back and handed me my change, he said: "Not very talkative are you?"

"Is that a fuckin crime?" I asked him. "No, but causing bother in my pub is. So just remember that," he told me. "Who the fuck do you think you're talking to, cunt?" I asked him, putting the tray back down on the bar.

"Look, son, I don't want any trouble in here, okay?" "No, it's not fuckin okay," I told him "and I'm not your fuckin son. I came in for fuckin a beer, not the Spanish Inquisition, so don't start your fuckin pish with me. If you've got something to say then spit it out or shut the fuck up!" I screamed at him.

He was genuinely taken aback. I guessed no one had spoken to him like that. But I had my colours on and there was no way I was going to take threats from a prick like him.

Julie came to the bar and tried to defuse the situation by talking to the barman on my behalf, but I told her to shut the fuck up and go and sit on her fuckin arse, which she did rather sharpish.

He was still staring at me and hadn't said anything, so I started again.

"Well? Am I going to sit down and have my drink or do you have something else in mind?" I asked him.

"Look, I told you, I don't want any trouble. If you behave like everyone else then I'll have no problem with you having your drink, but don't ever call me a cunt again." I interrupted him, "Or what?" I asked. "If you do, I'll be forced to have you removed," he told me.

I picked up the drinks then said: "Well, that's your call, cunt," then walked over to the table to be greeted by five very nervous people.

"Shug, what was that all about?" Julie asked me. "Sorry, Julie, I didn't mean to go off on one, but that prick at the bar was coming the cunt and you know I can't let that go."

"Oh yes, the colours' thing, you can't walk away, I know that very well. Come on, Shug, this is my local, please don't start anything, the next pub is miles away and we don't want to be barred," she told me.

"Julie, as long as he doesn't start anything, I promise I'll let it go." I picked up my bottle of Newcastle, filled up my glass, raised it up and said: "Cheers!"

You could have cut the atmosphere with a knife, nobody seemed to know what to say, so I started the ball rolling.

"Becky, have you ever been on a bike?" I asked her. "No, not really, I've sat on a couple, but never actually been on one when it's going," she told me. "You still up for a blast tomorrow?" I asked her. "Yes, too right I am," was her reply.

I thought she would've been put off after my altercation with the barman, but she didn't seem to be. The other girl, who I found out later was called Lisa, asked me to tell her about my colours and what Julie meant about not walking away, so I gave her the briefest of explanations I could, which she seemed to accept.

I turned to Julie and asked her if she was okay. She said she was then told me she'd forgotten about all the shit like this, that went on when she was dating Rooster, and that this had brought it all back.

I again apologised to her, but also reminded her that she knew the drill and she just nodded. Calum (the poof) then went and got some drinks in. From then, the night improved greatly. I kept my eye on the barman throughout the night, but he never looked over at our table once.

There was a steady stream of girls, around my age, coming in and Julie said that most of them worked in the hospital, which ticked another box for me in terms of a job.

'Oh, fuck!' I just had a sudden thought about the job. 'Julie's never going to recommend me now. Fuck, Shug, what a prick you are. 'Why didn't you think of that earlier?' I wondered. Then I thought 'Ah, well, fuck it!' and decided to forget about it and pick it up the next day.

It was my turn for the round and after five minutes of everyone trying to tell me they would get it, rather than have me go to the bar, I told them I was going and that was that, which provoked another awkward silence amongst the group.

I headed to the bar and, low and behold, it was the same cunt from earlier who made a point of coming to serve me.

"Yes, sir, what can I get you?" he asked. 'Fuck, a far cry from earlier!' I thought. "Same again, please," I told him. "No problem, sir, coming right up, would you like me to bring them to your table?" he replied.

"No, you're fine, I'll carry them back myself," I told him. 'Right, what the fuck's going on?' I wondered, 'Is he taking the piss? or has he maybe arranged a surprise for me later?'. Who knew what the fuck he was up to, but I was so used to people acting weird with me since I got my colours that I decided not to think about it anymore.

He put the drinks on the tray and I went to hand him the money. "No, sir, this one's on me," he told me. "I want to apologise for my behaviour earlier and I hope you can forgive me, please just put it down to a big misunderstanding on my part."

"No probs, already forgotten," I told him as I lifted the tray. He then said: "Thank you, sir, much appreciated," then left to serve another customer.

'Fuck, how weird was that?' I thought, 'What a strange cunt he was! One minute, he's threatening me and the next, he's treating me like a king. Fuck, sometimes I just don't understand people'.

As I put the tray of drinks down on the table, all eyes were on me, dying to know what happened. Julie asked if everything was okay and I told her I wasn't sure.

I explained my conversation with the barman and everybody agreed it was well weird. "But, hey, fuck it," I told them. "Never look a gift horse in the mouth," I said, raising my glass to them all.

After a few more, Julie suggested we head back as one of the girls was having a party, which we were invited to, and we needed to catch the garage to buy some drink before it closed.

We finished up our drinks and headed to the door. As we were about to go out, the barman came running over and asked to speak to me.

'Ah, this is it now,' I thought, 'I knew he was taking the piss earlier'. "What the fuck do you want?" I asked him, in a really aggressive tone. "I just wanted to make sure we were cool before you left and to let you know you're welcome here anytime."

Well, fuck me senseless. That was the last thing I expected, but I was still on my guard, wondering if he'd set something up outside.

"We're cool, everything's fine," I told him. He then thanked me and offered his hand for me to shake, which I did before heading out.

Julie stuck her arm through mine and snuggled up to walk beside me. She then asked what I'd done to get him to behave the way he had.

I told her nothing had happened and I didn't understand it either. "But, hey, it's better than rolling about the floor, knocking fuck out of him," I suggested, then we both had a bit of laugh about it.

As we came to the brow of the hill, a bunch of girls were coming towards us, heading to the pub. One of the girls shouted out my name and made her way towards me. It was Anna, the girl from earlier on, who'd given me directions.

"Hi, Shug, you ready to get your temperature taken yet?" she asked, with a big smile on her face. I looked her up and down and thought she was well fit.

"Hi, Anna, didn't recognise you with your clothes on," I remarked, which led to a roar of laughter from her friends and some light-hearted ribbing.

"Anna, this is Julie, my friend I told you about." The girls exchanged a nod, with both of them looking each other up and down. "You fancy coming back to the pub with us?" she asked.

"Nah, no thanks, we're heading to a party at the nurses home. Maybe I'll catch you there later?" I suggested. "Okay, see you then," she told me, then touched my face with her hand and smiled before heading off.

"Well, Shug, come on, spill the beans," Julie demanded. "What?" was all I said. Julie then started on one of her rants, "What! Is that all you've got to say, what! Right, here it is, Shug: a girl approaches you, you tell her you never recognised her with her clothes on, she invites you for a drink, you tell her you'll catch her at the party later. You've been with me all day and never mentioned her, and you say 'What?'"

"Okay, okay, let's get the drink and head to the party, I'll tell you all about it there," I told her. She reluctantly agreed, reminding me that she wouldn't forget.

We went into the garage and the girls, and the poof, were picking up half and quarter bottles of spirits. Calum grabbed a six pack and I lifted a slab of lager. They all looked at me as if I had horns.

"Fuck, I thought you said it was a party we were going to. That shit's not going to last you very long, is it?" I declared, but they just shook their heads in unison and offered me some very wry smiles.

We paid for our drink and headed up the back road. I split the case and took out a beer, offering everybody a can, but they all declined.

On the way, I told them the story about my arrival: how I'd met Anna, the patient I thought was a doctor and the run to the ward on my bike, which made them all shriek with laughter. This raised their spirits and I'm sure they were still laughing when we arrived at the room where the party was being held.

After seeing Julie's room, I wondered how it would be possible to have a party in such a small area, even the living room in my flat was bigger than her whole room, but I needn't have worried.

The girl, Debbie, who was having the party, had the biggest room in the home. She had a double bed, a two-seater couch, a desk and a couple of chairs. It was at least two and a half times the size of Julie's.

Debbie opened the door and greeted everyone like long lost pals, kissing and cuddling everyone until she came to me. Julie introduced me to her and she held her hand out for me to shake, which I did.

"Come in, Shug, Julie's told me so much about you, I'm dying to hear some of your stories," she said, as she gestured me in and closed the door behind us.

There were about sixteen people in the room, a few more girls than boys, but a pretty even mix. Debbie then announced over the music, "Everybody, this is Shug, Julie's friend, he's a real biker," then turned and smiled at me. 'Fuck, what a stupid cow' I thought to myself 'A real biker, what in fuck's name does she think that means?' I thought about having a go at her for embarrassing me, but decided she didn't know any better and let it go.

Julie whispered in my ear that she was sorry for her friend's choice of words. I told her not to worry about it and suggested we grab a seat on the floor.

The poof sat down beside us and asked if he could have a word and I told him to go for it. He started by telling me he wasn't a poof and was disappointed I thought he was.

I told him it made no odds to me what the fuck he was, poof or not, it wouldn't affect me in any way. He then said that he was a black belt in Karate and fought for the Scottish team and would have had my back tonight if anything had kicked off.

Well, fuck me! Talk about first impressions! I was glad I never took the piss out of him. How fuckin embarrassing would that have been? - getting slapped around by a cunt who everybody thought was a nancy boy!

He then told me he had a steady girlfriend back home and hated the fact everyone thought he was gay. I told him not to worry about it and suggested he stop drinking gin and fuckin tonics and get wired into some beer. I handed him a can and we both had a laugh.

During the night, I changed my whole attitude towards Calum and found out he was a pretty sound dude.

Julie, by this time, was starting to get a bit pissed and I asked her if she wanted to split. She told me she would be glad to go, but didn't want to spoil my night. I told her it'd been a long day and I would be glad to head.

I shook hands with Calum, told him he was sound, but needed to work on the old handshake, then we went back to Julie's room. I wondered about the sleeping arrangements as there was only one bed and I didn't see a sleeping bag or any spare covers lying around. Julie went to the sink and started washing off her makeup. I ditched my jacket and boots, sat on the bed and opened one of the beers I'd brought back with me.

"Thanks for a great night, Julie, it was nice meeting your friends, and sorry about the thing with the barman earlier"

"Don't worry about it, Shug, it turned out okay," she told me.

She then started to strip off in front of me, which delighted me. "Where am I going to crash?" I asked her.

By this time, she was down to her bra and knickers and I was waiting to see what else was coming off.

She leaned over and pulled a long t-shirt out from under her pillow and put it on before taking her bra off, much to my disappointment. "You'll just have to cuddle in with me, but it's only to sleep remember, I don't want any of your funny business," she said, laughing.

"No probs, Julie, I remember you saying earlier you were off men and I would never do anything to wreck our friendship." What I really meant was that I wouldn't do that to Rooster, he was a proper mate and a great bro.

I stripped down to my pants and got into bed. Julie put her arms around me, cuddled in, then very quickly drifted off to sleep. I lay for a minute thinking about Rooster and again wondered what had gone on with them.

I could feel Julie's erect nipples up against my back. When she moved, they pressed into me and it was giving me a raging hard-on. Try as I might to think about other shit, it just wouldn't go away.

Finally, I drifted off to sleep. When I woke, I was lying on my back and Julie had her leg, as well as her arm, wrapped around me.

As usual, I had the early morning totem pole struggling to get out my pants, but Julie's leg was lying on top of it, and to be honest, I didn't really want to move it, but nature called.

I slipped out of bed and headed into the corridor, looking for the piss house. I eventually found it after five minutes of walking both ways.

I went in and relieved myself. When I came out, there were four girls walking towards me, all with their uniforms on, and there was me, standing in a pair of scants with a semi.

"Morning, girls," I remarked. One of the girls then replied "Good morning to you too, looks like you're happy to see us," then pointed to my pants.

This made the other three laugh. As they passed, I told her I was, but if she would like to strip for me, I would be even happier. I gave her a kiss on the cheek which made her go instantly red and the others laughed even more.

I was smiling as I entered the room. When I walked in, I caught a glimpse of Julie, naked. She was getting changed and when I went in, she was taking a bra out of her drawer and turned around to see who it was and I got a real eyeful.

I turned away and apologised, but she just said: "Don't worry about it, Shug, I'm sure it's nothing you haven't seen before." I closed the door and turned back around, just in time to watch her put her knickers on.

She then nodded in the direction of my underpants. "I guess you liked what you saw," she said, laughing. I looked down at my dick, it was nearly bursting out of my pants.

I wasn't sure about what to say next so thought I would tell her the truth. "What's not to like, a beautiful girl, naked in front of me. You're lucky we're friends or I would've been chasing you around the room, hoping for a shag," I told her, laughing.

Julie never said anything, just smiled then put on the rest of her clothes. I told her I would grab a shower and asked if I could borrow a towel. She explained there was no need to borrow a towel as they were already provided in the bathroom, so I grabbed a pair of scants from my bag and, armed with Julie's girlie shampoo, I headed back out into the corridor.

There were three showers in the bathroom, three sinks and two urinals. I went into the cubicle, closed over the curtain, and began giving myself a good wash. I was bollock naked and covered in soap when the curtain was suddenly pulled open.

"What happened to you last night, Shug? I went to the party looking for you, but you'd already left!" Fuck, I wiped the soap from my eyes and there was Anna, standing staring at me, with only a towel wrapped around her. "Nice to see you too," I told her. "Don't you think you've found the wrong bathroom?" I asked.

"Not at all, I've found exactly what I was looking for," she told me. She then dropped the towel to reveal a stunning body, a shaved pussy, and a gorgeous set of tits.

She stepped into the shower, pulled the curtain over and started kissing me while fondling my dick at the same time. I couldn't believe what was happening; I had to pinch myself to make sure I wasn't dreaming.

She pulled her tongue from my mouth, slid down until she was kneeling on the floor, then expertly began sucking and licking my cock. She had certainly done that before, that's for sure. I had to fight with all my might to stop myself from shooting in her mouth.

I pulled her back up, started kissing her and got my hands on her lovely breasts. I started tweaking her nipples, which made her groan out loud. I then grabbed her arse and lifted her up so she could wrap her legs around me. As soon as she did, I rammed my cock into her pussy.

I leaned her gently against the shower wall and started shafting her. She was squeezing her legs tightly around my back, using her arms around my neck to give her leverage to buck up and down.

She seemed to be in some kind of frenzied state, like she hadn't had it for a long time, and I was fuckin loving it. She seemed to be coming for ever, I could feel myself going weak at the knees, so I suggested we sit on the floor. She never said a word, just nodded, and carried on bouncing up and down.

We slipped to the floor and she rearranged herself: putting her hands on either side of my knees, leaning herself back, and lowering her head behind her. She continued to bounce up and down on top of me and I was greeted with a perfect view of her tits swinging all over the place as we fucked.

She became increasingly noisy as she brought herself to yet another orgasm. By this time, I was aware of other people using the bathroom. I'd heard the other showers going and someone doing a pish, but Anna was way too far gone to notice anything.

As she shot her load for the umpteenth time, she leaned forward and put her hands on my shoulders. She was making some strange faces as her bucking slowed down until eventually, she stopped.

She then slumped on top of me, as if she'd died, and we sat for a few minutes saying nothing, letting the water from the shower beat down on us.

I whispered in her ear that she was a great ride and thanked her for abusing me, then laughed. She told me I wasn't so bad myself and also had a bit of a snigger.

She then told me to 'shush' as she thought someone else might be there. I told her people had been in and out of the bathroom for the past fifteen minutes.

She freaked a bit at that point and told me she needed to get the fuck out and couldn't be seen.

I told her I was sure that more people than her had fucked in the showers before and that she shouldn't worry about it. Then she dropped the bombshell.

"Shug, I'm married. If anyone sees me, they'll tell my husband. I can't afford that, he's a nursing officer here and it would kill him."

"Fuck's sake, Anna, why didn't you tell me that before we fucked? I'm not into marriage wrecking! Jeezus Christ! You've fucked it all up now!" I told her.

"Shug, what are we going to do?" she then asked, with an almost terrified look on her face.

"What are WE going to do! I think you mean: 'What the fuck are YOU going to do?' This doesn't affect me in any way, Anna," I reminded her.

"I wouldn't be here if you'd told me you were married. I can just walk out and head back to Julie's room, without giving a fuck about anything."

"Shug, please, you need to help me here. I need to get out without getting caught," she begged. 'Aagghhh, I can certainly pick them' I thought to myself. I stood up and switched the shower off. I then looked down at her sobbing and shivering and thought 'Here the fuck we go again! Just for once - Why can't anything in my life be fuckin simple?'

I told her to stay in the shower for a minute as I got out and started to dry myself. There was a guy brushing his teeth and one of the toilet cubicles was locked, so I guessed there were only two dudes to worry about.

The guy brushing his teeth looked at me and gave me the thumbs up (I'm guessing he thought I was cool because I'd just shagged someone in the shower). I just nodded and continued to dry myself.

I saw Anna shivering so handed her towel into her and she wrapped it around herself. The guy who was brushing his teeth then nodded in the direction of the shower, gave me the thumbs up again, then left.

'One down, one to go' I thought, as long as no one else came in. I looked outside and realised the girls' bathroom was directly adjoining the boys'. As no one was in the corridor, I motioned for Anna to come out, which she did.

She then slipped into the girls' bathroom unnoticed and I headed back up the corridor towards Julie's room.

Chapter 10

When I went in, I was surprised to see Julie back in bed. She was sleeping again, now lying on her front, with her t-shirt half way up her back. I could see her skimpy white knickers and a lovely view of her pussy edging out of them.

Even after my exertions in the shower, I could feel the old hard-on coming back so grabbed my fags and headed towards the window to take my mind off her.

I pulled the chair over and sat down, lit up my fag, lifted the window open a little, and stared at the view. I smiled, thinking about Anna, then started to wonder what the fuck she was all about.

She'd made a clear play for me and I hadn't even given her any encouragement. She'd shagged me into the quick then told me she was married, what the fuck's that all about? I wondered. I must have been laughing out loud, thinking about it, because Julie woke and asked me what was so funny.

She sat up, gave her head a bit of a rub with both hands, messing her hair all over the place, then swung her legs out of bed. She stretched her hands above her head and yawned out loud. Again, I was focused on her body as her nipples were erect and I found myself not being able to look anywhere else.

I turned the chair around to face her and wished I'd just waited another minute or so to do it as my dick was again trying to burst out my pants. Just as I was looking at her, she had a quick squatch at me.

I offered her a fag, which she took. We never mentioned our ogling at each other, but we both knew we'd done it. "How was your shower?" she asked. "Well, Julie, you're not going to believe what happened," I told her.

Intrigued, she told me to continue. "Remember that girl Anna we met last night? Well, she accosted me in the shower this morning and we ended up fucking, and then she tells me she's fuckin married!" I then filled her in with all the details and she burst out laughing.

"What?" I asked her. "Ha ha, it could only happen to you, Shug." "What do you mean by that?" I asked her.

"Well, think about it, Shug. You've only been here five minutes and so far you've been told off by a patient who thought he was a psychiatrist, you got in a fight with a barman, you cuddled in with your mates 'ex' all night, then you shag a married woman in the fuckin shower first thing in the morning. Come on, who else do you know that has twenty-four hours like that?" she asked, still laughing.

"Well, when you put it like that, maybe you've got a point! Anyway, what do you do for breakfast around here? I'm starving. All I had yesterday was a bacon roll and loads of beer." She told me there was a kitchen and dining room in the nurses home and we would head there if I fancied it.

"Let's go then, that'll do for me," I told her. "Eh, Shug, we don't have any clothes on. I think it would be best if we got dressed."

I agreed and put my jeans on then grabbed a t-shirt from my bag. I sat on the bed to put my boots on, watching her as she stood at the sink. Then I remembered that Julie was up and dressed before I went for my shower. "Hey, Julie, how come you were back in bed when I came back from my shower?" I asked her.

She told me she'd borrowed the spare key from the warden the day before and had to return it first thing. She carried on having a wash at the sink, bent over just enough for me to see her arse bulging out her knickers.

I couldn't help thinking how horny she looked and what I wouldn't give to fuck her.

She dried herself with a towel then opened her cupboard, lifted out the jeans and a blouse she had on earlier, and threw them on her bed. She grabbed her bra off the floor then removed her t-shirt, revealing her tits to me.

She stared at me for a minute, but my view was transfixed on her tits, and her growing nipples. "What?" she said, looking at me. "Julie, your tits are a fuckin sight to behold," I told her. "Shug, you shouldn't be looking," she reminded me. "I know I shouldn't, but I can't help myself, they're fuckin awesome."

She then put her bra and blouse on and hid them away, but I swear she was smiling.

"Sorry, Julie, I'm bang out of order, it won't happen again," I said, quite apologetically. "Don't worry about it, Shug, if I was bothered about you seeing me then I would've chucked you out."

I wondered if that was a come on, but decided just to ignore my thoughts. "So are we ready for breakfast then?" I asked. "Yep, let's go," she agreed.

"I wonder if your 'shower sex partner' will be in for breakfast?" she asked, nudging me in the ribs as she said it. "Fuckin hope not, that might be a bit uncomfortable for her," I suggested.

Julie then said: "What if she's there with her husband, enjoying a romantic breakfast? After all, he does work here - you told me." "Julie, don't even fuckin joke about it, that's the last thing I need." We both looked at each other and burst out laughing.

We got into the dining room and to my surprise, it was really busy. We picked up our trays and slid them along the railed counter.

I missed out all the cereal, the fruit and shit and went straight to the cooked stuff. I asked the lady for a bacon roll, a sausage roll and a black pudding roll. She looked at me like I had two heads as she served me, but I just ignored her. I ordered a cup of tea and waited on Julie, who was pissing about with fruit and cold meat and stuff.

She joined me at the till and I paid for it while she went and found us a seat. She sat with some of the people I recognised from the party the night before. When we sat down, she was chirping away, but I concentrated on wolfing down my rolls.

I knew I was in need of a good feed, but I didn't realise just how hungry I was until I started munching away. I was well on my way through my last roll when Julie gave me a dunt on the leg. I looked at her and she nodded towards the till.

Fuck, it was Anna! And she was with some old dude. The minute she turned around, she noticed me, then instantly looked away and went to the tables furthest away from us, out of my line of sight.

Julie whispered to me, "Fuck, Shug, she's with nursing officer McKay. You don't think that's her husband, do you?"

"Don't be fuckin stupid," I told her, "he's old enough to be her fuckin grandad." "Yeh, you're right, Shug, but it would've been funny if he was," she suggested. "Funny? Funny for fuckin who? Certainly not her, that's for sure," I reminded her.

We had a bit of a snigger and I continued with my roll. Julie chatted away with some of the people at the table then grabbed a hold of my arm and told me she'd just found out that it was her husband and that he'd just finished the night shift and had come to pick her up for breakfast.

'Holy shit, that's a turn up for the books' I thought. I reckoned he must be at least fifty and wondered what the fuck she was doing with him? Then I thought 'No wonder she was gagging for it!'

Julie was ready to go and suggested heading back to her room as she wanted to get a shower. As we all walked along the corridor, Becky asked if I would give her a run on my bike, like I'd promised the night before, and I told her I would love to.

I headed up to get my keys and helmet and told her I would meet her at the bike in five minutes. She then ran off, saying she was away to get a jacket.

As she ran up the corridor ahead of us, I thought to myself she was a bit of a big girl and worried there wouldn't be room for both of us on the seat.

I picked up my gear and headed out. Julie told me she would leave the door open, in case I was back first.

When I got outside, Becky was already standing looking at my bike. I handed her my helmet and told her to put it on and I clipped her up.

"What about you?" she asked. "What will you wear?" "Don't worry about it, I'll be fine," I reassured her. I jumped on and started it up. As it roared into life, she let out a loud scream. I just smiled and told her to get on.

She struggled a bit, but eventually managed to get on, with a bit of a pull up from me. She instantly wrapped her arms around me, squeezing really tight, like her life depended on it.

As I drew away, she started squealing again. Fuck, it was right in my ear. I just ignored it and headed for the back road. I stopped at the back entrance and asked her where the road went. She told me it led down to some cottages and farms.

'Perfect. No chance of the pigs being about.' I thought. I drew out and turned left. Again, Becky let out a squeal - fuck knows what she would've been like if we were going fast!

I headed along the road and came to a really sharp corner with four large houses on it. I remember thinking 'Fuck, I wouldn't like to live on that corner. There's a chance you'd get hit every time you came out your drive.'

I followed the road for a couple of miles until I came to an underpass, then turned around and headed back. When I stopped and got Becky off, she was flying, telling me how great it was and that she really appreciated it.

We then headed into the reception area and I went to go up the stairs. She grabbed me and planted a smacker right on my lips then said: "Shug, that was great, thanks very much," then disappeared along the corridor.

I headed upstairs, shaking my head and smiling away. I opened the door of Julie's room and noticed she still wasn't back so I kicked off my boots, planted myself on the bed, and lit up a fag.

Julie came in about five minutes later with a towel wrapped around her, still dripping from the shower.

"Oh, hi, Shug, I thought you'd still be away, how did it go? Did she enjoy it?" she asked.

"Yeh, she said she had a ball, and she gave me a big smacker on my lips, so I guess she was quite happy. You know what, Julie? I get the feeling I could like it here. Everyone wants to kiss or shag you, it's fuckin great," I told her, smiling away.

Julie just laughed and told me I wasn't right in the head, then plugged in her hair dryer and began drying her hair. I leaned back on the bed and lit up another fag, pulled the ashtray onto my knee, and watched her.

I noticed how long her hair had grown and just realised she'd dyed it a bit lighter. Even with a towel wrapped around her, you could see her shapely body and I started to hope the towel would fall to the floor.

She must have noticed me gawping at her in the mirror, "Shug, stop staring at my arse!" she shouted, laughing. "Well stop having a sexy one and I might," I replied, also laughing. She just shook her head and carried on.

I started to feel a bit of sexual tension between us, with all our flirting, and I guessed Julie was feeling the same. Almost every time I looked at her, I got a hard-on, but I wasn't sure how much of it was because she was forbidden fruit or how much was her natural sexiness.

I wondered how she was going to get changed? If she would ask me to leave or turn away or something? I really hoped not, as I was looking forward to getting another eyeful.

Julie finished drying her hair then asked me what I thought. I told her it looked great and commented on the length and colour, which seemed to go down well. "Can't believe you noticed," she replied with a smile.

"Course I noticed," I told her. "How could I not, it adds to your perfection," was my reply. The minute I said it, I thought 'Fuck's sake, Shug - adds to your perfection - what a cheesy fuckin thing to say. Aagghh, my brain's turned to mush with all the horniness in my head and I can't think of anything normal to say'. I decided to shut up and try my best not to say anything else so fuckin stupid.

Julie then said to me, "Shug, if I was listening to you in a pub or something, I would think you were trying to get into my pants."

She then looked at me, as if waiting for a reply. My mind was racing. All I could think was 'Come on, Shug, say something sensible, for fuck's sake. But don't say anything else so fuckin stupid.'

"Julie, if you were in a pub looking like that, everybody in there would want to get into your pants." 'There.' I thought to myself 'That was okay, Shug, well done!'

"Ha ha, you're some man, Shug, sometimes I think you're from a different planet," she told me, again laughing, but this time with a bit more purpose. I joined in, relieving a bit of my tension. She then dropped her towel and stood straight in front of me, bollock naked. She picked her knickers up off the bed and started to put them on.

I quickly stood up, turned to the window and fixed my stare on the view. "What's up, Shug?" she asked.

"What's up? Fuck's sake, Julie, what do you thinks up? You stand in front of me, with fuck all on, giving me a raging hard-on, knowing I fancy you like fuck, and you ask me what the fuck's up? Come on, Julie, you know what you're doing."

She then put her arms around me from behind, and again, I could feel her nipples pressing into my back.

"Sorry, Shug, I honestly never realised. I should've been more discrete about getting changed, but I feel so comfortable with you I didn't give the sexual thing a thought."

"Well, Julie, neither did I at first, but since we cuddled in bed last night, I've thought about fuck all else." I then stupidly told her that when I was banging Anna in the shower, I was imagining it was her. "That's how bad I've got it, Julie."

She then turned me around and looked straight at me. She put her arms around me and started kissing me. I responded. Fuck, she tasted great.

I pulled back from her. "Sorry, Julie, as much as I want to, I can't do this. Rooster's my best mate, I couldn't do it to him."

Again, she stared at me, "Listen, Shug, Rooster and me are finished for good, there's no way back for us. I won't ever be going back home. When I finish here, I'm going abroad, so I'll never see him again. So if you don't tell him, he'll never know."

"Yes, Julie, that's true, but if we did it I don't know how I'd ever be able to look him straight in the face." She sat on the bed, still dressed only in the skimpiest of knickers, and placed her hands between her knees.

"Shug, please sit down and I'll tell you something about your precious 'Rooster'," she said, patting the bed beside her. So, feeling a bit confused, I joined her on the bed as requested and looked at her, waiting for her to talk.

"Shug, the reason we split up was because I got pregnant." I interrupted her, jumping up from the bed, "Fuck! You're pregnant! Holy shit, Julie, that makes this even worse. What are you thinking about?" I demanded to know.

She then said, really quietly, whilst patting the bed beside her again, "Shug, sit down please, and listen for a minute." I sat down again, thinking 'Fuck, this is bad, this is really bad.'

She began speaking again. "Shug, I found out I was pregnant and was really excited, even though it wasn't planned, but these things happen. Rooster came to see me and I sat him down and told him. He was over the moon, jumping up and down like he does, all excited, telling me how great it was, and talked about all the things he wanted to do. He talked about us getting a place together and stuff like that, everything was great. I then told him that certain things needed to change, like he would need to put me and the baby ahead of the Bats. It was then that everything broke down. He asked me what I meant and I told him I didn't want him to leave the Bats or anything, just make sure that he would be here for us first, and that if I needed him at the same time as the Bats then he would choose me. Then he dropped the bombshell and told me he couldn't do that. He said that the Bats would always come first, no matter what, and that it was something I would need to live with. I then said that if we were having a baby together I couldn't accept that. He told me there and then to get rid of it. He stood up, took a hundred pounds out of his pocket, threw it at me, and said 'That'll cover the abortion', then left."

I looked at her and could see the tears running down her cheeks, so I put my arm around her, but in a comforting way rather than a sexual way. She then leaned her head on my shoulder and continued.

"I cried my eyes out. I'd gone from being worried about what he would say, to watching him jump up and down with excitement and feeling great, to being totally devastated, in the space of ten minutes. I couldn't believe his reaction. I wasn't asking him to leave or anything, just to consider his family first, that's all. Surely that wasn't too much to ask, was it?"

She started crying a bit more outwardly and I gave her a bit of a squeeze, hoping I wouldn't need to say anything, then the bombshell - "What do you think, Shug? Was I asking too much?"

Fuck, now she wanted me to say something. All I could think was 'Please, Shug, for fuck's sake, don't say anything that'll make her cry anymore'.

"Well, Julie, I really don't know what to say. You know being a Bat demands that your first priority at all times is them. Rooster is no different from anyone else, he has to honour that or he would face serious consequences. The commitment is for life, there are no exceptions. Perhaps he felt you were pressuring him to choose and he freaked or something. I'm not really sure what to say, Julie, I think it's a conversation you should be having with him, don't you?" I asked, hoping I wouldn't need to say anything else.

By now, she was sobbing really hard. When she started talking again it was difficult to hear what she was saying. I thought she told me that she'd had an abortion and I asked her to repeat what she'd just said.

"I tried to talk to him a hundred times, Shug," she repeated, "but he wouldn't listen. So I told him to fuck off and went and had an abortion, which broke my heart. I then spoke to my boss and explained my position and she got me on this course." Fuck, I HAD heard it right! Jeezus, what the fuck do you say to that? I for one had no fuckin idea.

By this time, Julie's crying was almost out of control, she was jerking up and down and the tears were flooding from her eyes. Sadly, I noticed her tears were dripping onto her tits, making her nipples erect once again.

'Fuck, Shug, how could you think about sex at this time, get a fuckin grip, man', I told myself. I decided it was best not to say anything else and got Julie to lie on the bed.

I cuddled her into me and told her everything would be okay. I tried to reassure her by telling her that this was probably the best thing for her in the long run and that being with a Bat was not a good thing for any girl.

She kissed me on the cheek, thanked me, then closed her eyes and cuddled in. I suggested we have a kip and see what the rest of the day brings when we woke and she agreed.

I kicked off my jeans, removed my t-shirt, and pulled the covers up. As I lay back down, Julie wrapped herself around me as she had earlier, but this time she had no top on and I could feel her warm body and those fuckin gorgeous nipples directly against my skin.

Julie's leg was again over my dick - there was no way she couldn't have noticed I was getting an erection. Fuck, I felt like I was lifting her leg up with it, but she never said a word.

We drifted off to sleep, but not before I tried to make some sense of what had gone on with them. I knew Rooster could be a cunt when he needed to be, but I never imagined for a minute he could do this to her. 'Hey, you think you know people, but do we ever really know anyone?' was my last thought.

Chapter 11

I woke up and looked at the clock, we'd been sleeping for over three hours. Julie, by this time, was lying on her back and had kicked her covers off. I sat up a bit, facing her, placed my elbow on the pillow, and rested my head in my hand, watching her sleeping.

I looked at her body; her tits were perfect and I could see her bush, straining to get out the sides of her tiny pants. Her stomach was so flat that her pants rested on her hip bones, again allowing me to see her bush straining to get out.

I've no idea why, perhaps I just got lost in the moment, but stupidly, I leaned over and started sucking gently on one of her tits. I didn't even realise I was doing it until Julie woke up and asked me what the fuck I was doing!

I immediately apologised to her, telling her I didn't mean it, and started bumbling my way through a million excuses until she interrupted me.

"Shug, stop, it's okay, don't worry about it, you're fine," she told me. "I just got a bit of a fright, that's all."

Again, I apologised, feeling like a right prick for doing it. "Sorry, Julie, I couldn't help myself, I was just looking and the next thing I …" She interrupted me, "Shug, I've told you, it's okay. Now relax, everything's cool. Actually, it felt quite nice, if truth be told," she said, starting to laugh.

Fuck, I felt so stupid. I went to get up, but Julie stopped me. "Shug, don't get up, give me a cuddle, please."
"You sure?" I asked. "Of course I am, come on, lie back down."

I lay back down on my back, not sure where to put my hands, but she sorted that out. She lifted my arm and put it over her head until I was touching her back. She then assumed the position she was in when we went to sleep, again with her leg over my dick.

All I could think about was 'Don't get hard, please don't get hard'. But unfortunately, as we all know, we have no control over our dicks and away it went again.

I knew she would be able to feel it, but decided not to say anything. I was embarrassed enough and couldn't face apologising for anything else.

We lay still for a few minutes, me with my heart racing and my mind going a mile a minute, then, fuck, out of the blue, Julie slipped her hand into my pants and started massaging my balls.

I lay with my eyes closed, wondering what the fuck to do next. "Julie, I don't think that's a good idea," I could hear myself saying to her. "Don't know why, Shug, it seems like a good one to me," she told me.

She then started rubbing my dick and kissing my nipple. 'Oh fuck, come on, Shug, think, for fuck's sake, man,' I screamed inside my head. I was so turned on, but knew it was so wrong. 'Fuck, fuck, fuck, stop her, Shug' I said to myself, but then a louder voice took over and it said: 'Aaagghh, Shug, fuck it, let's do it'.

I decided, at that point, to worry about the consequences later. I lifted her head, kissed her on the brow, then on her mouth and she responded by sticking her tongue in my mouth and rubbing her hand up and down my shaft.

We kissed softly and I placed one of my hands on her breasts. I started gently massaging it and could feel her nipple growing in my hand. Julie then rolled herself on top of me and slowly started pushing her hips into my groin.

I ran my hands softly over her back and down to her bottom. I squeezed her buttocks and ran my fingers down between her legs and felt her pussy. She was already moist and squirmed a bit, letting out a quiet sigh as I gave her a little rub.

I slid her pants down a bit and she kicked her legs until they were on the floor. At that point, I rolled her over and got on top of her and we continued kissing. We were now holding each other's faces, with the intensity of two people deeply in love.

I then took hold of my dick and directed it into her willing pussy. She groaned as I slowly slid it in as far as it would go. Julie wrapped her legs around me and began digging her nails into my back. I started moving up and down on top of her, pulling my dick almost out of her then slowly sliding it back in as far as I could. With each stroke, Julie dug her nails in and pushed her heels against the top of my legs.

We continued making love without sharing a single word, our tongues never left each other's mouths. Almost at the same time, we started to pick up the pace and burst into a frenzied race to come. Julie started moaning louder and I was almost grunting every time I thrust into her.

I'm sure her nails were drawing blood and her legs got tighter and tighter around me. She then let out a massive squeal as she burst into climax and within seconds, I came as well.

I collapsed on top of her, like a crumpled heap, as Julie squeezed every last bit of pleasure out of her climax, holding tight and gently bucking until she went limp as well.

I rolled off her and we cuddled in together, we were both panting like we'd ran two marathons back to back. At this point, we were now staring at each other and I could see that she had tears in her eyes.

"Are you okay, Julie?" I asked her, wiping away her tears with my finger.

"I'm fine, Shug," she told me. "In fact, I'm better than fine, that's the first time I've felt close to someone in a very long time. Please hold me for a minute will you?"

I put both arms around her and snuggled her into my chest. I was thinking about what she had said and thought the last time I'd felt like this was with Lorraine, and that wasn't yesterday either.

We fell asleep again and only woke when we heard the door being banged. Julie was at the front of the bed and got up, put her housecoat on and went to answer it.

I could hear her talking, but couldn't make out what she was saying. She then opened the door and in walked Anna.

I sat bolt upright in the bed, "Anna! What the fuck are you doing here?" I asked. "Shug, I need to talk to you," she started. I looked at Julie and she just shrugged her shoulders and sat on the chair.

"What is it?" I asked as if I didn't know. "Shug, about earlier, I know I shouldn't have done it and I know I should have told you I was married, but I just got carried away. I need you to promise you won't tell anyone. I've only been married six months and this would destroy my husband if it gets out, please tell me you'll keep this to yourself."

"Of course I will, Anna, don't worry about it, I have no need to tell anybody anything. I'll be away tomorrow so you can relax, no one's going to find out."

"Thanks, Shug, I really appreciate it, if there's anything I can do for you, just let me know."

Straight away, I thought about the job and suggested she could maybe help me out. "Well, actually, Anna, there's one thing you could maybe help me with," I told her. "I was thinking of applying for a job as a nursing assistant here, maybe you could mention to your man that he should look favourably at my application?"

"Yes, I'm sure I could do that, what's your second name?" she asked, looking much more relaxed than when she'd come in.

"Actually, my proper name is Ochil Kinnaird. That's what I would put on my form, so if you don't mind putting a word in his direction, that would be great."

"Okay then, and if you don't mind, I'll give your friend my number and get her to call me when you submit your application and I'll have a word with him. Promise that if I do this then you won't say anything."

"Anna, relax, even if you don't, I won't say a word. I told you, I'm not a marriage wrecker, and I meant it."

She then thanked me, wrote her number on a piece of paper and handed it to Julie.

"Thanks, Shug, good luck," she told me, as she went to leave. "Anna, before you go, can you come over here?" Anna walked towards me and I stepped out of bed, bollock naked, and gave her a cuddle, "Don't worry, everything's cool," I reassured her.

She burst out laughing and Julie and I joined in. Shaking her head, she made her way to the door then left. Julie and I then burst into a proper giggle, she dropped her housecoat and we got back into bed and cuddled in.

"What now, Julie?" I asked her. "What do you mean, Shug?" "Well, where the fuck do we go from here? We've just had a session of what I would probably call 'sensual love making', rather than a fuck, and just wondered what you were thinking about?"

"Shug, I wasn't actually thinking about anything, I was just enjoying the moment: knowing that tomorrow you'll be away and we'll go back to our normal shitty lives. Why? What were you thinking?" she asked.

"I don't really know, Julie. I'm just appreciating how nice this is and mulling over what happened with you and Rooster, and how it's going to affect me when I go back home."

"Shug, you think too much, and you worry about everything, just relax and take things as they come," she told me. She then gave me a kiss on the cheek and cuddled in.

I thought maybe she had a point, but I was still concerned about Rooster and how I would be with him.

Julie suddenly sat up and looked at me. "Shug, I can't believe you just asked Anna to help you get a job, you certainly know how to pick your moments, I'll say that for you."

"Well, I was going to ask you, but it just seemed like the right thing to say, she could hardly refuse me, now could she!" I said, laughing.

"What a man you are, Shug, you'd get a piece at anybody's door."

"Hey, Julie, never look a gift horse in the mouth …. you never know when it's going to come around again," I told her.

She lay back down and we chatted for a while. I then suggested going back to the pub for some grub and getting plastered, and to my surprise, she agreed to it.

We both got up and got dressed. I was feeling a bit awkward about what we'd just done and when I sat on the chair to put my boots on, I noticed Rooster's unopened letter still lying on her desk.

Fuck, it gave me a massive pang of guilt. I couldn't believe I had betrayed him; I'd seriously let myself down.

I wondered how I would have felt if he had shagged Lorraine. I think I would've been well pissed with him, and I knew if he found out about this that he would go fucking apeshit.

I must've been lost in my thoughts again as Julie gave me a tap on the shoulder, "Shug, are you okay? I thought we were going?" she asked. "Yes, Julie, I'm good to go," I told her, as I stood up.

We headed out and began our walk to the pub. I had my hands in my pockets and Julie put her arm through mine as we walked.

Fuck, here I was, arm in arm with Rooster's ex, after spending the last fifteen hours or so in bed with her, now heading for a few beers, and no doubt more shagging when we get back to her room.

It's unbelievable the mess I get myself into. How the fuck I manage it, God only knows! I thought about what had happened to me since I arrived and burst out laughing thinking, 'Fuck, only you, Shug!'

"What's the joke, Shug?" Julie asked. "Come on, share it with me." "Nothing, Julie, just thinking about some shit," I told her. "Come on, let's get a move on, I'm starving and could murder a beer."

We stepped up the pace and arrived at the pub in jig time. I went to the bar and Julie went to grab us a seat. The pub was pretty busy, as busy as it had been the previous night, and again, there was a fair scattering of girls in, all around the same age as me.

I muscled my way to the bar, looking to order the drinks, when the barman who was on the night before clocked me and made a beeline for me. "What can I get you, sir?" he asked. The bloke beside me told him he was first and the barman told him to shut up as he was serving someone.

I ordered my drinks and the guy next to me continued to moan at the barman, who told him if he didn't be quiet he would be barred. The guy then looked at me and asked if I was his boyfriend or something, I told him if he said another word that I would cut his tongue out and stick it up his fucking arse. That seemed to do the trick and he moved further along the bar, shaking his head. The barman came back with my drinks, put them on the bar and told me again they were on the house. I asked him what the fuck this was all about and he said it was his way of apologising for being rude the night before. I just picked up the drinks and went looking for Julie.

I saw her sitting with a couple of girls and she waved me over. I put the drinks down and asked the girls if they wanted refills, but they both said they were fine.

After Julie introduced me, I told her what had happened at the bar and she thought it was as weird as I did.

One of the girls asked me what the name on my patch was and I told her it was the Black Bats. She then said she thought she might know what was going on with him.

She told me that a couple of years ago, two people who were in the Black Bats had got beaten up. The next night, about forty of them came back and wrecked the place. They beat everyone up and threatened the owner that if anything else happened they would be back to kill him.

"My guess is, when he saw your patch, he thought you may be back to get him." I started laughing and told her that I didn't know anything about that, but it made much more sense than anything I could come up with.

We all had a laugh about it then chatted away for a bit before ordering some food. We had a fair bit to drink before we decided to head up the road and I had to support Julie as she staggered most of the way.

When we got back into the room, Julie stripped off, saying nothing, almost like she was on autopilot, got into bed and was asleep in an instant. I sat on the chair and lit up a smoke.

The room light was off, but the moon illuminated the room with an eerie glow, stopping it from being in total darkness. I blew the smoke up into the air and watched it circulate around the room.

I thought to myself, 'What a fuckin day that was! Another really bizarre one. Seems like my plan for a nice normal weekend has again, 'all gone tits up!'

I wondered if trying to quit the Bats was a good idea and started thinking about what it would be like if I did move here. If this weekend was anything to go by, I decided I wouldn't mind a bit of it and if I did get a job then I would stay with the Bats, almost like a part-timer, giving me the best of both worlds.

I looked out the window for a bit, thinking how calm and peaceful it was. Yep, decision made. I now had a plan in place which I thought would be perfect for me at this stage in my life.

I stripped off, got into bed, and cuddled in with Julie. We slept for a good ten hours and she was the first to wake. I felt her kissing my neck, as she wrapped her arm and leg around me.

"Morning, Julie, how's the head?" I asked her. "Seems okay so far, Shug, fingers crossed. You know what? I can't even remember getting back home last night! What time did we leave the pub?" she enquired.

"We left at closing time, came back here and had an amazing couple of hours of sex. You were like a wild animal, it was fuckin awesome," I told her.

"Holy shit, Shug, please tell me you're winding me up."
"No way, Julie, I'm on the level, and I think you'll have a bit of explaining to do to your neighbours. At one point, you were screaming so loudly that they started banging on the wall, telling you to shut up. You roared back to them, telling them to fuck off and stop being boring bastards."

That seemed to do it for her, she lowered her head under the covers and let out a scream. "Oh fuck, Shug, I'll never be able to look them in the face again. What a red neck, I'll never live it down."

I couldn't control myself at that point and burst out laughing, telling her it was just a wind-up. She started slapping and punching me, in a joking way, telling me I was a bastard and that she would get me back.

I grabbed her and pulled her on top of me, holding her close to prevent any more slaps. We both laughed and Julie relaxed. We were looking at each other for a minute or so then the inevitable happened.

We started kissing, but this time it wasn't the soft gentle way of the night before, but a forceful one, with frantic purpose. Julie was biting and started bucking her hips and I felt my dick on her pussy, which fired it into life.

She grabbed hold of it and almost pulled it off, trying to force it into her pussy. As I entered her, she sat up and started bouncing away on me.

I hadn't ever imagined Julie as the racy type (Oh, how wrong was I!). She had her arms by her sides, slightly leaning over me, and her hands on my chest. This position pushed out her already swelling breasts, making them compulsive viewing.

I grabbed hold of them and started giving them a bit of a rub. "Shug, pull my nipples and twist them really hard," she told me, staring straight into my eyes. She almost looked like she was drug crazed.

I did as I was asked, at first not being too forceful, until she stared at me again and told me she needed it harder and wanted the pain.

I did as I was told and she started bucking like a mad woman, bouncing up and down on me like her life depended on it, making all sorts of weird and wonderful noises.

Fuck, I thought she was going to snap my cock in half, it was that frantic. She then changed her position, now leaning back with her hands placed firmly on my shins. It made it almost impossible for me to keep hold of her nipples so instead, I started flicking them with my outstretched hand.

Fuck, I didn't think it was possible for her to go any harder at it than she already was, but she did.

I could see the sweat starting to run down Julie's body, and by the way she had slowed to a grinding motion, plus the deep throaty sounds she was now making, I guessed she'd shot her load.

I pulled her towards me, expecting her to cuddle in, hoping to give my dick a bit of a rest, but she had other ideas. "Shug, I want you to fuck me from behind," she told me, getting up and grabbing a pillow.

"Come on over to the chair, I always fancied getting fucked at the window." I got out the bed, dick in hand, and followed her. She placed the pillow over the chair, leaned her belly on it, and held on to the arms.

I grabbed hold of her arse and rammed my dick home. What a weird sensation I had, looking out of the window, sun shining, glorious view, and here I was, fucking a grunting woman from behind. Fuck, I was loving it.

I don't think Julie had stopped coming from earlier, she was already gone with her quiet moaning and heavy panting.

The back of the chair was just a bit lower than my waist and Julie's feet were lifting off the ground as I banged into her.

I lifted up her legs then held tightly to her waist and thrust as hard as I could. I saw Julie's grip on the arms of the chair tighten and she lifted her head back towards me.

"Oh, Shug, don't stop, for fuck's sake, fuck me harder," she demanded. I rammed into her for all I was worth and at that point, we were almost grunting in unison.

The next thing, Julie let out a scream, then shouted, "Oh, Shug, fuck, I'm coming, aggghhh, fuck, I'm coming."

Her panting got heavier and heavier then she collapsed. I almost came, but as she slumped over the chair, I pulled out of her and took hold of my dick, turned Julie around, sat her in the chair, and wanked for all I was worth.

Julie started rubbing my balls and within seconds, I shot my load all over her face. Julie opened her mouth as I came and managed to swallow a fair bit. She then took my dick in her mouth and sucked me dry.

She then got up and we stood at the window, kissing and cuddling for a minute. Fuck knows what anybody looking up would have thought, but at that point, we didn't give two fucks about anything.

"Julie, that was fuckin awesome." "You know what, Shug? I can't remember the last time I came so much." "It's just because you haven't done it for so long," I told her. "Next time, you'll be back to normal."

"After that, I don't think I'll ever be normal again," she suggested. "Join the club, Julie. I haven't felt like that for ages." We both laughed and Julie pulled us towards the bed.

We lay down and cuddled in. I could feel her heart beat against me and it was still beating really fast. We both closed our eyes as we relaxed and I started thinking about how great I was feeling.

"What time are you leaving, Shug?" she asked. "Why? Are you wanting rid of me now you've had your wicked way?" I said, laughing.

"Actually, I was hoping you could stay another night. I'm not working again until tomorrow. I'm starting on shifts and don't need to go in until one and I'm having a really nice time with you."

"I don't know, Julie, it's Provo's funeral on Tuesday and I thought I should go to the farm on Monday to see if there was anything needing to be done."

"Oh, so you're just going to run away now, after taking advantage of me" "Julie, that's ..." "Shug, stop, I'm only kidding," she interrupted, laughing loudly.

"You know what, Julie? I could stay and just get up early. I could still make it there by lunchtime." Julie then slid her hand onto my dick and gave it a squeeze.

"Don't put yourself out on my account," she told me. "I wouldn't want you to think I was being needy," she said, sarcastically.

That was enough for me, decision made. I lifted her head level with mine and kissed her and, hey ho, we ended up at it again. This time, however, it was much more controlled, almost a replica of Friday night.

While we were making love, I was starting to worry how much I liked her and wondered what would happen if I did move here.

I wondered if Julie was feeling the same or if she was just enjoying it because she hadn't been with anybody for so long.

I reckoned, that when I left, she would probably forget all about it and put it down to experience. So I put all my thoughts about it to the back of my mind and decided to concentrate on the matter in hand.

We were lying on our sides, me between Julie's legs, slowly moving in and out of her. Our mouth's locked together, exploring each other with our tongues, and me gently massaging her left breast with my hand.

I rolled her onto her back and moved my mouth down her body, kissing both her breasts, her stomach, and then kissed her pubes before exploring her pussy.

I started by teasing her clit with my tongue, before licking her all over. She let out a few pleasurable groans and grabbed my hair a couple of times with her hand, pushing me deeper inside her.

She tasted and smelled lovely and felt I could have continued all day, but after Julie came yet again, she pulled me back up and demanded that I fuck her.

I entered her and she wrapped her legs around me. As she started bucking underneath me, she then started licking her come off my face and mouth, then told me she loved the taste of herself and I started to think that every woman was the same.

As she started bucking a bit more wildly, I grabbed her pillows and stuffed them under her back, allowing me a bit more purchase.

I lifted her legs up until they were spread wide above my shoulders and I went hard at it. Within minutes, I shot my load then rolled off her and lay beside her.

We were back to lying beside each other, both sweating and both breathing heavily. I gave her a kiss on the forehead then cuddled her in.

"Fuck me, Julie, you certainly know how to knacker a man," I suggested. "Well, Shug, you certainly know how to fuck a woman," she told me back.

I thought, 'Fuck, Shug, you've come a long way since that first night at the farm!'. It was nice to know that you could do it okay - that was always something I worried about after a shag.

"Hey, Julie, you say the nicest things," I told her. "Oh, and by the way, you're not so shabby yourself. I think I really need to go home, though, you've shagged me into the quick, I'm not sure if my dick will ever be the same again."

We then both started laughing and Julie playfully slapped me a couple of times. I looked at my now limp bright red dick, smiled to myself, then glanced at the clock. It was almost five. And with no chance of me being able to provide a repeat performance for a while, I decided to get up and have a smoke.

I poured us both a drink of juice, sat on the chair and lit my fag. Julie sat up and wrapped the cover around herself. She took a sip of her juice then asked me, "Shug, what do you think this is?"

Fuck, I nearly choked on mine as I absorbed her words, I still wasn't actually sure she'd just said them.

Oh, fuck, I knew exactly what she meant, and how this conversation was going to go.

"What do you mean, Julie?" I tried to sound as surprised as I could.

"This, Shug! Us! What we're doing? What is it?" she asked, with her eyes firmly fixed on mine.

"I never gave it much of a thought," I lied to her. "I'm not even sure how it happened. Are you?" I said, trying to put it back into her court.

"Well, I'm pretty sure we have feelings for each other," she began. "The way we made love made me feel that, and I know you couldn't have been the way you were with me if you didn't feel the same."

For some reason, at that point, I started to get a sickly feeling in my stomach as I knew exactly where she was coming from.

I started to think back to some of the good times I'd had with Lorraine and the feelings we shared. I knew that the feelings I had for Julie now were similar to how I felt then.

'Holy shit' I thought, 'If I was actually in love with Lorraine then … Oh, fuck, Shug! Don't say you're falling for Julie? Fuck, how did that happen?', I could feel myself breaking out in a cold sweat as I started to think of the ramifications if I exposed my feelings to her.

"Shug? Shug?" Julie said, as she kicked at my knee. "Shug, are you okay? You're miles away, eh… Hello? Are you with us?"

I could hear Julie talking to me, but it sounded like an echo in the background, I was so absorbed in my internal debate.

She gave me another kick, this time a bit harder, and raised her voice as she spoke. "Shug, are you okay? You seem to be in a bit of a trance there!"

At that point, I managed to snap out of it. "I'm fine, Julie, I was just thinking about what you said," was all I could muster.

"I'm not sure, Julie. I'm having a really nice time and I'm enjoying the closeness we're sharing. The sex was fuckin awesome, but I am really concerned about Rooster," I told her, trying to put my feelings to the back of my mind.

"Shug, I wasn't asking about anything else other than how you felt about us. Rooster is out of the equation, it's no longer anything to do with him what I do."

"Maybe that's how it is for you, Julie, but he's my best mate and a brother, I wouldn't want anything to wreck that."

Fuck, as I listened to myself I thought what a hypocritical cunt I was. I'd just spent the last two days fucking his ex, who I'm sure he still has feelings for and would happily get back within a heartbeat.

What a wanker I was, some fuckin mate I turned out to be! I felt like a right bastard now. How the fuck did I manage once again to get things so fucked up?

I decided I needed to play down my feelings for her and try and get myself out of this fuckin mess.

"Julie, there's no doubt I have feelings for you, you know that. I've always liked you, right from the very first time we met in the hospital. And if the circumstances were different, I would love to get into a relationship with you, but right now that's impossible. Maybe if I do get a job here, and you and Rooster resolve your issues, then perhaps at that point, we could give it a go. What we've done this weekend doesn't put either of us in a good light, and as much as I have really enjoyed myself, I'm starting to think about how the fuck I'm going to face him when I get back."

Julie's reply kind of stunned me a bit. "Shug, I don't give a fuck about Rooster. Fuck, he made me have an abortion, for fuck's sake. I had to move away, change jobs and start again. And what did he do? Oh, yes, …. he sent me a fuckin letter. Well no, he didn't actually send me a letter, he wouldn't even pay for the fuckin stamp, he gave the fuckin thing to you to give to me. And you think I should be concerned about his fuckin feelings?"

Julie, at that point, had tears streaming down her cheeks and was sobbing uncontrollably. I moved onto the bed and went to put my arm around her to comfort her, but she pushed it away.

"Shouldn't you be heading back to your precious Rooster?" she asked. "Maybe you should save your sympathy for him."

She then turned away from me and lay down on the bed, still wrapped in the cover. By this time, she was crying really loudly, making lots of throaty sounds and shaking like she was freezing.

I lay down beside her and grabbed hold of her. At first, she tried to push me away, but I held on to her tightly, until she cuddled into me.

The minute she was in my arms, she became even worse, her crying got louder, the shaking more violent, and her tears became a continuous stream of water.

I just held on to her, wondering why she was taking this so badly, until the penny dropped ... the abortion! I wondered if she hadn't been able to cry at the time and this was her first opportunity.

'Holy shit, how the fuck do I deal with this if it is that?' I began to feel pretty scared, having never experienced anything like this before. I was shitting myself, I knew that I'd need to say something to her soon.

I decided just to cuddle her and wait until she said something. I patted her back and gave it a bit of a rub. My chest was soaking from her tears and she looked like she had the worst cold ever.

Suddenly, she jumped up and went to the sink. She turned the tap on, slunged her face with the water, and took a drink from the tap. She then picked up a towel, dried her face then turned around and looked at me.

"Shug, I'm sorry for that, I should've controlled myself much better," she told me. I got out of bed and went over to her. I cuddled her and told her it was okay, and that I was glad she did it.

"Julie, it's good to get it out," I told her. "I was the same when Malky died. I bottled it all up then one day, it all came to a head. Afterwards, I felt much better and was able to see things much more clearly. Hopefully, you'll be the same."

"Thanks, Shug," was all she said. We stood cuddling for a few minutes and it was only when I caught a glimpse of us in the mirror that I realised we were both still in the scud.

I looked at us a bit more, my arms were wrapped around her, and she was snuggling into my chest. It looked very much like a romantic hug, one a couple in love would share.

I started laughing. When Julie asked me what I was laughing at, I told her I'd seen us in the mirror and realised we were still in the buff. She turned her head to have a look and burst out laughing as well.

She seemed to be back to normal so I ushered her onto the bed and we both lay down. I knew at some point we were going to need to discuss what just happened, but I was hoping Julie would save it for another day.

"What do you fancy doing for food?" I asked, changing the subject. "Do you want to go out or will I grab something from the canteen?"

"Shug, don't you see the state of me? I couldn't go anywhere after all that crying; people would think I had two black eyes."

"Sorry, I never thought, I'll just go and get us something in then. Anything you fancy?" I asked her. "Just get me whatever you want, I'm not fussy," she told me.

I tried to lighten the mood by cracking a joke. "I know you're not, you've just spent your weekend off with me," I said, laughing, but it hardly raised a smile. "Hey, Julie, you'll come through this much stronger," I told her, as I got up.

"Thanks, Shug, I know you mean well." I kissed her on the forehead then got up. I stuck on my t-shirt, jeans and my boots, and headed for the canteen.

Walking along the corridor, I was thinking of Julie and wondering why Rooster had been such a cunt to her. What was in the letter? I wasn't sure if Julie would open it or not, and if she did, how would she react if Rooster wanted her back?

I was jolted out of my thoughts by someone grabbing my bum. It was Lisa. "Hi, Shug, how's things?" she asked. "Yeh, great," was all I could muster. The last thing I wanted right now was to be jolly with someone I didn't really know.

"Where's Julie? Hope you haven't tied her to the bed," she said, laughing. "Actually, I have, and she's loving every minute of it," I told her.

"Ha, ha, you're some man, Shug, I wouldn't put it past you," she said, laughing again. I just joined in with a bit of a forced laugh.

"You going to the party in the common room tonight? It's one of the girls twenty-first birthday, it should be a bit of a laugh."

I told her I would see if Julie was up for it, and if so, we would see her there. "Okay, great, hopefully, see you then," she said, as she headed off down the other corridor.

'Thank fuck she's away!' I thought to myself. I couldn't be arsed with any of her shitty chit-chat. I walked down the corridor and into the canteen without needing to speak to anyone else and surveyed what was on offer.

I grabbed some sandwiches, crisps, chocolate, and a couple of cans of Irn Bru, paid the lady then headed straight back to Julie's room. I had visions of bumping into Anna and her man again, but thankfully, I never saw anyone.

When I got into the room, I noticed Julie had moved from the bed and onto the chair. She had the cover wrapped around her so I couldn't tell if she'd got dressed or not. I kissed her on the top of the head and sat down under the window, facing her.

"I just got sandwiches and shit," I told her, dumping it all on her knee. "Take your pick, I'll eat whatever you don't want."

"Thanks, Shug, but I'm not really hungry," she replied. "I'll just have a drink of juice and get something to eat later." "Okay, if you're sure, but I'm going to have something, I'm starving," I told her.

I opened a sandwich and a packet of crisps, and as I ate, I watched Julie just sit there, staring out the window. She looked like she was in a trance: she wasn't blinking and never even noticed me looking at her.

"Penny for them?" I said, to her trying to get her attention, but she never moved her gaze. I tapped her on the foot, "Julie, are you with us?"

"Sorry, Shug, what is it?" "You're miles away, Julie, what's up?" I asked her.

"Oh, I'm just thinking about this … us … you … what we've done. You know, the stuff we spoke about earlier. I really loved Rooster you know, I thought he was 'the one', despite all his faults, and, by the way, he had a few. I loved him to bits. I couldn't believe how he reacted when I told him. It's those fuckin Bats, that's what fucked it all up, and now I'm here with another one, what in fuck's name am I thinking about?" I tried to interrupt her at that point, but she just talked over me.

"I promised myself that I was finished with men and then you came to see me. I was drunk, glad to see you, horny and starved of affection for so long … and bang! I'm not blaming you, Shug, it was my doing, I know you didn't want to at first, but I did. And, hey, here we are. Don't worry, I won't be telling anyone about this, so your precious 'brothers stuff' won't be affected."

Again, I tried to interrupt, but again, she raised her voice and kept talking.

"It's probably for the best if you leave tonight, we'll only have a repeat performance and tomorrow we'll feel shitty again. There's an application form in the drawer, if you fill it in when you're finished eating and leave it on the desk, I'll hand it into the Senior Nursing Officer in the morning."

She dumped all the food stuff on the floor, lifted the cover and got into bed. She positioned herself facing the wall, making sure I knew she didn't want to talk, but I was having none of it.

I stood up and went and sat on the side of her bed. I put my hand on her shoulder and turned her around. I went to speak to her, but she spoke first. Her eyes were closed, but I could see the tears on her cheeks.

"Shug, please don't say anything, I really can't talk anymore. I'm tired and I would really appreciate it if you would leave me be. I'm sorry for being like this, but I just need to be alone right now."

Fuck, another situation unfamiliar to me. I just stared at her, not having a clue what to do. Should I fuck off or go find one of her pals? Or should I try and get her to talk to me? Holy fuck, I was well out my depth here.

I took a minute or two to compose myself then decided I would have a smoke, give her a minute. Then, if she still felt the same, I'd fuck off or hey, maybe I'd take Lisa up on her offer and go to the party.

I sat on the chair, turned it towards the window and lit up. The darkness was descending on the sky and the sun was really low.

I always liked when I could see both the sun and the moon in the sky at the same time. I remember someone telling me, when I was really young, that if you saw them in the sky together, something good was going to happen to you.

Looking at them now, I laughed to myself thinking, 'Fat fuckin chance of that!' I stood up, threw my cigarette out of the window and took in a last view of the hills before lifting the application form out of the drawer.

I stood with it in my hand for what seemed like an age. I then decided moving here, when Julie was still here, would be a bad idea so placed it back in the drawer and closed it.

I grabbed what stuff was lying around and stuffed it into my bag, put on my jacket, then leaned over and kissed Julie on the head, but I guess she was sleeping as she never moved.

I picked up my bag, put a tenner on her desk for her hospitality and left, closing the door quietly. I walked along the corridor and down the stairs where I was met with the Warden, standing at the door to her office.

I got to the bottom of the stairs, just ready to go out the door. "Excuse me, who are you?" she asked. "Who the fuck are you?" was my reply. "Don't you swear at me, young man, or I'll report you to the Matron."

"You can report me to whoever the fuck you like, Mrs, I really couldn't give a fuck, I'll never be back here again so why don't you go and take a flying fuck to yourself," I told her as I left.

I went out, thinking to myself, 'What a nosey cow she was!' I tied my bag to my bike and fired it up. I left it to tick over a bit, put my helmet on and had a look around. I thought to myself, 'What a pity, I could've had a great time here, but hey, Que sera sera …'

I got on my bike and drew away. As I checked my mirror, I thought I could see Julie running behind me. I turned my head around, just to make sure I wasn't seeing things, and Fuck, it was her!

I wondered what the fuck was she doing, so turned my bike around and headed back towards her, thinking I must've forgotten something.

As I approached her, I noticed she had a housecoat and slippers on and watching her run, I could quite clearly see she had fuck all else on underneath.

As I drew up alongside her, she put her arms around me, placed one of her hands on my helmet and started snogging the face off me. I pushed her back a bit.

"Julie, what the fuck are you doing? What the fuck's this?" I asked her.

"Shug, please don't go, please come back, I need you to stay tonight. Come back to my room and I'll explain. Please, Shug, say you will!"

"Okay, Julie, no probs, just let me park my bike first, okay?" I told her, completely confused by her actions. I slowly made my way past her, turning back into the car park, now totally bamboozled. I had no idea what the fuck was going on.

I parked up my bike and undid my bag. By this time, Julie was standing at the door and I went and joined her. We walked in and I was greeted by the Warden. Fuck, I'd forgotten about her. She stood in front of me and asked me where I thought I was going.

"Look, I'm going back up to the room, I forgot to take some stuff with me so I'm going to get it, then I'll be on my way," I told her.

"You'll be going no further than this until I get an apology," she demanded. "Listen, bitch, if you want an apology then you'll need to say sorry to me first for your fuckin cheek."

"I beg your pardon? I have nothing to say sorry for. It was you that was rude and abusive to me. And now I want you to leave. If you don't, I'll call the police."

"Do what the fuck you want. I've told you already, I don't give a flying fuck. I'll only be five minutes, so by the time they come, I'll be gone. And if not, it's your word against mine, so why don't you go fuck yourself!" I told her, then brushed past her and headed up the stairs.

"Five minutes, and no more!" she shouted after me. "Then I call the police!" She then had a go at Julie, who apologised on my behalf before running up the stairs at the back of me.

When she caught up with me, she asked what that was all about and I told her it was nothing, that she was just being a 'jobs worth' cow.

We got to the room and went inside. I dropped my stuff back on the floor and asked Julie what the fuck was going on.

She undid her dressing gown and let it fall to the floor, stepped towards me and removed my jacket. I asked her again what the fuck was going on, but she just kissed me and pushed me onto the bed.

She started undoing my belt, unzipping my jeans and pulling them down along with my scants.

"Julie, you need to speak to me," I told her. "What the fuck's going on? One minute, you're telling me to fuck off, the next thing, you're undressing me. Come on, spit it out!" I almost demanded her to tell me.

"Not now, Shug, I'll tell you everything later. Right now, I need you to fuck my brains out."

She undid my laces and threw my boots on the floor, then yanked my jeans and scants off, discarding them as well.

Julie then came back onto the bed, cupped my balls in her hands then lowered her mouth onto my dick. She began softly sucking me and I could feel myself growing in her mouth.

Here I was, lying in her bed again, with only a t-shirt on, getting my dick sucked. Fuck, five minutes ago I was on my bike heading home! 'Jeezo, how the fuck do these things happen to me?' I wondered.

I started rubbing Julie's head and playing with her hair and she began to suck me a bit harder. Her mouth was now moving up and down a bit faster and she also started rubbing me with her hand.

I told her if she didn't stop that I would come and there would be no fucking, but she didn't seem to hear me.

I raised my voice a bit "Julie, you'll need to stop unless you want me to shoot my load in your mouth!"

She lifted her head up and said: "Don't you fuckin dare come, Shug," in a very aggressive tone. She then moved her head up beside mine and gave me a kiss.

"Shug, I need you to fuck me hard, and I need you to do it now," she told me, again, in a very aggressive tone.

"Julie, what the fuck's going on with you?" I asked her again. "Fuck all, Shug, I'm great, come on, let's do it," she demanded.

I thought 'Well, fuck it, she's not going to tell me so I should do my best to accommodate her request'. I turned her over and went to get on top of her, but she stopped me.

"No, Shug, I want you to fuck me from behind," she told me and turned herself around and went on all fours. I moved behind her and slipped my dick into her now wet pussy then grabbed hold of her hips and started banging away.

"Harder, Shug, fuckin harder! Come on, slap my arse!" she screamed, so I obliged and satisfied both her requests.

We were banging away for all we were worth and Julie was panting and moaning as if she was ready to climax, then the next thing we heard was the door being banged.

Someone was shouting on Julie and demanding she open the door. "Julie, someone's at the door," I told her. "I know, Shug, I'm not fucking deaf. Whoever it is can go fuck themselves, and don't you dare fuckin stop," she screamed at me.

Fuck, Julie was wild, I couldn't believe what I was hearing - never in a million years would I have thought she could be like this. The door was still being banged, and now much more loudly than before. Whoever it was, was not taking no for an answer. He kept shouting Julie's name, but she completely ignored him.

The next thing, she let out an almighty scream and started furiously banging her arse into me. I was hoping that she was coming and my prayers were answered.

She collapsed in a crumpled heap in front of me and I pulled out my aching cock. I don't think I'll ever dislike a ride as much as the one I'd just had, I just couldn't get into it, she was acting way too weird for me and she seemed like a completely different person.

I told her she needed to answer the door, but she told me to answer it. I got up, put on my scants, and opened the door.

Fuck, it was him, Anna's husband, and the poxy fuckin Warden.

"What?" was all I said, as I looked them both up and down. I could see the Warden staring at my pants and when I looked down, I realised why.

I still had a hard-on and my pubes were sticking out all over the place. Fuck, in my rush to answer the door, and in the dark, I'd put Julie's pants on. Fuck, how embarrassing was that!

Anna's husband then told me he wanted to speak to Julie, to make sure she was okay.

I asked him why and followed it up by wanting him to tell me if he thought I'd hurt her or something?

"I heard her screaming and I just want to know if she's alright." "Of course she's alright, we were fucking, that's why she was screaming," I told him.

At that point, Julie came to the door and ushered me back into the room, telling me she would deal with it, and that I'd said more than enough.

Julie went outside into the hall with them and closed the door. I pondered whether or not to go out, but decided to let them sort out whatever it was themselves.

I guessed it was the fuckin Warden moaning about me and running away to the boss to get me thrown out.

I started putting my clothes on, thinking I should leave, to avoid getting Julie into any more trouble, so got dressed. Then, as they were still outside, I opened the door and interrupted the discussion.

I focused on the boss. "Look, I'm sorry for being rude to the Warden and I don't want to cause any more trouble for Julie, she has nothing to do with this and the person you should be speaking to is me. I'm getting ready to leave now and you won't see me again, so please, can you just go and forget all about this?" Julie then asked me to go back inside, but I stood where I was.

Senior Nursing Officer Mckay repeated the request and told me Julie was not in any kind of trouble, he just needed to speak to her. I looked at Julie and she nodded to me before pushing the door open.

I went back into the room and closed it. I then sat myself down on the chair and lit up a fag. 'Fuck, I've done it again! Jeezo, Shug, when the fuck are you ever going to learn?' I pondered. I stared out the window, wondering what the fuck was going on outside.

I heard the door open and turned around to see Julie standing with her back leaning against it. "Julie, what the fuck was that all about?" I asked.

"What else, Shug? It was all about you," she told me. "I've just been given a final warning. If I step out of line again, or invite any more unsavoury guests, I'll be put out of the nurses home and lose my place on the course."

"Fuck, Julie, I'm sorry, I'll go and speak to him and try to get him to change his mind." "No you won't, Shug, you'll do nothing of the sort, you've already done enough," she told me, as she made her way back to bed.

"Julie, remember Anna? Well, I could speak to her and get her to make him withdraw it." "Shug, for fuck's sake, just stop. You're not going to do anything. He said you can stay 'til morning, then you need to go, so best you stop thinking about anything and leave it be."

I looked at her sitting on the bed, with her knees up to her chin and her arms around her legs. She was just staring into space and looked like a lost soul.

I removed my jacket and sat down beside her, putting my arm around her. I kissed her on the top of her head and she rested her head on my chest.

"Julie, I'm really sorry, I never meant to get you into any trouble. I thought I was leaving and that cheeky fucker of a warden was giving me a hard time so I told her where to go."

Julie never said a word, she just lay down on the bed and assumed the foetal position. I rubbed her head then removed my boots.

I snuggled in with her, almost mimicking her position. I put my arm around her and gave her a squeeze. She patted my arm then held on to it.

I was thinking about Julie and started to wonder if she was depressed or something. I thought back to her tantrums and her need for both love and crazy mad sex.

That was nothing like the Julie I'd first met, who was full of life, calm assured and very switched on.

I began to wonder if she'd changed because of the abortion or if she was actually always like this. Although I'd met her loads of times, I didn't really know her.

I decided to try and get to the bottom of what was going on and asked her if she wanted to talk. Her reply kind of shocked me a bit.

"What do you want me to tell you, Shug? That I'm a wreck ... that I'm not coping ... that I really miss Rooster ... that I'm struggling with my course ... that I'm lonely ... that I cry myself to sleep every night ... that I'm drinking way too much ... that I can't face my parents and that I really, really wish I could turn the clock back ... Is that really what you want me to tell you?" she blurted out, while sobbing all the way through her rant.

I never said a word for a few minutes, until her sobbing stopped. I turned her around and cuddled her into me, and just held her. I had no idea what else to do.

It seemed that most of my weekend had been like that, finding myself in strange emotional situations that were foreign to me.

"Shug, I'm sorry for being a drama queen. When I heard your bike starting up, I just realised how lonely I really was and didn't want you to go. I didn't want to be on my own. And, after spending all this time with you, I knew if you left with us not talking that you wouldn't come back. I'm really sorry for being such a bitch."

"Julie, listen, we all feel fucked up at times, I know that more than most. Remember the state I got myself in after Malky? But there is always something or someone that gets you out of it, but it takes time. At least you've got your studies, you're lucky that you're here and no one knows your past. Fuck, my situation was the talk of the village and every cunt I met had advice for me. I wished then that I could've fucked off until it was forgotten about and that something else happened that people would then run with, but hey, I got through it, and whatever this is with you, you'll get through it too," I told her.

"What snapped you out of it, Shug?" she asked.

"A letter from Malky's mum and a big fuckin biker called Rooster. I attacked him and he gave me one 'fuck off' tanking," I told her and she burst out laughing. I joined in, trying to tell her that it wasn't funny at the time, but she was gone.

We continued laughing for a bit then she sat up and looked at me. "Thanks, Shug, I'm feeling much better. You're right, I need to get a fuckin grip, get my act together, and stop wallowing in the past," she told me, as she got up and headed to the fridge.

I thought to myself, 'I've never said any of that stuff, but hey ho, if she's feeling better for it, then fine'. I laughed a bit and wondered then if maybe I should fill in the application form - I seemed to have the gift of the gab for cheering people up!

Chapter 12

I started to recall the events from earlier and offered myself a wry smile, then quickly dismissed my idea, thinking that it would never get off the ground. I sniggered then looked at Julie, who was pouring us both a drink.

She'd wiped away her tears and had given her face a bit of a splash with some water and she looked much brighter for it. She handed me the glass and sat on the chair, lifting her knees to her chest again, after turning it to face me.

I spotted, when her dressing gown dropped down from her knees to her side, that she still hadn't put her knickers back on and was getting a lovely view of her snatch.

I looked at her, smiling, and asked her where we went from here. "I'm going to give myself a good kick up the backside and get myself back on track. How about you?" she asked.

That, for me, was the million-dollar question. Right up until tonight, I thought I had it all planned out, but now, I had no fuckin idea.

I told Julie all about where I thought I was going and how I'd managed to fuck it up yet again, and that I would just suck it and see for a while before coming up with a plan 'B', whatever the fuck that was!

I lifted my glass up and said: "To the new Julie, onwards and upwards!" I then had a drink of the juice and told Julie I could murder a beer.

"Fancy going for a beer?" I then asked her. She looked at the clock and reminded me that it was getting late and that the garage would be closed in five minutes.

"No, I meant going out to the pub," I told her. "I would need to get dressed and put on some make-up to cover my panda eyes, I don't want to frighten the natives," she said, laughing. I pointed to her snatch and suggested she should get a move on, starting with knickers, then laughed.

"Shug, you're unreal. Were you sitting there looking at me all that time?" I just nodded and smiled. She got up and slapped me on the head.

"You're a fuckin nightmare, Shug, I'm pouring my heart out to you and you're sitting staring at my fanny!" "Julie, it would've been rude not to," I said, still smiling.

She then started getting dressed and I watched her until she'd covered up the best bits. I then told her I would go and ring for a taxi.

I went back down to the front hall, called the taxi and was told he would be here in ten minutes. I heard music coming from the common room and guessed Lisa's party was now in full swing.

I told Julie when I got back to the room that the taxi would be here in five minutes. She said she would be ready as soon as she put on her lippy.

I looked at her and noticed she'd put on a pair of tight jeans that showed off the shape of her arse perfectly. She had a pair of short high-heeled ankle boots and a tight white blouse on. Her hair flowed down past her shoulders and she looked great.

She turned around to me and said: "Well, will I do?" "Fuck, won't you just," I told her. "Julie, you look good enough to eat."

"Ha, you say the nicest things, but there'll be none of that shit tonight! We need to get back on track, remember? Come on, let's go," she said, walking towards the door.

'Fuck, Shug, you and your big mouth' I thought, 'If you'd just shut the fuck up, you may have been on to a promise later, but, as usual, you've fucked it up'.

Ah, well, if ever there was a reason to get blootered then this was it.

We got outside as the taxi was coming towards us and within minutes, we were at the pub.

It was very busy and there didn't appear to be any seats available. I squeezed my way to the bar, hoping to see my 'best friend' the barman, but he didn't appear to be on. Eventually, I got my drinks and went back to where Julie was standing. I handed her her drink and asked if she'd spotted any seats.

"No, but I have spotted Mr Mckay and his wife with another couple, sitting over in the corner. Shug, you have to promise me you won't say anything to them."

"Julie, relax, I won't say a word. In fact, I won't even look at them, how's that?"

"Great, Shug, I'm glad. Come on, let's go through the back, out of their way." 'Through the back. Fuck, I never even knew there was a *through the back* – I'd been under the impression that it was just one big room'.

We went through and I noticed that it was surprisingly big. There was a pool table, a dartboard, and a jukebox that was blaring out some sounds. There were a few seats to choose from and Julie made a beeline for two in the corner, next to the window.

We sat down and Julie finished her drink so I went to get her another, but she told me to sit where I was and that she would get it.

There was also a bar in this lounge and because it was less busy, Julie was served fairly quickly.

I watched her at the bar as she ordered and noticed how much male attention she was getting and thought that it would boost her confidence. She smiled and talked a bit with a couple of guys while she waited, but didn't look to be taking any of them on.

When she turned around, I saw she had a tray of drinks: two bottles for me and a couple of halfs for herself. "Somebody's thirsty!" I suggested to her.

"The pub will be closed in less than an hour and as this is my last night before I put my sensible head on, I plan to do my best to get pissed, so drink up."

"No problem, you won't get any arguments from me," I told her and proceeded to do my best to keep up with her. I said to her that I'd noticed her getting chatted up at the bar and asked her if she fancied any of them.

"Give me a fuckin break, Shug, have you seen them in here? They're either gay or fucking ugly," she moaned at me. "Anyway, I told you, I'm done with all that for a while. Now get the drinks in!"

Julie downed what was left of her second drink with a bit of a purpose. I poured some Newcastle into my glass and slid it over to her "Here, that'll keep you going until I get back."

I went to the bar and ordered another two bottles and got Julie a couple of doubles. I was waiting on the barman fixing them up, looking through the hatch into the other lounge, when I saw Mr Mckay heading to the toilet.

I paid for the drinks, noticed Julie had emptied the glass I gave her, so put the drinks on the table and told her I was going for a pish.

He was washing his hands when I went in. I looked around and noticed there was no one else about. "Mr Mckay, nice to see you again," I said politely. He looked startled.

"Listen, sonny, I don't want any trouble from you, I was just doing my job," he replied, very nervously. "Mr Mckay, you've got the wrong end of the stick. I just want to apologise again for my behaviour, I was upset and perhaps said a few things I shouldn't have. Please let me buy you and your wife a drink by way of trying to make it up to you."

"You're fine, son, we're just leaving, but thanks for the offer," he said, as he headed to the door. "Okay, no problem. Thanks for listening," I remarked. He nodded in my direction then hurriedly left.

I stood in the toilet, looking in the mirror, my hands on the sink, thinking that he was a right fud. 'I should've just punched his fuckin lights out. *Fuckin Sonny* that's what he called me, *Fuckin Sonny*, fuckin wanker, aaagghh. I've just fuckin apologised to him for Julie's sake and he called me *Fuckin Sonny* ... bastard' I thought.

Just then, two guys came into the toilet and one of them gave me a right look.

"Who the fuck are you staring at, ya fuckin prick?" I said as I turned around, squaring up to him. I was right in his face, begging him to say something.

"Whoa, mate, settle down," he said, "I wasn't staring at you, I was just looking at your jacket. I'm sorry if I upset you, I didn't intend to." He then took a step back, holding up his hands.

I thought about apologising, as my rage was nothing to do with him, but I thought better of it and told him he was lucky I was in a good mood.

When I turned to go, I looked at him again, giving him a proper stare. I saw the relief in his eyes as I backed off. I knew he hadn't intended to offend me, but I was so wound up that I didn't give a fuck about him.

I left the loo and headed up the corridor towards the lounge, the exit door was on the right-hand side at the end of it. Just as it opened up into the lounge, Mr Mckay, Anna, and the other couple they were with, were just about to go out when I entered.

I looked at them, nodded, and said: "Mr Mckay, Anna, folks, enjoy the rest of your evening." I then opened the door for them and smiled.

Mckay looked at me then at Anna, who by this time was scarlet, then back at me. His brow was wrinkled and he had a very confused look on his face. As Anna passed, she stared at me open-eyed, as if to say: 'Thanks a fucking lot!'

I knew if I left it like that she would get the third degree when she went home so I said, in a loud enough voice for her man to hear, "I bet you're wondering how I know your name, Anna?" "Yes, I am actually," she replied, with a real worried look on her face.

By this time, her husband had come back to join her and the four of them were staring at me, waiting for my answer.

"I saw you yesterday morning in the canteen and asked my friend who you were because I thought you were pretty, but she didn't know you. However, one of the others at the table told me who you were then followed it up by telling me you were married."

I could see the relief immediately oozing from her. She smiled, said thanks for the compliment, and they all left. I laughed to myself, thinking how well that had gone, feeling content with the game I'd just played.

I was sure, that if I did want a job here, I would have a better chance now than I had earlier in the evening.

I headed back into the other lounge where Julie was sitting. She was now chatting with the bloke who she'd spoken to at the bar earlier.

He had his back to me as I walked over. Julie was facing me and she put her hand under the table, giving me the wanker sign. I tapped him on the shoulder and he looked up at me.

"What?" he said. "You're in my fuckin seat, prick," I told him. "So be a clever little cunt and get the fuck up and piss off." He got up from the chair and squared up to me. "Listen, you, I'm talking to the lady so …"

I'd had enough at that point and stuck the head in his nose, before hooking him right on the jaw and watching as he collapsed on the floor.

As he landed, I booted him in the ribs with my steelies, which seemed to do for him. I leaned down beside him and told him to remember his manners in future. I then stood up and kicked him again, just for good measure.

Some of the guys stood up from their barstools, watching what was going on. A couple of girls were squealing, but no one came near me.

I sat back down to have a drink, but Julie suggested a sharp exit. So I picked up the two bottles I had on the table, one in each hand, held by the stalks, just in case anyone had an idea for revenge.

Surprisingly, none of the bar staff said a word, and as we walked out, there was an eerie silence, but nobody moved anywhere near us. When we got outside, Julie started moaning at me, telling me I was a fuckin nutter and that I shouldn't have done it, but all I heard was blah, blah, fuckin blah.

I drank my beer, not listening to a word she said. By the time we reached the garage, she realised she was talking to herself.

"Shug, you never listened to a fuckin word I said. Did you?" "Nope, not a fuckin thing," I told her and started laughing.

She got pretty mad, slapping me about the body. "Aaagghh, you're so like fuckin Rooster, it's scary!" she screamed. "I'll take that as a compliment," I told her.

"Well, it wasn't fuckin meant to be!" she screamed again. "Cheers, Julie, I love you too," I said, raising my bottle towards her.

I finished my bottle and threw it in the field as we headed up the back road towards the hospital. I put my arm around her and gave her my other bottle. She took a drink and relaxed a bit.

She handed me the bottle back and said: "Shug, what the fuck am I doing? First, Rooster, and now you."

"I have no idea, Julie, but I reckon, deep down, all the girls love a bad boy, don't you think?" I said, laughing.

"I know about that saying, everybody thinks that, but I've gone way further than a fling with a bad boy. I've had a relationship with a proper madman and now I'm out with another one - after promising myself never again. Do you think there's something wrong with me?"

"Julie, Rooster and I aren't madmen and there's nothing wrong with you, maybe you just think too much and fuck, I know all about that. Come on, let's see if the party's still on and forget all this heavy shit," I suggested.

"Okay, Shug, I'll go, but you better promise me you'll be on your best behaviour."

"Scouts honour, Julie," I told her, holding my three fingers up. "You better not let me down, Shug. Remember, I'm on my last fuckin warning because of you."

"Don't worry, Julie, I've told you, I won't fuck it up for you."

We arrived at the nurses home and could see the party was still on: the curtains were closed, but the disco lights were still shining through them.

When we went in, Lisa clocked us and came straight over. She looked pretty pished and gave Julie one of those cuddles that always make a man horny.

As they cuddled, their tits were pressing hard against each other and they were squeezing each other tightly, kissing each other on both cheeks.

Lisa then kissed Julie on the mouth and Julie was quite happy to respond by kissing her back. It only lasted a few seconds, but I was sure I saw tongues.

She then turned her attention to me and did the same. We had a quick snog and she pressed herself against me then whispered that she was having a party in her room afterwards

173

and, if I kept my nose clean, I would get an invite. I just smiled at her and told her I would see how things went.

During the party, Julie and I mainly kept ourselves to ourselves. But because of my encounter with the warden and Mckay, people kept coming up to me and telling me how cool I was and saying that they wished that they'd been there to see it.

All I could think was, 'Fuck, if you think that was something cool then you cunts need to get a fuckin life!', but I smiled politely, remembering what Julie had said and looked like I was interested in what they had to say.

Every time someone came over to me, Julie would give me the lowdown on them as they left.

I couldn't believe how many of them were in relationships, but shagging someone else seemed like it was the norm here.

They were told that the party had to finish at one o'clock. And to make sure it did, a senior manager was there bang on 1a.m., and he made sure everyone headed to their rooms and the place wasn't damaged.

Fuck, it was like being back at school: all these fuckin adults cow-towing to some fuckin jobsworth and scurrying away like fuckin sheep - I couldn't believe it.

As we were leaving, I started moaning to Julie about it, but was interrupted by Lisa who came over to us and reminded me about going to her room.

I was well up for it, but I wasn't sure about Julie as she was pretty pished. I guessed she would want to go back to her own place.

"You fancy going to Lisa's, Julie? They're going to continue the party there," I asked her.

"I don't know, Shug. I think I should just go to bed, I feel kind of drunk." "Come on, Julie, let's just go for an hour or so, maybe I'll even see you two snog again."

"Even if I do go, Shug, there's no chance of that happening, it's just what Lisa does when she's a bit drunk. Everyone thinks she swings both ways because of it, but let me tell you right now, I, as sure as fuck, don't."

"Come on, Julie, are you telling me you've never thought of it?" I asked.

"I never said that, Shug, and I never said I hadn't tried it. What I said was that I don't do it now."

Fuck, I could feel myself getting a hard-on just thinking that Julie might have fucked another woman. But when I looked at her, I realised she was taking the piss.

"You can be a right shite sometimes, Julie," I told her.

"Ha ha, I know that, Shug, but I didn't half get you going there," she said, laughing at me. "Come on then, stuff it, let's go for an hour or so and see if I can pull a chick, ha ha."

"You're so full of shit tonight, Julie, but I'll tell you what, if I can get someone at the party who wants to fuck you then you're well in trouble."

"You think so, Shug? I think it may be you who'll be in trouble. Just think, if I take you up on that offer then you'll be sleeping under your bike tonight."

She looked at me, smiled, kissed me on the cheek, then headed up the corridor.

Fuck, my mind was racing about the amount of drink she'd had, and the way she was acting - it made me think there may be a chance of her actually doing it and there's no way she would chuck me out if she did!

I reckoned if she didn't let me join in that she'd at least let me watch. I thought if I could get another few drinks down her neck, and Lisa to chum her up a bit, you never know, I might be on to a winner.

I smiled to myself, thinking what a great plan I had and decided to work it for all I was worth.

I caught up with Julie just as she'd knocked on Lisa's door.

"Julie, if you did get a click tonight, would you really chuck me out?" I asked. "That really depends on who I'm fucking, Shug," she said, devilishly.

Lisa opened the door and invited us in, again pulling Julie close and planting a smacker on her lips.

This time, though, Julie put her hand on her tit and gave it a bit of a rub and a squeeze.

All the time she was doing this, she was looking at me. I swear to God I was getting one of the biggest erections I'd ever had.

The next thing, Lisa put her hand on Julie's arse and started massaging it. Fuck, at that point, I nearly shot my load.

They parted, looking and smiling at each other, and Lisa came towards me. I asked her if she could just do the same to me and she said: "Of course, and a bit more if you like." "Sounds good to me," I told her.

We started having a bit of a snog and I followed Julie's lead, rubbing her tit. To my surprise, she didn't flinch, quite the opposite, in fact, she started rubbing my dick.

I was watching Julie as this was going on and she appeared a little agitated so I cut it short and pulled away.

"Thank you, Lisa, for a very warm welcome," I told her. She replied by telling me that later it might get even hotter. I just smiled and thankfully, at that point, she went to greet someone else.

"Quite the show you put on there, Shug," Julie remarked. "Just following your lead, Julie, that's all," was my reply.

We both burst out laughing and I gave her a cuddle. I grabbed us a couple of beers and we sat down on a large beanbag under the window.

The room was exactly the same size as Julie's. There were already about a dozen people in, and another couple at the door. Any more and there wasn't going to be enough oxygen for everybody.

Julie gave me the lowdown on who was who and pointed out the good guys and wankers. Looking around, I never really thought that I wanted to talk to any of them although I wouldn't have said no to a shag with most of the girls.

Lisa announced that it was time to play spin the bottle and I told Julie that was my cue to head for the door. She agreed, saying that it was a pretty shit party anyway and that we could have more fun on our own.

"Is that an offer?" I asked her. "That depends, Shug, on whether or not you can behave yourself," she told me, as she ran her finger over my lips then stuck it in her mouth, mimicking a blowjob. She then winked at me and said now it really was time to go.

"Julie, I'll be the best behaved dirty bastard you could ask for," I whispered to her, smiling.

"Oh, Shug, you say the most romantic things to a woman. How could anyone resist you?" she replied, sarcastically, placing her hands on her heart and trying her best to look all girly and vulnerable.

I grabbed her and cuddled her, telling her she could be a right little cockteaser sometimes. She cuddled me back and we laughed. I thought to myself that I was on to a good thing when we got back to her flat.

We headed to the door with a bit of urgency, probably me more than Julie, but I didn't want her mood to change as I thought the quicker we got out of there, the better chance I had of fucking her.

As we opened the door, Lisa came running over to us and asked why we were leaving. I told her, jokingly, that it was because I thought we were coming to an orgy and when I realised it wasn't, I saw no point in staying.

"Well, Shug, let me tell you: if it's an orgy you want then all you have to do is start it. I'm sure everyone else will join in."

Fuck, I didn't know what to say, I wasn't sure if she was calling my bluff or if she was being serious, so I winked at Julie then blurted out, "Right, Lisa, if you're serious, let's go. Get your kit off and let's fuck."

"Okay, Shug, that's great, I'm up for it if you are!" she told me, as she kicked off her shoes. She motioned to Julie, reaching her arm out towards her.

"Right, Julie, come and join us, let's fuckin do it," she said, raising her voice a notch. She then started kissing me, slipped my jacket off and started fumbling with my belt.

I started unbuttoning her blouse, waiting for her to stop me in my tracks and tell me she was taking the piss, but no, to my delight, she kept on going.

I was watching Julie, unsure how she felt as she surveyed me snogging, fondling and stripping her friend right in front of her.

However, I needn't have worried, because she was smiling at me and she then moved towards us, removing her jacket and dropping it to the floor. I couldn't believe it when she came between us, moving me out of the way and planting a kiss on Lisa's lips.

Lisa immediately turned her attention to Julie and started fumbling with her blouse. I stood behind her and unbuttoned her jeans then stuck my hand down her pants.

Lisa had a short skirt on and I also slid my hand into her pants. Fuck, I was in heaven; the girls were snogging the faces off each other and massaging each other's tits in between removing their clothes.

I was rubbing their pussies at the same time and could feel they were both as moist as each other. I had a quick glance around the room to see what everyone else was doing, and most of the people had started doing something sexual.

I lowered the girls to the floor and Julie ended up on top of Lisa. I was on my knees beside them and looked around the room again, then said to everyone, "Come on, folks, look a bit more fuckin lively, for fuck's sake. We're trying to start a fuckin orgy here, so get your kit off and let's get fucking each other."

At that point, two of the couples got up and left, but the rest stayed. There was a big fat girl who was sitting on the edge of the bed, kind of squirming a little and trying to hide her face with her glass, not knowing what the fuck she should do.

Everybody else was following Lisa and Julie's lead and were removing clothes, touching up whoever was closest to them and generally getting into it.

She was the only one in the room who wasn't engaged in anything so I made a beeline for her. I never said anything, I just knelt down in front of her, spread her legs with my hands, allowing me to get close enough to kiss her.

I took the glass from her and put it on the floor. I put my hand on her face, stared straight at her, and told her how pretty she looked.

I kissed her on the lips and slowly slid my tongue into her mouth, she responded and we kissed for a few minutes.

When I thought she was a bit more relaxed, I placed my hand on her breast. She jumped a little, but never removed it.

I asked her name and she told me she was called Elsie. I reckoned she was about nineteen and I was getting a feeling that she was still a virgin.

While we kissed, I removed her jacket then went to take off her t-shirt. She stopped me, telling me she was too fat and didn't want anyone to see her naked.

I told her not to be silly, that she was no such thing, and suggested she look around the room at everyone else and she would see none of them was perfect and that every one of them had something they would rather hide.

"Elsie, I think you look fuckin great, and tonight, I'm going to fuck you and you're going to love it. When we're done, I'll bet all the rest of the guys in the room will be queuing up to do the same, assuming you want it, that is."

I lifted her t-shirt again, and this time she let me remove it. I lowered her from her sitting position onto the bed and lay down beside her.

I started kissing her again and rubbed her tits for a bit. I then took her hand and placed it on top of my dick.

I put my hand on top of hers and squeezed it, letting her feel the outline through my jeans. When she started squeezing me, I removed my hand and went back to rubbing her tits.

She had one of those clip at the front bras, which I guessed she wore because she couldn't reach around the back. I unclipped it and, I swear to God, as they popped out, they grew to double the size.

I'd never seen such massive tits, far less man-handled them. Fuck, they looked awesome. I told Elsie this and she just smiled. I got up from the bed and removed my boots, jeans and pants.

I then lowered Elsie's skirt, slipped off her tights and pants then lay on top of her. I started kissing her again, trying to work out the best way to fuck her without embarrassing her.

She stopped kissing me and whispered in my ear that she hadn't done it before and was a bit worried. I reassured her that I would be very gentle and that she should just relax and enjoy it.

We kissed again for a bit then I made my move. I knelt down between her legs and went to give her pussy a good rub, just to make sure she was wet before I shagged her. I lifted her knees up and pushed her legs open, but I could hardly see her minge for her legs. I decided to give her a lick and see how that went.

I got myself positioned and pushed her legs as far apart as I could and began licking her. I felt a bit like I was being smothered and struggled to get a breath, but Elsie was fuckin loving it so I decided to carry on.

Within minutes, she was grabbing my hair and pushing me as far in as she could, then bang, she shot her load.

She was now pushing my head with both hands and I thought I was going to pass out, but I couldn't stop as she was in sexual fuckin heaven.

She slumped a bit and released her hands from my head and I removed my head from her pussy and moved back up to give her a kiss.

I was dripping in her come and I have to say it was one of the nicest tasting vaginas I'd ever licked.

Elsie started licking my face like she was eating an ice cream cone and I swear she licked my face clean in a matter of seconds.

We snogged again for a few minutes, giving me a chance to play with her amazing breasts, then asked her if she wanted me to fuck her.

By this time, Elsie seemed to be feeling much more confident about herself, either that or she wasn't giving a fuck.

"Of course I want you to fuck me, Shug, I thought you were never going to do it," she told me.

I grabbed both her tits, squeezed them together then started alternating my tongue between both of her nipples, biting and sucking, and enjoying watching her squirm.

"Shug, please fuck me, I need it now," she screamed at me, oblivious to her surroundings. That was all I needed and positioned myself between her legs, hoping I could give her what she wanted.

I pushed her legs apart and entered her. I'd been worrying over nothing. I managed with ease to get in and when I started riding her, it was fuckin brilliant.

She had the tightest pussy I'd ever been in and she was now bucking underneath me like a fuckin rodeo horse. I can honestly say it was one of the best shags I've had, even to this day.

I'm sure she started coming the minute I entered her and never stopped until I came out. I asked her how she felt and she told me she felt fuckin brilliant.

I kissed her and told her what a great fuckin ride she was and that she shouldn't give a flying fuck about any arseholes who thought she wasn't pretty because I thought she had it all.

She just smiled and thanked me for the compliments and asked me what happened now.

"Well, if you want to fuck with someone else then just point him out and I'll swap places with him."

She laughed and I could see her turning red. She then whispered to me, "No one in here would swap partners for me."

"You bet your arse they would when I tell them how fuckin awesome a ride you are."

"Come on, Shug, stop teasing me," she said. "Teasing you, Elsie? Listen here, hen, there's no way I'm teasing you, I've had a few old shags in my time and let me tell you, you're right up there with the best. Now, who are you going to pick?"

She looked around and pointed to a guy leaning against the wall with a chick bouncing up and down on his knee.

"Okay, let's do it," I told her. I leaned over, gave her a kiss on the cheek and told her to relax and enjoy whatever came next. She never said a word, just smiled and lowered her head.

I went over to the couple and started kissing the girl. I then started rubbing her tits, much to her enjoyment, which produced a look of confusion from the guy. I told him I was taking over and he should go and shag Elsie.

"I'm fine here, thanks," he told me. "Eh, no you're fuckin not. We're having a fuckin orgy and I'm sure you know how that works, so get your fuckin arse over there and fuck the life out of her or I'll beat the shit out of you to within an inch of your fuckin life - got it?"

I was staring straight at him and looking really threatening. "Listen, cunt, she's a brilliant ride, and up until half an hour ago, she was a virgin, so move your fuckin arse and do what you're told."

He looked at me, shook his head then lowered it, looking at the floor. I think he got the message. He got up and went to walk over to her, I grabbed his hand and said: "Now remember, play nice, I'll be watching." He just nodded.

I sat in the position he was and lowered the girl onto my cock. I watched him as he went over to Elsie. As he stood in front of her, to my surprise, Elsie cupped his balls with one hand, put her other hand on his arse, then took his cock in her mouth.

I thought to myself, 'Good stuff, young man, you just saved yourself from getting your cunt kicked in'.

I then focused on the chick bobbing up and down on my dick. "Hi, I'm Shug," "Andrea," was all she said, as she continued to bounce on me. I started fondling her tits and she started quickening up, which was really nice.

I looked around the room and noticed that everybody was shagging and wondered if they would have done anything like this if I hadn't suggested it, or if the spin the bottle thing mentioned earlier would have kicked it off anyway.

I saw Julie and she was still fucking about with Lisa, but there was also a couple of blokes and another girl with them.

I glanced back at the guy with Elsie and saw they were really getting into it. He was massaging her massive tits and she was sucking him for all she was worth while playing with his arsehole, which he appeared to be loving. 'Fuckin poof!' I thought to myself as I laughed a bit.

He looked over and nodded to me with a smile on his face so I guessed I could forget about him. I then turned my attention to Julie and saw she was on her knees, getting shafted from behind as she licked out Lisa.

Lisa also had a cock in her mouth and was sucking and licking it like a woman possessed. She was also rubbing her own clit for all she was worth. There was also another girl beside her who was playing with herself while sucking on Lisa's big tits.

All of a sudden, I started to get pangs of jealousy watching Julie getting shafted and almost went over to stop it, but knew I couldn't as it was me who'd encouraged her to get into it in the first place.

Just beside me, there was another girl who was kneeling on the floor. She had a dick in each hand, taking turns to suck on them. Fuck, it reminded me of a night at the farm.

I decided to put Julie to the back of my mind and concentrated on Andrea. I hadn't really looked at her until now; she had long dyed blond hair, very small tits and was a slim, fit looking burd.

I lifted her off me and suggested she turn around and go onto her knees, which she did very quickly. I rammed my dick into her from behind and started slowly pulling my dick back until I was almost out then slowly pushed it back in, as far as it would go.

Andrea let out a satisfied groan each time I did this and was urging me to speed up, but I continued to tease her while watching everything else that was going on in the room.

I looked over to Elsie and, unbelievably, she was on top of the guy with her arms at his side and hands on the bed. She was riding him like a wild mustang and he was sucking on her massive tits, loving every minute of it.

One of the guys, who had previously been getting sucked off, headed over to the bed and stuck his dick in Elsie's mouth. I swear if it was possible, she started to ride even faster.

The next thing, Julie came over to me and suggested that Andrea should lie on the floor, which she seemed more than happy to do. Julie then told me to mount her, which I did, then Julie sat on her face, staring straight at me.

She smiled, shook her head, then proceeded to snog the face off me. I could taste Lisa's pussy as we kissed, and it was lovely. I pulled away and asked her how she was doing.

"Shug, this is the first time I've ever been involved in a fuckin orgy and the first time I've fucked about with another girl. And you know what? I wish I'd did it yonks ago. Now keep rubbing my tits, shut the fuck up, and kiss me," she demanded. I did as I was told. I stuck my tongue in her mouth and started tweaking her nipples until she screamed.

Andrea then motioned for Julie to get off her. When she did, she told her she thought she was either going to suffocate or fuckin drown and we all burst out laughing.

I was feeling like I'd had enough, but wanted a ride at Lisa before I split. Andrea and Julie were having a kiss and that was my cue to move in on Lisa.

She was sucking a guy's dick as he was sitting on a chair and was rubbing his hands through her hair. I noticed she still had her hand on her pussy so I lifted her onto her knees and fired home my dick from behind.

She moved her hand onto his cock and while I was banging her, I stuck my finger up her arse, which made her nearly bite off his dick.

By now, she was ramming her arse into me and the bloke on the chair had a seriously worried look about him. I just smiled and told him to enjoy himself.

I looked over to see how Elsie was doing. She had her knees on the floor, a bloke fucking her from behind, and she was licking another guy's dick, who was sitting on the bed. I thought, 'Go on, Elsie, give it lalldy!'

I felt myself coming and beefed into Lisa for all I was worth until I shot my load. I then pulled out and sat down on the floor. I looked at my dick, watching it shrink in front of my eyes, and noticed how red fuckin raw it was.

I looked over at Julie and she was gathering up her clothes. "You ready to head?" I asked her. "Yeh, I'm done," she told me.

"Me too, give me a minute and I'll come with you."

I collected my clothes as well then thanked Lisa for a great night. She was still sucking away and only gave me a bit of a wave.

I went over to Elsie and said goodbye to her as well. She removed the cock from her mouth, lifted her head and said: "Thanks very much, Shug, this is the best night of my life."

I leaned over and kissed her on the cheek and told her I was sure she would have many more great nights." Then Julie and I left.

We walked along the corridor in the nude, carrying our clothes, and never said a word until we got back to her room. Julie closed the door and we dropped our clothes on the floor.

"Another blinding night, Julie, what do you reckon?" I asked her. Fuck, I could have bitten my tongue off the minute my words were out as I noticed Julie had tears running down her cheeks.

"Blinding night? Fuckin blinding night? You really do think that running around, shagging everything that walks, is the dog's bollocks don't you? What about tomorrow, Shug? When you've fucked off and I'm still here, seeing everybody that was in that fuckin room, every fuckin day ... I'll never be able to look any of them straight in the face again. Fuck, I won't even be able to look at myself in the mirror ever again. Whatever possessed me to fuckin do it?"

"Come on, Julie, don't you think you're over-reacting just a little bit? Fuck me, I think you need to stop being so fuckin mellow dramatic, it was just a bit of sex, for fuck's sake. By the way, from where I was standing, you looked like you were having a great time. Fuck, Julie, everyone in the room will feel a bit embarrassed in the morning, but I'm sure they all enjoyed themselves and I bet none of them will beat themselves up like you're doing."

"Oh yes, Shug, that's right, just play it down and make me look like the neurotic female. I would never have done anything like that if you hadn't got me pissed."

I forgot all about her tears and thought what a fuckin cow she was being so let rip at her.

"Oh, so it's my fault. I fuckin forced you to get pissed. I dragged you to a fuckin party. I made you get involved in a fuckin orgy. I fuckin forced you to fuck like a rabbit and told you to shag everyone in the room. You aren't half a piece of work, Julie. What about taking responsibility for what you choose to do yourself, instead of fuckin blaming me!"

I didn't realise until I stopped ranting how much I was upsetting her. I'd been walking about the room, shouting my mouth off, and not paying too much attention to her, but when I looked at her, I realised she was distraught.

The tears were streaming down her face and she was shaking like a leaf. I instantly changed my attitude and apologised to her for roaring like a banshee.

I walked towards her to give her a cuddle, but she walked away and went over and sat on the bed. I followed her and sat down next to her, but she moved away a little.

I wrapped the cover around her and offered her a hankie, which she took. She was now sobbing and jerking a bit.

I tried again to comfort her by putting my arm around her and this time she let me. "Look, Julie, I'm sorry for going off on one, it's just that I felt bad because you felt bad. Maybe you're right: if I hadn't talked you into it then maybe we wouldn't be having this conversation."

I cuddled her and she put her head on my chest. "No, Shug, you're right, I did want to do it. And while I was there, I had a great time. It's just the aftermath, thinking how much of a dirty cow I was and knowing that all those people were there to witness it. I just feel so cheap now. Everything you said was spot on, it was all my doing and it's me who needs to take responsibility."

"Come on, Julie, let's just forget about it, it's really late and I'm sure we'll both feel better in the morning."

"Yeh, I guess you're right," she agreed. "I'm glad, Julie, coz I'm freezing my bollocks off here." "Sorry, Shug, I never thought. Come on, let's get into bed."

We both got into bed and I checked the clock. Fuck, it was ten past four in the morning, no wonder I was shattered. Julie assumed what seemed to be her favourite position, cuddling into me with her leg over my dick.

I put my arm around her and squeezed her into me. I could feel one of her nipples getting erect against my side and that, coupled with her leg on my dick, was starting to give me a hard-on.

"Jeezus, Shug, have you not had enough tonight?" Julie asked. "Sorry, Julie, but I blame you. If you weren't so hot then I wouldn't get so many hard-ons, now would I?" I told her.

We laughed and I kissed her on the top of her head. Julie looked up at me, her face looking really earnest, and asked me if I thought she was a slut.

"Come on, Julie, you know I don't think that. Hey, it was just a one-off and we all had a good time, no one's going to think the worst of anybody, so stop fretting."

I lifted my head towards her and kissed her on the lips. She responded and placed her hand on my face. I put my tongue in her mouth and we started kissing properly.

Julie got on top of me as we continued kissing for what seemed like an age. She was gently grinding her hips, pushing her pussy towards my cock. I placed my hands on her arse and softly rubbed and squeezed it.

"Are we going to fuck, Julie?" I asked her. "I hope so, Shug," she told me. Fuck me, I was totally bamboozled. A minute ago, she was distraught because she felt like a slut. Now, she wanted me to ride her! Fuck, I'll never understand women as long as I live.

Julie grabbed hold of my dick, pushed it into her pussy then started grinding a little faster. She was kissing and licking my face while panting heavily.

I asked her to sit up, to allow me to see her, which she did. She was kneeling now, with her hands on my chest, and continuing to grind up and down on me.

I put my hands on her breasts and softly rubbed them. I then lifted myself up and started sucking and licking her nipples.

"Bite them, Shug, bite them hard," she told me. "Bite them? Are you serious?" "Yes, Rooster used to do it, I love it." Not one to refuse a request from a woman, I did as I was told and started biting away.

"Harder, Rooster! Oh, sorry, I mean, Shug." Talk about a passion killer, "Thanks for that, Julie, I guess I know who you're thinking about," I told her.

"Sorry, Shug, slip of the tongue, I didn't mean it, I just got carried away, it was something he used to do all the time."

"I think maybe it's time we went to sleep, Julie, don't you?" "Please, Shug, I'm sorry, let's keep going for a bit." "Sorry, Julie, games over for me, I can't do this any longer." I lifted her off me and she lay down beside me. "Shug, I'm really sorry, I didn't mean…." I interrupted her.

"Julie, honestly, it's okay. You don't need to keep apologising, I'm fine. It's nothing to do with you calling me Rooster, you could call me anything you want when we're fucking. I just felt really guilty, a bit like you did earlier. When you said: 'Rooster', I thought 'Fuck! I need to speak to him tomorrow and he's going to ask me all about you'. And I have no idea what the fuck I'm going to tell him!"

"Shug, please don't tell him anything about this, about us, or especially, about earlier."

"Fuck, Julie, do you think I've got a death wish or something? If I mentioned any of it to him then I really think he'd fuckin kill me. Fuck, he would probably come here and fuckin kill you afterwards as well. No, my real problem is not what to say. The big thing will be the letter. He'll want to know what your response is and you haven't even opened it."

"Shug, just tell him the truth about the letter - that I told you to take it back and before you left, you placed it on the table in my room and that sorts that problem. As for the rest, can't you just tell him about the pub and the party, but miss out the bits he won't want to hear?"

"That's my plan, Julie. But how the fuck can I look him in the eye when I'm telling him? He'll know I'm lying through my teeth. You know him, he's really good at sussing that kind of shit out."

"I know, Shug, but you're just going to have to do your best to convince him."

"Easier said than done, Julie. But hey, it's my problem, I'll sort it." "I know you will, Shug, I'm sorry for causing all this shit."

"Hey, Julie, this is not your doing; this is my shit, please remember that." "Shug, it takes two to tango, I think we're as bad as each other." "I suppose we are, but hey, let's stop thinking about it and we'll see what the morning brings."

I kissed her on the head and we cuddled down for a kip. I wrestled for a bit with my thoughts then drifted off.

We were wakened with the door being knocked. Straight away, Julie told me not to answer it. I asked her why and she told me it would be Lisa.

"How do you know that?" I asked her. "Because she always comes to see me first thing after a night out, to go over the gory details of it, and I sure as fuck don't want to hear anything about last night - especially not from her."

"Julie, you're going to have to face her sooner or later. Surely you'd be better seeing her when I'm here? That way you'll have a bit of moral support."

The door got knocked again, this time with a shout of "Julie, are you awake yet?" She was right, it was Lisa.

"Come on, Julie, what do you think? Will I let her in?" I asked her.

"Fuck, I suppose so, Shug," she said, pulling the covers over her head. I got out of bed, opened the door and Lisa smiled. "Hi, Shug, how are you this morning?" she asked me as she came in.

Before I could say anything, she patted my cock and said: "It's not how I remember it from last night," laughing away to herself.

She made a beeline for the bed and sat on the bottom of it. I climbed in and got under the covers. "How you feeling this morning, Jules?" she asked.

Julie removed the covers from her head and smiled, "Yeh, I'm okay. How's you?" "I'm great, did you enjoy yourself last night?" Lisa asked her.

Julie's face turned scarlet. "Well, it was certainly different from any other night I've ever had, that's for sure," she told her.

"What about you, Shug? Did you have a good time?" she asked me. "Sure did, Lisa. I had a ball, what about you?"

"Great, Shug. One of the best nights I've ever had. I couldn't believe how it turned out. Everybody said the same, we're all looking forward to the next time, especially Elsie." Lisa was smiling like the cat that got the cream.

I looked at Julie and she slid down the bed a bit, pulling the covers back over her head. Lisa asked Julie if she was okay and Julie resurfaced, this time sitting up a bit and resting her back on the headboard.

"Lisa, that was a one-off for me. I can't believe I got involved in it. It's not something I ever want to repeat and, if truth be told, I feel a bit embarrassed about the whole thing. Don't you?"

"Fuck, no way, Julie. I loved it. I don't understand why you're so upset. I can't wait for next weekend - we're all planning to do it again. Actually, I was hoping I was going to come in here this morning and have another session, that's how much of a good time I had. Guess what, Shug? I don't know what you did to big Elsie, but she had an absolute ball, and let me tell you, she was the surprise package of the evening, everybody certainly changed their opinion of her - what a great girl she is."

"Well, as much as I'd like to fuck you again, Lisa, I think it's off the menu this morning. Isn't that right, Julie?"
"Definitely!" was all she said.

"Ah, well, it was worth asking I suppose. Okay, folks, I'm heading down for breakfast now, anyone want to join me?" she asked.

Straight away, Julie said she couldn't as she would need to have a shower first. Lisa then said that was okay as she wasn't in a rush. And if Julie didn't mind, she would just hang around until she was ready.

Julie went to protest, but I quickly intervened and said that would be fine.

Julie gave me one hell of a dirty look, but I knew she wouldn't go to the dining room if I didn't force the issue and I wanted to be there when she met them all for the first time.

She got out of bed, closely watched by Lisa, and grabbed a towel. She then wrapped it around herself, picked up her soap bag and headed towards the door.

I shouted to her and asked her if she wanted me to come and scrub her back, but she turned around and gave me a real cold stare and said: "I think you've done enough in the shower this weekend, thanks, don't you?" then left, slamming the door behind her.

The door was hardly closed and Lisa was pulling back the covers and fumbling for my cock. "Lisa, what the fuck are you doing?" I asked her. "Come on, Shug, we've got plenty time for a fuck before she comes back." "Whoa, Lisa, hold the bus, we can't do this. Julie would be well pissed if she comes back and catches us at it!" I told her.

"Well, best we get a move on then," she replied. She started stripping off and wouldn't take no for an answer. Within seconds, she was in bed, sitting on top of me and directing my cock into her pussy.

"Come on, Shug, fuck me, make me cum," she whispered. I just nodded and smiled at her. I wasn't doing a fuckin thing, she was in total control and bucking away like her life depended on it.

I almost felt like I wasn't interested and wished to fuck she would cum quickly and get it over with. The last thing I wanted to do was upset Julie any more than she already was. I knew if she came in and caught us that she would probably never speak to me again.

I then thought the best thing I could do was to make her cum and get it over with as quickly as possible. So I grabbed her tits, tweaked away at her nipples then grabbed both of them, squashed them together and started biting the fuck out of them, like Julie had asked me to do earlier.

Fuck, that certainly did the trick! She let out a roar and started bouncing on me like a kangaroo in heat.

I kept biting away at them and within seconds, she was screaming herself to an orgasm. I put my hand over her mouth and told her to shut the fuck up, but she was so far gone that she wasn't taking incoming calls.

She eventually calmed down and got off me. She lay beside me, out of breath, and asked me if I'd come. I lied, telling her I had, which seemed to satisfy her.

I got out of bed and started putting my clothes on and suggested to her that she do the same.

We were both up and dressed, just before Julie came back. Lisa was sitting on the bed and I was on the chair having a smoke when she entered.

"Hi, Julie, nice shower?" I asked. "You fucked her, didn't you?" "Eh, no," I replied, pretty unconvincingly. "Shug, I know you did. You fucked her in my fuckin bed, how could you?" she said, making her way to the mirror.

"Hang on a minute," Lisa said, "if we'd fucked, don't you think I'd tell you? It's not like you're an item or anything, is it? So if we'd fucked, it's no big deal to tell you. I think you need to relax, Julie, you seem well stressed today."

Julie was standing with her hands on the sink, staring at herself in the mirror. I went over to her and put my hand on her shoulder, but she shrugged it off.

"Julie, what the fuck's got into you? Why are you behaving like this?" I asked her.

"Leave me, Shug, please. Look, why don't you and Lisa go for breakfast? I just need to be on my own right now," she replied.

I tried to cuddle her, but, again, she stopped me. I looked at Lisa and nodded towards the door. She nodded back then got up to leave. "I'll pop back later to see how you are, Julie, if that's okay?" Lisa said as she left. I just said: "Thanks," as she closed the door.

I got hold of Julie by the arms and asked again what was up. "You know what's up, Shug. Fuck's sake, I'm not going over it all again. You know I thought having a shower would wash it all away, but last night's going to live with me for a very long time."

She then burst out crying and again, asked me to leave, but I just pulled her towards me and held her in my arms. She was sobbing uncontrollably like earlier, but this time, she was also heaving and making all sorts of noises.

I just kept rubbing her back and telling her everything would be fine, but to be honest, I don't think she heard a word. She eventually stopped crying, but I think it was because she'd actually ran out of tears. I manoeuvred her on the bed and sat down beside her.

"Shug, what the fuck am I going to do now?" she asked. "I've blown everything, I fucked it up at home and now I've fucked it up here. There's nowhere else for me to go, I think I'm a waste of space, I fuck up everything I do."

"Julie, come on, you need to stop this wallowing in self-pity pish. Trust me, I know, I've been there, done it and got the fuckin t-shirt. All it does is drag you down and you never get out the bit. You need to get the notion right out of your head that you did something wrong last night. It's now history and by tomorrow, somebody else will have done something way worse than us and that'll be the front page news. You need to get dressed, put your brave face on and I'll take you for breakfast. We'll go into the canteen with our heads held high and eat, smile and chit-chat, like we did yesterday."

"No fuckin way, Shug, I'll never go in there again, especially not today."

"You fuckin will, Julie, even if I have to carry you down with your towel wrapped around your fuckin arse, you'll be there. And we're leaving in five minutes - so best you get dressed," I told her.

"Shug, you can do what you like, but I'm not going anywhere and that's the end of it!" she screamed back at me.

"Okay, Julie, your choice," I told her, then lifted her, put her over my shoulder and edged towards the door. Julie started roaring, telling me to put her down and was hitting me on the back. I ignored her and put my hand on the door knob. "Okay, last chance, Julie," I told her. "With or without clothes? You decide."

"Okay, Shug. Put me down, you fuckin arsehole. I'll go, but afterwards, I want you to leave and I never want to see you again, got that?"

I put her down and told her that was okay by me. She removed her towel and threw it at me. While she was changing, she was calling me all sorts of names, but I just ignored her.

The minute she was dressed, I opened the door and gestured for her to go out. "I fuckin hate you for this, Shug, I'll never speak to you again."

"No probs, Julie, just be polite until we're fed, then we can go our separate ways," I told her. "Fine," was all she said. We walked along the corridor and down the stairs. As we walked towards the canteen, I couldn't help thinking maybe she'd meant it, about not wanting to speak to me ever again.

I couldn't think of any other way to get her out and really hoped that when she got to breakfast she would be fine, but now I was having my doubts.

We went in, grabbed what we were eating and turned to find some seats. I clocked Lisa sitting with some of the people from the party and whispered to Julie that's where we should sit. "In your dreams," she whispered back.

"Julie, that's where we're sitting and if you don't get your arse over there then I'll cause such a major fuckin scene that you'll never be able to show your face here again."

"I fuckin hate you so much, Shug, I can't wait until you fuck off out of my life." "Well, not long to wait now, Julie, then we can both be happy," I told her.

We went over and sat down. The mood at the table appeared fairly sombre and I guessed more than Julie were feeling a bit uncomfortable about the previous evening's events.

Julie just smiled as she sat down and everyone either returned a smile or nodded, but no one said a word.

"Good morning, folks, how are we all this fine morning?" I asked them all. Lisa was the only one who replied and told me she was great. I looked at Julie. She put her elbow on the table, her hand on her brow, and tried to cover her face with her hand as much as she could. She picked up her fork and started playing with her food.

I directed my statement at everybody. "Great night last night, folks, I really enjoyed myself. Lisa, thanks for the invite, I look forward to the next one."

No one responded and Lisa just smiled. As I looked about, shaking my head, I caught Elsie out of the corner of my eye looking for a seat. I waved her over and pulled a chair from another table and positioned it next to me.

She came over and sat down. "Hey, Elsie, how you doin?" I asked her. "Shug, I'm doing great, I had a brilliant night last night. Everybody was getting into it and having a ball, best night I've ever had, thanks to you all."

"Me too," I told her, "but everybody seems a bit embarrassed about it and I don't know why."

"Listen, if anybody should feel embarrassed about anything that happened last night then it should be me. I was a virgin until last night and I ended up fucking everyone in the room. And for the record, I fuckin loved every minute of it and would do it again in a heartbeat. We did absolutely nothing wrong so why should we be sitting here all concerned about what someone might think? Having a nice time is not a crime in this country, as far as I'm aware, and anyway, it's not like we killed anyone, I think you all need to remember that," she exclaimed to them in a sharp whispery tone.

"Here, here, Elsie, well said," I told her, patting her on the back. Then Lisa began, "You know what? I agree with Else, we really do need to get a fuckin grip of ourselves and lighten up a bit," she told everyone.

I couldn't believe it, almost instantly, the mood lifted. One of the girls then said: "You know what, Elsie? You're right, it was a great night. And you're right, we shouldn't be beating ourselves up about it. Lisa, the next time you fancy doing it, count me in."

Then everybody started talking about their part and within seconds, they were all smiling and chatting away. I looked at Julie and saw she was still sitting in the same position. I nudged her and said: "See! I told you. Not only do they not give a fuck anymore, they're looking forward to doing it again."

She lifted her head, gave me an awful stare, then lowered her head again and went back to looking at her food. "Come on, Julie, lighten up, for fuck's sake," I told her, but she never responded.

Lisa then got up and went and sat next to Julie. She gave her a hug and started whispering in her ear then kissed her on the cheek and went back to where she was previously sitting.

I have no idea what she said, but I wish to fuck I could have bottled it because Julie then kissed me on the cheek and said she was sorry for being a cow.

I told her to forget about it and we hugged. Julie then started chatting with everyone and even managed a laugh or two about the orgy.

I looked at Lisa and gestured to her to tell me what she'd said, but she just blew me a kiss and winked at me.

I finished my breakfast and said to Julie that I needed to go. So we both excused ourselves from the table and Julie agreed to meet up with the group for lunch.

When we got into the corridor, I asked her what Lisa had said, but she told me it was nothing, just a bit of girly stuff. I was dying to know, but I didn't want to push it, I was just glad that we were back on track.

I put my arm around her and we made our way to her room. When we got in, she told me that she thought I should fill in the application form before I left and she would hand it in.

"Why would you want me to do that, Julie? Surely you don't think I would still have a chance of a job here now?" "Shug, if you're serious about wanting to work here then fill it in and let me see what I can do."

"Okay, Julie, I'll do it, but I think it'll be a waste of time," I told her.

I sat down and spent half an hour or so filling it in. I then gave it back to her. I decided then that I really needed to go so got my gear together, picked up by bag, and told her I was heading.

"I'll walk you down to your bike, Shug," she suggested. "Is that to make sure I leave, Julie? Escorting me off the premises?"

"That's right, Shug, I don't want you sneaking back in. But especially, I don't want you giving the Warden another mouthful."

"Julie, if she's in her office then I'll go and apologise to her. After all, if I come back, I'll need to get her on my side."

We both laughed and continued to the door. When we got to the reception area, I noticed that the Warden was in her office and knocked the door. When she opened it, she asked in a very stern voice, "What do you want?"

"Sorry to bother you," I told her "I just want to apologise for my behaviour and language yesterday, it was completely inappropriate. I shouldn't have spoken to you in the way that I did. I hope you can find it in your heart to forgive me," I said, in the poshest voice I could muster.

Fuck, I thought she was going to faint or something. She was well taken aback that this greasy biker standing in front of her had taken the time to speak to her, and more importantly, apologise.

I think she was much more surprised about what I'd said today than what I'd told her the day before.

"Thank you for your apology," was all she said, with a bewildered look on her face, then closed her door.

I looked at Julie then smiled. "You're one smooth-talking bastard, Ochil Kinnaird, you'd get a piece at anyone's door," she remarked.

"I know, fuckin great, ain't it?" I said, laughing away as we went out.

I started my bike up, giving it a few revs, and tied my bag to the seat. "Well, Julie, that's me ready to go. Thanks for a great weekend. It was nice to see you and maybe I could spend another weekend here if you'll have me?"

"Fuck, Shug, I would like to say yes, but I don't know if I could cope with you for another weekend. You fucked up loads of people in such a short space of time. None of them will ever be the same again! Should I invite you back? Well…. Thankfully, my next weekend off is not for another seven weeks, that'll give me time to think about it."

I laughed a little at her comments then said: "Come on, Julie, we had a blast, you have to admit that. It was an interesting old weekend, if nothing else."

"Interesting? Well, that's one word for it, Shug. However, nightmare is another word I could use. I'm sure lots of the people you met might also use that instead of 'interesting'," she suggested.

"Julie, come on, you have to agree: at least it wasn't fuckin boring. I bet most people I came across were glad they met me."

"Try telling that to Anna!" she reminded me." "Hey, come on, Jules, remember it was her that wanted to fuck me, not the other way round," I reminded her.

"Shug, stop talking and give me a hug," she demanded. Again, I did what I was told and we cuddled for a bit. I gave her a peck on the cheek and told her it had been great to catch up, thanked her again for having me then got on my bike. I put my helmet on and went to leave.

Julie put her hand on the handlebars then said to me to remember and not say anything to Rooster. I told her she needn't worry on that score as there was no chance of that ever fuckin happening.

She stood back and I rode off. I slowly made my way through the hospital and decided to use the back entrance for my exit. I headed up the back road and turned right onto the main road.

As I passed the hospital, I noticed the row of houses on the left and wondered if they had anything to do with the hospital. I got to the roundabout and went onto the motorway.

It was pretty cold and the rain was spitting, but I felt glad to be back on my bike. I was feeling good, being on my own again, and looked forward to the journey home.

Chapter 13

I started recalling the weekend's events and couldn't stop myself smiling, I was even laughing out loud as I thought about certain parts of it.

Julie, Lisa, Anna and Elsie all sprung to mind, all for different reasons, but mainly because I'd fucked them all. I never in a million years thought the weekend would have turned out as it had.

Even with all the emotional shit Julie and I shared, and all her mental tantrums, we'd still parted friends. So, all in all, I decided it was a good one for the old memory bank.

As I got closer to home, the rain got heavier and so did my recollection of the weekend's events. Rooster was now at the forefront of my thoughts and what I should say to him was starting to prey heavily on my mind.

I knew the first thing he was going to ask me was about the letter and how Julie was. I'd already decided to go with Julie's plan and not deviate from it.

I had originally planned to head straight to the farm, but thought it would probably be better if I went to the flat first and grab a coffee. That way I could make sure I had a clear head for Rooster's impending interrogation.

My thoughts then turned to Provo and his funeral and what was going to happen after it was over. I wondered what Indie would do about the prospect's crash and when the voting would take place.

I arrived in the village, turned into my street and parked up. I lifted my bag and headed up the stairs. I opened the door and there was some mail, along with a piece of paper with the word 'Farm' on it.

'Fuck, I'm just in!' I thought to myself and now knew I would need to get to the farm as quickly as I could. I went into the living room, threw my bag on the couch and wondered what the fuck had happened now?

I opened the fridge and grabbed a drink of juice and stared out the window. As I drank, my mind was racing, wondering what I was heading into and I knew I'd better get my finger out.

I grabbed the knife I'd kept from our last skirmish from its hiding place under my bed, and stuffed it into my jacket.

I'd decided to keep it and carry it with me now that I had my colours. I now felt I should have some kind of protection with me at all times, just in case.

I ran back down the stairs and raced to the farm as quickly as I could. When I arrived, there was a fair old scattering of bikes outside and I noticed the barn door was open, which led me to believe there would be a few tucked away in there as well.

I guessed, by the number of bikes here, that something was just about to go down or they'd just arrived back from whatever it was. There were also a couple of cars sitting outside that I hadn't seen before.

I felt a couple of bikes engines and they were still pretty warm so presumed that they'd just arrived back not long in front of me.

I went into the kitchen and was met with total chaos. There were girls running around with basins of water, two girls were at the sink rinsing bowls and towels, it seemed as if everyone there was covered in blood.

Flick was lying on the kitchen table with Cowboy pressing a dish towel on an open stomach wound.

"Cowboy, what the fuck happened to Flick? What the fuck's going on, man?" "Shug, it's a fucking nightmare, we just got the shit kicked out of us and we have about a dozen brothers stabbed to fuck. Get me another towel will you?"

I handed him a towel and he removed the one he had on Flick's side and replaced it with the one I'd given him. I looked at Cowboy and noticed he was pretty bashed up as well. "What the fuck happened?" I asked him, repeating my earlier question.

"I'll fill you in later. Go and find out where the fuckin nurse is before he bleeds to death."

I nodded and went looking for her. Fuck, as I walked through the house, it looked like a fucking accident emergency unit on the front line: There were bodies everywhere, with people crouched over them and others running around with clean towels and water.

I noticed a girl stitching one of the guy's shoulders and guessed she was the nurse. I asked her if she could come to the kitchen and look at Flick.

"Give me a minute to finish here and I'll come through. Make sure you keep applying pressure to the wound," she told me.

I just nodded and went back to see Cowboy. As I walked, I looked around. There seemed to be about half a dozen girls that I didn't recognise who were tending to the injured. I wondered where the fuck they'd come from?

I went back into the kitchen and told Cowboy what she'd said. I noticed that Cowboy had a large cut on the side of his forehead and the blood was pouring out of it. I picked up a towel from the side of the sink and held it on his cut.

"What the fuck happened, Cowboy? I've never seen anything like this," I asked again.

"Shug, we were set up. A couple of the guys were at the park, doing a drug drop, and what seemed like a bunch of neds, chancing their arm, turned up and kicked the shit out of them. They told them if they saw them there again that they would give them another kicking. They then booted over their bikes, sat down with a carryout and started laughing, calling them pricks and stuff while drinking away. Because there were about ten of them, the guys just picked up their bikes, got on them, and told them they'd just got themselves involved in a war that they would regret. The neds laughed at them and told them to bring it on. When the guys came back and told Indie, we all jumped on our bikes, hoping to get them before they left the park. There was about twenty of us, a few two's up, and when we got there, we saw them, still sitting drinking. When they saw us coming, we expected them to bolt, but they stood up and started screaming at us, gesturing for us to come ahead. We got off our bikes, all tooled up, and made a beeline for them. When we were just about on them, they took to their heels and ran. As we charged at them, they turned and made their way up an alley, towards the road, with us in hot pursuit. The next thing we know, about forty guys, all tooled up, came racing towards us from the alley. The neds turned with them and we got involved in one fuck off fight. They all had baseball bats and knives and although we put up a fair bit of resistance, eventually, the sheer number of them allowed them to get the better of us."

"Who the fuck were they? Did anybody know them?" I asked him. "No one had a clue who the fuck they were, but they certainly knew us."

"Did they say why they were doing it?" "Nope, not a fuckin word. After they realised that we were all fucked, they just picked up their injured and fucked off."

"Holy shit, Cowboy, that's the strangest fuckin thing I've heard." "You're telling me, Shug! We're all scratching our heads about it. And Indie's fuckin raging, he was stabbed a couple of times and is pretty beaten up. But you know him, he's okay. He's had a few stitches, but the wounds were all pretty superficial."

The next thing, the nurse arrived and asked Cowboy to lift the towel off, which he did. I could see the blood bubbling out of Flick's wound.

I decided to go and see if I could find Rooster or Indie and see how they were. I met Indie. He was pacing up and down in the conservatory. As I walked in, he clocked me.

"Where the fuck have you been?" he roared at me. "I came over as soon as I got the note," I told him.

"I fuckin phoned Mark over an hour ago to get him to stick it in your door and you only show up now?"

"Indie, I just arrived back. Whenever I saw it, I dropped everything and came straight over."

"Well, a lot of fuckin use you are to us now. Have you seen the state of your brothers? That's the worst tanking this chapter's ever had, and let me tell you, it'll never fuckin happen again."

Fuck, he was sounding like he was blaming me. 'What fuckin good would I have been?' I thought to myself, 'It's not like we would've won if I was there'. I really wanted to tell him to shut the fuck up, but thought better of it.

Just then, Hotwire and another couple of guys arrived and Indie changed his focus from me to them.

"Where the fuck have you been?" he again screamed, this time at Hotwire.

"Hold it a fuckin minute, Indie, I never knew anything was up until I arrived. No cunt told me anything was going down. So back off, man, and tell me what the fuck's happened."

"You would know what fuckin had happened if you'd fuckin been here," he screamed again, this time squaring up to Hotwire.

Hotwire then said really calmly, "Indie, I know you're upset, but don't fuckin take it out on me. I'm asking you what the fuck happened here and I won't be taking any more of your fuckin screeching so best you calm the fuck down and tell me, okay?" He then put his arms around him and gave him a hug.

Surprisingly, Indie apologised. He then told Hotwire he couldn't help himself. They broke from their hug and Indie looked at me, "Sorry, Shug, didn't mean to go off on one." Fuck, I nearly passed out, Indie had just fuckin apologised to me, I couldn't believe it. "No worries, it's cool," I said.

'No worries, it's cool'- of all the fuckin stupid things I could have said, I reckoned that was the stupidest. 'No worries, it's cool'- Jeezus, what a fuckin tosser I could be!

Indie then sat down and Hotwire sat next to him. There were around a dozen or so guys there and they all looked pretty bashed up.

Indie started by telling us that the guys in the conservatory were the one's not seriously injured. That kind of unnerved me because they were all in a bit of a state.

He then explained what had happened, it sounded almost word for word what Cowboy had told me earlier.

I asked Indie where Rooster was and he told me he'd been stabbed in the leg and was in the big room. I got up to go and see him, but was promptly told to stay put and sit on my fuckin arse.

"Right, here's what's happening now: I want everyone in this room who's able to, to get out there, go around everybody you know and find out who these cunts are. Then get back here. Make sure you go in threes or fours. I don't want anyone else picked off. Don't be away any longer than an hour and, for fuck's sake, don't get involved in anything. Remember, it's Provo's funeral tomorrow and lots of our brothers will be arriving tonight and early tomorrow morning. We'll sort this shit out right after the funeral when we're at maximum strength. Okay, let's go and find out who these fuckers are."

He then stood up and headed to the door. I nipped into the room to see how Rooster was and when he saw me he shouted on me:

"How's it going, man? How was your trip?" he asked. "Yeh, it was okay, man," I told him. "I just popped in to see how you were, but I need to go, I'm heading out with Indie. I'll fill you in when I get back." "No probs, bud, see you then," he replied.

With that, we shook hands and I left. I almost ran to get outside, just in time to see Indie pointing to everyone, telling them who was going with who. As I went out, he shouted: "Shug, you're coming with me."

Everyone else had left apart from us and I was feeling a bit confused. "Indie, I thought you said we had to go out in threes and fours?" "That's right, I did. Why are you telling me this, Shug?" "Well, there's only two of us left," I reminded him. "Stop worrying, Shug, I'm sure we'll cope," he said, as he zipped up his leather jacket.

He turned to make his way towards his bike and it was then that I saw it. A gun! Fuck me, he was taking a fuckin gun with him! 'Holy shit!' I thought to myself, 'I never fuckin signed up for this'. I couldn't hold my tongue. "Why have you got that with you, man?" I asked, pointing at it. "To make sure no other brother gets hurt tonight. Come on, we're wasting time."

I jumped on my bike and chased him up the lane. All I could think was, 'I hope to fuck we don't find any of them tonight'. By the mood he was in, I was under no illusions that he would happily use it.

He headed straight to the park and stopped at the entrance to the small lane. I caught him up and drew in behind him. He was looking around then drove across the road to the pub and got off his bike.

He gestured for me to do the same, which I did. He then told me he was going in to see a couple of guys and for me to follow, but to stay 'schtoom'.

When we went in, looking around, I thought it was fairly busy for a Monday night, but then I saw that the darts team were playing. Indie went into the back room where there were a few people hanging around and playing pool. I followed him in and when he sat down beside a couple of guys, I did likewise.

One of the guys asked him what the fuck had happened to him and his reply was, "I was hoping you'd be able to tell me that."

The guy then said: "Honestly, Indie, I've no fuckin idea, man. All I've heard was that there was a punch up at the park earlier and it was a bunch of bikers who were involved."

"Who told you that?" he asked him. "You see the wee fat guy playing darts? It was him. His name is Chalky. He told us when he came in and asked us if we knew anything about it."

Indie then got up and went straight to the dartboard. The guy was just about to throw his dart and Indie stood straight in front of him. "We need to talk," he told him. Then, some random guy that was watching the darts shouted to Indie to get out of the fuckin way. Indie turned and looked at him with an ice cold stare and said: "One more word and I'll rip your fuckin head off, right here, right now, got it?" The guy lowered his head, looked away, and never said another word. Indie then looked back at the guy playing darts and said: "Chalky, get yourself through the back, now. I need to ask you something." I think the fact the big guy had shat himself, and that Indie knew his name, made him drain to a funny shade of white (a shade you don't normally associate with skin colour).

He put his arm out, in the hope someone would take the darts from him, so I obliged. I placed them on a table and followed the two of them back through to the pool room.

Indie sat him down in the corner, much to the amusement of everyone else in the room. He then sat down directly opposite him and I stood behind him.

"Right, I expect this to take two minutes," he told him. The guy just nodded.

"Tell me about the fight in the park earlier and don't miss anything out."

Chalky started by saying he didn't really know much.

"I met one of my mates, Alex, when I was coming into the pub and he told me he'd seen a pile of guys rushing out of the lane and onto a bus. And when he looked down he saw a lot of bikers getting up off the ground, some of them looked pretty badly beaten. Alex asked me if I knew anything about it and I told him it was the first I'd heard. When I came in, I asked Peter if he'd heard anything about it and he said he hadn't. That's all I know, mate, honest, that's the truth."

Indie kept staring at him for a bit then asked him where he could find his mate. "I'm not sure where he is just now, but I could give you his address," he told him.

Indie gave him a beermat and told him to write it down, which he did, then gave it back to him.

Indie took it from him then we headed out. As we went through the bar towards the door, we were given plenty of disgruntled looks, but nobody said a word.

When we got out, Indie showed me the address and asked me if I knew where it was and I told him I did.

"Take me there," was all he said. We jumped on our bikes and I took the lead. What a strange sensation it was, being in front of Indie, for some reason it felt really uncomfortable.

Within two minutes, we drew up at the address he'd given me. We parked up and headed towards the door. I went to give it a knock, but Indie just opened it and walked straight in. I followed, fearing the worst.

Indie opened the living room door. I noticed there was an older lady, with a baby on her knee, sitting on a chair and a couple, not much older than me, sitting on the couch. They were all relaxing, watching TV.

I swear to God I thought the three of them actually shat themselves. Indie went in and stood in the middle of the room. The guy went to stand up and Indie pushed him back down.

"Are you Alex?" he asked the guy. "Yes, I am. What the fuck's this all about? Who the fuck do you think you are fuckin barging in here?" he asked him. I must admit, I thought he showed some balls, considering the situation.

Indie then let rip, "Listen, you, and listen fucking good," which seemed to put Alex on the back foot, "Answer my fuckin questions and we'll be out of here in five minutes, okay?" Alex just nodded.

"I need you to tell me what you saw this afternoon," he told Alex, "and don't miss anything out."

Alex then said exactly what Chalky had earlier. "Anything else you can remember?" Indie asked. "No, that's it."

Indie then asked him if he remembered the colour of the bus, what size it was, which way it went, if it was a service bus or if not, and what name was written on the side of it.

Alex gave him a description of it, right down to the last detail.

Indie then thanked him, apologised for barging in, then told him he owed him one and if ever he needed anything, to tell Peter and he would sort it. He then tickled the chin of the kid, told the old dear it was a cute baby, smiled, then we left.

When we got out, he said: "We're heading back to the farm now," and blasted off.

As I chased him back, I thought about how he'd just barged into the house and wondered, if he'd got any resistance, if he would have used the gun in front of the woman and the kid. I was in no doubt that he would have, without a minute's hesitation, if he felt he had to.

The wind and rain made it a miserable ride back, but thankfully, it wasn't too far. When we got back, we were the last to arrive. Thankfully, everyone had returned unscathed.

Indie went straight into the conservatory, which was now packed with new arrivals. As he went in, the place fell silent.

He looked at Hotwire and asked him what info he and the rest of the guys had. It turned out they'd all got pretty much the same story to tell. The only thing extra Indie had was the name of the bus company.

"Right after Provo's funeral, we're all straight back here. We'll sort this then party like fuck for the big man. There's nothing else to do tonight so let's all get pished."

The noise returned to the room and there was a lot of back-slapping and handshakes as people started to filter out.

I decided to hunt for Rooster, Flick and Cowboy and check on the walking wounded. I spotted the three of them sitting together in the big room which, by the way, was no mean feat, considering the amount of people that were in there.

"Hey, guys, how's the war wounds?" I asked. Cowboy was first to reply, "Fuckin war wounds? Fuckin pussies! Leave them for five minutes and look at the fuckin state of them! A couple of fuckin blouses, Shug, that's what they are!" he said, roaring and laughing.

"Well, Cowboy, glad to hear you're as sympathetic as ever," I suggested. Rooster told me he was fine and it was just a flesh wound. Flick, on the other hand, was a bit more the worse for wear.

Apparently, his wound, although not life threatening, was much deeper and the chick who had fixed him up earlier, that I'd thought was a nurse, but was actually a doctor, had told him she would need to come back to see him in the morning.

I asked Rooster how the rest of the guys were and he told me no one was serious and that Flick was probably the worst off out of everybody.

I sat down beside Rooster, opened a beer and told him I needed to speak to him about Julie. "Sounds serious, mate. Is it about my letter?" he asked.

I told him it was, and that she'd refused to open it and told me to bring it back to him, but that I'd left it on her table. "I'm sorry, mate, but she said to tell you it's over for good." He then put his arm around me, raised his beer, offered a wry smile and said: "Well, Shug, you win some, you lose some. I've probably lost the best thing that ever happened to me, but hey, if there's no going back, then there's no going back, so fuck it, onwards and upwards, as they say."

Again, I apologised and he just pulled me into him then rubbed my head. Fuck, he was always doing that, and it really got on my fuckin nerves.

"Come on, Shug, let's get some more beers and you can tell us all about your weekend."

The four of us sat in a bit of a huddle on the floor and I told them the story about when I arrived and the patient masquerading as a doctor, which brought shrieks of laughter from the three of them.

When I told them the story about Anna in the shower and her husband, I thought the three of them were going to piss their pants, they were laughing that hard.

Flick looked in extreme pain as he laughed, but didn't seem to be too concerned about it.

I also told them about the lunatic barman. Rooster recalled the story, telling me the details which made it much clearer why the barman had been shitting himself.

Thankfully, that seemed to satisfy them and I never needed to say anything more so, as far as I was concerned, that was the last I'd say about it.

I asked the guys what the details were for Provo's funeral and Cowboy filled me in. I was a bit surprised when he told me that it was a cremation and not a funeral.

I'd never been to the crematorium and had no idea how it differed from a burial, but decided not to say anything and just wait and see for myself.

I told the guys I was going to split as I was totally fucked. I didn't mention, however, that it was because I'd been up half the night shagging Julie, just that it had been a long day.

Rooster suggested I should stay, but I told him I needed to go. I shook hands with them and told them I'd see them in the morning.

I was back in my flat within fifteen minutes and I was never so glad to be there. I sat on the couch and looked at the clock – Fuck! It was half-past-two in the fuckin morning, no wonder I was done in!

I thought I'd better set the alarm for nine o'clock, in case I slept late, the last thing I wanted to do was sleep-in tomorrow.

I thought about how lucky I was that there'd been a bit of a ruck today as it took the focus away from me needing to explain in any great depth to Rooster about Julie or answer any awkward questions he might've had.

I offered myself a bit of a smile and thought that, for once, things hadn't turned out too badly.

Chapter 14

I woke with the alarm sounding in my ear and jumped up. I'd fallen asleep on the couch and for some reason, I was cuddling the clock. I sat back down, laughing to myself as I'd thought I'd been shot or something when it had gone off.

The last thing I wanted to do today was wake up with a fuckin start. I switched it off then sat back down. I was really concerned with how the events of the day would pan out and wondered what part I'd need to play in it.

I got up, had a bath, got dressed, and headed to the kitchen for a bite to eat. I raked the cupboards and realised I didn't have a single thing in. I'd forgotten that I'd thrown everything out before I left.

"Shit! Not even a tin of fuckin beans. Aaggh, fuck it!" I shouted. I decided I'd just get something on the way. I, again, stuck the knife in my jacket, grabbed some cash and headed out.

I jumped on my bike and made my way to the paper shop for a couple of rolls. I ordered a bacon and sausage roll and was browsing at the papers when I noticed that Johnjo had got married. There was a picture of him and his Mrs, and in the background, I could see all my old mates.

I stared at it for ages until the shopkeeper shouted, telling me my rolls were ready. He gave me them along with the tea I ordered and I headed outside.

There was a bit of waste ground next to the shop and I sat on a piece of cardboard and rested my back against the wall.

The sun was out and the sky was clear, but it was still pretty cold. I was munching away and drifted off a bit, thinking about Johnjo, and wondered why I hadn't been invited to his wedding, but of course, I already knew the answer.

I was remembering how tight we all were, right through school, and some of the stuff we got up to. Just seeing them all smiling away made me feel pretty sad.

I started to think about what I was doing and what was going to happen to me, but stopped myself from going there. I decided that it was Johnjo who was wasting his life, more than me, by getting married at eighteen.

To my knowledge, he'd only ever slept with one woman and I reckoned that he would be divorced by the time he was twenty.

I finished eating, jumped back on my bike and went to head off. I was waiting for a break in the traffic and got a glimpse of myself in my mirror.

Fuck, I had to do a double-take. I looked again and realised that I'd turned into every single Bat in the chapter.

I was now sporting a proper beard and moustache, albeit a small one, my hair was now past my shoulders and here I was, sitting on a chopper with a pair of mirrored sunglasses and an open faced helmet, proudly displaying my colours.

'Huh, so much for individuality' I thought. Someone turning into the layby flashed me and I moved out. I headed to the farm, sun on my back, and the familiar sound of my throbbing engine underneath me.

Now this is what it's all about for me. I started to wonder about all the rest of the shit I was involved in, and how much I actually enjoyed it, compared with what Johnjo was doing, and a smile broke out the width of my face.

Would I give this up for a wife? "Like fuck I would," I said, laughing away to myself. Just then, I was distracted from my thoughts by what could only be described as the sound of exploding thunder.

The Devil Angels were coming up behind me and it looked like there were hundreds of them. I indicated to turn up the lane then decided to block the road to oncoming traffic, which got me a nod from their Sergeant at Arms as he turned in.

I waited until everybody had turned off the main road before I made my move and laughed at my initial estimate of hundreds. I counted around forty bikes, with just over half a dozen them 'two's up'.

When we got to the farm, I couldn't believe the number of bikes that were there; there was hardly any room for any more. The Angels just abandoned theirs where they could and some of them, along with myself, parked on the lane.

Most of the Bats were now outside to greet our guests. Indie and the Angels SAA were already embraced in a manly hug.

I started chatting away with a couple of guys, asking how their trip was and they told me it had been uneventful.

As we talked, I noticed out the corner of my eye that the Devils SAA had summoned a couple of his guys. And along with Indie, Hotwire and Jelly, they disappeared into the farm. I presumed he was filling them in about the spat we'd had and his plans for retribution after Provo's funeral.

I excused myself and went looking for Rooster. But, after checking the barn and the house, I gave up. There were just so many people that it was impossible to find anyone.

Just then, Indie came out and stood on the steps and whistled really loudly. People came out from the barn and the house to join us outside.

My best guess of the number of people, at this point, was about two hundred and fifty to three hundred. There were more people here than at most of the rallies I'd been to.

Indie eventually got everybody's attention and began: "Brothers, firstly, I'd like to thank you all for coming, I'm sure the big man would be well proud." A roar of approval then went up for what seemed like an age.

"Today, we bury not only our President, but our friend. I'm sure you'll all agree: he was a man among men." Again, a huge roar went up.

"When Provo took over as the Bats President we were going nowhere, but he turned it around, and turned us into what we are today. I've never met a man so committed to a cause. His legacy here will live on, way beyond all of us. I just want to say that he was one of the best people I've ever had the pleasure to know and anyone who knew him well would surely agree."

This brought a lot of 'here here's' from people. Indie then said: "I don't want to say anything more just now, but I would like everybody to respect a minute's silence, on behalf of the big man."

Everybody, to a man, lowered their heads; you could have heard a pin drop. Indie then thanked everybody for their respect and told us to make sure we all came straight back to the farm after the funeral.

At that point, it was a mass scramble for everyone to get their bikes. Indie and the Devils SAA had decided we wouldn't be riding in two chapters, but that we would be mixed and had already nominated the outriders.

They both led the procession up the lane, everyone without helmets. It was the biggest I'd been involved in. It was not only an awesome sight, but a fearful one - God forbid that anyone would try to break the ranks.

When we arrived at the Crematorium, the bikes extended from the entrance gate all the way to the service room. There was a contingent of police officers who were trying to direct us to the parking at the rear of the building, but there was no way that we were all going to fit in.

We ended up parking all over the place: on grass verges, next to headstones, and along the side of the road.

We all made our way to the service room. By the time I got there, it was mobbed. I was one of the last to get into the main room (everyone else was directed into the two waiting rooms adjoining the service room).

When we went in, there was some soft classical music playing in the background, but it was switched off as soon as the minister began speaking.

Provo's coffin was sitting on what looked like a table with rollers on it, in front of a couple of small curtains. All the seats were taken, it was three deep in the aisle and all the girls were sitting on people's knees.

The minister began by reminding everyone that they were in God's house but, at the request of the family, this would not be a traditional service. He spoke for a while about Provo: from his childhood, through his teens, and touched briefly on his role within the Black Bats.

I couldn't believe it when he mentioned that Provo had been the dux at his school - that was something no one who knew him recently would ever have imagined.

One of the weirdest things was that the minister never used Provo's real name once. Here I was, sitting at his funeral, and I didn't even know his fuckin name.

The minister then told the congregation to bow their heads and to think of the way Provo had touched their lives during the piece of music which was going to follow and to pray for his soul.

The music began and straight away, I recognised it. It was a song I'd heard a million times at the farm; it was a Moody Blues song called 'Nights in White Satin'.

Listening to the lyrics, it seemed a strange choice of song, but it certainly moved a lot of people. I guessed it was because it was one of his favourite songs and we could all remember him singing along to it.

When it finished, the minister moved over to the coffin and said a few words, followed by the commitment.

The curtains then opened and, as the coffin started to move through them, another song was then played.

It was a Neil Young song called 'Hey Hey, My My (Into the Black)'. This was another one of his favourites. Again, a song I'd heard many times at the farm.

This time the lyrics were spot on and described the big man to a 'T'. The line 'The king has gone, but not forgotten' has stuck with me ever since as a memory of him.

Once the coffin had disappeared and the curtains closed, the minister held his hands up and did the benediction. He then started walking up the aisle and everyone parted in front of him to allow him through.

The next thing, Meatloaf's 'Bat out of Hell' blasted out the speakers and the whole place burst into roars of involuntary laughter.

'Fuck, what a way to go!' I thought to myself. I wondered if he'd told anybody what music he would want or if Indie had picked it.

Waiting to leave the service room with 'Bat out of Hell' ringing in my ears almost made me cry. Just as I got to the door, the words, 'Like a Sinner before the Gates of Heaven, I'll come crawling on back to you' rang out and changed my tearful mood to one of joy, bringing a smile back to my face. I looked around and most of the guys were also smiling.

We all hung around for a bit and I noticed Angel and Fiona standing with Indie at the funeral car. I hadn't seen them since before Provo died and we were told about Stiff. I walked over and touched Fiona on the shoulder. When she saw me, she burst out crying.

I gave her a cuddle and she began to sob much harder. As we cuddled, Angel held her hand out to me and I squeezed it. I told her how sorry I was about Stiff and asked how she was, but she just squeezed my hand back then shook her head, released her hand, then went into the car.

I kissed Fiona on the cheek and told her to look after herself. She kissed me back, never said a word, then joined Angel in the car.

When the car left, Indie started mustering everybody up, telling us it was time to go. We all split up and went looking for our bikes. Indie and the Devil's SAA followed the car to the Crematorium gate then waited for everyone to get in line.

It probably took around fifteen minutes or so for us all to get organised. Indie then set off with everyone following. The police escorted us up the road and shut off the dual carriageway on both sides, allowing us all to leave together.

At the next roundabout, they'd done the same, with motorbike cops at each of the exits, except the one we were turning off.

After this, we were on our own and continued through the next three villages with guys going ahead and closing every exit we were approaching.

We arrived at the lane and turned down, heading to the farm. I wondered where everyone was going to go (as it wasn't possible to fit the amount of people who were there into the farm) but I needn't have worried as Indie had already sorted that out.

He'd emptied the barn. And, after parking up, all the guys followed him in and the girls were directed into the farm. When we got in, the doors were closed and everyone fell silent.

I always thought the barn was huge, but today, it seemed so much smaller with us all crammed in it. Indie stood on a box and started to tell us that he'd arranged for us to go to the local social club later and had agreed with the committee for us to have the whole place to ourselves, which brought a loud cheer from everyone.

He then explained that we were going to attend to our problem from the previous day first. It turned out that the football supporters from a week ago were responsible for the attack and Indie knew they had a home match tonight and told us we were going to pay them a visit at their club.

We were all to head to the social club first, have a couple of beers, then most of us would go sort them out, then return, giving us an alibi for the full day.

The Devil Angels SAA then stood up and asked his guys if they would like to join us and they all roared a resounding 'yes'.

Indie then told us to double up as he wanted as few bikes as possible going. He also said he would be taking the van, which we could probably squeeze around twenty guys into the back of, along with all the weapons we would need.

We all scattered at that point, leaving the prospects to fill the van, then decided who was taking bikes and who would ride pillion. Rooster shouted me over, said he would drive and suggested I jump on the back, which I did.

When we got to the club, the females were already there and the guys who'd arrived before us had already started drinking. The bar was already full of pints and open bottles of beer and the bar staff continued to pour. The people arriving picked up two and three at a time then went to find a seat.

By the time everyone was in, the place was packed and the music was blaring. I sat down with Rooster. We had two bottles of Newcastle each in front of us and were chatting away when I noticed Indie, Hotwire and Jelly going around the room, telling people something.

I asked Rooster what he thought was going on and he told me they were telling everybody who was going and who was staying.

"How the fuck do they decide that then?" I asked him. "Who knows, Shug. Indie will have some daft system worked out, that's for sure."

"Do you reckon we're going?" I quizzed. "Fuck knows, Shug. I expect we will be, but you never know."

Within two minutes of us talking about it, I saw Hotwire walking towards us. I was hoping that he would tell me I was staying, but at the same time, if I wasn't picked to go, I would've been pretty pissed off wondering why.

He came to the table and said: "You two are staying here," then turned to walk away. Now, I understood Rooster not going because of his leg, but why not me? I asked him to wait a minute and he turned around.

"What about me? Why the fuck am I not going?" I demanded him to tell me. "How the fuck should I know, Shug? Best you speak to Indie; he made the decision, not me."

"That's fuckin pish," I told Rooster. "I'm going to see the cunt and find out why the fuck I'm not going." "Shug, I think you should just leave it. He won't take too kindly to anyone having a go today, just relax and enjoy the beer, man."

"It's alright for you to say that, but I want to know why the fuck he's left me out." I then got up and went to speak to him. I saw Cowboy and asked him if he was going and he said he was. 'Fuck, how come he's going and I'm not' I thought.

I approached Indie and asked him why I wasn't going. He said because he'd decided to leave me here. When I asked again, why? He said because I was, and that was the end of it, and to go and sit on my arse.

"That's pish, Indie. I just want you to know I'm not happy ... but I respect your decision," I told him as I walked away. He never said a word and carried on going around speaking to people.

I went back over to Rooster, who was now joined by Cowboy and Flick. "Well?" Rooster asked. "Well, basically he told me to fuck off."

"I fuckin told you, Shug. I fuckin told you to leave it, but you just couldn't, could you? Sometimes you need to listen to people who are giving you good advice and take it on board."

"Oh, like you're the man full of good advice are you?" I ranted back. "What the fuck is that supposed to mean?" he said, in a very aggressive tone, demanding to know.

I then checked myself, realising I nearly mentioned the abortion, then changed what I was really going to say.

"Come on then, Mr Advisor, tell me why Cowboy was selected and I wasn't? Can you advise me on that?" I asked.

"Yes, I can actually, I reckon it's because you act like a dick half the time. My advice to you right now is: shut the fuck up and get the beers in."

Just as I was about to go off on one, he smiled and told me to relax, he was only winding me up. Then the three of them started laughing.

I joined in, more with relief about getting away with what would've been a major disaster and headed to the bar. I let out a sigh as I approached the bar and stood in the queue. I was actually glad to be standing in the queue, it gave me a bit of time for a reality check.

Why the fuck was I so concerned about not going? - I didn't want to go in the first place! Rooster was right about me being a dick half the time.

Why would I want to ride thirty miles to get involved in a fight, then ride thirty miles back, probably bashed up a bit, then lie to the police later that I'd been here all day?

I was nudged out of my daydream by a guy behind me telling me the barmaid wanted my order. "Sorry, mate, miles away there," I told him. "Six Newcastle, please," I told her.

She dumped them in front of me, unopened, pointed to a bottle opener on the wall and started serving the next guy. I guessed somebody would be around for money later.

I got back to the table just as Cowboy was getting ready to leave. I dumped the bottles on the table, shook his hand, told him to be safe, then sat down and watched them all head out the fire doors.

I counted around forty odd guys leaving, at least ten of them were Devils. "Rooster, why do you think the Devils are going and we're left here?"

"Eh, come on, Shug, even you can work that out," he told me. "Well if I could, I wouldn't be asking, now would I?" was my reply.

"Shug, their SAA is showing his support to Indie. That's how it works, man." "Ah, right, I never thought about that, Rooster, it makes sense," I agreed.

"Shug, why don't we change the subject and forget all about it until they come back. Come on, tell me some more about your weekend."

"There's nothing much else to tell. I caught up with Julie and her friends and we spent most of the time talking a lot of shit and curing the world through drink," I told him, hoping that would be it.

"How's the war wound, Flick?" I asked him, changing the subject. "It's okay, Shug, plenty of liquid painkiller is helping me. The doc says I'll be back to normal in a couple of weeks." "I'll drink to that," I told him, raising my glass.

We'd been drinking for about an hour and a half when we heard the bikes arriving back, so someone opened the doors and the guys poured in. I noticed straight away that none of them seemed to be bashed up and as they were all smiles, I guessed that it must've gone pretty well.

The doors were quickly closed and people started gathering around, trying to find out what had happened. We waited at the table, looking for Cowboy to join us and tell us the script.

Within a couple of minutes, he came and sat down, grabbed a bottle, opened it on the side of the table, and took a long drink.

Rooster then said: "I take it you stayed in the van then, pretty boy, I don't see any signs of battle," then laughed.

"For your information: there wasn't a single injury, it went like a dream. I don't reckon they'll be heading back down this way anytime soon," he said, directing his conversation at Rooster.

"Well, come on, spit it out, tell us what happened?" Flick demanded.

"Dead simple: six bikes drew into the car park. They saw us coming and about a dozen of them came rushing out, full of bravado, ready to lay into us. As they approached us, the rest of the guys came around the corner with bats and chains and we kicked the absolute shit out of them. Then we went in and did the same to everybody else in the club. When we came back out, we smacked all the ones who'd got up again, jumped on the bikes and here we are, job done."

There was now a lot of back slapping and cheering going on and the party really began to take off. It was at that point I started to wish I'd brought my own bike so I could fuck off. I just wasn't in the mood and could have seen it all far enough.

A bunch of girls had arrived from fuck knows where and the guys were picking them off as quickly as they came in.

I noticed Indie and the Devils SAA deep in conversation and wondered what the fuck they were hatching now.

With no way of getting home and not wanting to ask anyone for a run, I decided it best just to 'go with the flow' and get pished along with everyone else.

I must have crashed out at some point because I woke up lying on the floor of the barn with a blanket over me, and no fuckin idea how I got there.

Later, it was explained to me that I was put in the van, along with a pile of others, and dumped in the barn.

I was standing outside, the sun was splitting the trees, and felt as rough as a badger's arse so headed into the kitchen for a glass of water. I couldn't believe it! The party was still going on. I grabbed my drink of water and headed back outside, taking a seat on the steps.

I started to think about the elections and who would get what, knowing that it would be happening very soon.

I thought about Angel and Fiona and wondered if anyone from the Bats had visited Stiff. I made a mental note to ask Rooster the next time I saw him.

I decided to have a smoke then head back to the flat. I looked around at all the bikes and noticed that no two were the same.

I could see mine in the distance, at the start of the lane, and thought it was up there with the best of them. I wondered about the individuality of the bikes and how everyone did something that would make theirs slightly different from the rest.

I then thought about the way we dressed. I looked at myself and realised that it was the complete opposite of the bikes, which made me laugh.

I remembered asking Stiff about this not long after I met him and he told me the bike was the mark of the man and the look was to make sure the cops, or anybody else, couldn't tell us apart. I'd been growing my hair and remained unshaven ever since.

I noticed people in the barn starting to come out. Some headed into the farm, nodding as they passed. I decided that it was time for me to split and went back into the house in search of my helmet.

The place was still rocking. There was a chick lying on the kitchen table getting fucked and sucking a dick. I walked through to the hall where lots of the helmets had been dumped, wondering where the fuck all these slutty women actually came from? And why the fuck they wanted to come here?

After a bit of raking, I eventually found my helmet and made my way to my bike. Just as I got to it, I heard Cowboy shouting on me. 'Fuck! Caught!' I thought to myself, 'I was nearly away'. Cowboy came over to me. "Hi, man, what's up?" I asked him. "Just wondered where you were off to? That's all," he replied.

"Need to head home, do some shopping and get cleaned up and shit," I told him. "Thought you may be heading to avoid Rooster," he told me. "Why would I want to do that?" I asked him.

"Come on, Shug, you're not telling me you can't remember arguing with him last night."

"I can hardly remember anything about last night, Cowboy. I don't even know how I got back to the farm, far less any argument."

"Well, Rooster was raging with you so I chucked you in the van, brought you back and dumped you here. I threw a cover over you and left you to sleep it off."

"What were we arguing about?" I asked him. "Well, you told Rooster he was a cunt for wrecking Julie's life and that he should be ashamed of himself. When he asked you what the fuck you were talking about, you jumped up and started pointing at him, telling him he knew why. He then told you that if you mentioned Julie again that he would rip your fuckin head off and so you asked him outside. That's when I intervened and threw you in the van."

'Holy shit, well done again, Shug,' I thought, 'How the fuck am I going to get out of this?' I wondered. I decided that it would be best to deal with it before I left.

"Fuck, Cowboy, do you know where Rooster crashed? I think I need to apologise to him before I leave, for being a dick."

"He's in the farm. But I would be careful what you say; he was proper raging at you. I asked him when I went back what the fuck it was all about and he told me to shut the fuck up, that it was no cunt's business, bar his, then disappeared and I never saw him again."

"Cheers for the heads up, Cowboy," I told him and shook his hand then headed back in. I quickly decided what to tell him and hoped it would be enough to satisfy him. I convinced myself that if I started with an apology that it would defuse some of his anger.

I eventually found him crashed in the conservatory, half-dressed, and guessed he'd had a good night. I kicked his feet and he stirred, looking up at me. "What the fuck do you want?" he asked. "I see somebody had a good night," I told him.

"What the fuck do you want? I asked you," he repeated. "I want to apologise for being a dick last night," I told him.

"You're always a fuckin dick. Why are you only apologising for last night?" he said, sounding pretty aggressive.

"Rooster, sit the fuck up, man, I want to talk to you about Julie." "Don't you think you said enough about her last night?" he warned.

Rooster sat up and rested his back against the wall and I sat down beside him. "Listen, man, I should never have mentioned her last night and, if truth be told, I can't even remember it. Cowboy filled me in earlier."

I gave Rooster a fag and began my story, "When I went to see her, she seemed okay. But after a few drinks, she told me that her life was ruined when you broke up with her and she felt she couldn't stay here. She said she moved away from her job, her family and her friends because she couldn't stand seeing you and not being with you. Then she told me she would never date another man as long as she lived. I asked why she didn't just patch it up with you, but she told me that would never happen as you made it clear that you loved the Bats much more than her and at that point, I thought, 'What a right cunt you were'. I guess I just had way too much to drink on an empty head and started thinking about it. I don't know, man, I can't remember, but I'm sorry for going off on one." I held my hand out, hoping for a handshake, and he obliged.

"Shug, there's more to it than that, but I'm not getting into here. Just remember, there are always two sides to every story, maybe I'll let you know my side one day, but don't ever fuckin mention her to me again, got it?" "No probs, Rooster, consider it done."

Then he did that fuckin thing again - grabbing me and rubbing his fuckin knuckles on my head.

"Why the fuck do you always fuckin do that to me?" I asked him. "Because I know it annoys the fuck out of you, that's why," he said, laughing.

I stood up as he continued to laugh, "We good, man?" I asked, shaking his hand again. "We're good, Shug," he replied. I told him I had to split, but that I would catch him later. He just nodded.

I was heading back for the door, feeling pretty good about squaring things with Rooster, and walked into the kitchen.

The chick on the table now had two dicks in her and one in her mouth. She was lying on top of the guy who was fucking her arse. Another bloke, who was standing at the end of the table, was ramming his length into her pussy while she was sucking the third bloke, who was standing beside the table. There and then, I made a mental note never to eat there again. I noticed that the three guys fucking her were all Devils. I smiled and nodded to them as I passed. 'Fuck me!' I thought as I looked at the clock, it was ten past nine in the fuckin morning. Let me tell you, it's not a sight you'd ever expect to be greeted with at any time, especially not on the table at breakfast. I think I laughed all the way out to my bike.

I headed into the village, picked up a couple of rolls, then made my way to my flat. I went in and closed the door and thought 'Thank fuck!'

I grabbed some juice from the fridge, planted my arse on the couch and wired into the rolls. I started to think about what came next, but really …. I had no idea.

I wondered if Julie would actually submit my application form or if she was just humouring me? I thought again about the elections, about the prospects lying in hospital and about Indie's promise to them that he would sort everything out after the funeral.

I also couldn't understand why there'd been only one visit from the police? Considering all the shit that had gone down in the past couple of weeks, I expected the farm to be crawling with them, but not a single one reappeared.

I finished my rolls and decided to have a kip and try to leave all my woes until I got up.

When I woke up, it was mid-afternoon. I jumped into the bath then grabbed a change of clothes and headed to the shop for some provisions.

The weather was still nice and I could feel the sun warming me as I walked along. I hit the shop, grabbed a rake of stuff then headed back home.

I fired it all into the cupboards and fridge then gave the place a tidy up, wishing to fuck I'd done it before I left.

I filled a couple of rubbish bags with all the shit that was lying around then took them out to the bin.

I met Mark on the way back upstairs and we had a bit of a catch-up. He told me he'd heard that the pigs had been compiling a case against the Bats and were going to be making some arrests soon and suggested I stay clear of the farm for a bit.

I told him I would need to go and let Indie know, but he said that he was already aware of it. I thanked him for the advice and went back into my flat. I sat down, lit up a smoke and as usual, my mind was working overtime.

I began to wonder if they had info on specific people or if they just had evidence on the Bats as a whole. Either way, I was preparing myself for a bit of time in the cells.

I wasn't sure whether to follow Mark's advice or if I should head to the farm and see what they knew. Fuck, another dilemma - my life always seemed to be full of them.

I was at a bit of a loose end for the first time in ages and wasn't sure what I should get up to. I thought about going to the local pub to see if anyone I knew was in. I wondered if I should go back to the farm and talk to Indie? Then I thought, 'Maybe I should give Julie a call and see if she'd handed in my form?'

It was Wednesday afternoon and I decided the pub was out, as most people I knew had jobs. Julie would probably be working as well, so that was out too, so the farm won.

I was curious about how the rest of the night had gone and wondered if all the guys would still be there? I grabbed my gear and headed out.

It was like a proper summer's day and I was glad the sun was out. I jumped on my bike and rode off. The roads were very quiet so instead of going straight to the farm, I decided to take a detour.

I had no idea where I was going and didn't care, I just felt the need to ride around for a bit and enjoy the freedom that it offered.

I rode through the village and decided to head for the seaside. I chose all the side roads I could, doing my best to avoid the motorways and dual carriageways.

I rode for almost an hour and arrived at a seaside car park. It was even warmer there than when I'd left my flat. There was a barrier and a dude sitting in a little hut, like a sentry box.

I drew up at the barrier and he told me I had to go to the 'top car park'. I told him I wanted to go down to the beach, but he insisted I would need to park here and walk down.

'Fuck that' I thought to myself. "Lift the fuckin barrier and let me drive down," I shouted at him "Stop being a fuckin prick, there isn't a single cunt here, bar me."

"Don't you swear at me or I'll call the police," was his reply. Then he started spieling a lot of shite about rules and regulations and I thought 'Fuck him!'

I drove around the barrier and proceeded down the hill with his threats of the police 'being on their way' ringing in my ear.

'Fuckin police on their way, his arse. It would take him half an hour to get to the phone box. Fuckin idiot!' I mumbled to myself.

As I drove down the hill, I could smell the sea air and inhaled it deeply. The sun was shining on the water and the reflection was blinding, the sea was a bit choppy and the tide looked like it was coming in.

I followed the winding road to the beach and stopped my bike in a small car park that was right on the seafront. I kept thinking about the dick at the top, wondering why he was being such a wanker.

I stood there, looking about the place for a bit, and noticed there was only a scattering of people around. 'And he wanted me to walk half a mile for fuck all, fuckin dick,' I mumbled to myself.

I then noticed an ice cream shop and decided to treat myself to a chocolate wafer. I bought it and sat on the beach.

As I ate, I tried to remember the last time that I'd had one. I must have been about eleven or twelve. Usually, when the icy came, my mum was out and I never had any money. I would watch everybody else gather around the van; they always left smiling happily with their purchases, and I would always feel really sad.

One particular night, my mum was in when he came and, as usual, she had a man in her bedroom - if I wanted anything then this was always the best time to ask.

I heard the chimes and knocked her door, asking for money. She shouted, "Take some money from my purse, darling." Which I did, then raced out. I was standing in the queue, really excited, wondering what to buy.

My choice was a chocolate wafer, a '99' or an oyster. When my turn came, I decided on a '99' with sauce and sprinkles. The man asked what I wanted and I told him. "Nae flakes, I'll gie yie a wafer," he told me as he took my money. He then handed me my '99' cone with a wafer on top, minus the flake, and said: "Next!"

I went around the back of my house, sat on the steps, looked out across the park, and ate it like I was eating a king's banquet.

I smiled to myself as I finished and wondered if anyone else at that age would've been so excited just to get something from the ice cream man?

It made me feel really sad that this was one of the outstanding highlights of my childhood. Others spoke of holidays, and stuff they had been bought. And me? ... A fuckin cone with a wafer! It almost brought a tear to my eye just thinking about it.

I was miles away, staring at the sea, enjoying the sun, and at the same time depressing myself with my shitty fuckin memories, when someone tapped me on the shoulder.

I turned and looked up, it was a woman about thirty. I stood up and asked her what she wanted and she asked if the bike in the car park was mine, which made me laugh - there wasn't another person within five hundred yards and I was sitting with a bike jacket on and a helmet next to me.

I thought she was something to do with 'Mr Jobsworth' from earlier on and I was getting ready to tell her to fuck off as well when she pointed over to a little boy standing beside my bike. "That's my son over there," she told me. "He's mad on motorbikes and I can't drag him away from yours. Is there any chance you could hold him on it and let me take a picture?"

I looked at her and thought how lovely she looked. She had a tight fitting blouse on and you could just see the very top of her cleavage, nothing showing, just the shape of the start of her tits. Her skirt was knee length and she had flat shoes on. Her hair was short in a side shed and she was very pretty.

"No problem," I told her. "I'd be delighted." She smiled and said: "That's great, he'll be over the moon, thanks very much."

As we walked towards my bike, she told me that she'd spent the last ten minutes wondering whether or not to come and ask me. "If truth be told, I was a bit frightened to ask. I wasn't sure what kind of reaction I would get from you and thought you may think I was stupid."

"Did you think I might rape you and eat your son or something?" I asked her, laughing.

"No, nothing like that, but you hear such terrible stories about people in biker gangs and when I saw your gang thing on the back of your jacket, I have to admit I was really nervous asking."

"Don't believe all you read," I told her. "A reporter once told me that when they write anything about bikers and their exploits: half of it is made up and the other half is lies."

I knelt down and spoke to her son; I reckoned he was about four or five. "What's your name, son?" "I'm James. Can I sit on your motorbike, please?"

"You're very polite," I told him. "Can I please get a shot on your motorbike?" he said again, ignoring my compliment.

His mother told him not to be rude, but he just looked at her and said he wanted a shot on my bike.

"Okay, come on then," I told him and lifted him on. I put him on the seat and straight away, he leaned forward, reaching for the handlebars.

He was just able to touch them and no more. His mother got out her Polaroid camera and went to the front of the bike.

I was holding the kid and asked him if he wanted me to let him go for the photo. He just nodded so I stood back and she took a couple of shots.

She put her camera back in her bag and stood with the photos, waving them about, waiting on them developing.

I asked James if he wanted to have a ride and he squealed with excitement, shouting: "Yes please" half a dozen times.

His mother tried to coax him out of it and suggested to me that she didn't think it was a good idea, but I reassured her he would be fine and told her that I'd give him my helmet.

I got on behind James and fired it up, pulling the throttle right back at the same time, making as much noise as I could. I wasn't sure who got the biggest fright out of the two of them, but they both jumped.

I backed out of the car park with his mother's shouts of 'Be careful' ringing in my ears. James held onto the handlebars as we rode out.

I headed along the path a few hundred yards then turned and came back. When I stopped, she asked if she could take a photo of the both of us on the bike and I agreed.

Again, she took two snaps before I rolled the bike back into the car park. I then lifted James off and parked it up.

James asked his mum to see the photos and she gave him the first two. She was waving the other two about like she did before.

I sat on the grass and lit up a fag. I offered her one and she said she would have it when she was done with the photos.

She chatted with James, talking about the pictures in his hand, and he told her how cool it was getting a ride on my bike. I looked out at sea, thinking I'd done my good deed for the day.

She gave James the other photos and he headed down the beach, smiling like he'd won the football pools. His mum sat next to me and I gave her a fag.

"I'm Beth, by the way," she told me, holding her hand out. "Shug," I said, giving it a bit of a shake. "Thank you very much for that, he loved it, he'll talk about this incessantly for a long time. Ever since his dad's funeral, he's been obsessed with bikes; he never passes one without stopping. He has hundreds of toy ones in the house."

"Why did he become obsessed after the funeral?" I asked her, curiously. "One of his dad's best friends had a motorbike. Like you, he was in a gang and he turned up at the funeral on his bike, dressed like you, and James couldn't keep his eyes off him. When we went outside, he ran over to the bike and stood staring at it for ages. When I pulled him away, he burst out crying. Everyone thought it was grief. But when we got into the car, I tried to console him and he told me he was upset because I'd taken him away from the motorbike, that's when his obsession began."

I asked her when her husband died. "When James was three, which is nearly two years ago now," she told me. "If you don't mind me asking, what happened to him?" I enquired.

"Cancer, we didn't even know he had it. He collapsed at work and was taken to hospital, but he never came back out. They discovered a massive brain tumour and he died within two weeks."

"James was too young to understand and never asks about him. I guess I'll need to tell him all about it in a few years' time."

I didn't really know what to say and told her it was a shame when people die unexpectedly, especially young people, and she just nodded in agreement.

She then stood up and said she would need to go and get James. She then thanked me again for giving him a run on my bike.

I stood up and told her it was my pleasure and that I'd enjoyed it. Then, out of the blue, she asked me if I wanted to join them for a fish tea.

The invite kind of threw me a bit and I blurted out, "A fish tea? Sure. Whereabouts?"

"There's a great place on the main street we always go to when we come to the beach and the food is delicious," she told me, then ran off down the beach to get James.

I thought to myself 'Widowed, invite for tea and very fuckable'. I hoped I wasn't reading the signals wrong, but I was beginning to think she may want a bit more than company over dinner, or so I hoped.

I was still daydreaming about the possibility of shagging her when she arrived back with James.

"Our car's at the top of the hill. We'll meet you there and you can follow us to the café."

"Don't be silly, I'll take you up on my bike. James, do you want another ride on my bike?" I asked him and he nodded and let out a cheer.

Beth then said she would just walk. But, after a bit of coaxing, I got her to agree to ride pillion.

I started my bike up and lifted James onto the front. He was sitting half on the tank and half on me. I put my helmet on him then concentrated on his mum. Beth swung her leg over and sat behind me. I told her to wrap her arms around me and relax.

She told me she'd never been on a bike before and was absolutely terrified. I reassured her by telling her I was a great rider and that she had absolutely nothing to worry about.

We moved off slowly and, at every turn of the wheel, I felt Beth squeezing tighter and tighter. James, on the other hand, was having a ball.

We got to the top of the hill, went around the barrier, and I drew up alongside the only car in the car park, assuming it was hers.

She got off and I lifted James onto the ground, "Well, how do you feel after your first time on a bike?" I asked her.

"It was certainly an experience," she told me, "but I had my eyes closed all the way." I laughed and suggested she should come for a proper ride some time and surprisingly, she said she would like that.

They jumped into the car and she gestured for me to follow. As we headed out the car park, old 'Mr Jobsworth' held his hand up for me to stop, but I just growled at him on the way past and he returned to his little hut.

The café was only a couple of minutes from the beach and Beth went into the car park at the rear and I parked right outside in front of the window.

I went inside and Beth was already there, talking to a waitress. She'd come in the back door and was already heading for a seat.

"Hope you don't mind, I've ordered for you," she told me. "No, that's no probs. So what do I fancy eating then?" I asked her, smiling.

"A fish tea with mushy peas, bread and butter, and a cup of tea," she told me.

"What are you having, James?" I asked him. "Fish," was all he said. He still had the photos in his hand and when I asked him which one he liked the best, he showed me the one of both of us on the bike then continued to look at them.

I then turned my attention to Beth. "So where do you live, Beth? Are you close to here?"

"About fifteen minutes north of here," she told me. "I'll need to get James home and into bed after his tea, he's got school tomorrow. We like to come to the beach as often as we can and we always end up in here. I normally have him in bed by eight most nights. So by the time he's eaten his dinner, he'll be ready to go down for the night. I don't want him falling asleep in the car or he'll not settle."

I wondered if she was telling me this to let me know she would be alone or if she was just making conversation.

The dinner came and while we ate, we chatted away about superficial stuff. When we finished, I went to pay for it, but she was adamant it was her treat, so after a bit of toing and froing, I agreed to let her.

When we were getting ready to go, I thanked her for a lovely day and told her it was a pleasure to meet her and her son, then gave her a cuddle.

She then told me that after meeting me, I'd totally changed her opinion of people with bikes. I reminded her that there WERE lots of crazy dudes out there with bikes who DIDN'T give a shit.

We laughed and I walked her to her car. She put James in his car seat and closed the door. We cuddled again and I asked her if I was getting invited for coffee, but she told me she didn't think it was a good idea. "Okay, no probs, just thought I'd chance my barra," I told her.

She laughed and said: "Anyway, Shug, you'd just be disappointed," smiled then got into the car. I laughed to myself as she left, thinking 'What a dick I was. Why would someone like her ever want to shag me?'

I walked around the side of the building to get my bike and she was sitting waiting to get out onto the main road. I walked past her and we both waved.

I got on my bike and drew out onto the road then stopped to let her out. She turned the same way as me and I followed her for a couple of miles before she indicated to turn right.

She rolled her window down, stuck her arm out, and pointed the way she was turning. I thought something was wrong and turned in behind her. I was expecting her to stop, but she carried on for about half a mile then turned left.

We headed into a new estate and she turned into a driveway. I followed her in and switched off my bike. Beth got out the car and told me to wait a minute.

She opened the door of the double garage and drove her car in. She then told me to go around the back as she was taking James up the stairs, then she would open the door.

I walked around the back and sat on the step. I lit up a fag and wondered what the fuck was going on. One minute, I've had a knockback, the next, I'm being directed to her house.

Beth opened the door and ushered me in, telling me to be quiet. I walked into her kitchen and she pointed to a door and told me to put my bike in the garage.

"Make yourself comfy. Get a coffee or grab a beer from the fridge. I'm going to put James to bed, I'll be about fifteen minutes or so," then she went back upstairs.

I opened the garage door and wheeled my bike in. I reckoned she wanted me to stay the night. I started to think about the older chicks that Malky and I had shagged in the caravan and hoped she would be just as raunchy.

I closed the garage door, grabbed a beer from the fridge, took my jacket and boots off, and planted my arse on the couch.

Her house was pretty big for just two of them, and it looked like she had a few bob. I wondered what the fuck she was wanting with me and decided she must have fancied a bit of rough.

I'd just got myself another beer and sat back down when she came into the room. I noticed she had changed and now had a pair of jogging bottoms and a t-shirt on. She'd let her hair down and cleaned her makeup off.

I guessed my plan of her wanting to shag me was off the table. I thought if she'd brought me back to seduce me then she would've dressed a bit differently.

"Going to grab myself a drink, do you want another?" she asked. "Just got one, thanks," I told her.

To my surprise, she came back with a can of beer. I expected her to bring a glass of wine, or at least something in a glass.

She sat down beside me on the couch and I asked her why she'd changed her mind about inviting me back. She said she'd felt guilty about not inviting me back after I'd been so good with James.

"I guess you wanted my bike in the garage to hide it from the neighbours, in case they saw you with an undesirable in your posh estate?"

"Actually, I thought it would be better in there if you were staying over. It's forecast for rain later," she told me. 'Fuck', I thought to myself 'She does want to shag me after all'.

"Is that an offer?" I asked her. "Do you want it to be?" she replied. "I would love it to be," I told her. "Okay then, it's an offer." We smiled at each other then laughed.

"Shug, just to let you know, I've not been with anyone since my husband died and I've no idea how I ended up inviting you back. I think you're probably the first person, out with my family and close friends, that I've connected with in a long time. Everybody sees me as the poor widow and they've all forgotten that I'm still a person in my own right."

"Listen, Beth, I don't have any preconceived ideas about anyone or anything. I take everybody as I find them. All I give a fuck about is how people treat me and how I get along with them. If they have shit going on then that's their business."

"Shug, I can't believe how mature you are in your thinking, that's really refreshing," she told me.

I laughed and told her she wouldn't have been thinking that if she knew what was going on in my head on the way there.

"Go on then, Shug, tell me what you were thinking." "You sure you really want to know, Beth? It's not pretty," I told her. "Of course, I do. I wouldn't have asked if I didn't." I thought 'Fuck it, I'll tell her it all'. So I told her about the caravan adventure then about how I'd hoped for a similar experience with her.

She seemed a bit shocked, but not so much that she looked like she would throw me out. I thought, however, I best change the subject a bit so asked her what she'd meant earlier when she said 'I'd only be disappointed'?

"Well, Shug, I've only ever been with one man, but I'm guessing that you would have seen a fair bit of sexual action being in a bike gang if all the stories we hear are true. So I was thinking that you doing anything with me would probably be pretty boring by comparison. Anyway, I'm not exactly an oil painting at my age," she told me.

"Well, firstly, you shouldn't believe all you hear," I told her "and secondly, I've seen loads of people your age and you're well up there with the best of them in terms of looks, and you've still got a great figure, so you should stop putting yourself down."

"Thanks, Shug, I appreciate the compliment, even if it's just because you're trying to get into my pants, it's nice to hear."

"Beth, as much as I would love to fuck you, I'm not just saying it because of that, I'm telling you the truth." She then leaned over and gave me a kiss on the cheek and said: "Thanks."

I was getting a bit bored with all the chit-chat and decided to go for it. "So, Beth, are we going to fuck or not?" I asked her. "Holy shit, Shug, that was a bit direct," she told me.

"Well, Beth, I need to know if you want to fuck or if you're just wanting a bit of company. I don't want to read the signals the wrong way and end up making an arse of myself."

"Jeez oh, Shug, you don't beat about the bush, that's for sure," she told me. "When I asked you to come for coffee I did have it in mind, but I didn't know if I'd be able to go through with it." "And what about now?" I wanted to know.

"Can we just kiss and cuddle for a bit, and see how it goes?" she asked. "Beth, that's fine by me, I just wanted to know where I stood."

We then had a bit of an awkward moment where we sort of sat looking at each other. I lifted her can from her and put both of them on the table.

I took her hands in mine and told her I was fine if she didn't feel she could do it, but she told me she felt she needed to.

I leaned forward and kissed her, firstly on the lips, then the cheek, then I moved down to her neck. I put my arms around her and gently massaged her back. She then cuddled me and was panting a bit and I could feel her shaking.

I told her to relax and pulled her on top of me, letting her feel like she was in control. We kissed for a bit and I stuck my tongue in her mouth and she responded by doing the same back.

I slipped my hands under her t-shirt and continued with the gentle massage. I had my legs open and Beth was in between them. I felt myself getting a bit of a hard-on and I knew Beth could feel it.

I slid one of my hands down into her trackies and started rubbing her bum, she responded by grinding softly into my dick.

I put both hands on her bum, massaging her cheeks, then slid them under her knickers.

My hands were now on her bare arse and I was pushing her hips and groin into mine. She started panting again and began biting my lip.

By now, I was sliding my hand down between her cheeks and rubbing a bit of her pussy with my fingers. She was already soaking wet, and every time I tickled her, she groaned and pressed herself hard against me.

She was now tugging at my t-shirt and trying to unbuckle my belt so I pulled off her top and suggested we got on the floor. She just nodded and never said a word.

When we stood up, we started kissing again and she removed my jeans. I unclipped her bra and pulled down her trackies and pants. She yanked my t-shirt off and we were now both bollock naked.

I picked her up by the arse and she wrapped her legs around me. I walked over to the fireplace and laid her down on the sheepskin rug.

I got on top of her and pushed my cock between her legs, resting it on her pussy. I fondled her breasts and we kissed some more. She was tugging and pulling at my arse, trying to get me inside her.

"Come on, Shug, please put it in, I need it so much," she told me, almost begging. I never said anything, I just continued to tease her.

She was bucking underneath me and trying to edge her pussy in the direction of my cock, but every time I felt the tip on her lips, I moved away.

"Come on, Shug, please stop fucking about, I need you to shag me right now," she told me. Then she grabbed my dick with her hand and rammed it home. She wrapped her legs tightly around me and dug her nails into my back, causing me to let out a roar.

She was shagging me from underneath; I was no longer in charge, I just had to go with the flow. She was biting at my face and ears and I was starting to get the feeling she was out of control.

Then she screamed and squeezed even harder for a few seconds, then relaxed. She was panting really heavily now and her body was covered in sweat.

"Oh, Shug, you've no idea how much I needed that. In fact, I had no idea how much I needed that," she whispered, laughing in my ear. "Come on, Shug, turn over, I want to fuck you until you come."

She moved off me and I rolled onto my back. She then mounted me, slipped my dick into her pussy, leaned back, then gyrated up and down, pushing her pussy as far onto me as she could.

I was really enjoying the position, but not as much as Beth as I watched her come again and again. Eventually, she couldn't go any more and collapsed beside me, out of breath and still dripping in sweat.

"Did you enjoy that, Beth?" I asked her, cuddling in. "Jeezus, Shug, did I enjoy it? You have no idea how much. I think I've just had an internal explosion."

I laughed at her description of coming, I'd never heard of it as an 'internal explosion' before, but thought it sounded quite cool.

As she got her breath back, she started rubbing my dick and it instantly returned to all its glory. "What about sucking me off?" I asked her.

What she said next shocked me to bits. "Shug, I don't really know how to do it. I've never actually done it before, but I'm willing to give it a try."

"You're shitting me, Beth, come on, you're at the wind-up?"
"No, honestly, Shug. My husband was always on at me to do it, but I told him I couldn't. The thought of it always made me feel sick. It's one of the things I now regret as I was his only partner and he never had a blowjob in the whole of his life. So I promised myself, if I ever had another partner, I would try it with them."

She then knelt beside me and took my dick in her hand. She cupped my balls with her other hand and gently lowered her head. She closed her eyes, stuck out her tongue, and licked around the tip. She said it tasted strange, but nice. I told her she was licking her own juices off it and she pulled away.

"Beth, relax, most females I've been with love the taste of their own juices. Come on, keep licking, trust me, you'll enjoy it." She lowered her head and this time put my dick into her mouth. I held her head and guided it up and down in a slow and steady motion until she got the gist of it, I then removed my hands.

I lifted her onto me and manoeuvred her pussy towards my mouth. I then started to lick her out, paying particular attention to her clit. She started bucking up and down and I had to stop her sucking on my dick as she started biting it really hard.

She sat up and put her hands on my stomach and continued to bounce up and down on my face. She was coming again and this time I thought she wasn't going to stop. Then she let out a scream and, as she did earlier, collapsed in a heap on top of me.

I turned her around and cuddled her again, letting her get her breath back. "Well, how do you feel about blowjobs now, Beth?" I asked.

"Shug, that was just so good. And you're right, I did enjoy the taste of my own juices. But I have to admit, I loved you doing it to me much, much, more. That was the first time anyone has ever put their tongue down there and it felt awesome. I can't believe how much I enjoyed it. I could never get away from the fact that I thought it was a really dirty thing to do, and stupidly, I thought if he put his mouth down there that I would never be able to let him kiss me again."

I looked at her and burst out laughing and she joined in. Fuck, I couldn't believe what I was hearing, someone of her age not giving or getting a blowjob, what a fuckin waste of life!

"Beth, I can't get my head around why your man didn't force the issue with you. If it had been me, I would have needed to know what you liked and didn't like way before I even thought about marriage."

"Shug, Colin, my man, was so sweet and gentle. He never forced me to do anything I thought I wouldn't like to and just accepted it was one of the things that was 'off-limits'."

I thought to myself he sounded like a 'right fud' but never said anything about him. "Have you ever had it doggie style?" I asked her.

"We tried it a few times, but we never seemed to get it right. It always seems such an awkward thing to do so we eventually just stopped trying."

"Right, Beth, come on, let's do it." "Shug, I don't think I could. I'm done in. I'm not sure if I'll ever come again, I've come so much already," she told me.

"Beth, you let me worry about that. Come on, get up. She stood up and I picked up the sheepskin and led her to the dining table. I pushed all the shit on it out of the way then threw the rug on it.

I stood her at the end of the table and bent her over. She rested the top half of her body on the table, gripping the sides with her hands.

I slipped my dick into her and started gently moving in and out. As I entered, she was squirming a bit and making a few noises. I started tickling her arsehole and putting the tip of my finger in, just, and no more.

Beth, by this time, was ramming her arse against me, using the table for leverage. She was fuckin loving it and was telling me not to stop and to keep fucking her hard.

As I fucked harder and faster, her moans and groans got louder and louder, I could actually feel her cum running down my leg, she was that wet.

The table we were fuckin on was right next to the window so I decided to open the blinds and see what was outside. Fuck, Beth nearly had a heart attack and screamed at me to close them. "Beth, it's dark, and it's just your garden, no one will see us," I told her.

"Shug, shut the fuckin blinds, now!" she demanded. I closed them over and she let out a sigh of relief and we continued fucking.

I started sticking my finger further and further up her arse and eventually, I had three fingers in. Beth, by this time, was so out of it that I'm not sure she knew what was going on. So I decided to fuck her up the arse (I guessed this was something else she wouldn't have tried!). I whipped my dick out and pushed it straight into her arse and she let out another scream.

"Shug, what the fuck are you doing?" she asked, turning her head around. "Beth, relax, take it easy, you'll love it," I told her. I picked up the pace and started ramming into her as fast as I could while rubbing her clit with my hand. She was screaming so loudly that I had to put my other hand over her mouth to muffle the sound. I took my hand from her pussy and grabbed her hair, pulling her head back, and she started biting my hand.

I felt myself going to cum and went for it for all I was worth. By this time, Beth was grunting and heaving. I pulled out and turned her around, sticking my dick in her mouth and shooting my load.

Beth started spluttering and choking before pulling my dick out of her mouth. She swallowed some of it and the rest was running down her chin and onto her tits.

I grabbed hold of her and cuddled her (I was actually holding her up, she seemed unable to stand on her own accord).

I lifted her up and moved over to the couch. I then sat down with her on my lap. She had her arms around my neck and I gave her a kiss. She started sobbing, then crying, and the tears were flooding out of her.

'Fuck, here we go again' I thought to myself, 'First Julie, now Beth. What is it with me that every time I shag someone they end up in fuckin tears?'

I tried to console her as best I could and asked her what was wrong. She took a minute to answer as she tried to compose herself.

"I have no idea why I'm crying, Shug. Suddenly, I feel really emotional and it's all just coming out. I'm sorry, I can't help it," she told me.

I cuddled her in some more and told her she was fine and she should get it all out. Fuck, she sobbed for about another ten minutes. I tried to talk to her a couple of times, but she just nodded.

My chest was soaking wet from her tears and I decided enough was enough. "Come on, Beth, let's get cleaned up," I told her, moving her from my lap. "Where's the loo?" I asked and she pointed to a door.

"Through that door, first on the right," she told me. I got up and headed out. I stood in the loo, staring at the mirror above the cistern. I thought to myself 'Fuck, Shug, you can pick them, that's for sure'.

I finished my pish and went back into the living room. Beth had already dressed, put the sheepskin back on the floor, and was rearranging the table.

I picked up my clothes and started dressing. While I was putting my clothes on, she went into the kitchen. When I was dressed, I went to see what she was doing.

She was standing at the sink, staring out the window. I went behind her and put my arms around her waist. "You okay?" I asked her. "No, not really, Shug. I can't believe what just happened. I was like a whore in there. I feel so dirty - like I've just desecrated my husband's memory."

I could see in the reflection of the window that the tears were running down her cheeks again. "Hey, come on, Beth, you've done nothing wrong. He's been gone for two years. You're still a young woman; he wouldn't expect you to be celibate for the rest of your life."

She never even turned around, she just kept staring out the window, then said: "Shug, I'm sorry, but I need you to go."

"What?" I said. "Please, Shug, can you just go?" I tried to ask her why, but she just repeated her request. I thought 'Ah well, fuck it, I suppose she's embarrassed'.

I kissed her on the back of the head and went back into the living room. I sat down, put my boots on then stood up, put my jacket on, grabbed my helmet, glanced at the clock then went back into the kitchen.

Beth was still staring out of the window. "Beth, that's me ready to go," I told her, then stupidly asked, "Will I see you again?"

"Oh, I don't think so, Shug, this was a one-off for me." She never took her eyes off the window as she spoke. "Okay, Beth, thanks for a lovely day," I told her and headed into the garage for my bike.

I opened the garage door and wondered if I should let it rip outside, or if I should push it down the street a bit.

I closed the door and went back inside. "I'm off, Beth, sorry it didn't turn out how you wanted it to, take care of yourself." I went back into the living room and was going towards the front door when she came running through.

"Shug, wait." I turned around and she put her arms around me. "I'm sorry, I didn't mean to act like an idiot. It's just I felt so dirty and I didn't know what to do. I just wanted you to go, I couldn't look at you because of how I felt about myself, I'm really sorry."

"Beth, listen, you're fine, it must have been really hard for you. After having such a good time - you're bound to feel guilty, but trust me, I've been there, by tomorrow morning, you'll be smiling and thinking about what a nice time we had."

"I hope so, Shug, and thanks for being so understanding," she told me. We then kissed for a bit and I told her I should really go.

She said I was welcome to stay, but I declined her offer. I couldn't face listening to any more of her guilt-tripping shit; I had enough of my own pish to deal with.

I went out, pushed my bike down the street a bit then fired it up. It was after two in the morning and it was pitch black. In the quiet of the night, it sounded like thunder. I clicked it into gear then shot off.

I started laughing to myself, thinking I should go to the seaside more often. I could feel the cold biting and I wanted to get home as quickly as possible so I didn't hang about.

Chapter 15

I hardly saw another vehicle all the way home. I really enjoyed the run: it was pitch black, I had my full beam on, the moon was shining bright and if it hadn't been for the cold wind, it would've been perfect.

It took me around forty minutes to get home. I opened the door and, again, there was a note on the floor: 'Farm'. Fuck, does it never stop!

I wondered how long it had been there and wasn't sure if I should go just now or leave it until morning. I decided I'd better go and see what the fuck was going on.

I about turned and headed back downstairs to my bike. Again, I rolled it down the street a bit, this time not wanting to wake Mark's kid.

I arrived at the farm ten minutes later and it looked pretty quiet. I was hoping that, whatever it was, it was now dealt with.

Then, I thought if it was, would Indie throw another wobbly at me? 'What was the worst?' I wondered, 'Better with a bollocking than a kicking' I decided as I headed in.

The place was eerily quiet. I went into the kitchen then the conservatory and there was no one there. I went into the big room and it was empty as well. I headed upstairs to check the rooms. I opened the first one and it was empty.

I was starting to panic a bit. Never, in all the time I'd been coming here, had it ever been empty. I opened the next room and thankfully, there was someone there. I switched on the light and there were four girls sleeping on the bed.

I recognised them. They were all girlfriends of the guys. I woke one of the girls, her name was Lizzy.

"What the fuck's going on, Lizzy? There's not a single cunt here. Where the fuck is everybody?" I asked her.

"Shug, is that you?" she asked. "Yes, it is, where the fuck is everybody?" I asked her again. "Not sure, they all raced away a couple of hours ago, must have been something important, though, because Indie told the guys to go and get everybody before they left."

I turned around and went downstairs. 'Holy shit' I thought to myself 'What the fuck's going on? What the fuck will I do? Where the fuck are they?'

I walked through the house and back out the door. I stood outside, looking up the lane, wondering if I should go and have a look around.

Then, I thought about it and decided that was a stupid idea as they could be absolutely anywhere.

I lit up a fag and sat on the step. It was now after three and I knew it must be something big as they very rarely sorted business out at this time in the morning.

I sat staring into space for about ten minutes then headed back inside. I felt pretty agitated and started to wonder if I should go home or if I would be better to stay and greet them when they arrived back.

I must have crashed out as I woke with the smell of bacon coming from the kitchen. I walked through and checked the clock, it was now half past nine and still no one had returned.

Lizzie was cooking breakfast and the others were sitting at the table, smoking and drinking tea. I asked if anyone had heard from anybody, but they all shook their heads.

I poured myself a cuppa and sat down. "You must have an idea where they went?" I suggested to everyone.

"Come on, can't you think of anything that was said before they left? Did anyone mention a person, a place or some fuckin thing that might give me a clue?" I asked.

I stared at them all, waiting for some kind of response, but they just shrugged and looked around at each other. Fuck, I was getting nowhere fast and didn't have a clue what to do next.

Lizzy then told me I should just relax and wait on them coming back and then I'd find out where they'd been.

"Aye, guid yin, Lizzy, why didn't I think of that! Fuck's sake, I'm trying to find out where they are so I can go and help out with whatever the fuck they're doing and you come up with that, fuckin great plan, well done."

I got up from the table, shook my head at her and walked out, mumbling to myself about her being a thick cunt. I went back outside and planted my arse on the step.

I decided to have a fag then go for a scout around. If I couldn't find them I reckoned I should head back to the flat and give Mark a shout and see if he knew anything. He always seemed to know more about what was going on than anybody.

I'd just started my bike up and was putting my helmet on when I clocked a bike coming down the lane so I switched it off and removed my helmet. As the bike drew closer, I realised it was Flick and thought, 'Thank fuck, at last someone who'll know what's going on'.

He drew up and parked alongside my bike. I hardly let him get off it before I asked him if he knew where the fuck everyone was.

"Shug, give me a minute, for fuck's sake, man," he told me. "Sorry, man, but I've been going off my fuckin nut here, wondering what the fuck's going on."

"Come on, let's go inside and I'll tell you all about it," he suggested. We went in and straight through to the conservatory. "Right, Flick, spill the beans," I almost demanded of him.

"Fuck, Shug, you need to calm your jets, man," he told me.

"Calm my fuckin jets! Fuck's sake, Flick, you've no idea what's been running through my mind all night. I've been going off my fuckin nut trying to find out where the fuck everybody is so come on, man, spit it out."

Flick then started to explain: "Indie got a call from one of the Devil Angels, telling him that their clubhouse had been destroyed and that they'd all been wasted. He said that it was down to a new biker gang called 'The Cannibals', who'd just moved into the area. He told him that they'd tied a few of them up and that their President then beat some of them to a pulp and told them that they'd to get out of town as they were taking over. Then he burned their patches. The guy reckoned that they decided to strike because the Devils President and some of the officers were still in jail. Indie asked him where they could meet then told him he would bring everyone up and help sort it out. Within an hour, everyone was off. I was arranging to get a lift home to get my bike, but Indie told me I wasn't going, that I would be more of a hindrance than a help, he said my wound would fuck me up and told me to stay at the farm. I got

Cowboy to drop me off so I could pick up my bike, just in case I needed it, and decided to crash at home to get a decent sleep."

"Holy fuck, Flick, how serious is this? And how come Indie is rushing up there to get involved when really it's nothing to do with us?" I asked him.

"Well, Shug, Indie told us he'd already heard of this new mob and knew they were planning to take over Scotland. He said they'd already secured a base way up north and were now starting to work their way down. Apparently, Indie and the Devils Prez had agreed to join together to sort it out. They'd concocted a plan at the last run to go up north and wipe them all out, but it had to be put on hold when the guys got jailed. So, whenever he got the call, he decided we needed to go straight away and deal with it."

"Fuckin hell, man, that's some pretty heavy shit that's going down. And here I am, sitting here, twiddling my thumbs, doing fuck all. Do you think I should head up north and join them?" I asked him.

"Shug, they're probably on their way back home by now. If I was you, I'd sit tight," was his advice.

"You're probably right, Flick, but I fuckin hate sitting about waiting, plus I know Indie will go off his fuckin nut at me for not being there."

"Shug, listen, I've missed a few, as you know, and when it happens there's nothing you can do. By the time they get back Indie will have way much more to do than bollock you, so I wouldn't worry about it."

I knew he was right, but I still couldn't help thinking that he would find time to have a go, he always did. "Where the fuck were you anyway, Shug?" he asked.

I told him all about going to the beach, about meeting Beth, her kid with my bike, and the whole saga of ending back at her place.

While I was telling him, I could see a broad smile coming over his face and by the time I'd finished, he was doubled up laughing.

"What the fuck are you laughing at?" I demanded him to tell me.

"Ha ha, only fuckin you, ha ha. I bet you're the only cunt who could pick up a neurotic, psychotic, widowed, fuckin born again virgin, mother at a beach then go back to hers after a fish tea and bang her fuckin brains out, ha ha. You just couldn't make it up; that's fuckin brilliant. Remind me to tell the guys when they get back, that's sure to cheer them up, ha ha."

"You'll be telling them fuck all," I said, smiling. "One word from you and I'll be poking you in the guts with a sharp stick," I said, smiling at him. We both had a bit of a laugh at that point and it seemed to lighten the mood.

The rest of the day was really long and if it hadn't been for the girls walking about half naked and feeding us, I think we would have gone stir crazy.

We both crashed out around eleven. When I woke up in the morning, I had a cover over me. I guess one of the girls must have thrown it over me before they headed to bed.

Chapter 16

I got up and noticed Flick was still sound asleep. I went to the kitchen to check the time. It was nine-thirty and still no sign of them. I stuck the kettle on and went outside.

I stood, staring up the lane, almost wishing them to turn in, but there was hardly even a motor on the road. I was starting to get a really bad feeling about the whole fuckin thing and, as usual, my mind was working overtime.

They'd now been away nearly two full days and we had no way of contacting them. I couldn't decide if they were in hospital, jail or just staying on to celebrate a victory - not knowing was driving me crazy.

I went inside and made myself a cuppa then went back outside, sat down and lit up a fag. I was miles away when Lizzy came out. She had a blanket wrapped around her and she sat down beside me. She also had a cup of tea in her hand.

"What do you think has happened, Shug?" she asked me. "I've no idea, Lizzy. I've covered every possible scenario and never really settled on anything. I don't reckon they're in jail, though, because if they were, someone would've called looking for the lawyer. My best guess is that they got a result and are staying on for a couple of days to make sure everything is settled before they split, or at least that's what I'm hoping for," I told her.

"What about you, Liz?" I asked her. "How do you cope with all this shit? What makes you hang around? It can't be much fun when it's like this."

"I don't know, Shug, probably the same reason you and everyone else does. I didn't really have anything else before this and I'm treated well here. I think, though, the most important thing for me is that I feel really safe for the first time in my life, why are you asking?"

"No reason, I can understand the guys being here; I just wondered what made females commit to this kind of lifestyle."

"Shug, male, female, at the end of the day it makes no difference, I think we're all looking for the same shit," she told me.

"Yeh, I suppose you're right," I agreed. We then fell silent for a while, staring up the lane and enjoying the sun. We were then distracted from our thoughts by Flick coming out.

"Anything stirring, guys?" he asked. I just shook my head. As he sat down, Lizzy got up. "Something I said?" Flick asked her. "Just going to get changed and put on a bit of breakfast," she told him as she headed back inside.

Flick was chatting away, but I wasn't really paying any attention to what he said. I was deep in thought, still worrying about what was going on up north.

I then remembered that I was supposed to be meeting with Lorraine at the weekend. Fuck, I then wondered why the fuck I'd agreed to that?

Flick was still blethering away when I interrupted him, "Flick, what day is it?" "Thursday, Shug, Why? You got a hot date on?" "Thank fuck," I told him, "I thought it was Friday." "What's so special about Friday?" he wanted to know.

"Nothing special, man, it's just that I'd arranged to meet with someone, but I didn't really want to leave, in case I missed the guys coming back. Right, Flick," I told him, "I need to split for an hour or so, I've got a couple of things to do. You need me to pick anything up?"

"Nah, I'm cool here, man, thanks," he told me. I went back in, put my boots on, grabbed my jacket and lid. I pinched a couple of bits of bacon from Lizzie's pan on the way out, then blasted up the lane.

I decided to head straight home and relax in a bath for a bit, then find Lorraine and tell her I didn't want to see her at the weekend.

I reckoned, after thinking about what Lorraine had said to me at the garage, that she was really keen for us to start up our relationship again.

I had already made up my mind that I had no interest in that so, in my wisdom, seeing her would be pointless.

I arrived home, went straight in and ran a bath. I put the kettle on and stared out the window for a bit. All I could think about was what was going on with the guys and just hoped, when they eventually did come back, that Indie wasn't going to be too pissed at me.

I made myself a coffee, went into the bathroom, slid into the bath, lit up a fag, and relaxed. I swear it's one of the best feelings in the world: your body, warm in the bathwater, a freshly made cuppa and a smoke - and not a single sound.

After about half an hour or so, I got out feeling relaxed and fully recharged. I decided to write Lorraine a note, in case I couldn't find her. It was short, sharp and to the point, telling her we'd had a great time, but that we couldn't go back and there was no point in meeting as I had no interest in rekindling our relationship.

I stuck it in an envelope, got changed, grabbed some cash from my drawer, then headed out in search of Lorraine.

I drove around the village for a while then stopped at her house. I put the letter through the door and made my way back to the farm.

I wondered if I'd done the right thing as I started to recall all the good times we'd had, and decided it was and that I no longer felt the same about her.

As I approached the farm, I saw a couple of bikes parked outside and I felt my stomach starting to churn, wondering how they'd got on and what Indie was going to say.

I parked up and rushed inside. Flick was sitting in the kitchen with two guys and Lizzy. "What's happening, Flick?" I asked.

"Shug, this is Scribe and Tosh. They're just back from a trip down south and I'm giving them an update about the Angels," he explained.

I shook hands with them both. I knew Scribe from his previous visits to the farm and a couple of runs.

Scribe was a tattoo artist and had done most of the guy's tats. He had a shop in the next village. I'd been there a few times, dropping off dope and stuff, which he dispersed on behalf of the Bats. Twice I'd arranged to get the club tat done on my back and still never got around to it, something else always seemed to get in the way, I thought it was fate.

Flick finished telling them the script and Tosh reckoned the four of us should head up north and meet up with the guys. I was well up for it and agreed to go straight away.

We all bounced the idea around for a bit then decided to go.

As we walked out, Scribe told me that when we got back I should get my arse into his parlour for my tat. I told him I would and we shook on it.

We decided on the quickest route there, thinking that if the guys were on their way back that's the way they would choose, as they would be keen to get straight home and we would meet them on the way.

We were about twenty miles into our journey when we saw them coming towards us, so we did a U-turn and stopped at the side of the road. Indie drew to a halt, with everyone else behind him doing the same.

Indie removed his sunglasses and looked at Scribe, "Where the fuck are you cunts going?" he asked him. "We were coming to get you," he replied. "Well, you're a bit fuckin late for that, are you not?"

"Indie, we were down south, man, we just got back," he almost pleaded. As they spoke, I noticed Indie was looking a bit battered and bruised. I thought I best get out of the way, in case I was next to get it in the neck, and went in search of Rooster. I noticed him about four back, he also looked pretty bashed up.

"Hi, man, how's things with you?" I asked him. "Yeh, doin okay, man, I'll fill you in when we get back," he told me.

Just then, Indie drew away, followed by everyone else. I jumped on my bike and nipped into the pack, just in front of the prospect.

Within half an hour or so, we were all back at the lane. As we went to turn in, some of the guys headed elsewhere, but the majority made their way towards the farm.

My mind was racing and my stomach was spinning like a washing machine, to the point that I thought I was going to be sick. By the time we drew up at the door, I was officially shitting myself.

We all headed inside and a bunch of the guys, including Rooster, followed Indie straight into the conservatory, and he closed the doors behind them.

Scribe was talking to one of his close mates in the kitchen so I sat beside them. He started explaining that when they got there, the Cannibals were already inside the Angels clubhouse and it looked like they'd taken it over.

"Indie instructed us to park up our bikes a bit away then we charged in, all guns blazing. There was about twenty of them and we wasted the fuckin lot of them before we kicked the fuckers out. Indie grabbed one of the guys and told him to tell their Prez that he wanted a meet. We then got one of the Angels to rally round his troops.

"Within half an hour or so, about thirty Angels arrived and Indie spoke with the Sergeant at Arms. Indie demanded he tell him what the fuck happened and why thirty of them couldn't keep their own fuckin clubhouse secure. He explained to Indie that they were driven out by over fifty of them and that three of their guys had nearly been killed. He then went on to say that they were trying to regroup and were just about to come and get the bastards when we'd shown up. Indie then asked him what their plans were to sort the mess out and the SAA told him that they were going to protect their clubhouse and get some guys to head up north and see what kind of strength the Cannibals had. When they got the info they would then decide on how best to wipe them out. Indie sniggered at him and asked if he thought that's how his Prez would have approached it and the guy told him he wasn't too sure. Indie then started ranting at him, telling him he knew exactly what the Prez would have done and that we were going to sort it his way. He asked him if he knew where they were based and he said he did. The next thing, Indie's telling us all to tool up and get on our bikes. He told us we were going into their backyard to wipe them all out. We rode for about an hour and a half and Indie brought us to a halt. We all got off our bikes and made our way to the Cannibals clubhouse.

"When we burst in, it looked like they were preparing for a war: they had all sorts of chibs in a pile on the floor and were all standing around talking. We burst in and started getting into it, it was fuckin awful, man, probably the worst I've experienced. There must've been well over a hundred guys knocking fuck out of each other, both inside and outside. The place got wrecked and we smashed up their bikes. We thought a couple of them were dead, or at least seriously injured, and there wasn't one of us without some kind of injury. We eventually got the better of them and Indie totally wasted their President. He ripped off his cut, set it on fire, then threw it on top of him. He just managed to remove it before he got too seriously burned, although he'd lost almost all of his hair. Indie then picked it up with the end of a pool cue and used it to set fire to the curtains.

"Within about half an hour or so of arriving, we were off again, heading back to the Angels clubhouse. When we got back and everyone had cleaned up, Indie told the SAA that he'd already spoken to his Prez about both clubs becoming one and felt that the time was now right for them to patch over as Bats, and that he should go and speak to the Prez in jail about it. The rest of us got the party in full swing, oblivious to this conversation. Around eight o'clock, the SAA arrived back and, for about half an hour after he returned, him and Indie were locked in the corner, chatting away. Nothing was said until the next day. Indie was up early and off with the SAA. We had no idea where they went and we still didn't know anything about Indie's patch over plan from the night before.

"They both arrived back around lunch time and Indie told us all to gather in the lounge. He sat on the bar and the SAA stood beside him. He told us all to settle down and explained that he'd been to see the Devil Angels President in jail and they'd both agreed on a patch over, but he didn't mention who was patching over to who. We were all stunned, to say the least, and the room turned into a wash of muffled whispers. Their SAA brought us all to order again, telling us to shut up and listen. Indie started again, 'Just to let you know, the Prez of the Angels reckons he and his VP are getting at least 8 years and as you know, we've just lost our Prez and VP too. So, because of this, we've agreed the time is right for us to become one.

We've ran together for years and we've always supported each other so we've agreed that the time is now right for us to amalgamate and stop anyone coming into Scotland and threatening us'.

"Somebody then shouted out 'Who's patching over who, then?' Indie then replied by telling us that they thought it made sense for everyone to become Bats as they'd been about the longest. But if there was strong resistance from the Angels then they were happy to rename as a new club. He then said: 'Guys, remember, the name isn't as important as it seems. The real important thing is that we combine our resources, become one, and have two chapters, then eventually three. We need to take control of Scotland or we'll continue to get arseholes, like we've just had, springing up, thinking they can do what they want. It makes sense if one club controls the north, one controls central and one the south. Then we can make sure no cunt takes anything in Scotland unless we agree to it.'

"At that point, lots of cheers went up, with shouts of 'Black Angels' and 'Devil Bats', a few wanting the Bats and the Angels to keep their original names. One of the Angels asked Indie how he was going to decide and he told him he wasn't going to, that the decision was up to everybody. He then told us that he'd agreed with the Angels Prez that we would select four names and would ballot them. Every member of both clubs would get one vote each. He told us what the choice of names were, the two existing ones and the two shouted out earlier. 'One of the guys is in town now, getting the ballot papers done. So if there's anyone you think should get a vote, who isn't here, then go get them now. We'll be doing this in two hours', he told us, then got off the bar and went through to the backroom with the SAA. At that point, we all looked at each other, wondering what the fuck had just happened. To say we were all a bit shell-shocked was putting it politely. And as we mingled, we realised everybody was feeling the same. It seemed everyone, to a man, thought it was a great idea to become one, but nobody could decide on the name.

"I think most people there wanted to keep the names they had, but knew, that if we joined up, we would be twice as strong and it would send a signal to anyone who thought they could muscle in that it wasn't going to be worth it. We thought about calling the farm and getting the rest of the chapter up, but realised, other than you three, no one else would've been able to make it in 2 hours and we were probably only talking about another ten or so active members. Some of the Angels headed off at that point, looking to rally round the rest of their troops, but only another half a dozen or so came back with them. The guy returned with the ballot papers. Indie and Ammo (the Angels SAA) dished them out and told us to put them in the box they'd placed on the bar when we'd made our selection.

"When the vote was counted, Indie told us eighty-four votes had been cast. Indie then read out the results: Black Angels - 10, Devil Angels - 16, Devil Bats - 20, Black Bats - 38. He then told us that from now on the new club would be called 'Black Bats' and that we would have three chapters: the original 'Central', plus one in the north, 'North' and one in the south, 'South'. Then he said that next weekend we'd have our first meet at the farm and elect all office bearers for the two current chapters. Anyone who didn't want to sign up for the new club should let it be known there and then. The last thing he said was that everyone should now look towards the future by embracing a new start with old friends. Ammo then stood up and told us he'd voted for Black Bats as the new name because it was more established, respected and feared in Scotland and he couldn't wait for everybody to be one. He turned to Indie and they shook hands, then they hugged and suggested to us that we all get pished, and get to know each other better. Other than the party afterwards, that was the gist of it."

I looked at Scribe and saw he was as gobsmacked as me, "Fuckin hell, talk about missing something important!" I said. Scribe then agreed and excused himself, saying he needed to go and see Indie.

I watched him go through to the conservatory and barge straight in. I thought he would get a right mouthful for interrupting, but he closed the door and we never heard a thing.

I watched the door for a couple of minutes, thinking he would be thrown out, but he wasn't. So, feeling the need to do a bit of regurgitating, I got up and went outside. I sat on the step and lit up a fag.

From everything I was told, the part about 'leaving if we wanted to' was the bit that was imprinted on the front of my memory bank. I wondered if that was just for the Angels or if it applied to everybody?

I was thinking that maybe I could get out after all so decided to see if I could do a bit of digging and thought that the best person to explain it to me would be Rooster.

I thought, if I could engage him in conversation about the whole thing, then at some point, he wouldn't be too suspicious of me asking him about the 'leaving' bit.

I was mulling over my plan when I was joined by Cowboy. "Thought I'd find you out here," he said as he sat down.

"What's happening, man? What about that news? Did you see that coming?" I asked him. "Certainly didn't, bit of a surprise, to say the least. It seems that Provo, Stiff and the Angels Prez and VP had been discussing it for months. Apparently, the only thing they were undecided on was the name and when they were going to do it," he explained to me.

"Just shows you. You think you know what's going on, but really, we have no fuckin idea," I suggested.

"Hey, Shug, I'm glad I'm not part of the bigger picture. It must be shite trying to look after the club and all the stuff that goes with it. For me, ignorance is bliss, and I like it that way."

"You've certainly got a point there, Cowboy," I agreed.

I asked him about the leaving part and wanted to know if he'd been told about that and he nodded to me that he had. "Do you think it applies to everyone or just the Angels?" I asked.

Cowboy then said: "Just the Angels, I reckon, because they're the ones who need to patch over. I think it would only apply to everyone if the two clubs had chosen a different name. And only then because everyone would be patching over so we would all have the same choice. Why? Were you hoping to do a trap five?"

"Not sure if I was, I just wondered if I had the option, that's all," I told him.

Cowboy then suggested to me to be careful who I spoke to about it, because he knew from the guys that a few of the Angels were planning to dig their heels in about the amalgamation.

"We don't want them to get wind of any Bats wanting out, it would play right into their hands," he added.

"Cheers, man, thanks for the heads up. Don't worry, the only people I would have spoken to about it would be you or Rooster," I told him.

We continued to chat about the whole thing for about half an hour and we also debated about the new chapter, wondering if there was already a club down south that they wanted to take over or if they would start a new club altogether.

Rooster then came out with a few others, who all headed to their bikes. "What's going on here, ladies? What plans are we hatching today? Don't tell me, I bet it's the Girl Guide Bible group coup, ha ha," he told us.

Straight away, Cowboy told him we were planning his murder and were at the bit where we were chopping up his body and feeding it to the pigs, which made us both laugh.

"Clever little fuckers today, are we not?" he replied. "Well, anyway, can't stand here chit-chatting to you pair of pricks, I need to head off, I've got a bit of business to attend to."

"Where you headed, man? You needing a hand?" I asked. "Come if you want, it's up to you," he told me. "I'm just going for another little nosey at both the hardware stores to see if there are any changes in the staff and shit."

"Has Indie decided when he's going to do him?" I asked. "Not sure, he just said he wants me to check it out. But my guess is he'll want it sorted before next weekend," Rooster told me.

I reckoned that it made a lot of sense to get all these loose ends tied up before we joined together, plus everyone would remember that Indie sorted it, which would stand him in good stead for the President position.

It was just after four when the three of us set off. We went to his main shop in the town first and agreed that Rooster would go to the counter, I'd check the back room, and Flick would check the shop floor.

When we went in, Rooster made a beeline for the counter and I noticed the Thatcher prick was serving. Just seeing him made my blood boil. I had an overwhelming sense of anger towards him, making me want to grab a crowbar from the shelf and knock fuck out of him.

I decided to check the room then go to the counter and see if he recognised me. The room was closed, but I opened the door anyway.

There were two girls about my age sitting having a cup of tea. I apologised to them for barging in and told them I thought it was a toilet. They just sniggered at each other and told me it was a staff room.

One of them told me they had a toilet there if I wanted to use it and pointed towards a door directly opposite the one I was standing at. I thanked her and went through. The door opened into a small corridor with a fire exit at the end of it. I located the toilet and noticed another door as well.

I tried the door, but it was locked. I pushed open the fire door to have a look outside, but the fuckin thing was alarmed and I closed it quickly and jumped into the toilet.

One of the girls knocked on the toilet door, asking me if I was okay, then reset the alarm. I told her I was fine, that I'd fallen over and pushed the door open. I could hear her laughing on the other side of the door and thought she must have bought it.

I gave it a couple of minutes and then went back out, just in time to be greeted by Thatcher himself. He asked me what the fuck I was doing in his office and toilet and why I'd opened the back door.

I told him the same story I told the girls, but he didn't seem to be convinced. Then he asked me if we'd met before and I was dying to tell him we had, but just said I didn't think so as this was the first time I'd been in his shop.

I could see Rooster and Cowboy hanging about just inside the door. Rooster was shaking his head, with his finger in front of his mouth, gesturing for me to say nothing.

I turned away from Thatcher and thanked the girls for letting me use the loo. I then went to walk out. He then shouted me back so I stopped and turned around. He walked towards me and told me that, in future, if I came into his shop, that the back area was off-limits to me.

Fuck, I've no idea how I managed to control myself. I just looked at him for a bit and said: "No probs," then about turned and walked straight out.

I got outside and my blood was boiling and I had to take a few minutes to compose myself. I then had a smoke and calmed myself down before getting on my bike.

When Rooster and Cowboy came out, I told them I was going back in to 'kick his cunt in' there and then, but they talked me out of it, reminding me Indie wanted us to come back later and that I would get my revenge then.

We headed to the other shop and checked it out too. It was pretty much the same as the last time we were there so we rode back to the farm. Rooster went in and had a word with Indie and I stayed outside, moaning the face off Cowboy about Thatcher.

About ten minutes later, Rooster came out and sat down beside us, "Right, guys, it's on for tomorrow night," he told us. I asked him what the plan was and he told us that the shops close at five-thirty and the staff leave right away. However, Thatcher and his dad didn't leave their shops until around six'ish.

"We're going to wait until his father leaves his shop then torch it. But at Thatcher's shop, we'll wait until his staff have gone then go in and waste him, take what we can carry, then burn the cunt with the shop."

Even though Rooster was talking about killing someone, I think, for the first time, I never actually felt a single bit of guilt and would gladly have torched the place myself just to see what I thought would be rightful justice.

"Did Indie say I could go to Thatcher's shop?" I asked him. "Nah, he never said who was doing what. But I'm sure, if you put your case forward to him, he'll be fine with it, but leave it until later before you speak to him." I agreed and told him I would catch him before I headed back to my flat.

We went back into the farm and grabbed a couple of beers. Each of us went into the big room. We were sitting chatting when Flick came through and told me there was a chick at the door for me.

I told him to fuck off, thinking he was taking the piss, but then he told me her name was Lorraine. 'Fuck's sake,' I thought to myself, 'that's all I fuckin need, her coming here!'

Rooster was already laughing away, having a go at me, remarking that my ball and chain had come to take me home, but I just told him to shut the fuck up.

I went outside and noticed she was standing at the tree where we'd shagged the last time she was at the farm.

"Lorraine, what the fuck are you doing here?" I asked her. She fumbled in her bag then pulled out a piece of paper. "I got your note," she said, with tears in her eyes.

"Why are you doing this to me, Shug? I thought you were going to give us another chance. I've sorted it all out with my parents and told them how much I love you. They've only just accepted that it's us or nothing, then you send me a letter telling me it's over!"

She slumped down on the grass and started crying even more. I knelt down in front of her, feeling really guilty, but at the same time, knowing that I no longer wanted her and that I wasn't ready for a long-term relationship.

I decided to be up front with her and make sure she got the message, guessing that when I told her, she would storm away, hating me, and get on with her life.

"Listen, Lorraine, I'm sorry you're upset, but I explained to you in the letter that what we had is now gone for me. I no longer feel the same. You know, as well as me, that I would never be accepted into your family - no matter what your father says. I've chosen what I want to do with my life and it's here with the Bats, you know this is no place for somebody like you. You have much more to offer, and deserve more than this. I'm in another relationship now and I'm happy with it, so please don't make this any harder than it already is."

I then got up and walked towards the farm, waiting for her to start ranting and raving, but she didn't, she just kept crying. Inside, I was crumbling, but I just couldn't go back and comfort her because I knew, deep down, how much I loved her. If I had, I would've ended up crying with her and taking her home.

I went in and closed the door. I leaned my back against it and instantly, I could feel the tears starting to well up inside; I couldn't stop then from rolling down my face. I ran upstairs to the bathroom, locked the door and sat on the pan. By this time, the tears were flooding down my cheeks and I was starting to sob.

I stood up, opened the window, and watched her walk up the lane. My heart was in my mouth. I felt like a pure bastard, but convinced myself what I was doing was the best thing for her in the long run.

I never took my eyes off her until she got to the top of the lane. I kept watching until she got on a bus, then closed the window. I turned around and looked at myself in the mirror, the tears were still rolling down my cheeks. I must have been crying the whole time I was in there.

My eyes were like big red balloons and my face looked like it was all puffed up. I ran the tap and began slunging my face with cold water, in the hope of returning it back to normal.

Someone then knocked the door, asking to get in. I told them I'd just be a minute before drying my face and opening the door. It was Rooster. As soon as he saw me, he knew something was up.

"You okay, man? You've been in there for nearly an hour," he told me. "Yeh, I'm fine," I told him, trying to get past. But he grabbed hold of me and asked me again what was up.

I gave him a very quick version of what happened, missing out the bit about me being in floods of tears and told him I was sorted. He then gave me a hug, said he understood what I was going through, and assured me I'd be fine.

I felt myself going to cry again so stood back and told him I had to go back to the flat for a bit and he offered to come with me. I told him I needed to go on my own and he just nodded.

"Remember, Shug, be back here tomorrow before four." I told him I would be back in plenty of time then quickly went downstairs and headed out. I fired up my bike and shot off up the lane.

I got back to my flat, went in, locked the door, and lay down on the couch. I started crying again for no reason; all I could think about was how much I'd hurt Lorraine.

I must have dozed off fairly quickly. When I woke up, there was daylight shining through the window. I stood up, went to the loo, then checked the clock.

It was eight-thirty in the morning, I'd slept for almost twelve hours. I couldn't remember the last time I'd slept so long. When I got up, I noticed something lying on the mat in the hall and went to get it. It was an envelope with my name on it.

I recognised the handwriting, it was from Lorraine. God knows when she'd stuck it through my door. I went back into the living room and sat down. I stared at it for ages, wondering whether or not I should open it.

I decided to go out for a roll and a newspaper first and would open it after I'd fed myself. As I made my way to the paper shop, I started to wonder about the content of the letter.

It was a beautiful day: the sun was shining and it was really warm. I could actually feel my face burning, it was so hot. I got my rolls, grabbed some other stuff, then went straight back to my flat.

I went in the close and up the stairs. I noticed someone standing, knocking at my door, and realised it was Lorraine's dad.

I thought to myself 'this is the last fuckin thing I need right now!' I got onto the landing and looked him straight in the eye.

"What the fuck do you want?" I asked him. "Shug, I need to talk to you. Can we please do it inside?" "Just say what you have to say out here, then fuck off," I told him.

He then said: "Please, Shug, I don't want any trouble. I just want to talk. Can we please do it inside?" he asked again. I pushed past him, opened the door and went in. He followed me, closing the door at his back.

I went straight into the kitchen, dumped my stuff, then sat down on the couch. "You've got two minutes, so start talking," I told him.

"Do you mind if I sit?" he asked. I just nodded. He sat on the chair opposite me and began,

"Look, Shug, I know we didn't see eye to eye after the incident at my house, but you have to understand how it made me feel. I've gotten over it now and realise that you and Lorraine were in love and perhaps I overreacted. I guess it was just my fatherly instincts taking over."

I butted in, asking him where this was going, then he started to tell me that Lorraine had changed and had become very withdrawn, not speaking to anyone and not going out, taking time off Uni and falling out with the family all the time.

He then went on, "When we eventually got to the bottom of it, she told us that she hated us for ruining her life and that she loved you and that we'd chased you away and that she would never forgive us for that. At that point, we realised it was more than just a fling for her and agreed that we were wrong to split you up, so we gave her our blessing to pursue her relationship with you and she instantly became her old self again. When she told us she'd seen you at the garage, and you'd agreed to meet up with her yesterday, she was floating about like she'd won the football pools. Last night, she came in hating the world again and blaming us for you telling her it was over for good. I just wanted to ask you why and if it had anything to do with our relationship?"

"Look, I told Lorraine it was over because I'm in a fuckin motorcycle gang, for fuck's sake. I don't want her getting mixed up in all my shit, she's way too good for that. I told her I didn't love her and that I had someone else. It's best for both of us that we stay apart. I've already fucked up my life and I sure as hell ain't going to fuck her's up as well. You can go back and tell her I told you that I don't love her and that I've got someone else, or tell her whatever the fuck you want, just don't tell her I still love her, okay?"

I stood up, walked into the kitchen and told him to go, as I didn't want to talk about it anymore. He stood up and thanked me, saying I was a much better man than he'd initially given me credit for, and would always remember what I'd done for his baby girl.

I shouted to him to take the letter from the table and tell her I didn't want to read it. He lifted it, put it in his pocket then left, without saying anything else.

By the time I heard the door slam shut, I was looking out the kitchen window with tears streaming down my face.

I watched him get in his car, and I swear he was grinning from ear to ear. For a second, I thought I should go down and punch his fuckin lights out, but resisted because I knew it would cause more problems than it would solve.

I wiped away the tears and tried to give myself a bit of a shake. I grabbed my rolls and can of juice then planted myself back on the couch.

I finished eating and decided to head straight back to the farm, thinking it would be better to be there than here - as I would just sit there, wallowing in my own pish.

I changed my scants and t-shirt then headed out. I rode straight to the farm, enjoying the sun on my back, the quiet roads, and the warm wind on my face.

When I arrived, I saw the usual scattering of bikes outside and the noise of bikes being revved up coming from the barn.

I wondered about these familiar sights and sounds. Very rarely was the barn ever empty, it always seemed to be the same guys messing about with the bikes. It seemed like their whole life was in the barn.

I went into the kitchen and grabbed a beer from the fridge. There didn't seem to be anyone about so I went into the big room.

There were about a dozen or so guys and girls sitting around, some chatting, some sleeping. At the window, there was someone sitting on a chair, facing the wrong way, with his hands over the back of it. Scribe was busy with his tattoo gun, beavering away on him.

Some guys were sitting around watching and I noticed Rooster was one of them. He nodded to me and I made my way towards him. I then recognised that the person being tattooed was Cowboy.

I looked at his back and realised he must have been there for ages, as Scribe was just putting the finishing touches to it. I wondered how long he'd been sitting there and if he was in a lot of pain. I looked at his tattoo and it was stunning. The centre of his back now had the same image as our colours.

Scribe had also put some black bats flying around it, and a motorbike underneath it, with skulls and chains at the bottom. I nodded to Scribe, told him how cool I thought his work was, then sat down beside Rooster.

We were both looking straight at Cowboy and I asked him how he was feeling and how painful it was. He told me he was fine and that it wasn't as bad as he thought it might be.

I was looking straight into his eyes and they told me a completely different story. He looked like he was in fuckin agony. "How long have you been sitting there?" I asked him.

"A couple of hours or so, I think," he replied. Rooster said it was nearer three than two. Then Scribe piped up, telling us it was just under two and a half and that he would be finished in five minutes and that I was next!

Fuck, I could feel my heart sinking, that was all I fuckin needed today! I'd already dodged it a couple of times, but I couldn't see a way of getting out of it this time.

"I'm fine with that, man, as long as you're not too tired," I told him, lying through my teeth. "I'm good, Shug, I'll get to you in about fifteen minutes," he told me.

I looked at Cowboy's face and thought to myself 'Fuck, he looks like he's in a whole world of pain - and he's already got some tattoos! I've never even had a small one and I'm getting my whole back done in one fuckin go!'

When Scribe told Cowboy he was finished, you could actually see the colour returning to his face, the relief was pretty evident. He got up, shook Scribes hand, thanked him, and then said he was going to the bathroom to check it out in the mirror. My guess was he was away for a good fuckin greet in the privacy of the loo.

Scribe left the room with some of his gear. I guessed he was going to give it a clean or something, in preparation for me.

Rooster started winding me up a bit, telling me how he'd cried like a baby in front of everybody on a run when he got his because he couldn't cope with the pain.

"Very fuckin funny, Rooster, your patter's shite," I told him. "Straight up, man," he said, "it was fuckin agony. Didn't you see the state of Cowboy there? He'd just stopped moaning two minutes before you came in."

I asked Rooster if everyone had their back done and he reckoned that the majority of the guys had, but Scribe was now catching the ones that he'd missed.

Scribe came back in with his gear and a handful of beer. "Right, Shug, stick a couple of these down your neck and we'll get started," he told me.

I drank two of them in about five seconds, much to the delight of Rooster, who was sitting staring at me and smiling like a right fuckin dick.

I removed my top and sat down in the same position I'd seen Cowboy in earlier, except I got my hands in a position that allowed me to squeeze the chair, just in case I needed to.

Scribe wiped my back with freezing cold water and I nearly shit myself, much to the amusement of everyone else. He then shaved my back with a disposable razor and told me he was ready to start.

I asked him if he was going to draw it on or something first, but he told me not to worry, he was going to do it freehand, as he'd done it a million times before. Talk about panic stations! I started to think about Malky and his tattoo; Scribe could be doing anything on my back and I wouldn't know what until he was finished.

The next thing, I was brought back to the real world when he started with his gun. Fuck, he was all over my back; I guessed he was marking it out or something.

It was like a proper burning sensation and, if truth be told, it was fuckin sore. Not sore like a kicking, but sore like someone putting a hot poker on you.

I could feel my hands tighten on the chair and concentrated all my efforts on not moaning like a pussy. Cowboy reappeared with his shirt back on and looking much more like his old self. He sat down beside Rooster. He had a few cans with him and gave one to Rooster.

"Has the little pussy had a cry yet?" he asked Rooster. "Nah, not yet, but I can see it coming very soon," he replied, and then they both raised their cans and started laughing. I did my best to ignore what they were saying, but it was good to listen as it was taking my mind off the pain.

After about an hour, I couldn't actually feel very much and in some sort of sick way, I was actually enjoying the pain. Scribe stopped and told me he was breaking for a rest and needed a can of beer.

Rooster then got up and had a look at my back. "What do you think, Rooster?" Cowboy asked him. "Looking good, Cowboy, I reckon another couple of hours and it'll be done," he told him. Fuck, all I could think about was doing another two hours of this - I might pass out!

A few people were popping in and having a look, everyone trying to be a smartarse with some kind of wisecrack at my expense. Scribe came back in, finished his beer, let out a loud rift, then started beavering away again.

When he started again, it was worse than when he'd begun, but very quickly it numbed back into the good pain. Less than an hour after he started again, he told me he was done.

Casually, I got up from the chair, thanked him and shook his hand. He gave me the small hand mirror he'd given Cowboy and told me to go and have a look at it in the loo, which I did.

As I walked up the stairs, I felt like my back was on fuckin fire. Fuck, it felt like I was lying on a hotplate or something. I got into the loo, locked the door, sat on the toilet and sighed a few times, wondering how best to cool down. I stood up and positioned the hand mirror in a way that enabled me to see my full back in the wall mirror.

I was well surprised how cool it looked, enough to make me smile. At that point, I forgot all about the last two hours of pain and reckoned I was the dog's bollocks.

I then had a bit of a laugh to myself as one minute I'd been looking for a way out, the next, I was getting the club tattoo on my back. 'What a crazy fucked up guy you are', I thought.

I went back downstairs and noticed Scribe rubbing cream over Cowboy's back and guessed I'd be next. "What's that for, Scribe?" I asked him. "It's just a bit of cream to stop it scabbing over, you'll need it as well," he told me.

After we'd both been creamed up, Cowboy suggested we go outside for a chat. When we got to the step, we both sat down and I asked Cowboy what was up.

"Nothing, man, just wondered how you felt after getting your tat done?" "Okay," I told him, deciding not to mention the fact that my back was on fire. "What about you?"

"Yeh, I'm fine now, although I thought some of it was pretty sore, didn't you?" he asked. "Some of it," I let rip. "Fuck, I thought my back was on fire all the way through it. At one point, I thought he was actually colouring in my kidneys."

"Ha ha, me too. Thank fuck you felt like that, I thought it was just me that was the pussy." We then both burst out laughing (I think it was more in relief than in humour).

We'd just about finished our fag when Rooster came out and slapped us both on the back, making both of us roar at him. "Oh, sorry, guys, I forgot," he said, smirking. "Come on, Indie wants us in the conservatory."

He called us a pair of pussies then went back inside, laughing away to himself. Cowboy and I both agreed we would get him later for doing that then followed him inside.

When we went in, there was already about twenty or so guys sitting about and Indie nodded for us to close the door.

"Right, guys, here's the script for later: I only want two on one bike going to the old man's shop, but we'll do that bit later on, okay? I want half a dozen of you, on three bikes, to go to Thatcher's shop and park up a bit away from it. Once his staff have left, I want you in and the door locked. Tie the bastard up, make him shit himself. Then get anything you think is of value to us, rob the cunt of any money or shit lying around. When you're done with that, I want his legs and arms broken, and give him a proper kicking, make sure you tell him why you're doing it, but don't kill the fucker. Make sure he knows that if he tells the cops anything that the next time we visit him: he'll need a coffin! Untie him then throw him out the back of his shop, torch it then split. I'm going with Jelly and Hotwire to his fuckin house. I guess, when they get word the shop is on fire, they'll all rush over there. When they leave, we'll break in and have a rake around, then burn the fucker's house as well. Right, who wants to do Thatcher's shop?"

Straightaway, I told him I'd like to do it. Then, Cowboy, Flick and Rooster said they wanted to go as well. Lots of the other guys also said they wanted to take part.

Indie picked Scribe and Tosh, telling them they should do it, as they missed the north run, and they both nodded in agreement.

We had our six, and I was really pleased that I was going with people I knew pretty well. Even though I didn't know Scribe and Tosh that well, I knew enough about them to know that they were sound guys.

Indie then sorted out who was doing the rest of the stuff. I never paid any attention to it as I wanted the six of us to get round the table and plan who was doing what in our group.

Indie then told us we were leaving in an hour then arranged the other times with the rest of the guys. When Indie had finished, I grabbed Rooster and suggested we all get together and plan our strategy.

He started laughing and was looking at me in a very odd way. "What?" I said. "Strategy? Fuckin strategy?" he replied. "Ha ha, you sound like a fuckin war general or something, ha ha, fuckin chill, man, we're going to have a blether and sort it out." Then he grabbed me and did that fuckin thing to my head again, aarrghh, I could fuckin slap him sometimes!

The six of us headed through to the big room and grabbed a corner. Rooster started the conversation by announcing that 'Field Marshall Shug' would be coordinating the strategy group for the assault on target Thatcher, much to the amusement of the others.

"Very fuckin funny, Rooster," I told him. "Now, can we get on with deciding who's doing what?" I suggested, hoping to draw the attention away from myself.

To my surprise, Tosh (who was always very quiet anytime I'd been in his company) spoke up first: "I think that me and Scribe should go into the shop five minutes before it closes and wait until the staff fuck off, then we'll grab the bastard and let you lot in the back door, and take it from there."

Everybody nodded in agreement and then Rooster said: "Cool, that's us sorted, meet outside in forty-five minutes," then got up and fucked off. I thought to myself 'Some fuckin plan that was! What about the rest? No one mentioned any other part of it'.

I spoke with Cowboy and Flick, suggesting we needed more of a plan, but Cowboy then referred to Rooster's earlier comment.

"Don't worry, 'Field Marshall Shug', everything's in hand, the rest will happen with military precision, the SAS would be proud of us," he said, saluting me while he and Flick roared with laughter.

"Okay, ya pair of pricks, I get the message," I said, joining in with their laughter.

We had a beer and changed the subject until it was time to go. I jumped on the back of Rooster's bike, Cowboy had Flick on the back, and Scribe doubled up with Tosh.

As we left and rode towards the shop, I could feel the cold air cooling my back. I was enjoying the sensation, not thinking too much about what lay ahead.

We headed past the shop and Rooster drew in at the car park at the rear of the shop. A separating wall meant we couldn't be seen from the back door. We got off the bike and I reminded Rooster that Indie had told us Thatcher wasn't to be killed. Rooster laughed and said: "Let's just see how it goes, Shug, okay?"

When we were all there, Rooster checked his watch and nodded to Tosh, telling him the time was right for them to go into the shop. As they went around the corner, out of sight, the back door of the shop opened and the two girls I'd spoken to the last time I was there came out the shop, got into a car and left.

A couple of minutes later, Tosh and Scribe came back. Tosh stuck a knife in one of the Volvo's front tyres and Scribe told us they were too late in arriving as Thatcher had shouted from inside that he was closed and had told them to come back tomorrow.

Flick burst the tyre, knowing he would have to fix it before he left and at that point, we could get him back into the shop.

The plan worked a treat. He came out, swore at the car, kicked the wheel, and headed back into the shop. We watched as he came out with a trolley jack and pushed it under his car before starting to jack it up.

Rooster and Flick walked towards him, grabbed him and pushed him straight back into the shop. We all followed them in and closed the door. By the time we got into the main part of the shop, Rooster had already gagged him and they were both taping him to a chair.

Once they had him secure, Rooster nodded for us to search the shop. I stood in front of Thatcher and could feel the rage building up inside me as I looked at him. I hit him a really hard punch on the face, bursting his nose and eye. He tried to squeal, but only offered a muffled grunt from behind the duct tape.

I think that was one of only a few times in the whole of my life that I took satisfaction from hitting someone. Normally, I felt pangs of guilt hitting someone, especially someone who was unable to defend their self.

However, this time it felt so good that I did it another few times. I told him he deserved it for what he'd done and that I was going to enjoy watching him being tortured. I then smiled at him before walking away.

Rooster put his arm around me and asked if I felt better now, having given him a few smacks. I told him I did, even although it didn't. Hitting him had just made me feel angrier.

By this time, the rest of the guys had raided the place, taking money from the till and some small stuff from the shelves.

Rooster found a safe under the counter and asked him for the key. He gestured to his jacket pocket with his eyes and a nod of the head. Rooster put his hand in, lifted it out then proceeded to open the safe.

He found a couple of hundred quid, which he reckoned must've been a good few days takings, and stuffed the cash into his pocket.

Tosh then came out from behind a row of shelves and placed a hammer, a saw, and a screwdriver on the floor, in front of Thatcher. "Bet you can't guess what I'm going to do with these?" he teased him.

I looked at Thatcher closely, he already had tears streaming down his face and was trying frantically to talk.

Flick patted him a couple of times on the cheeks and started to tell him what he was going to do with the tools, whilst holding them up to his face one at a time.

Before he put the hammer down, he whacked him on the back of the hand with it, and again, he let out a muffled roar. He then handed the hammer to Scribe who did exactly the same with the other hand, which provoked the same response from Thatcher.

Rooster then picked up the screwdriver and placed it on top of Thatcher's shoe. He took the hammer from Scribe and smacked the screwdriver right through his foot then threw the hammer to Scribe.

Thatcher passed out at that point, and his head dropped onto his chest. Just then, I started to feel some pangs of guilt and suggested we just torch the place and fuck off.

Cowboy agreed that it was a good idea and looked at the others, awaiting their response. Tosh then reminded us that Indie wanted his arms and legs broken and that we were nowhere near that stage yet.

I suggested that there was no point in doing anything more to him as he wouldn't feel it, but Rooster had other ideas. He came out from the back room with a basin of cold water and chucked it over him.

Thatcher responded, and although he wasn't too coherent, he was now awake. Scribe picked up another hammer from the shelf, kneeled down in front of him, and whacked both hammers off either side of his right ankle at the same time.

You could actually hear the bones being crushed, I thought I was going to throw up. Thatcher passed out again, which I thought was the best thing all round.

"Come on, guys, that's enough, he clearly can't take anymore. Let's just drag him outside and split," I suggested. Thankfully, Rooster agreed and we untied him then dragged him outside.

He was moaning as he lay on the ground, but was still pretty much out of it. The other guys then came out and told us it was time to split. Tosh grabbed Thatcher by the hair and slapped him a bit until he returned to semi-consciousness.

"Remember, Thatcher, if you tell anyone about us, we'll be back. We'll rape your wife while you watch then kill your kid and then I will personally fuckin kill you, very, very slowly, got it?" Thatcher almost managed a nod before passing out yet again.

"Fuck's sake, Tosh, that's a bit harsh," I told him. "It's harsh, fuck all. Just remember, we have two brothers in hospital because of that bastard. If it was left to me, I'd burn the bastard with his fuckin shop!" he roared at me.

Tosh then went back inside and lit half a dozen rags, placing them in different parts of the shop before casually walking out.

We all then ran to our bikes and headed off in different directions. I sat on the back of Rooster's bike and, as he drove back to the farm, I started thinking about what we'd just done.

I was well up for it initially, as I wanted justice for the prospects, but when it came down to it, I'm not sure I could've managed to do some of the things the others had done.

Just watching had made me feel physically sick, and knowing what the guys were capable of made me feel like I really didn't belong.

I wondered, if push came to shove, would I really have been able to smash someone's ankle with two hammers? I didn't think so.

Fuck, here I was, psychoanalysing everything again. I wondered if any of the others would be thinking the same way as me, or if they were just happy that he'd been paid back for what he did to the prospects. I convinced myself that the bastard deserved it and that what we did was totally justified.

As we neared the lane, we saw a couple of bikes head off in the other direction and I guessed that they were off to complete the final part of the 'master plan'.

When we stopped at the farm, I decided to have a word with Tosh.

As got off the bikes, I asked him if I could have a chat before he went in and waited until the rest of the guys were inside. I went to speak, but before I said anything, Tosh interrupted.

"This better not be about that prick Thatcher! Because, as far as I'm concerned, he deserved everything he got and more. If it had been left to me, I would have killed the bastard. So, before you say anything, just remember what the cunt did to the prospects. We should have killed the bastard. So if you're going to give me any pish about how harsh we were then you can fuck off, coz I don't want to hear it."

"Whoa, man, take it easy. Fuck, it's nothing like that, I just wanted to say I was sorry and that you were right. I just had a bit of a wobble when I saw the state of him, but I'm cool now, we still good?" I asked him.

"Shug, now we're perfect," he told me, then gave me a hug and suggested we get a few down our necks and chill out. I nodded in agreement, feeling a bit better that I'd spoken to him.

I made yet another mental note to myself: 'Don't be so open about your true feelings and make sure you never appear like a shitebag in front of another brother again!'

When we went in, it seemed that there was a bit of a party going on. I checked the clock, it was ten to seven, we'd been away for a couple of hours and yet, in my head, it only seemed like five minutes.

Tosh grabbed a couple of beers from the fridge and threw one to me before heading inside. I sat on the edge of the table, looking out the window, wondering if the police had arrived at the shop yet?

I opened my beer and had a couple of swigs. I must have drifted away as I thought about the whole sorry episode. I was wondering if Thatcher would say anything to the police or if he'd been scared enough not to.

I started to think about what Tosh said to him, about raping his wife and killing him, and wondered if that was just scaremongering or if he actually meant it. The next thing I knew, I was being brought back from my thoughts with a dunt in the ribs from Rooster.

"You okay, man?" he asked. "Yeh, fine," I told him. "Just me at my usual, mulling over what we've done." "What we've done, Shug, is: we've paid back a fuckin arsehole for a crime he'll probably get away with when he goes to court. So just think of us as public servants, doing our duty where the law has failed," he suggested. I just smiled, told him he was right then grabbed another beer and headed through to the party. About fifteen minutes later, Indie and the rest of the guys arrived back. Rooster headed into the conservatory at the back of them and closed the door.

Cowboy then asked me if I thought everything had gone to plan and I told him I guessed it had as they'd all come back together and no one looked the worse for wear. I decided that I'd wait until Rooster came out and gave us the lowdown before I headed home.

Rooster joined us about ten minutes later and told us everything was good: both shops were burned out, Thatcher was in hospital, his house was trashed and robbed. There were no casualties by the look of it and, so far, no witnesses either.

"That's great, man," I told him then stood up. "Right, guys, I'll see you all tomorrow. I'm heading off for a bit of a kip." "Come on, Shug, stay and have a few more beers, stop being a fuckin pussy, man!" Rooster shouted.

"Sorry, need to go, man, I'm feeling like shit. It's been a long one. I'll catch you all later, enjoy your night," I told them as I made a sharp exit, not giving anyone a chance to reply.

I jumped on my bike and raced away, feeling glad I'd got out without too much fuss. When I got back to the flat, I noticed Mark sitting on the steps, which wasn't normal. "You okay, man?" I asked. "My daughter's unwell and I'm waiting on the doc coming, just thought I'd sit here, in case he misses the house."

"Sorry to hear that, man, is there anything I can do to help?" I asked him. "No, not really, other than keeping the noise down," he told me. I reassured him he had no worries there as I was heading straight to bed. I gave him a bit of a pat on the back and told him I hoped that she got better soon then went upstairs.

I opened the door and lifted up the mail. I had three letters, which I threw on the couch. I took my jacket off, stuck the kettle on and made myself a cup of tea. It was only nine o'clock, but I felt like I'd been up for about a week.

I opened the letters: two of them were rubbish, but one was from the hospital. I couldn't believe it. They'd invited me for an interview the following week. I ran downstairs and headed to the phone box.

I dialled the number of the nurses home and eventually someone answered. I asked if they could find Julie for me and gave them the room number. The person asked me for my phone number and said they would get her to call me back.

I sat down on the pavement, leaning against the door. I wondered if it was Julie or Anna who'd managed to wangle this for me. I thought about the interview: I hadn't really had a proper one before and had no idea how it would work.

Just then, the phone rang and I answered before it had a chance to ring twice. It was Julie. "Shug, it's Julie, what's wrong?" she asked.

"Hi, Julie, there's nothing wrong. I just rang to let you know that I've got an interview at the hospital next week, and to thank you for putting a word in."

"That's great news, Shug, what day is it on?" "It's next Thursday at nine-thirty in the Admin block," I told her. "You should come on the Wednesday night and stay at mine, then you can just walk to the block in the morning," she suggested.

"Thanks, Julie, I'll do that. What if I come around lunchtime? Do you think you could go shopping with me for a suit and stuff? I don't have any dress clothes, other than the black suit I wore at Malky's funeral."

"Yes, that's no problem, I'm early shift on Wednesday and finish at two. So, if you come then, I'll meet you at my room." "That's perfect, thanks very much, Julie, I look forward to seeing you then." She said she was looking forward to seeing me as well then hung up.

I ran back up the stairs, two at a time, thinking what a fuckin great way to end a shitty day. Just as I got to the landing, Mark and his Mrs were coming out his flat with his kid and the doctor. I stepped aside to let them pass, I nodded to everyone and whispered good luck to Mark and he nodded back.

I went inside and closed the door, 'At last!' I thought, 'something to look forward to'. I sat back on the couch, picked up the letter again, read it, then smiled to myself.

I went to bed and lay thinking about the job. I wondered if I got it: When I would start? Would they give me a room in the nurses home? How would Julie feel about it? And more importantly, how would Rooster feel about it?

I thought about not telling him until I found out if I got the job and decided that would be a bad idea. I wondered if he would be happy for me or if he would be pissed. I decided I would tell him about the interview in the morning and take it from there.

Next morning, I was up around ten and decided to head straight to the farm. I stopped to pick up a paper, interested to see if there was anything in it about the shops.

I couldn't believe it when I picked it up. The front page headline read: 'Family targeted in triple attack' and underneath there was a picture of both shops burning.

I handed the money to the shopkeeper and walked out the shop. I read the article before getting back on my bike. As I rode to the farm I tried to digest the words: 'Local businessman critical in hospital', 'Gang target family in shocking attack', 'Parents and wife treated for shock', 'businesses ruined', 'house theft', then a bit about police having a number of leads they were investigating.

As I mulled it over, I thought 'Holy shit, we've gone way too far this time. There's no way we're going to get away with this'.

I approached the farm, half expecting the pigs to already be there, but to my surprise, it was all quiet. When I drew up, I noticed Cowboy and Flick sitting on the step, chatting and smoking. "Hi, guys, how's tricks?" I asked them. They both nodded, as if to suggest they were fine, then Cowboy told me he was as rough as a badger's arse.

Flick then told me that Cowboy had ended up totally blootered, and kept telling everyone it was purely medicinal, and that he was only drinking for its painkilling properties.

I had a bit of a laugh at Flick's description and asked Cowboy how his back was and he said: "It's way less painful than my fuckin head today, that's for sure."

We all burst out laughing. Then he wanted to know how I was and I told him my back was fine. I then asked if Rooster was still here and Cowboy said the last he saw of him was when he fucked off upstairs with a chick.

Flick then pointed towards the barn, picking out Rooster's bike. "There's his bike, I guess that means he's still inside," he told me. I handed them the paper, told them they should read it, then went inside.

I went straight upstairs and stuck my head into one of the rooms. I saw plenty of bodies in the bed, but not him. The next room I tried, I found him lying in between a couple of naked chicks.

I gently grabbed hold of his nose, pinching his nostrils together with my fingers. In a matter of seconds, he was awake, spluttering and struggling for breath.

He let out a roar, saw it was me, and asked me what the fuck I was playing at. "Get up, I need to talk to you about a couple of things," I told him, then turned to walk out. I noticed his jeans and cut-off on the floor so picked them up and threw them at him. "I'll be outside when you're ready," I told him.

"Fuck you, I'm going nowhere," he shouted, then threw his jeans at the door. I knew he would be down in five minutes or so, as curiosity would get the better of him, so ignored his rant.

I went into the kitchen and made us both a coffee, taking them outside, and joining Flick and Cowboy on the stairs. We discussed the article in the paper and started debating whether or not we thought the police actually had any leads.

Just then, Rooster arrived, as predicted. "Right, where's the fire then, ya little cunt?" he roared at me. "No fire, big man, just coffee, a smoke, and a bit of a chat."

I asked Flick and Cowboy if they could give us a minute and they got up and went inside. We sat down and I handed Rooster his coffee and a fag.

"Rooster, I've been offered an interview at the hospital, it's next Thursday morning, I wanted to ask you how you felt about it?"

"Ya little prick!" he roared at me. "You've just got me out of a warm bed, with a bit of pussy on either side of me, to tell me that! Fuck's sake, Shug, I thought it was something fuckin serious."

"Eh, pardon me for wanting advice from my mate regarding the rest of my life, how stupid am I? You know what? I should've realised that you wouldn't give a fuck about my problems. You're right, Rooster, that's not as important as a couple of bits of skirt in your bed. So why don't you just fuck off back there and forget I ever fuckin asked you!"

I put down my coffee, threw away my fag and lifted my helmet. As soon as I had it on, I got on my bike and fucked off. I kept waiting for him to shout me back, but he didn't.

As I headed home, I thought 'Fuck him and his fuckin attitude. I'm going to go to the interview and I'll try like a bear to get the job and, if I'm lucky enough to get it, I'll move there, lock, stock and barrel. I'll give up my flat and they can all go and fuck themselves, especially him.'

I arrived home, stopped outside the flat and parked up. Just as I was heading into the close, I saw Mark and his Mrs drawing up in a taxi so I waited to ask him how his little one was.

The minute I asked him, I wished I hadn't. He told me his little girl had passed away. Fuck me, my heart was in my mouth; I had no idea what to say.

I just told them I was really sorry and his Mrs burst into tears. Mark ushered her up the stairs and into their flat.

Fuck me, it doesn't half make you put your own life into perspective when you hear of a little one's passing. It makes you realise that the moaning, bickering and arguing you do is totally irrelevant and completely insignificant.

I followed them upstairs, trying to make as little noise as possible. I went into my flat, closed the door as quietly as I could, made my way into the living room, dropped my jacket and helmet to the floor, and sat down.

I started thinking about Mark and the sadness he must be feeling right now. I thought about the Bats and the coming weekend when the Devils were patching over and all the officers were being selected for both chapters.

I wrestled again with my thoughts of quitting the Bats. Thinking again about Mark's loss made me start to look at my own tragedies, and how many of them could have been avoided if I'd chosen another path.

I thought about The Reaper, and the trail of destruction that followed him, and began to feel like my life was following the same route.

I must have dozed off as I woke with a bit of a start. I heard the door being banged and raced to open it before it was knocked in again; I opened it to find Rooster standing there.

I told him to shut the fuck up and stop making a noise and the cunt punched me right in the face, dropping me to the floor. He stepped over me and walked through to the living room, ranting away.

I picked myself up and closed the door quietly. I went into the living room and saw he'd sat his arse on the chair and was taking his helmet off.

"Don't you say another fuckin word," I told him. "Mark's baby's just died and they need some quiet, so if you're here to cause any bother then you can fuck off right now and we'll pick this up later."

I went into the kitchen and put a damp cloth on my nose. Rooster followed me through and asked me quietly about Mark's kid and I told him all I knew.

I pushed past him and walked back through to the living room and sat down. Still holding the cloth to my nose, I started talking:

"Rooster, you're a fuckin wanker, why the fuck would you do that to me?" I whispered at him, demanding that he tell me.

"Because you deserved it for fucking off in the huff, like a pussy," he said, as quietly as he could.

"You woke me up, telling me you needed to talk. I thought something had happened to you. Then you started prattling on about a fuckin interview."

"Well, at the time I thought it was important and I wanted to make sure you were okay with it. But, as you clearly don't give a fuck about me, I won't ask your advice again," I told him.

"What the fuck did you want me to say? Hey, Shug, I think it's a brilliant idea for you to fuck off, fifty miles away, and start afresh. Oh, and when you're there, why don't you give my ex a good seeing to?"

"Ah, so that's what it's all about. It's fuck all to do with me leaving; you think I'm just going there so I can jump on Julie's bones. For fuck's sake, Rooster, you need to get a fuckin grip of yourself, man, this has got fuck all to do with her. It's not my fuckin fault you two fucked it up, my only interest in Julie is as a mate, and if you can't see that then you're even more fucked up about it than I thought," I lied.

Rooster then lowered his head, breaking eye contact for the first time.

"Sorry, man, you're right," he told me. "I guess I'm just looking for someone to blame, even though I know it's all my own fault. I still can't believe we're finished. But you're right, I need to get a fuckin grip. I must have shagged a dozen different chicks since she fucked off and I still can't get her out of my fuckin head. By the way, I'm sorry about your nose as well," he said, pointing towards my face.

"So you fuckin should be, it's fuckin gowpin," I reminded him. "Look, Rooster, I only wanted to ask you if you thought it would be a good idea for me to move on. You're the only person I really trust to give me good advice. You must realise, I'm still not sure whether I'm cut out for the whole Bat thing.

When I got the letter about the interview, I thought it might be a good way for me to forget about my past and start again amongst cunts that I've no history with."

"Look, Shug, I hear where you're coming from, but I'm the last person you should be asking advice from. Everything I touch goes tits up, you know that. As for the Bats, this weekend will herald a new beginning for everyone and I think it's a pretty exciting time to be involved. However, as you know, it's also a chance for anybody who no longer wants to be part of it to fuck off. I don't know what you're going to do, but if you really want my advice then I reckon you should hang in there with the Bats. Think about it, Shug, what's your alternative? Do you really want to work in a fuckin looney bin for the rest of your puff? I sure as fuck don't think you do. Hell, you're daft enough as it is!" he said, raising a smile.

"Rooster, I don't plan to stay there all my life, I just want to put some distance between me and the Bats for a while, just to suss out whether or not I'm as committed to the Bats as the rest of you. I still have nightmares about Malky and my mum, and I know they'd both still be here if I hadn't joined the Bats. I'm not sure if I can have anybody else's death on my conscience, it's way too much for me to carry around."

We then spent about half an hour or so debating the whole issue of me fucking off until Rooster said something that struck a chord with me and made me decide what I was going to do.

He said, pretty casually, "Hey, Shug, when you think about the big picture, does it really matter a fuck what any of us do? I remember Provo telling me something when he saw I was struggling to get to grips with the Bats lifestyle, he said: 'Hey, Rooster, remember: the only thing that's right is what's right for you at the time, you'll always know, deep down, what that is'."

I don't think he realised when he said it how much of a profound effect it had on me. As he continued chatting away, I was deep in thought, analysing Provo's words.

The bit about 'what's right' and 'deep down, knowing what to do' switched a light on in my napper and straight away, I decided that I would follow my gut instincts and no longer dwell on any 'what if's?'.

I had no idea what Rooster was saying, but I interrupted him, telling him to stop talking and listen to what I had to say for a minute.

"Rooster, thanks for the advice, I really appreciate it. You'll be glad to know I've now decided what I'm going to do," I told him. "I'm going to do both. I'm going to stay in the Bats and I'm also going to take the job if I get offered it."

He then interrupted me and asked me how the fuck I was going to manage that. I explained to him that, after this weekend was over and both the chapters were sorted, Indie's plan was to start another chapter in the south, and if that was still the case, then I would ask him if I could be part of that.

"Don't you see, Rooster? This solves all my problems," I explained. "I could help set it up and maybe even become one of the officers. Hey, you could even become President, how cool would that be? Just think, we could talk Cowboy and Flick into it as well, now that would be brilliant, wouldn't it?"

Rooster then burst my bubble a bit. "Shug, whoa, hold your horses, man, stop fantasising for a fuckin minute and listen to yourself, for fuck's sake. You need to take a fuckin reality check on this. For a start, what makes you think Indie would want me to run the new chapter? Have you even considered the thought that any of us would even want to do it, or more importantly, if we would actually be able to? I think it sounds like a great idea and I would be well up for it, but there are way too many factors to consider before we get all excited about it. The main one being that none of it would be our decision."

"I know that, Rooster, but you've got Indie's ear, and if you put it to him before Saturday, that we would be willing to help start the new chapter, then I think he'd be well up for it. Think about it, Rooster, Indie would rather have people he trusted setting it up than cunts he wasn't sure of. Come on, man, you know it makes sense. All you have to do is plant the seed and convince Indie that it's a good idea. I'll have a word with the other two and find out if they'd be up for it and we'll take it from there, what do you think?" I asked him.

"Shug, I'm not sure if this is just another one of your hair-brained fuckin schemes or a brilliant idea. It all sounds a bit farfetched and I'm not sure if I really want to do it," he told me, deflating me a bit.

"Right, I'm going to tell you something, but you need to keep it to yourself for now, okay?" he said. I just looked at him and nodded in agreement, still thinking of ways to convince him about my plan, but the minute he started talking again, he had my full attention.

"Indie has already asked me to be his SAA. He told me if he is elected Prez that he wants me by his side, and I told him I would be delighted to do it if I'm nominated. So here's my dilemma, if I now go to him with this idea, and he knocks it back, then he might change his mind and that would fuck it right up for me."

I got up and leaned over to shake his hand. "Rooster, that's brilliant news. Congratulations, man. If I'd known about it, I probably wouldn't have mentioned this," I told him.

"The thing is, though, Rooster, I really want this and I know we could do it. What if you just told him that you were thinking about the new chapter and, if he wanted you to, you would be happy to take some guys and try and get it up and running for him and see what he says? That way you're not putting yourself at risk of losing your stripes," I suggested.

"Shug, that sounds a bit better, I suppose, but let me think about it for a while, to make sure I don't fuck everything up. I think I need to cover all my bases." "Hey, that's all I'm asking, man," I told him.

"Okay, what if we head back to the farm just now and I have a quiet word with Cowboy and Flick, just to see if they would be interested? I won't mention you, that way I can gauge how they feel about it. If they're up for it, I'll let you know, then you can decide if you want to take it to Indie or not. What do you think of that?" I asked.

There was a bit of silence between us for a few minutes as I watched Rooster appear to mull it over, then he spoke,

"Okay, Shug, fuck it, let's do it. But remember, it needs to be kept between the four of us until I speak to Indie, got it?" I nodded and smiled in agreement. "And take that stupid fuckin grin off your face, it makes you look like a fuckin halfwit," he said, smiling back.

I jumped up and grabbed my gear, ushering him out the door before he had a chance to change his mind.

Chapter 17

When we arrived at the farm, I noticed there was a fair sprinkling of bikes scattered around and guessed people had already started arriving for the weekend patch over.

We got off our bikes and went to head in, Rooster grabbed my arm, reminding me again not to talk to anyone, except Cowboy and Flick, about our plan and I reassured him that I wouldn't. When we went in, Rooster went straight into the conservatory and I went into the big room in search of the pair of them.

I couldn't see them and asked one of the guys if they were here and he told me they were in the barn. I headed back out and over to the barn. There was a lot of shouting and cheering coming from inside and I wondered what was going on.

When I opened the door, I soon realised what it was all about. There were about twenty guys and they had a couple of airguns, which they were shooting at targets with. It was a drinking game that I'd played before and, by the state of some of them, I reckoned they must've been playing for a while.

I spotted Cowboy and told him I wanted a word with him and Flick. He told me he would grab him and meet me outside in five. I went out and lit up a fag and thought about how I was going to ask them.

When they both came out, I walked a bit away from the door and they followed. "What's up, man?" Cowboy asked. "Nothing's up, I just need to run something by you both," I told them.

I explained my plan to them, without mentioning Rooster, as we agreed, and waited for their response. They both looked at each other, then at me, then back at each other and burst out laughing.

"What's the fuckin joke?" I asked them, sounding pretty aggressive. Cowboy then spoke, "Are you drugged up or just fuckin mental, Shug?" he asked me, still laughing.

"What the fuck do you mean by that?" I again replied, with aggressive undertones. "Look, Shug, you might want to fuck off somewhere else and start a new life, but we're happy here, you know that. What makes you think that we could start up a new chapter anyway? Fuck, we wouldn't know the first thing about it. I don't even know anything about how this one runs, for fuck's sake," he told me.

"We might not, but Rooster does, and he's in," I told them, then remembered what Rooster had said. Fuck! I quickly realised I'd said way too much.

"Hey, guys, you know what? Just forget it, okay? It was only a thought, and please don't mention this to anyone, especially Rooster, I promised him I wouldn't tell you he was up for it," I pleaded with them for their silence as I walked away.

Flick then jumped in, "Shug, hold it, man, wait a fuckin minute. Come on, come back here." I about turned and walked back towards him, waiting for him to say his bit.

"Are you saying that Rooster wants to do this as well? Have you two been speaking about this? Come on, man, let's hear it, spill the fuckin beans."

"All right, I'll tell you the whole thing if you promise me it stays between us?" I looked at them and they both nodded in agreement. I told them everything Rooster and I had discussed. I explained that if they were up for it then he was going to take it to Indie.

Cowboy asked me to tell him exactly what Rooster was going to say to Indie and if he would be mentioning their names.

I reassured him that no one's names would be mentioned and told him how he was going to approach it, which seemed to relax him a bit.

"So, guys, what do you think then, in or out?" I asked them. Flick was first to speak. "Fuck, Shug, I thought you were having a laugh at first, but now I know you're serious, I'm interested. I'm not saying I'm in, but I'll certainly give it a bit of thought," he told me.

"Cowboy, what about you - are you up for it?" I asked him. "Shug, I'm a bit shell-shocked with the whole fuckin thing. I'm with Flick on this, I'll think about it as well."

"Okay, I'm cool with that," I told them. "I'm going in to see Rooster, I'll catch up with you later, you can let me know then what you've decided." I then about turned and headed in.

I saw the two of them deep in conversation as I closed the door and reckoned they would eventually be well up for it, although I was a bit worried that they might slip up when they spoke to Rooster.

I caught up with Rooster and told him that the guys were on board and suggested he should put it to Indie tonight, as he may not get a chance when everybody else arrived tomorrow.

He told me he'd just told Indie about Mark and thought it best to leave it until later. "I'm heading out with Indie for an hour or so and, if I get a chance, I'll speak to him when we get back. Rooster then left and I grabbed a beer and had a chat with a few of the guys.

I was sitting relaxing when Cowboy and Flick came in and joined me. Cowboy told me they were up for it and wanted to know when I'd be seeing Rooster. He said they wanted to be there when I spoke to him.

I told them I'd already spoken to him about it and that he was going to try and have a word with Indie when they came back. Before we had a chance to have a chat about it, we heard the roar of bikes coming up the lane so we followed everyone outside to see who it was.

It was the Devil Angels arriving, and I reckoned that every one of their members had come. There must have been over thirty bikes and a good few were two's up. As they drew to a halt, they were all revving up their bikes and tooting their horns, we could hardly hear ourselves talk.

All of our guys were gathering around our visitors, shaking hands and hugging each other. I clocked Fixer and made a beeline for him, welcoming him to the farm.

We were standing beside his bike, chatting, when I noticed Indie and Rooster returning in the van.

They drove it straight into the barn. When Indie made his way out to greet Ammo, I made my excuses to Fixer, telling him I had a bit of business to attend to and would catch up with him later.

As I headed in to see Rooster, I laughed to myself, thinking that I'd just told Fixer 'I was going to do a bit of business' - I was now using the same phrase that had so often been a source of my frustration in the past.

As I entered the barn, Rooster shouted to me, "Excellent timing, Shug, you're just in time to help me get this stuff out the van." I went around to the back door and couldn't believe my eyes, the van was full to the brim with cases of beer and bottles of spirits.

"Fuck me, Rooster, there's enough drink in here to sink a battleship," I remarked. "Listen, with the number of people we're expecting, we'll be lucky if this lasts us through the night," he replied.

"I've got another couple of runs to do in the morning, Indie wants to make sure we're fully stocked for the whole weekend," he told me.

I started helping him unload the van and we fired the cases into the store. I asked him if he'd spoken to Indie yet, about the south chapter, and he told me he had, then grabbed another three cases from the van and headed to the store.

I jumped in front of him, eager to hear what Indie had said. "Well, Rooster? Don't keep me in suspense, man, tell me what the fuck he said."

"Shug, relax, man, I'll tell you when the four of us get together," he told me, pushing past. I followed him into the store empty-handed and when he dropped the cases on the shelf and turned around, I was right in his face.

"Will you fuck," I said. "You know I can't wait that long, you need to tell me right now. Come on, man, I'm going to explode if you don't spit it out." He started laughing loudly then grabbed me and rubbed his knuckles over my head, making my frustration even more evident.

"Okay, Shug, take a breath or two, man, and for fuck's sake, relax. If you stop freaking out then I'll tell you." He went back to the van and sat on the floor, in-between the open doors. I followed and sat down beside him and he eventually began speaking.

"Right, I asked him, if he became Prez and I became SAA, would he consider letting me be involved in setting up the new chapter. And, to my surprise, he told me that he was actually thinking of asking me to oversee it. He then said that we needed to leave it until everything else was sorted and, if things go according to plan, we would pick it up again next week."

"That's fuckin brilliant, man, I just hope to fuck everything goes according to plan." I grabbed him and gave him a hug, and told him I would go and tell Cowboy and Flick the news.

He then said I was going nowhere until the van was empty. We must have emptied the van in record time and he told me I needed to calm the fuck down as I was racing around like a rabbit on speed during the mating season.

When Rooster picked up the last three cases, I reversed the van out and parked it in the garage. I jumped out just as Rooster was closing the barn doors and threw him the keys before running into the house.

Cowboy and Flick were sitting in the kitchen, smoking and drinking with a few of the Angels, and I composed myself as I walked in.

"Hey, guys, Rooster wants you to come outside and give us a hand," I told them. A couple of the Angels offered to help as well, but I told them it was cool, that we were just picking up some drink.

We just got outside as Rooster was making his way up the stairs. I closed the door and started to tell them our news, but Rooster interrupted, reminding me that it hinged on a lot of factors panning out the way we hoped.

He then told them the same story he'd told me, both Cowboy and Flick seemed quite happy about it, without being overly excited.

"What do you reckon then, guys? Great news, don't you think?" I said, looking at the both of them. Before they could reply, Rooster interrupted again, telling us that we should keep a lid on it and not mention it again over the weekend, and we all nodded in agreement.

Rooster, at that point, headed into the farm, leaving the three of us on the steps. I looked at Cowboy and Flick and noticed they were both staring at me so I asked them if everything was okay.

Cowboy then started, "Well, Shug, actually, were both pretty fuckin pissed with you right now, you had no fuckin right telling Rooster that we were up for it when we hadn't even had a chance to fuckin discuss it. That's not a fuckin cool thing to do to your mates and it better not fuckin happen again."

I knew I was well in the wrong and immediately apologised to them both. I tried to explain that I was just overly enthusiastic and in a hurry to get Rooster to talk to Indie.

Flick interrupted me and gave me a bit of a mouthful, telling me never to speak on his behalf again, and I offered yet another apology. Cowboy then started sniggering and said that he was used to me being a dick and knew I didn't mean anything bad by it, but reminded me, if it happened again, he would be seriously pissed.

I held my hands up, ready to offer another apology, but they both grabbed me and we all started laughing. We had a bit of a hug then I suggested we go inside and get plastered and forget all about my stupidity and, surprisingly, they both agreed.

We headed back in and grabbed some beers out the fridge then made our way into the big room. By this time, it was standing room only everywhere in the house, even the garden at the back of the conservatory was heaving.

Everybody seemed to be getting on really well and there was a lot of laughing and joking. It had been a long time since the mood of the place had felt this good.

I was feeling pretty pleased with myself, knowing that everybody was on board and was keeping my fingers crossed that everything worked out.

Between the music and everyone trying to shout over it, the place was jumping. It was so loud and busy that I was starting to feel a bit claustrophobic so I suggested we head outside for a bit of air and see if it was any quieter and they agreed it was a good idea.

It wasn't much better in the garden, but at least we were able to hear what we were saying to each other.

Cowboy told me that Indie had arranged for us all to go to the social club on Saturday, after the patch over and voting had been done, for a serious party.

"Yeh, they're giving us the big hall. The prospects will be taking a fiver a head at the door, it's to be a free bar all night."

While we were talking, I thought I saw Angel and Fiona in the conservatory. When I finished talking, I told him I would go and grab some more beers for us, but I really wanted to check if it was them I'd seen.

I went back into the conservatory and noticed it was them. Angel was cuddling with Indie and Fiona was standing next to them, looking around. I went up to her and put my arms around her, giving her a hug. She responded by doing the same. As we cuddled, I told her it was great to see her and that she was looking lovely. She said she was glad to see me, told me she was okay, then asked me how I was doing.

We broke from our embrace and I told her I was doing good and asked how Stiff was. Fiona said he was still in hospital, but they were considering where to put him as he really should be in some kind of care home rather than the hospital.

I asked if anyone had seen him yet and she told me only Angel and Indie had been in and that they weren't allowing anyone else to visit. We chatted for a few minutes about his condition and tried to surmise what would happen to him next.

Just then, Angel interrupted us, giving me a hug, telling me she was glad to see me. She also asked how I was doing and I told her the same as I'd told Fiona minutes earlier.

I asked her the same question and she said she was okay, but would be even better when all the club stuff was sorted out.

I told her that we were all feeling the same and that everyone was rooting for Indie to become the new President and that I hadn't heard of anyone opposing it.

She whispered in my ear, telling me she would rather he walked away from it all and then they could maybe lead a normal life as a couple, but knew that it would never happen.

I never responded to that, I just told her I thought Indie was a good bloke and that I was sure, no matter what happened, she would be safe with him. I then excused myself and headed to the kitchen to grab more beer.

The rest of the night was just about everyone getting pished, me included, and all the talk was about the two clubs becoming one. The thing that stood out for me the most was that all the Angels we spoke to were really looking forward to becoming Bats. I thought that there would have been at least a few of them who would resent the fact that they were being patched over, but if there was then they were hiding it very well.

When I woke the next morning, I was lying in bed with Fiona, we both had all our clothes on and I had no idea how I'd got there. The last thing I could remember was having a debate with Cowboy about who could drink a pint the quickest.

I gave Fiona a bit of a shake to wake her then asked her how we'd ended up there. She told me that she had no idea how I came to be in the bed. She'd been looking for somewhere to crash and when she opened the bedroom door, she saw me already sleeping and decided to join me.

I tried to retrace my steps from the night before, but my last memory was still the discussion with Cowboy about the beer.

I felt a bit worried about my apparent memory loss, the last few times that I'd had a skin full, it had happened and I couldn't decide if it was because I'd had way too much to drink or if I just wasn't able to handle it the same.

I suggested to Fiona that we get up and grab a coffee and a bit of breakfast, but she told me she couldn't as she and Angel had loads of stuff to organise for later that day.

We both stood up and had a bit of a kiss and cuddle. As usual, I misinterpreted the situation and stuck my hand down the back of her jeans and started rubbing her arse.

Fiona then pulled back, removing my hand, and told me she couldn't do it. I tried to apologise to her, but she put her finger on my lips and told me to be quiet, that everything was okay, it was just that she just didn't have the time, but would be happy to get together later.

She gave me a kiss then told me she had to go, leaving me standing there, thinking of what might have been. As I left the room, I saw her going into Indies room then made my way downstairs.

I headed to the kitchen in the hope of grabbing a coffee. The place was silent and, as usual, there were people lying all over the place, looking much the worse for wear.

There were a few people sitting around the table, looking a bit subdued, having a coffee and smoking. A couple of girls were making a fry-up. I acknowledged everyone and poured myself a coffee then headed outside.

I opened the door and was blinded by the bright sun shining directly on me. I closed the door and lifted my hand up to my face, shading my eyes.

I noticed Rooster sitting alone on the step and joined him. "Hey, man, you're up early!" I suggested as I sat down beside him.

"Never slept much, Shug, couldn't get my head to switch off. I kept trying to work out how things would go today and what the fuck's going to happen next."

"Ha ha, welcome to my world, Rooster, I thought I was the only eejit who did that. Were you not the person who told me I thought too much and that I should just go with the flow? Why don't you take a bit of your own advice and let it go?" I suggested. "In my experience, whatever conclusion you arrive at never pans out. Something you've never thought about always slips into the mix and fucks you right up."

"I know that, Shug, but the thing I'm wrestling with is the 'New Chapter' gig. I keep asking myself, would I really want to be involved in setting it up if you hadn't wanted it so badly? And the answer's no. It just seems like way too much hassle for me, I keep thinking I'd be better off here with Indie and focusing on stabilising this chapter."

"Fuck's sake, Rooster, you told me you were well up for it. What the fuck's happened to change your mind, man?" I demanded him to tell me.

"Listen, Shug, I was well up for it when you made the suggestion. At the time, it sounded dead exciting, but since then, I've had time to weigh up the pro's and con's and I'm not sure if I want it. Hey, if I decide not to do it, it shouldn't make any difference to you. Indie's already said he wants it set up; I'm sure he'll be glad to have you involved if it's what you really want."

Before I got a chance to reply, the door opened and lots of the guys started pouring out. We both almost jumped up from our sitting position to move away from the steps.

"What's happening, man?" Rooster said, grabbing one of the guys. "Indie wants us all in the barn, looks like the patch over's happening now," he told him.

Rooster looked at me and remarked that he thought something else must be going down. He reckoned it was way too early to get started, but when I told him it was well after eleven, he seemed to change his mind.

We all gathered in the barn, as Indie had requested, and when he entered with Ammo, all eyes were on him. He stood on a couple of crates, raised his hands above his head and let out a loud whistle, which brought everyone to order.

As the place fell silent, he started talking, "Guys, today we will unite two clubs. Our clubs have been like one, for as long as anyone can remember: We share the same values, we operate the same way and all the members of both clubs have treated each other like true brothers. Today, we will unite as one club with two chapters." He then pointed to Ammo, getting him to join him on the crates. He helped him up and put his arm around him then faced us all.

"Ammo, as you all know, is acting Prez for the Angels, due to the fact that her fuckin Majesty decided she wanted to provide board and lodgings to Dog and Bootsie for the foreseeable future," he shouted, amidst roars of laughter. "So, guys, I would now like to hand you over to Ammo, who's going to say a few words."

Indie then jumped off the crates, amid a loud succession of roars and cheers, leaving Ammo to say his bit. "Thanks for that, Indie, it's much appreciated," he told him, clapping his hands above his head.

"Brothers, I would just like to say that it is a testimony to our relationship with the Bats that every Angel in our chapter agreed to the patch over, without objection. As you all know,

Dog and Bootsie had already set the wheels in motion for the patch over with Provo and Stiff and were ready to discuss this with us before their untimely removal by the local constabulary. They felt that, by doing this, we would be able to grow, become stronger and be part of something that would control the whole of Scotland, not just our own little bit."

Again, roars and cheers resonated around the barn as everybody hugged and backslapped each other.

Ammo then restored some order, removed his cut-off and asked all the Angels to do the same, which they did.

I watched the Angels as they did this, wondering what they would do with their existing cuts. Most of them just removed them and held them in their hands, while others took a bit of time and care to fold them neatly and place them inside their leathers.

At that point, the whole place seemed to dull to an eerie silence until Ammo started talking again.

"Brothers, both myself, as acting President of the New chapter, and Indie, as acting President of our Mother chapter, would now like to present each and every one of you with your new Colours."

He then jumped off the crates and stood directly in front of Indie. Indie had a box on the floor beside him which was full of new cuts. He bent down and picked out the first one.

He asked Ammo to turn around, which he did, then placed the cut over his leather jacket. When Ammo turned back around, he shook him by the hand and gave him a hug. Everybody, again, started roaring and cheering.

When we all calmed down, Ammo asked for all his officers to come forward, which they did. There were seven of them. Ammo shook all of their hands then looked to Indie who handed him a cut.

Every time Ammo put the new cut on one of the officers, a massive cheer went up. The officers then all stood to the side and Ammo asked the remaining Angels to come forward to receive their Colours.

Between them, Indie and Ammo placed all the cuts on the backs of every Angel, they all received a welcoming roar from us. As the guys filtered back amongst us, they were all received warmly with hugs and handshakes.

Indie and Ammo then got back up onto the crates and Indie roared, "Three cheers to the Black Bats, hip hip," Fuck, I thought the barn roof was going to lift off, such was the din made by everybody roaring and cheering. Again, Indie shouted 'hip hip' and there was another explosion of noise. When the third one was delivered by Ammo, you couldn't hear yourself think.

Indie and Ammo then tried to restore a bit of order which, under the circumstances, was proving to be a bit of a tall order.

Again, they both held up their hands, hoping for some silence. This time, however, it must have been a full five minutes before it was quiet enough for any of them to be heard.

Eventually, they managed to bring everybody back to order and Ammo was able to start talking.

"Indie, I'd just like to say thank you very much, on behalf of the North chapter." As he said the words 'North chapter' everyone cheered and roared as loud as they could.

Ammo then paused again, letting the cheers subside before he spoke again.

"Indie, as acting Prez, and on behalf of all brothers the North chapter of the Black Bats, I would just like to thank you for your support and diligence in making the transition so smooth for us." Ammo then turned to Indie and said: "Indie, I want to assure you, and all our new Brothers, here and now, that your new 'North chapter' will never allow anyone to disrespect the patch, we will wear it with pride, honour and loyalty."

They both shook hands and hugged and we all followed suit by doing the same. Indie then asked for some quiet, wanting to tell us what was coming next.

"Gents, as you know, we at the 'Central chapter' now have the pressing matter of electing our officers, which we'll be doing at the local social club. I would now like to invite everyone to attend. After I finish talking, I want everybody to make their way there. As there is limited parking, I'll be taking the van and we also have a couple of cars going. If you're not going in the van or the cars, make sure you double up. The prospects will collect a fiver from everyone at the door, which will cover your food and drink for the whole night. I just want to say thanks to everybody for your attention during the patch over, it was much appreciated. So come on now, what are you all waiting for, let's get the fuck out of here and have a party! See you at the club in five!"

At that point, the barn emptied and the bikes were fired into life. We all went two's up, as Indie requested. I went to get my bike, but saw Rooster sitting waiting for a passenger and decided to go with him.

"Come on, ya poof, what the fuck are you waiting for? Let's get going," I screamed in his ear, making sure he heard me over the din of the bikes.

Rooster never said a word, he just smiled, shook his head, then he shot us off up the lane, avoiding everybody that was scrambling about, still trying getting organised.

We were about to turn onto the main road when I realised I had no helmet on. I told Rooster he would need to take me back to the farm for my helmet. He told me to fuck off and carried on towards the club.

Thankfully, we never saw any cops on the way and arrived relatively unscathed. We were greeted at the door by a prospect asking us for our fivers. Rooster walked straight in, pointing at me, which meant I was left to pay both.

Surprisingly, we were the first there. By the time I got into the main hall, Rooster had disappeared. I had no idea where he'd gone. So, after a couple of shouts, I lifted a bottle of beer from the bar and sat at the first table I came to.

I was in a good position to watch all the guys pouring in and it wasn't long before Flick, Cowboy and a couple of others joined me. I asked if any of them had seen Rooster, but they all shook their heads.

Just then, he came in with a pile of paper, pens and a couple of small boxes, both about the size of a shoe box. Indie had already got a couple of tables moved into the corner, directly opposite the bar, and that's where Rooster headed to dump all the stuff.

He then went to the bar, grabbed a beer and joined us. Within five minutes, Indie banged a glass on the table and asked for order. The whole room then fell silent and all eyes were on him.

I was really looking forward to the election. I'd never been to one, but I vaguely remember when I was at school, getting a day off for the local election. I'd seen similar boxes to the ones Rooster had brought in in the gym hall, along with booths for people to fill in their voting forms.

"Gents, can I have your attention for a minute. Brothers from the North chapter, I know this election doesn't concern you, in terms of voting, but I hope you'll bear with us for half an hour or so before the party begins properly."

A chorus of 'here, here's', and some table banging, echoed around the room before the silence returned.

"Thanks for that, we're now going to crack on. I'd like to explain, for anyone who has not done this before, how it works."

Indie took about ten minutes to explain the process then invited us to collect ballot papers for voting.

I picked up mine then went back to my table to look at it. On the top it had a sentence telling you to select your choice and to write the name of your selections in the space provided.

The first box said President and had a blank box next to it. Underneath it was the same with Vice-President in the first box. I made my choice, opting for Indie as President and Jelly as his VP, then placed my paper in the ballot box.

I went back to the table via the bar, picking up a bottle for everyone on the way. Rooster was already seated and I asked him who he'd voted for and he told me he opted for Indie and Jelly. When I told him I had voted the same, he just smiled.

Cowboy and Flick joined us and it turned out the four of us had voted the same way. Indie then announced that that the voting was over and that Ammo and his SAA would count the votes and announce the results.

Indie then headed to the bar, grabbed himself a drink then wandered around the room, chatting away to everybody. Within five minutes of sitting down to count, Ammo announced that they'd counted the votes and had a clear majority for both positions.

It was no surprise when he announced Indie as the new President and invited him to join him at the table. We all cheered for Indie and, as I looked around, I never heard or saw a single person who didn't look happy about the result.

Indie then took the floor, thanking everyone for voting for him and told us he was going to announce who his VP would be. Ammo handed him another piece of paper and, after a quick glance, Indie then told us that the new VP was going to be Hotwire.

Hotwire joined him on the floor, grinning from ear to ear, and as everyone started cheering, we all looked at each other in a bit of disbelief. Cowboy was first to speak.

"Fuck, that's a surprise!" he suggested to us. "Didn't see that coming! Do you guys not think that Hotwire's still a bit part player? You know, in and out, just coming around when he got the shout?"

We all sort of mumbled and nodded our heads, except Rooster, who then started to speak. "Hey, come on, guys, fuck's sake! Remember, it was a fuckin vote, nobody controls that so let's just embrace it for a change, rather than fucking analysing it."

He turned to face Indie and Hotwire then joined in the clapping, lifting his hands above his head to do so.

I just followed his lead then began to wonder how and when the rest of the officers would be sorted.

Indie raised his hand in an attempt to get a bit of quiet and eventually, after a few minutes, got his wish.

"Guys, thanks again, I would just like you all to know both myself and Hotwire are delighted to be selected and Hotwire would like to say a few words."

Hotwire then said he was honoured to have been chosen and would do his very best to follow in Stiff's footsteps.

Indie then suggested we all get into the party mood and told us the ladies were in the other hall, waiting for the shout to come and join us, which probably got the biggest cheer of the day.

He asked all the other officers to join him and Hotwire in the committee room then they both made their way out.

We sat back down at the table and I asked Rooster what happened next. He then told me that Indie, Hotwire and the rest of the officers would now select the people they wanted to fill the vacant posts.

"How does that work then?" I asked him. "Fuck's sake, Shug, you're like a fuckin dug wae a bone. Do you never get fed up asking fuckin questions?" he replied. "Just like to know what's going on, Rooster, you know that," I told him, ignoring his aggressive tones.

Rooster then sniggered a bit and when he spoke, his tone suggested he was much calmer. "Okay, Shug, I'm not 100% sure how it works as this is the first time that we've had to replace more than one officer at a time, but, from what I've heard, I think what they do is that the Prez and VP nominate someone to be SAA, it would normally come from someone who is already an officer, and they then have an open vote on it. If they get a majority, it's a done deal. If they don't, they nominate someone else and do the same again. For the treasurer and secretary, they would normally discuss who they thought would be the best to do the job, based on any experience the guys had in that area. The last bit is the other officers, and we have eight altogether, so I guess they'll select brothers to make up the numbers."

"So is that what they'll be doing just now?" I asked him, wanting to know as much as he did. "Fuck, Shug, you just don't give up, do you?" he ranted at me, before carrying on.

"Right, this is the last bit you're getting, okay?" he told me, with one of his glowering stares. He looked straight at me and I knew he meant it this time so I just nodded. He was still staring straight at me and took a large breath before starting to talk.

"I'm not sure if they'll pick anyone tonight, or if they'll just discuss possible candidates. It's more likely that they'll announce their choices back at the farm, especially if any of the current officers want to stand down. Normally, when a new Prez is put in place, the officers can opt out if they don't want to be part of the new regime. I think the situation we have just now is probably pretty unique; I can't ever recall any biker chapter losing both the Prez and VP at the same time. So that's all I know, and now I'm done talking about it, so if you want any more info about it then you'll need to ask some other fucker, okay?"

When he finished, I just nodded to him and thanked him for the update. Cowboy then said he was going to get the beers in. Rooster then asked me if I'd made up my mind about the interview and I told him I'd decided to go for it.

He then asked me if I would say hi to Julie for him and I agreed I would. One of the guys then cranked up the music and grabbed the microphone. He started shouting that this was the most boring party he'd ever been to and pointed to the door, telling us it was time for everyone to rock.

We all turned to the door, wondering why he was pointing at it, and, right on cue, it swung open and a load of girls started pouring in.

All the guys Mama's and girlfriend's had arrived, along with the usual scattering of sad bitches from the village and surrounding areas. They all hit the dance floor and the guy's chicks were pointing to their respective partners, hoping to summon them to the dance floor (with little success). The rest of the girls were making their way to the tables, trying to coax somebody to join them.

A couple of girls came over to us, but Flick waved them away. I looked at Rooster. He hadn't spoken since he told us about the officer stuff and seemed to be lost in a world of his own.

I gave him a bit of a dunt, which brought him back to the land of the living. "Penny for them, big man, you're miles away."

"Sorry, Shug, just thinking a bit," he told me. "I know, I could smell the burning rubber," I said, laughing at my own joke. "Anything you want to share?" I asked him. "No, but maybe I'll tell you later. Come on, let's just get pished and see if we can get laid."

He then stood up, grabbed me around the neck, rubbed his knuckles on my head, and told me he was away to mingle. I told him he was a fuckin wanker for doing that again, but he just laughed as he walked away. 'Fuck, he knows how much that pisses me off, and he keeps fuckin doing it,' I thought to myself.

Cowboy came back, put the drinks on the table then asked where Rooster was. Flick pointed over to another table, where he was standing blethering away, and told him he was away looking to get laid.

The three of us spent the next fifteen minutes or so discussing what Rooster had told us and never really drew any conclusions from it, so decided to give up looking for one.

By this time, the party was starting to hot up and the girls were doing their best to keep it going. Three of them had pulled one of the prospects onto the dance floor and were circling him, while pawing at each other and trying their best to strip him.

He was trying to do the same to them, but they weren't having it. They removed all the clothing from the top half of his body then told him to lie on the floor, which he did.

One of the girls, who had a really short skirt on, that left little to the imagination, pulled her pants off then sat on his face. She then grabbed his hair and started gyrating on top of him, which raised a loud cheer from everyone watching.

The other two girls removed his boots, jeans and pants. One of them grabbed hold of his cock and slipped it into her mouth. The other girl then knelt down at the other side of him and joined in, sharing his cock between them.

The prospect looked like he was trying to lift the other girl from his face, without success, and seconds later he shot his load, much to the cheering onlookers delight.

The girls quickly licked him dry then started snogging the face off each other. By this time, the girl who was sitting on his face must've realised what had happened and got up.

The prospect looked really embarrassed and tried to get up, but was stopped in his tracks by the girls, who told him to stay where he was.

The girl who had been sitting on him, straddled him again, this time in the sixty-nine position, taking his now limp cock into her mouth. She then pushed her pussy back towards his mouth and he carried on where he'd left off.

The other two girls, who were now half-naked, came over to our table and pulled Cowboy onto the floor.

He didn't need to be asked twice, he was up like a shot. Again, they danced around him while undressing him, but this time Cowboy followed suit and within minutes, they were all bollock naked.

Cowboy lay down on the floor on his back, as requested, and this time one of the girls sat on his dick and the other on his face. They started kissing and fondling each other as they bounced up and down on top of him.

By this time, the prospect had got hard again and was now banging the chick 'doggy style' for all he was worth. My viewing was interrupted when I clocked Indie and the others coming back into the hall. They were all smiling and laughing so I guessed they'd sorted everything and were happy with the outcome.

I had a quick look around the room and realised that hardly anyone was still watching the floor show. Most of the guys who had a chick were involved in their own sexual activities.

Flick then got up and made his way to the dance floor. He pulled out his dick and knelt in front of the prospect's chick, offering her his dick, which she gratefully received. He grabbed her hair and started pulling her head back and forward, up and down his shaft.

By now, it was starting to look a bit like one of the farm orgies, but for some reason, I wasn't really getting into it and decided to head outside for a bit of air.

I'd just sat down on the step when I was joined by Fiona. "Hi, Shug, I was just coming over to have a chat with you when I saw you heading out, just wondered if something was up?" she asked as she sat down beside me.

"Hi, Fiona. Sorry, I never saw you inside," I told her. "Nothing's up, I just needed a bit of air, that's all. I take it the girls inside were you and Angels doing?"

"Yes, that's why I had to leave early this morning. We had a bit of organising to do, between picking people up from the train and bus stations and arranging to get them here without anyone knowing."

"Did you do it without Indie knowing about it?" I asked her. "Come on, Shug, don't be daft, it was his idea. We couldn't organise anything like this without his say so, he'd go mental!" she laughed.

I offered her a fag and asked her how she was doing. She told me she really didn't know. I couldn't be arsed asking why, because of all my own shit, so I changed the subject.

I asked her about Indie, Angel and Stiff and she gave me a bit of an update. "You seem a bit distant today, Shug, is everything alright?" she then asked.

I lied and told her everything was fine and that I was just thinking about all the changes that were happening within the club.

"So it's not because you're thinking of moving then?" Fuck, she didn't half know how to drop a bombshell. "Who told you that?" I asked her. "Angel told me, is it right enough, Shug?"

"Who the fuck told her that?" I asked, jumping right on the defensive. "Shug, it doesn't matter who told who what, I just want to know if it's true?"

I calmed down a bit, realising I was overreacting. My initial thought was that Indie had told her about the new chapter and I felt a bit pissed he was sharing club business with her, but then, when I thought more about it, I guessed he'd only told her I was going for an interview.

"Yes, I've got an interview lined up for Thursday and, if I get the job, I'll be moving, but I'll still be here on my days off."

"Why didn't you tell me about it, Shug?" she demanded to know. "Well, the truth is, Fiona, I didn't want to say anything to anybody in case I don't get it. I only told Indie because he found out and asked me about it."

"Why do you want to leave, Shug?" she then asked me. So I told her I felt I needed to empty my head a bit and the best way to do that was to put a bit of distance between me and the village for a while.

"I take it that includes me?" she then remarked. 'Fuckin typical' I thought, 'I'm telling her how I feel and she turns it round to her'.

"Listen, Fiona, this isn't about you, or anything in particular. I've had a bit of a shit twelve months or so and I'm not sure where I'm going, or what I want, so I've decided that, for now, this is the best thing for me to do."

We chatted a bit about things in general and about our friendship. I must've touched a bit of a nerve with her when I mentioned that I had no interest in getting involved in a relationship.

I started saying I felt I needed to have some alone time, but before I'd finished talking, she got up and headed back inside without saying a word. I called to her, asking her to come back, but she just ignored me.

I took a long draw on my fag and decided not to go looking for her. I thought to myself 'Fuck her, I owe her fuck all. If she's not happy then she can go take two fucks to herself'. I stood up, threw away my fag and headed back to the party.

I had a quick scan as I entered, but couldn't see her, and made my way to the table. By this time, Rooster was nowhere to be seen and Cowboy and Flick were entertaining a couple of chicks.

Flick saw me coming and shouted me over. I sat down and he introduced me to the girls. I just gave them a nod, picked up my beer and took a large swig from it.

One of the girls, who was sitting on Flick's knee, reckoned she knew me and started asking questions about who I was and where I was from. I looked a bit closer at her and recognised her from the weekend we'd had just before Malky died.

I told her I remembered her from the last run we had up north, and had shared a fag and a chat at the fire with her the morning before we headed home.

She then told me that she had remembered and was sorry to hear about Malky dying. I just smiled at her, excused myself, then headed to the bar for a refill.

I stood at the bar, waiting to be served, and had a good look around the room. I, again, started to wonder if I really did want this. It seemed, lately, that every party I'd been at was the same as the last, and what initially was unbelievably exciting, now seemed a little flat.

I got served, picked up my two bottles from the bar and turned around, only to be greeted with a slap in the face. It was Angel and she was calling me all sorts.

"What the fuck are you doing?" I demanded her to tell me. "You're a fuckin wanker, Shug, a real piece of fuckin work," she screamed at me, slapping me again. "I can't believe what you did to Fiona; I never thought you were like that," she continued. I put the drinks down on the table and told her if she slapped me again that I would slap her back.

She did try again, but this time I grabbed hold of her arms. Within seconds, Indie was in my face. "What the fuck's going on, Shug?" he demanded to know. "Indie, I have no fuckin idea," I told him. "You'll need to ask your mental fuckin girlfriend."

He then grabbed me by my jacket lapels and aggressively pulled me even closer to him. "You apologise to my old lady, or I'll rip your fuckin head off," he said, staring straight at me.

"Indie, hold it a fuckin minute. What the fuck do you want me to apologise for? I've done fuck all. She slapped me twice and screamed at me like I'd murdered her fuckin mother or something. I only grabbed her to get her to stop slapping me. I've got no idea why she's going mental at me."

"Tell her you're sorry for grabbing her and we can talk," he told me. I then stupidly said: "Okay, if I apologise, do I get an apology back from you and her for embarrassing me in front of everybody?"

He then replied even more aggressively, "You get to continue breathing, and take it from me, that's a fuckin bonus for you, the way I'm feeling right now."

At that point, I really felt that I wanted to punch his fuckin lights out, but knew that was never going to happen, so told him to let me go and that I would talk with her outside.

Surprisingly, he then let me go, or rather pushed me away, and told me to go into the committee room and he would join me in two minutes.

I walked away from him and made my way to the committee room. All I could think about was what a fuckin cow Angel was and what a fuckin prick he was.

I went in and slammed the door behind me, took out a fag and lit up. I inhaled deeply and tried to gather my thoughts. I stared out the window, looking out onto the park.

I saw some kids playing football and they looked like they didn't have a care in the world, the only thing that mattered was the next goal in the game.

I laughed a bit, remembering when I used to be like that. I almost began to feel sorry for myself, thinking about the way things had turned out for me.

My thoughts went back to Indie and the matter in hand and I decided that I wasn't going to take any shit from them, and if I ended up getting a kicking, so fuckin what - it wouldn't be the first time!

I felt I'd done nothing wrong and was prepared to stand by that.

I was still staring out the window when the door opened. I wanted to turn around to see who it was, but decided not to. I listened as the door was closed and I heard my name being called. Fuck, it was Fiona, why in fuck's name had he brought her in?

I turned around and saw she was joined by Indie and Angel. I looked straight at Indie and asked him why the fuck Fiona was here. "Because I want her here, that's why, okay?" was his response.

"What are we doing here, Indie?" I then asked him. "You know fine well why we're here, so sit the fuck down and shut the fuck up," he told me, in a really aggressive tone.

I decided that I was best just doing what I was told, until I saw how things were going to transpire. I slumped down on the chair and opened my hands wide in front of me then said, sarcastically, "Okay, I'm sitting, what's the script?"

I could see that I'd pissed him off big time and noticed him clenching his fists. For a split second, I wished I hadn't, but then Angel started talking and Indie seemed to calm down a bit.

"Shug, look, I'm really sorry for making a scene and for slapping you, I totally over reacted. I guess I was just sticking up for Fiona. When I saw her coming in and running to the loo, crying, I knew you must have upset her and I lost it."

I was kind of thrown a bit by her apology and no longer felt the need to be aggressive. I told her it was fine, but that I was disappointed she didn't try to talk to me about it first.

I then apologised for grabbing her wrists and also apologised to Fiona for upsetting her.

They both smiled then came over to me and gave me a hug. Fuck, how weird was this! One minute, I'm being hated and the next, I'm being cuddled.

Fiona started sobbing as we cuddled and whispered in my ear that she loved me and was sorry for getting me into trouble with Indie. I kissed her on the head and told her everything was alright.

I then looked at Indie and asked him if we were cool and he said we were. He asked the girls to leave then sat down. As he sat, he pointed to the chair next to him and I sat down as well.

"Shug, I didn't know what was going on with you and Fiona until Angel filled me in. My only thought was to protect Angel and I don't give a shit who upsets her, you know that. Now I know all the facts, I'm happy to let it go."

I really wanted to have a go at him for being a dick with me, but decided it best to digest his words for a moment before I spoke. I reckoned that was the closest I was going to get to an apology from him so told him it was fine and that I understood where he was coming from.

I asked him again if we were cool and he told me we were so I got up to leave, but he asked me to sit back down, which I did.

I was wondering what the fuck else I'd done to piss him off and waited for the hammer blow to come. He then stood up, took out his fags and threw one on the table for me before lighting up his own.

He started walking around the table and I watched his every move as I lit up. I started to get that goose bump feeling you get when something bad is about to happen to you so. As he came around the table, approaching my back, I turned to face him.

I decided I needed to take the initiative and asked him what he wanted.

As he walked past me and sat back down on the chair, I turned to face him. "Shug, that's one thing I've noticed about you, you're dead impatient, sometimes that can be a good thing, but other times, it fuckin sucks. I think you're a bit like me in that respect."

I felt that he was just talking for the sake of it and wished he'd cut right to the chase so interrupted him. "I don't know if I'm anything like you, Indie. I think you're way much more controlled than I could ever be and I don't think for a minute that I could run a club. However, you, on the other hand, seem to be taking it in your stride," I told him then asked him again what he wanted to talk to me about.

"See, Shug, that's what I'm talking about. There you go again, that's you to a tee, wanting everything yesterday. Okay, here's the deal, I know that you're hoping to move away, but I need you to tell me the real reason you want to go. You see, I have a proposition for you, but I wouldn't want to share it with you if I thought for a minute that you're running away from being a Bat."

"Indie, I've told you why I wanted to move, we've already had this discussion. It has nothing to do with the Bats," I reminded him.

"Yes, I know that's what you told me before, but that was during all the shit we were going through. But now I'm the Prez, I need to know for real what your intentions are."

"Indie, I'm a Bat now and I swore that I'd be a Bat for life - nothing will change that. I have no intention of leaving. If anything, I now feel much more part of it than ever and if the South chapter is a goer then I would ask you if I could transfer when it was up and running."

"Good, that's what I wanted to hear," he told me. "Shug, I want to talk to you about the new chapter. I was going to wait until tomorrow, but seeing we're talking now, I would be as well just telling you. We will be setting up the South chapter very soon, Ammo has identified four members from the North chapter and I have four in mind from here, you being one of them, and I just needed to know if you were really up for it."

I told him he could count me in and that I was definitely up for it, but reminded him that I had no knowledge or experience in setting up a club so wasn't sure how much use I'd be.

He then told me that I didn't need to worry as he'd already arranged a patch over with one of the MC's that already exist in the South and that one of the guys, Brutis from the North chapter, was well up to speed with how it all worked.

"Who else are you thinking of from here?" I asked him."
"I'll tell you tomorrow, it wouldn't be fair to tell you before I speak to them, okay?"

He then stood up and said: "Right, let's join the party. Oh, and by the way, if anyone asks you what we were talking about, tell them it's none of their fuckin business, okay?"

I stood up and just nodded in his general direction as he left. I followed him out.

'Fuck!' I thought to myself, 'What another crazy fuckin day it's turning out to be'. I decided to head back outside rather than go into the hall. I felt I needed to clear my head before I went back in.

I stood outside, smoking, and tried to come up with something tangible to tell the guys and decided the best thing would be to play on the Fiona thing and keep it as brief as possible.

As I went to go back inside, I was again confronted with Angel and Fiona, but this time, there was no aggression. They both looked a little sheepish and were again full of apologies.

I told them to stop apologising, that everything was cool, and we had a bit of a group hug. Angel then pulled away, telling Fiona she would get her at the car then left.

It was then that I remembered that Fiona had told me she loved me and knew the next part of the conversation was going to be awkward. So, being the pussy I am, I decided it would be best to let her speak first.

We were still cuddling when she whispered in my ear, "Shug, I meant what I said in there, I do love you, you know that, right?" As she spoke, she lifted her head from my ear and started kissing me on the lips. I responded, but after a minute or so, I pulled away.

"Fiona, listen, I'm really flattered," I told her, "but I'm not ready for a committed relationship just now, I couldn't cope with it."

"I know you're not, Shug, but I need you to know that when you are, I'll be waiting." She then kissed me on the cheek and left.

I stood still for a bit before turning around to watch her leave then started walking back to the big hall. Holy shit, just when I thought it couldn't get any weirder she goes and dumps that on me!

I went back into the hall with all sorts of shit swirling around in my head - so much for going outside to clear it!

The place was jumping, but I couldn't see what was going on, there was a circle of people surrounding the dance floor and they were all cheering and laughing.

I went straight to the bar for a beer and noticed a guy sitting at the end of the bar with a beer in his hand. I asked him what the fuck was going on and he told me that the prospect who was getting fucked earlier was doing his last challenge before getting his colours.

I walked over to the crowd and muscled my way in until I was in a position to see what the fuck was going on. The first thing I saw was the prospect. He was blindfolded and had only his jeans and boots on.

He had his hands tied behind his back and two of the guys from the North chapter were giving him drinks to taste. He shouted out whisky and was told he was wrong then the other guy touched him with a lit fag, forcing him to let out an involuntary scream, much to the amusement of the crowd.

I noticed he already had a few burn marks on his back and stomach and guessed he wasn't particularly good at guessing. I didn't watch any more, I just headed back to the table and noticed Rooster sitting by himself and looking a bit down.

I sat beside him and asked him what was up. He told me he had just spoken with Indie and he'd told him he wasn't going to select him as the SAA and that he was giving it to Jelly.

"He fuckin promised me if he got elected, that he would put me in as SAA and now he's fuckin shafted me. I never thought he would do that to me. What a cunt!"

I intervened, suggesting that maybe Indie had bigger plans for him and that he should wait until tomorrow before drawing any conclusions.

"Fuck tomorrow, fuck him, fuck every-fuckin-thing, I've had enough," he told me. He then got up and headed towards the door. I followed as fast as I could and grabbed hold of him just as he entered the corridor.

"Hold up, Rooster, I need to tell you something." "Not interested, Shug. I'm sick of the whole fuckin thing, I'm off." He then walked towards the outside door, pushed it open and stormed out.

As he made his way to his bike, I grabbed him again, "For fuck's sake, Rooster, just stop for one fuckin minute and let me say my piece. Then you can do what the fuck you like, okay?"

He let out a large sigh then said to me: "Okay, Shug, let's hear it, say what you have to and be quick about it."

I told him about the conversation I'd had with Indie and suggested to him that I thought he was going to be offered the Prez or the VP role in the new chapter and that was probably why Indie didn't offer him the SAA gig.

"So why the fuck didn't he tell me that then?" he asked. "Listen, Shug, I know you mean well, but Indie knew I was well pissed when he told me so if there was anything else in the offing then I'm sure he would have shared it with me, especially now I know he's spoken to you about it."

I found it hard to argue with his logic, but somehow managed to convince him to stay and wait until the following day's events transpired before doing anything rash.

We went back inside and sat back down at the table. The place was back to normal and the music was blaring away, people were dancing and it appeared that the prospect's ordeal was over.

I told Rooster I was glad that I never prospected for the Angels if that was the kind of initiation rituals you had to endure. He just laughed and called me a pussy.

We spent the rest of the night drinking and chatting away, hardly speaking to anyone else, then decided to split back to the farm around midnight.

When we got on Rooster's bike, I realised just how pished we actually were. He was all over the road and I wasn't much help as I was swaying about behind him.

How we managed to get back to the lane without a crash was a minor miracle. We turned off the main road, heading down the lane towards the farm, but for some reason, Rooster didn't realise there was a left-hand turn and drove us straight into the field.

The bike hit a felled tree and catapulted us both into a gorse bush - Oh how I wished I'd had a fuckin helmet on!

I started shouting at him, asking him what the fuck he was playing at, but he just started roaring and laughing. I was in fuckin agony, ripped to fuck with the gorse, and I thought I'd broken my arm.

"What the fuck are you laughing at?" I shouted at him. "Are you fuckin blind or something? How in fuck's name could you not see the turning? For fuck's sake, man, you've ridden up here a million times!"

He never even answered me, he just laughed harder. "Rooster, what the fuck is wrong with you, man," I roared even louder. This time, however, he did speak.

"You know what, Shug? I was that fuckin mad, thinking about what that bastard Indie had done to me, that I forgot to fuckin turn at the corner!" then he burst into laughter again amid moans that he thought he'd broken his back.

When I looked at him, I could do nothing else but join in with his laughter, even though I was in agony myself. After a couple of minutes, we settled down a bit and I asked him if he could move. He told me if I pulled him up then he'd be okay.

By this time, the effects of the drink were starting to wear off and I could feel the pain kicking in for real. I somehow managed to get myself out of the gorse and into an upright position.

I realised that my arm probably wasn't broken, even though it hurt like fuck. I stuck out my other one and Rooster grabbed hold of it with both hands. As I started to pull, he let out a scream, telling me his back was fucked.

I kept pulling until I managed to get him up, amidst his moans and groans. When he was standing up, he put his hand on his back and realised he was bleeding.

He brought his hand back around to his front and it was red, his whole hand was covered in the stuff. I quickly pulled him towards me and put his arm over my shoulder and dragged him onto the road.

I sat him down and looked at his back. I could see a hole the size of a tennis ball at the bottom of his back, just to the right of his spine. I removed my jacket, pulled off my shirt, removed his and stuffed my shirt into the hole.

While I was doing this, Rooster passed out and I laid him down on the road. The shirt seemed to have stopped the blood coming out, but I had no idea what to do next.

I thought about running to the farm, but didn't want to leave him so just pressed my hand over his wound, applying some pressure to it, and waited in the hope that someone else would come down the lane soon.

I sat there for about ten minutes, but it felt like I'd been there for hours. How I wished I'd gone to the farm, knowing if I had that we could have called an ambulance and it would have been there by now.

I kept talking to Rooster, telling him to wake up, but I never got a response. A couple of times, I thought he'd stopped breathing, but I think it was just my imagination.

At last, I saw some lights heading towards us and knew I'd soon be getting help. As they approached, I realised it was a motor and not two bikes. It was Indie in the van and he was up and out like a shot.

"Holy fuck, Shug, what happened here?" he shouted at me. "We crashed, Indie. Rooster's fucked and needs to get to the hospital sharpish, man," I told him.

By this time, a rake of guys and girls who were in the back of the van had piled out and were standing around us.

Luckily, a couple of the girls there were nurses and immediately took over from me. One look from them, and they both agreed that he needed to get medical treatment straight away.

We lifted him into the back of the van as quickly as we could. The girls then went in with him and I jumped in the front with Indie. He turned the van around and shot off, making his way to the hospital, driving like a maniac.

"What the fuck happened, Shug?" he asked. "Rooster missed the corner and we ended up in the bushes. He landed on a tree stump and a branch stub went right into his back."

"How the fuck did he manage that?" he wanted to know. Fuck, I didn't know if I should tell him what he'd told me or just blame the drink.

"Fuck knows, man. One minute, we were heading towards the farm the next, we were lying in the bushes - I've no idea how it happened," I lied.

We got to the hospital and Indie went straight into the area reserved for ambulances at the casualty entrance. As he jumped out, he told me to help the girls take Rooster in.

I opened the back door and the three of us carried him inside. When we got in, a doctor came rushing towards us, with Indie, and directed us to a treatment room. We laid Rooster down on a trolley on his side and the girls started talking with the doctor.

I went back to the waiting area and saw Indie giving a nurse at the reception Rooster's details. I went over beside him and listened to them talking.

She asked him what had happened and he told her he'd fallen. When she asked where from, Indie gave her a cold stare and said: "He fell and landed on a tree, okay?" I think she realised that asking anything else would prove futile so she noted his response and told us to take a seat.

We sat in the waiting area beside a scattering of people who were waiting to be seen. I looked down at my hands and realised not only were they covered in blood, but my chest, jeans, jacket and cut-off were all soaked in it as well.

I told Indie I was going to look for a loo to get cleaned up and he just nodded. I found some nearby and went in. The first thing I did was look in the mirror. Fuck, my face and hair were also covered in Rooster's blood.

I removed my jacket and filled the sink with water. The minute I stuck my face and hands in it, it became red. I pulled out the plug and turned the tap back on. I removed as much as I could from my face and hands then grabbed some paper towels and started cleaning the rest of me.

It took me about fifteen minutes to get scrubbed up. When I was done, I put my jacket back on and went back out to the waiting area, hoping there would be some news.

The girls were standing talking to Indie and I interrupted them by asking how he was. One of them told me he was going to be fine and that he was very lucky that I'd stemmed the flow of blood when I did as his condition could have been much more serious if I hadn't.

"So what's up with him? Why was he bleeding so much?" I asked her. "Well, the doctor said that he had extensive bleeding due to the tree piercing some small veins and capillaries and he also has some tissue damage."

"Sorry, what the fuck does that mean? Please tell me in idiot speak as I didn't understand a fuckin word of that." I replied.

She gave me a bit of a stare and shook her head, "He's going to have a small op to repair the damage on his back and if there are no complications, then he'll be back to normal in a week or so, okay? Is that simple enough for you?" she said as if she was talking to a five-year-old.

"Now I understand, thank you very much." I was going to remark on her sarcasm, but decided to let it go. The other girl then told Indie that it was pointless hanging around as we wouldn't get to see him until at least late afternoon.

He thanked the girls for their help and asked them if they were coming back to the farm. They both looked at each other and decided that they would just head home. So he offered them a lift, but they declined it, telling him they only lived five minutes away anyway.

We got back in the van and made our way out the hospital grounds and onto the main road. "Thank fuck it's not serious," I remarked. "I'm glad the girls were there. At least they knew what they were doing."

"You didn't do too badly yourself, Shug. How did you know to put pressure on the wound?" Indie asked. I told him I remembered when Flick got stabbed that the doctor at the farm had told me to do it with him.

"Ha ha, have we've got a right little Florence fuckin Nightingale here or what?" he said, laughing away to himself.

He then started thinking out loud, saying he wondered what made Rooster crash and that it wasn't like him and that he'd ridden his bike with way much more drink that he'd had tonight.

"What do you reckon, Shug? Do you think he had something on his mind that made him lose concentration?" I thought about telling him the truth, but wasn't sure how he would react so decided just to feed him a little info.

"Not really sure, Indie. The only thing I can think of was that he seemed upset about not getting the SAA's gig, but I don't know if he was dwelling on it."

Indie then started banging his hands on the steering wheel and started shouting, "Fuck, fuck, fuck." I'd never seen him like this before, he was normally so calm.

"Jeezus! I thought about telling him the rest of it, but thought it better to wait until he was sober. Aaahhggg, what a fuckin idiot I am!" he announced.

I had no idea what he was ranting about. But when he stopped, I asked him what he meant.

"I had lined him up to be Brutis's VP in the South chapter, but I wanted to wait and tell him tomorrow when we announced who the other officers were going to be. Fuck, I should have just told him tonight."

I tried to defuse his anger by telling him I didn't think that it had anything to do with it and it was more likely that I had snaked the bike by not going with him at the corner, but he wasn't for having it.

We never spoke another word from then until we reached the farm. When we passed the scene of the crash, I noticed that Rooster's bike had been lifted and guessed it would be in the barn, waiting to get repaired.

When Indie stopped the van, he reminded me that I should keep schtum about our discussions and I told him I would.

When we went into the farm, it seemed like everybody from the social club had landed back and that they'd decided to continue the party.

We'd hardly got in the door when we were confronted by a rake of the guys enquiring about Rooster. Indie kept it short, telling them that he was a bit bashed up, but would be fine in a few days.

Everybody seemed happy enough with that and then turned their attention to me, slagging me off for the state of my face. I just smiled with them and grabbed a beer from the fridge.

The guys then went back into party mode and I went out onto the stairs and lit up a smoke. Within minutes, I was joined by Cowboy and Flick who wanted to know all the gory details.

They both stood in front of me with expectant looks on their faces. I looked up at them and Cowboy said: "Come on, Shug, spill the beans and tell us what the fuck happened."

"Indie told you what happened, why the fuck would you think there was anything else to tell?" I lied. "Don't give us that pish, Shug," Flick replied. "We know you better than that, there's no way Rooster would have missed the corner. So come on, spit it out."

"Fuck's sake, guys, this is heavy shit. If I tell you then you need to promise to keep it to yourselves." They both assured me they would and I trusted them so told them everything.

Cowboy was first to speak, "Holy fuck, Shug, that isn't half a turn up for the books. I can't believe Indie would tell him about Jelly then not tell him the rest. He was well out of order; no wonder Rooster was pissed."

I told him to keep his voice down and forget all about it until everything was sorted and that when Rooster got out of hospital, we'd all sit down and discuss it.

Flick went to say something, but I told him to forget it and save it for another day. Flick then said that he wasn't going to mention it, but wanted to know what happened with me, Angel and Indie earlier.

I almost felt relieved when he asked me that so I told them all about it, right down to the bit about Fiona telling me she loved me.

Well, if nothing else it lightened the mood, that's for sure, and I couldn't get the pair of cunts to stop laughing. I eventually, after some light hearted ribbing, joined in and felt much better for it.

Chapter 18

We all went back inside and noticed the party had ground to a halt, apart from a few stragglers who were trying their best to keep it going. After having a bit of a look around for somewhere to crash, I decided I'd be better off heading back to my flat.

Cowboy suggested that he and Flick join me, and I told him, as long as he wasn't looking to party, it was cool. We walked back through the kitchen and I checked the clock, it was twenty to four, and Indie wanted us all back at the farm for twelve.

When we got outside, I reminded the guys about Mark and told them I needed them to be as quiet as possible when they arrived at the flat.

In contrast to that, we jumped on our bikes and started them up, making as much noise as possible and laughing aloud as we negotiated our way through the large number of machines abandoned all around the building.

Eventually, we got onto the lane and headed to the flat. The dawn was just breaking, the sun was starting to filter through, and there was hardly a sign of life anywhere.

We never saw a single car on the road until we hit the village, and then it was only the bread van making a delivery at the newsagents.

As I passed it, I got a whiff of that smell you only get from a baker's shop or van, which made me smile and took me back to when I delivered milk.

Any time we met the baker, he used to give our boss a dozen rolls in exchange for four pints of milk and I always got two of them.

Those were always the best mornings, as there's nothing better than a freshly baked warm roll, especially in the winter.

We arrived at the flat and the guys were true to their word, killing the engines as early as they could and then quietly parking up. When we hit the flat, I went straight into the bedroom, grabbed my sleeping bag and chucked it on the couch without saying a word.

I left them to decide who was sleeping where and jumped into bed without even bothering to take off my jacket or boots - I was that tired. I think I was almost sleeping before my head hit the pillow.

I never woke until just after eleven and saw the bed next to me was empty. I lay for a bit, listening for any noise, but I couldn't hear a sound coming from the living room.

It was so quiet that I began to wonder if the guys had split without wakening me up and felt a bit miffed that they'd do that. I opened the door into the living room and was a bit surprised when I saw them both, sitting reading newspapers and drinking tea.

Cowboy looked at me and told me I looked rougher than a badger's arse and offered to get me a brew. He headed into the kitchen and I sat down on the chair.

"How you feeling, Shug?" Flick asked me. "Still a bit fuzzy," I told him, then asked him how long he'd been awake. "Cowboy got me up about ten and we went to the shop to get stuff for breakfast."

Cowboy then came back through and handed me two bacon rolls and a mug of tea. "Get that down your neck, it'll revive you," he told me, then sat down and started reading his paper again.

I hadn't really thought too much about the age gap between us, but as I sat eating my rolls, I watched them both, sitting silently reading and suddenly felt like I was a kid having breakfast with his parents.

It's funny how a simple thing like that changes your perception of people. It was the first time I'd actually seen Cowboy and Flick as 'older people' and laughed to myself as I ate.

I finished my rolls then went to the bathroom for a wash before hitting the bedroom for a change of clothes and grabbing some cash from my drawer.

When I went back into the living room, the guys were getting ready to go, reminding me that Indie wanted us back at the farm for twelve.

As we headed out, I told Cowboy and Flick I wanted to swing by the hospital to check on Rooster before heading to the farm and they both said they would come along.

When we got there, we were told that Rooster was now in the surgical ward so we made our way there. We went to the reception area and I asked the receptionist if it was possible to pop in and see him for a couple of minutes. She told me to take a seat and she would get a nurse.

The nurse who came to talk to us was one I recognised from my time in the ward and she remembered me as well. We had a brief chat, asking each other how we were and shit like that, then I asked her if I could see Rooster. She told me I couldn't get in until visiting at two. I then lied, telling her I was going to work at one and only wanted to see Rooster for a minute to pass on a message to him.

After a bit of persuasion, she reluctantly agreed to take me to him. He was in a little side room and she pointed it out, telling me she would be back in five minutes to get me. I thanked her and told her she was a star. She smiled at that and told me flattery would get me everywhere.

I went into the room and closed the door. "Shug, how you doin, man? How's my bike? Did you get it back to the farm?" he asked. "Rooster, relax, man. I'm fine, the bike's fine, everything's cool. How are you feeling?"

"I'm good, man, doc say's there's no lasting damage and I'll be out in a few days." I told him that was great news and mentioned that Cowboy and Flick were here as well and that I was the only one allowed in.

"I only have five minutes so I need to be quick. After the crash, I had a chat with Indie and told him you were a bit pissed with him. He was pretty upset that he'd pissed you off and blamed himself for you being in here."

Rooster then tried to interrupt, but I told him to be quiet until I'd finished. I then shared the whole conversation with him and, thinking he'd be happy about the news, I stuck my hand out to offer him congratulations.

However, his reaction was nothing like I expected and he let rip.

"What a fuckin wanker! Who the fuck does he think he is, deciding where I'll be going? He can stick his VP up his fuckin arse! In fact, he can stick his Bats up his fuckin arse as well. I'm finished with that prick, and the sooner I get out of here, the sooner I'll let him know that!" he ranted.

I tried to intervene, "Whoa, man, settle yourself down, for fuck's sake. You'll burst a blood vessel or something. Right now, you need to calm down and focus on getting well, and fuck all else. Jeez oh, man, I wish to fuck I hadn't told you now, I thought you'd be fuckin pleased."

"Pleased? Fuckin pleased? Why the fuck would you think I'd be pleased? Are you fuckin thick or just taking the fuckin pish? He wants me to fuck off somewhere else, with cunts I don't even know, and help start up a new chapter, instead of being the SAA in my own chapter! Think about it, if it goes tit's up then I'm back with my tail between my legs and some other cunt is the SAA, and I'm back to being a fuckin foot soldier. Listen, he fuckin promised me that position, but now it's the old pals act and he's pumping me away under the pretence that I'm getting an even better gig. Well, fuck him!"

He then stared at me and started pointing, "You know what, Shug? I fuckin blame you for this. If you hadn't started this pish, and got me to talk Indie about it, then I would be the SAA and I wouldn't be lying in here. So why don't you just fuck off and give me peace before I say anything I might regret."

"Hey, Rooster, hang on a fuckin minute here. I know you're pissed, but don't start fuckin blamin me for all this!" I replied.

He didn't answer me, he just shouted on the nurse, telling her to get me out. I looked directly at him and told him he was an ungrateful self-centred prick and if that was how he felt then he could go fuck himself. I then about turned and walked away.

As I was leaving, I heard him shout, "You know what, Shug? Fuck you! Fuck your bullshit and fuck your hair-brained schemes! You've fucked me up, this is all your fuckin fault, and I won't fuckin forget it, ya bastard!"

I stopped in the ward when I got out of Rooster's line of sight. I was welling up and felt like I was going to cry. I couldn't believe the things he'd said to me and had to compose myself before I faced Cowboy and Flick.

I went back out into the corridor, hoping that they hadn't heard him roaring at me, and thankfully, they weren't there. I guessed they must have headed back to the bikes for a smoke or something.

The nurse followed me out then tapped me on the shoulder and told me not to worry about the things Rooster was saying as he was full of painkillers and would probably not remember a thing. I just smiled at her then walked away.

I went outside and sat on a bench. I played back our chat in my head, but couldn't think clearly about it all. I kept coming back to the bit when Rooster told me I'd fucked everything up for him and that he thought I was a complete bastard.

I could actually feel the tears running down my cheeks and I only hoped that he was fucked up with the medicine and that, like the nurse said, it was the drugs talking and not him, but deep down, I knew that wasn't the case.

I was getting ready to head back to my bike when an old lady sat down beside me. She looked at me and told me not to worry because whoever I'd lost would now be safe in heaven.

I looked at her and said: "Sorry?" not as an apology, but in an inquisitive way. "I don't know what you mean."

"It's okay, son, I've just lost my husband, 46 years we were married. I know you're grieving, but don't be sad, just concentrate on the time you had together, that's what I'm doing."

I tried to tell her I hadn't lost anybody, but she just patted my knee and carried on speaking.

"Before my husband died, he told me, 'Elsie, you remember all the good times we had, not what's happening now, and make sure you have plenty more once I'm gone. If you're not going to do that then you should change places with me because, as sure as hell, if I was left, then that's what I'd do. Don't waste what time you've got left moping over me, it's not worth it'. So, son, that's exactly what I'm going to do and you're way too young to mope around. So think about what comes next for you and make the most of it. Remember, nothing's ever as bad as it seems."

She leaned over, kissed me on the cheek, then got up and left. As I watched her hobble away, reliant on a walking stick to support her, I felt really bad.

She obviously thought I'd lost someone and I suppose in a way I thought I had, but what an incredible old lady she was.

I couldn't help thinking, 'There she was, she'd just lost her husband of 46 fuckin years, and yet she was still able to make time to support someone else she thought needed help, during her own time of need'.

'Fuckin hell', I thought to myself, 'If ever you needed an inspirational speech then you won't get much better than that'.

I started smiling and laughing to myself then looked up to see where she'd gone, but I couldn't see her anywhere; she seemed to have just disappeared. Holy fuck! I wondered if I'd imagined the whole fuckin thing! It made me give myself a bit of a shake.

I got up and headed back to the car park to get my bike. Strangely, as I walked, I felt less upset about Rooster and thought about the old lady's advice. I decided I was just going to take things as they came and would keep Rooster's rants and our disagreement to myself for now.

I saw Cowboy and Flick standing at the bikes and, as I approached them, I started telling them the good part of our conversation, about him having no lasting damage and about him reckoning he'd only be in for a few days. I then suggested we make tracks or we'd be late for our meet.

They seemed pretty happy with what I said and we blasted off with them in good spirits and me with a head full of shit.

The weather was stunning and the ride back to the farm was really good. I always felt much better when I got a chance to ride with the sun high in the sky. I stopped thinking about Rooster and started to concentrate on what I thought Indie was going to say.

When we arrived at the farm, there were loads of people outside and some of the guys were revving up their bikes. Indie and Ammo were standing on the steps, chatting, and I realised that the North chapter were preparing to leave.

We parked up then started chatting and shaking hands with the guys that were heading off. I ended up speaking to the prospect who'd been accosted by the girls on the dance floor the night before and found out it had been his birthday and that's why they'd abused him.

I suggested that he would be looking forward to his next birthday and he laughed, saying he couldn't wait. We shook hands and I wished him all the best.

By this time, Ammo was on his bike and motioning to the rest of the guys to move out. As they left, we all stood, watching and waving. I was transfixed by the new cut-offs they were all wearing and couldn't help thinking that, soon, I'd be changing my own bottom rocker.

When they were out of sight, Indie shouted to everyone that he wanted us in the barn in fifteen minutes then headed back into the house.

I followed him in and told him I'd been to see Rooster and gave him the news that he'd be out in a few days. He told me that was great and that he was planning to pop up to the hospital after our meet.

Fuck, my heart sank. I wanted to tell him what Rooster had said, to pre-warn him, but I just couldn't find the words.

I wondered if I should try and get there before him and try to talk some sense into Rooster. But then I thought that, if Rooster was still feeling the same, there would be no point and maybe I would end up making it worse.

I grabbed a can from the fridge and went back outside. I'd just opened the can when Cowboy came over and said: "Bit early for you, Shug, what's up?"

"Nothing, man, I just fancied it," I told him. But that wasn't enough for him, "Come on, spit it out, I can see it in your face, you're all fucked up about something."

I wondered for a minute whether I should tell him or not, but I knew if I didn't that he'd keep going on until I did.

"Okay, Cowboy, I'll tell you, but you need to keep it to yourself." "No probs, Shug, Scout's Honour," he said, offering me the scout salute.

I told him everything, right down to the old lady and my chat with Indie.

"Holy fuck, Shug, that's some heavy shit, man. Rooster can't be thinking straight; he would never say stuff like that. If he tells Indie what he said to you then he could fuck himself right up."

"Eh, don't you think I already know that? Fuck, man, I only told you because I thought you might be able to offer me some words of wisdom."

"Shug, I have no idea what to say. But if I was you, I'd stay away and let them sort it out among themselves. I think you should be more concerned about Rooster blaming you for everything and telling you he won't forget it."

"Thanks for reminding me, Cowboy! Eh, did you think I had forgotten that bit?" I replied, sarcastically.

We didn't get a chance to discuss it further because everyone started piling out and making their way to the barn.

We kind of nodded to each other, suggesting we would pick it up later, and joined the guys in the barn, waiting for Indie and Hotwire to arrive.

When they arrived, Indie stood on the crates, which were still there from the previous night, and Hotwire stood beside him.

Indie raised his hand and asked everybody to shut up. Very quickly the place fell silent. "Right, guys, we've now confirmed the officers and I'll tell you who's doing what. Remember, if there are any objections then raise your hand and state your issue. This is a unique situation for us, one I hope we never need to repeat. We're in a position where we've had to shuffle things around, bring in new officers, and also select people to help start up our new South chapter. I'll confirm the business for our chapter first, then I'll tell you all what's going on with the south. Okay, the new Sergeant at Arms, taking over from me, is Jelly, who has now vacated his post as Treasurer. Slim will stay on as Secretary and Bull will take over from

Jelly. The other three officers making up the committee are Robbo, Snake and Wolfie. Anyone with any objections should raise their hand now."

As Indie looked around, there was a bit of mumbling and the noise level increased as people chatted to each other about his selections. Cowboy suggested it was as expected, with the exception of Rooster, and I agreed. Flick, on the other hand, seemed a bit pissed and raised his hand.

Indie clocked it and told him to speak. "Indie, I want to know why Rooster wasn't voted in. Surely you've not excluded him because he's in hospital?" he shouted. Others then started shouting out things like 'here, here' and nodding in agreement with Flick.

Indie then said, that if everyone quietened down, he would explain. When there was a bit of quiet he began.

"Listen, there's no way anyone would be excluded because they were in hospital, or even jail for that matter. Rooster's not been excluded, I've spoken with him and he knows the script."

Flick then interrupted Indie, asking him to explain why he hadn't selected him. Indie told Flick he would explain in a minute then asked if there were any other objections.

No one else spoke up and Indie then told us that the selection of his officers was now complete.

He then explained to everybody what was happening with the South chapter and how he and Ammo had been in contact with the biggest of the local MC's who'd agreed to patch over.

He then said that they'd selected some people from each chapter who were going to transfer to the south for a period of time, to get the chapter up and running. He then went into a few details about how we would offer the rest of the local clubs the chance to patch over and that we would be visiting regularly, in numbers, to let everybody in the south know that we meant business.

The next thing he said got him roars of approval and cheers from everybody. He told us that he was going to organise his first run as Prez and that it would be a weekend visit to the new South chapter.

He explained that both the North and Central chapters would attend, and that all Brothers, without exception, would be there to celebrate the start of a new era.

After the cheering dissipated, one of the guys asked Indie which brothers were going and if Rooster was one of them.

Indie then said that Rooster would be going and that he would be acting VP, explaining that it was a temporary appointment until the chapter was established, then he and Ammo would select a permanent Prez and VP.

He then went on to explain that Brutis from the North chapter would be acting Prez, and the other three going from here were Flick, Cowboy and myself.

All of a sudden, all eyes were on us, most were nodding, but some looked surprised. I imagined a few of the guys would want to chat to us about it later.

Indie then called order again and everyone turned their focus back to him. "We're going to have a great weekend down south. All three chapters will be represented in full and I expect it to happen within the next four weeks." He then jumped down off the crates and left the barn, to a massive cheer ringing in his ears.

As everybody started to disperse, I almost felt like the whole thing had been a huge anti-climax. I guess, by falling out with Rooster and knowing most of what Indie had said beforehand, made it feel like that.

A few of the guys gathered around the three of us, some offering congratulations, others wanting to know the gory details of how we were picked. We chatted for about fifteen minutes or so and by then, most had drifted off.

I told Cowboy and Flick I was heading back to the flat, but they said they were going to speak to Indie and ask him what the fuck he was playing at, telling everybody they were moving without even asking them.

I'd forgotten all about that and decided I'd better go with them and see how things panned out. Indie was just coming out of the house as we went to go in.

Flick told Indie he wanted to speak to him, but Indie told him it would need to wait as he was off to the hospital to see Rooster. But Flick was having none of it.

"Indie, we need to speak now," he told him "Rooster's going nowhere for a while and this won't take long." Indie looked at him for a minute, then at Cowboy and myself, put his helmet on his bike, then nodded. "Okay, go for it, I'm all ears."

"Not here, Indie," Flick said. "I think we should go somewhere more private." "For fuck's sake, Flick, just spit it fuckin out. If you want to talk, do it here," he told him.

"Okay, fine, suits me. I just thought it would be better for you to do it in private, but hey ho, what the fuck do I know? Why did you just tell everyone that we were moving down south when you hadn't even spoken to us about it? Did it ever cross your fuckin mind that maybe we don't want to go?"

Indie looked at him a bit strangely and told him he had no idea what the fuck he was talking about. Then he replied, very aggressively, finger pointing and almost spitting with anger.

"Now you listen to me, Flick, and you listen fuckin good, that goes for the three of you, by the way. Rooster came and asked me if I would consider the four of you for the new chapter and I told him I would, but that I was disappointed you all wanted to go. He said that you had all chatted about it and were well up for the challenge and thought you could do a good job. I said, that if you did go, that it would only be until it was up and running as I wanted you to remain a part of this chapter. He said he was cool with that. If that's not the case then you better see him about it, oh, and by the way, Flick, you ever come across that aggressive to me again and I'll rip your fuckin head off!"

He then put on his helmet, jumped on his bike and fucked off. Flick tried to apologise, but he just waved him away.

Flick then turned to me and had a bit of a go. "Thanks for that, Shug, now he's pissed with me! This is all your fuckin fault. I hope you're fuckin happy." I tried to speak to him about it, but he just told me to save my breath as he wasn't interested.

Flick walked away and I went to speak to Cowboy, but he shook his head and told me Flick was right then followed him into the house. I decided the best thing for me would be to head home so I jumped on my bike and hit the road.

All the way home, I was thinking about what had just transpired, and my earlier disagreement with Rooster. I knew they were all right and that the whole thing was my fault, but I had no idea how to fix it.

I wondered if I should go to the hospital, to see Indie and own up, but thought it was best not to, just in case him and Rooster were having a ding-dong of their own.

I drove straight home and was never so glad to get in and shut my own door. I couldn't believe how everything had gone tits up: One minute everything was coming together nicely, then bang, the whole fuckin thing had blown up in my face.

I slumped down on the couch and closed my eyes, hoping to drift off to sleep and forget about the mess I'd made, but I couldn't settle.

I kept thinking over and over again about how I'd upset everyone, all because I wanted away. Why the fuck didn't I just say nothing, check out the job, get it, move away on my own, and pop back every now and then? Fuck, that was my original plan, why in fuck's name didn't I just stick to it?

I couldn't switch off so decided I needed to go to the hospital and face the music. I headed back downstairs, two at a time, and jumped on my bike like a man with a mission. Even though I had no fuckin idea what the fuck I was doing.

I arrived at the hospital car park and saw Indie's bike was still there. 'Shit, that's the last thing I needed', I thought to myself, as I looked for somewhere to park up. Then I noticed Cowboy and Flick's bikes were there as well, which made it even worse.

The minute I saw them, I got that really rotten sinking feeling in my stomach that you get just before something really bad happens to you.

I kept driving and did a couple of laps of the car park, wondering whether or not I should go in, until I eventually decided it was probably best to face them all at once.

I parked up and made my way along the corridor to the ward. I convinced myself that, if anything did kick off, I was in the safest place I could be. 'At least I won't need to wait for an ambulance!' I joked to myself, laughing nervously.

I went into Rooster's room and the three of them were sitting at his bedside. Rooster saw me first and spoke whenever I entered the room. "Well, well, well, if it isn't fuckin bunker gub himself. You should grab a seat, Shug, we've all just been talking about you."

"Look, Rooster, before you start, I just want to explain a few things. I know I...." "Shug, shut the fuck up and sit on your arse," he growled at me, stopping me in mid-flow.

I did as I was told and sat like a frightened puppy, trying not to make eye contact with anyone. It was now Indie's turn to have a go.

"Well, here we are with you again, Shug, right in the middle of a serious fuckin problem. A problem caused by you and your fuckin smartass scheming ways." I tried to interrupt again, but was told very quickly to shut the fuck up.

"Don't fuckin interrupt me again, okay?" Indie seethed at me, forcing me to nod very quickly in his general direction.

He started again, "I'm sure you'll be glad to know that we've now sussed out your grand little plan. Don't you think it's amazing, when you get the full picture, how everything just falls into place and you realise that some cunt's been playing you?"

I tried to interrupt again, but this time I was greeted with the four of them in unison, telling me to shut the fuck up.

Indie then prattled on about what a prick I'd been, and how I'd tried to shaft my brothers, and shit like that. But to be honest, by this time, I'd zoned out. All I could think about was what was coming next and how it was going to affect me.

I reckoned that the worst thing that could happen was that they would throw me out of the Bats and give me a proper kicking. The way I was feeling about it all, I really didn't give a fuck.

Rooster, Cowboy and Flick were my best mates - well, actually, when I thought about it, they were probably my only mates. So if they disowned me, there was nothing left here for me anyway.

The next thing, I got a dunt on the shoulder from Cowboy. I must have been miles away. I looked up and all eyes were on me.

"Well?" was all Indie said. 'Well, what?' I thought to myself. I hadn't heard a fuckin word of what he'd been saying, from when they all told me to shut fuck up, and now he expected me to reply to it.

'Awe, well, here goes' I thought to myself, 'Fuck it, tell them everything'. I guessed the topic was 'Shug the bastard' anyway, so I couldn't really make it any worse.

"Look, guys, firstly, I want to apologise to you all for all the shit I've caused you. But in my head, I thought it was what you all really wanted. Now, obviously, I realise it was only me. I was only trying to get things moving as quickly as possible. I honestly didn't think that I was doing anything wrong. Because I had this interview on Thursday, I was trying to see if I could have everything sorted out by then and that would have helped me decide whether to take the job or not. I realise now how it looks to all of you, and how selfish I've been acting, but I can't undo that now, no matter how much I wish I could. Honestly, I'm really sorry for upsetting you all."

I decided, at that point, it would be wise for me to leave and got up to go. I told them that I was heading back to my flat, just to let them all know where I would be, but I was told very sharply to sit back down on my arse by Indie.

I did as I was told, but then I asked Indie what the point of me staying was, when everybody was pissed with me. His reply was no less than I expected.

"Firstly, because I'm not fuckin finished with you yet," he growled. "And secondly, Shug, do you actually think that we're just going to let you fuck off and forget about what you tried to do to us? I don't fuckin think so."

I was past caring by this point and interrupted him. "Look, Indie, I couldn't really give two fucks what you or anybody else thinks anymore. I know I've fucked up big time, and I know there's no way back, so whatever you've got to say then just cut to the chase and say it, and let me get the fuck out of here."

Right away, the minute I'd said it, I realised that I did actually care. He almost jumped the bed to get at me and had to be restrained by Cowboy and Flick. I about shat my pants and instantly tried to apologise, but it totally fell on deaf ears.

Much to my relief, Indie then seemed to calm down a bit when Cowboy told him that he didn't think this was the time or the place to deal with it. However, it didn't stop me trying to continually offer apology after apology.

He told Cowboy he was right, and that he was cool, and that he would leave it until later. Then, the minute they let him go, the cunt swung for me, flooring me with one punch.

I fell to the floor, holding my face. Fuck, it felt like my jaw had been pushed up into my brain and, by fuck, it hurt like hell. Thankfully, though, I was still conscious, if only just. A couple of male nurses then came running in to see what was going on.

By the time they arrived, the others had sat back down and were chatting away with Rooster like nothing had happened. The nurses picked me up and sat me back on the chair, asking me if I was okay and wanting to know what had happened.

I told them I was fine and that I'd just fallen off the chair. They obviously knew I was lying and had a good look at me, then at everybody else, then they both walked out, closing the door behind them. I got the feeling they'd decided there was no point in pursuing it and left us to it.

I looked at Indie, stood up, and asked him if there was anything else he wanted to say before I left.

"Fuck me, Shug, you just don't get it do you?" "Look, Indie, I do, I know what's coming next and I just think I should go and we can deal with it elsewhere."

"No, Shug, when I say you don't get it, I mean you really don't. And, as for what's coming next, believe me, you have no fuckin idea. Now sit on your fuckin arse, shut the fuck up, and listen."

I sat back down, letting out a large sigh as I slumped back into the chair holding my jaw.

Indie then looked at Rooster, then Cowboy and Flick, then they all stared at me. Fuck, talk about cold sweats, I was crumbling inside and doing my utmost to look as cool as I could under the circumstances.

Then, together, they all burst out laughing and pointing at me, telling me I should see myself, as I looked like a right dick.

They kept laughing for a bit, but I had no idea why. Inside, I went from being a crumbling wreck to fuckin raging, before I eventually spoke. "Not sure what's so fuckin funny, guys, but I would appreciate it if you'd share it with me," I raged at them.

This seemed to make them laugh even harder and louder. I tried again to get some sense from at least one of them, but they just kept splitting their sides. I decided I wasn't taking any more of it and got up to go.

As I approached the door, a nurse pushed it open and told us all to be quiet or she would have us thrown out.

She was an older lady, and definitely not one to mess with. I apologised to her and told her we would be quiet. She just said: "Well, see that you do," then left.

I went to follow her out, but Flick and Cowboy grabbed me and closed the door. They were all still sniggering away, but this time, it was a more muffled version than before.

Indie told me again to sit down and he would tell me what was going on. I was completely baffled by their antics and certainly wasn't prepared for what came next.

They were all a bit more composed now, and again, all staring at me. Indie began, "Shug, before you came in, we'd already got to the bottom of what you'd done, and knew you were trying to do it for all the right reasons. But you really did piss us all off so we decided to let you suffer a bit. Cowboy clocked you driving around the car park and we knew you were shitting yourself to come in so we decided to have a bit of fun."

"Fun?" I squealed at him. "What's so fuckin funny about you trying to break my fuckin jaw?" "Ah well, Shug, that wasn't in the script. If you hadn't been such a cheeky cunt to me then that would never have happened."

I wanted to roar at them, and call them a shower of wankers, but I knew I'd got an 'out of jail free' card so bit my tongue.

I turned to Rooster and asked him if we were okay, after our earlier spat, and he said he really couldn't mind much about it, then winked at me so I wasn't sure what the fuck he meant.

Indie then told me that Rooster had agreed to be acting VP and that we would all be joining the new South chapter temporarily.

Fuck, I didn't know whether to laugh, cry or scream! But chose to smile and say how chuffed I was about it. I asked Indie when it was likely to happen and he told me that whenever Rooster was up for it, we'd be going.

The bell then went for the end of visiting and I shook hands with Rooster and told him I'd pop back in and see him the following day. He then said, sarcastically, "Hey, Shug, try and not fuck anything up between now and then, eh?"

We all left, and made our way to the car park. I was dying to get Cowboy on his own, to talk to him about what happened before I arrived, but Indie had other ideas.

When we got to the bikes, he told us he wanted us back at the farm so I guessed my explanation would have to wait. As we rode back, I felt so much better than I did on the way there and made a mental note to never put myself in a position like that again.

My thoughts then turned to Indie and wondered why he wanted us all back at the farm. It wasn't long before I found out.

Chapter 19

We all arrived together and when we got in, Indie headed straight to the office without saying a word. Flick went for a pish so I asked Cowboy if he'd tell me what had happened in the hospital, but he told me he would fill me in later.

"What do you think he wants us for now?" I asked him. "I've no fuckin idea, but you can bet your bottom dollar it won't be to invite us to a fuckin orgy, ha ha."

Flick came back and asked us what all the hilarity was about. Before we got a chance to tell him, Hotwire came out and shouted for us to go into the conservatory.

"I guess were going to find out right now," Cowboy suggested to me. I just nodded back without saying anything. When we went in, Hotwire closed the door behind us. I was a bit surprised to see that Indie, Hotwire and Jelly were the only ones there.

Indie told us to take a seat. He had a large box in front of him and lifted a cut-off out of it. He held it up, so we could all see it, and asked us what we thought of it.

It was the first one I'd seen with 'South' on the bottom rocker and was first to speak, telling him I thought it looked good.

Flick and Cowboy then repeated my sentiments. After which, Indie produced 3 separate bottom rockers, telling us that he wanted to get them on our cuts right away and asked us to give them to him as he had a couple of girls waiting to sew them on.

The three of us all took ours off and handed them to Hotwire who, by this time, had taken the rockers from Indie and was standing in front of us with his hand out.

We gave them to him and he disappeared, telling us he'd be back shortly. When he came back, he told us that he'd arranged for us, along with himself and his officers, to meet up with the Prez of the 'Mutts Nuts' (the club who were going to be patching over) on Saturday and wanted us to already be patched up before we went.

I asked him if the guys from the north would be going and he told me that they would. "The four of them, plus Ammo, are coming here on Friday. We'll change their rockers as well, before heading down on Saturday. We've agreed that the Nuts' current President, Gunner, will be the new SAA, which he's happy about, and we'll see if he is up to it when the chapter is up and running. If he's not, then there may be a slot for one of you guys."

Cowboy then asked Indie if they had a clubhouse and he told us that they didn't, but that they had a detached house at the end of a street that they ran out of, and used a local pub as their base.

I reminded Indie that I was heading down the following day for my interview and he said: "Eh, I know that, Shug, why do you think we're doing this tonight?"

I just nodded, wishing I'd kept my mouth shut. Thankfully, the conversation was interrupted by Hotwire's return. He threw us back our cut-offs and told us to put them back on.

I had a look at mine and felt a bit of a strange sensation, I wasn't sure why, but it just made me feel weird.

We all put them back on then Indie handed me a piece of paper with an address on it and told me that he'd arranged for me to meet with Gunner at ten on Saturday morning.

I slipped the note into my pocket and asked him when they would be arriving and he told me they would be there around three.

"Why am I meeting him so early?" I asked. "Would it not be better if we all met together?" "Shug, the reason I want you there first is so that you can have a look around and get to know them a bit before we get there. My guess is that you'll be able to do that much better on your own because they'll be more relaxed with one person than they will when we all arrive."

I nodded in agreement and told him I thought it made sense. But inside, I couldn't help feeling really nervous about the whole thing.

"Is there anything, in particular, you want me to do?" I asked him. "Yes, there is. I want you to pay particular attention to Gunner and see what kind of dude he is. I've only met him once and he seems okay, but I don't know what he's like with the rest of his troops. Try and get a feel for how he operates and see if there's anyone you think isn't happy about the patch over."

"No probs, I'll do that and fill you in when you arrive." He then said: "Shug, remember, don't fuck this up. You're going to be the first Bat that most of them have seen and you need to make sure that you make the right impression, okay?"

I told him he didn't need to worry on that score, that I'd make sure I represented the Bats well.

"Make sure you do. I can't afford for this to go tits up," he reminded me. He then told us that he was done and that he was off to see someone. He then got up and left. Hotwire and Jelly followed him out, leaving the three of us standing there, looking at each other.

I was first to speak, "Fuck, that was quick. I thought he said nothing was going to happen until Rooster was out of hospital?" "No, Shug, what he said was that he wouldn't be doing the patch over until Rooster was fit," Flick reminded me.

I decided I should go home and get packed up and told the guys I had to split. We shook hands and I told them I would see them on Saturday. They both wished me good luck for the interview and then I left.

I arrived back at the flat, pretty pissed that I'd got caught in the rain, and decided to have a bath to warm myself up. While the bath was running, I threw a few things in a bag and hung up my only suit on the door. I thought I better take it with me, just in case I couldn't get one there.

After my bath, I went straight to bed and began thinking about what the weekend would bring. It seemed my plan to spend more time with Julie was now going to be a washout and I wondered how she would react when I told her what was happening with the Bats.

I imagined that she would throw a wobbly when I got around to telling her that Rooster was moving and that he would be living less than fifteen minutes away from her. I decided it would be best not to mention any of it before the interview.

I reckoned the best thing for me to do was get the interview out of the way then take her out for a few drinks and tell her while we were in the pub. That way, she couldn't go too mental about it and it would save me a bit of grief.

Next morning, I got up and surprise, surprise, it was pissing down with rain. 'Fuckin typical' I thought, 'the only day you want it to be dry and it's pouring from the fuckin heavens'.

I wasn't sure how I was going to keep my suit dry so decided to fire it into my sleeping bag and roll it up as tightly as I could. I then put it into a couple of poly bags and taped it up.

I thought about having breakfast and couldn't be arsed making anything, thinking I would stop on the way. I grabbed some cash, picked up my holdall, then left.

By the time I'd tied my sleeping bag to the bike, I was already soaked, and cursed the Scottish weather with a vengeance. I started up and rode off, praying for a bit of sun, but with the look of the sky, I guessed that I was clutching at straws.

I had to keep my speed to a minimum as I could hardly see five feet in front of me, the rain was that heavy. I stopped off at a service station, just over half way there, and ordered a mug of tea and a full breakfast.

As I sat, the water was actually running off me and I noticed puddles gathering on the floor around my feet. The girl brought my tea over and also handed me a towel. She asked me if I wanted to use the staff room to get dried off. But I told her I was fine and thanked her for the towel. She then smiled and left, telling me my breakfast would be with me in a couple of minutes.

I gave myself a bit of a rub with the towel and tried to use it to absorb some of the water from my clothes. I then dropped it onto the floor to dry up some of the puddles.

Looking around the place, I noticed it was almost empty. Apart from myself, there was only a lorry driver and an old couple in the whole restaurant.

The girl arrived back with my breakfast and I thanked her and gave her back the towel. She again offered me the use of the staff room, but again, I declined.

She then said: "I could always come in and help you dry off if you like?" Fuck, I nearly choked on my sausage, I couldn't believe what I'd just heard. I cleared my throat then told her I thought that was a great idea.

"Okay, finish your breakfast then give me a shout and I'll take my break," she said, smiling, then headed back to the kitchen.

I rammed my grub down at breakneck speed, all the time wondering why she would want to fuck a manky looking guy that she'd never met before, who was soaked to the skin, at ten 'o'clock on a miserable Wednesday fuckin morning?

I'd hardly placed my cutlery back on my plate when she was back to collect it. "Go round the back to the fire door and I'll meet you there," she told me, smiling as she left.

I got up straight away and went to the till, paid for my meal then headed out. I was glad to see the rain had slowed a bit and kept my fingers crossed it would be dry before I left.

I walked around to the fire door and she was already standing there with the door open, ushering me in. I went in and she closed the door behind us. I'd hardly got my jacket off and she was already kissing me and trying to unbutton my jeans.

She was a really pretty girl with an okay figure and I couldn't really understand why she wanted to do this. She eventually pulled down my jeans and pants then quickly removed her own.

She had a yellow skirt and blouse on, which I presumed were the corporate colours, and I fumbled with her top until I got her tits out. She pushed me back onto a chair then sat on top of me, still kissing away. She then grabbed my cock and rammed it home. As she moved up and down on my shaft, she started moaning. The faster she went, the noisier she got.

I couldn't believe my luck. Here I was, chewing away on a lovely pair tits and getting my end away with a chick that I'd met for all of five seconds.

I wasn't aware just how loud she was until the door burst open. I couldn't see who it was, as I was sitting with my back to it, but to be honest, I wasn't giving a fuck, until she shouted: "Dad!" 'Holy fuck, not again', I thought to myself. She then jumped off and pulled her skirt down. I quickly pulled up my pants and jeans and turned to face him.

He started screaming at her, calling her all sorts of things, then grabbed her by the hair, slapped her face and told her to get home, out of his fuckin sight.

He then turned his attention to me. But instead of going mental, like I thought he would, he calmly walked towards me and asked me to leave. The girl was standing at the internal door, with tears rolling down her cheeks, calling him a variety of superlatives, but he wasn't taking any notice of her.

"Look, son, I need you to leave. My daughter and I are going through a difficult time and I'm afraid she's used you to get back at me. Now, if you'd be so kind," he said, raising his hand, motioning for me to go via the fire exit.

I wasn't sure what to do. I certainly never wanted to get involved in another father/daughter domestic, but I sure as hell didn't want to leave like this, in case he kicked the shit out of her.

I brushed past her father, ignoring his request, and went over to her and asked her what she wanted me to do. She said I should go, that she'd be fine, and told me that he wouldn't hurt her.

I wasn't so sure. So, before I left, I did a thing Provo always used to do. I went up to him, looked him straight in the eye, my nose almost touching his, and whispered, using my best aggressive tone.

"Right, you, listen, and listen fuckin good, I'm going to be back through this way with my mates in a couple of days, and when I stop in here, I'm going to speak to your daughter. If she's not here, or I see one bruise on her, I'll rip your fuckin head off, got it?"

He continued to look me straight in the eye as I spoke then just nodded to me and never said a word. There was something about him I couldn't put my finger on.

I got the impression he wasn't particularly worried about my threat, but at the same time, I never thought he intended to hurt his daughter. I brushed past him again, this time giving him a bit of a dunt with my shoulder, picked up my jacket and helmet then left.

I went out into the car park and the door was slammed behind my back. I stood at it, listening for a minute or so, but never heard a sound, so guessed they were talking rather than arguing.

Thankfully, by now, the rain had subsided, and there was a flickering of sun through the clouds. I jumped on my bike and headed back onto the motorway.

I realised, when I felt the wind against me, that I was still soaking wet and started to feel very cold. I hoped that, by the time I got to Julie's, I would be dry and I would be able to warm myself against her radiator.

As I travelled, I played back the situation with the girl and her father. At first, I couldn't believe I'd just been used, but when I thought about it, what better way to wind up your father than having sex with a stranger, especially a greasy biker. I sniggered a bit, deciding to forget about it, and put it down as another one for the memory bank.

Very quickly, I came to my turn off and pulled off the motorway. This time, I knew where I was going and within a few minutes, I was turning into the hospital grounds and making my way to the nurses home.

I parked up, grabbed my gear and headed in, hoping I wouldn't bump into the warden. Thankfully, there was no one at all in reception area so I just made my way upstairs and along the corridor to Julie's room.

I banged on her door a few times, but there was no reply. Then I remembered that she'd told me she was early shift and didn't finish until two.

I looked at the clock in the corridor. Fuck, it was only half past twelve; I had an hour and a bit to wait before she would be back. I thought about giving Lisa's door a chap then decided that would be a bad idea so went back downstairs and crashed in the common room.

It felt like I'd hardly closed my eyes when I was wakened by the noise of what sounded like loads of people chatting and rushing about.

I sat up, feeling a bit out of sorts, and looked out the window. I could see lots of people were coming in at the same time; it was like a bus trip had just arrived. Then I realised it was the change of shifts.

I went into the reception area looking for Julie, but was greeted with Lisa, who was standing waving a bunch of keys above her head. The minute she saw me, she shouted my name and made a beeline through the crowd, giving me a big hug and chatting away at a hundred miles an hour.

I told her it was nice to see her and asked her where Julie was. "That's what I was telling you, Shug, weren't you listening?" she replied. And, if I'm honest, I never heard a word.

"Sorry, Lisa, please tell me again, I missed that," I lied. "Okay, what's happened is that Julie's having to stay on 'til three, to cover for another nurse who won't be in 'til then, and she's asked me to look after you until she gets back."

"That's great. Just give me the keys and I'll go dump my stuff then grab a shower," I suggested. "No way, Shug, Julie asked me to look after you, and that's exactly what I'm going to do. So come on." And with that, she headed towards the stairs, waving the keys and gesturing for me to follow.

I picked up my bag and followed her up, wondering how I was going to get rid of her. We got to the room and she opened the door, again gesturing for me to follow her.

When we got in, I dumped my bag, hung my suit up on the back of the door and thanked Lisa for letting me in. I then told her I was going to crash, thinking she would leave me the keys and fuck off ... how wrong could I be?

"That's a good idea, Shug, I'm shattered as well. I think I'll join you for an hour," she told me. "I don't think that's a good idea, Lisa," I suggested to her. "I don't think Julie would be too happy to see us crashed in her bed."

"Shug, don't be silly. Julie will be fine, it's not as if we're going to be doing anything other than sleeping now, is it?" she said, smiling at me. I looked at her briefly and smiled back.

I sat on the bed, removed my jacket and boots, and watched as she removed her coat. I lay back on the top of the covers, having decided it best to keep my clothes on.

I watched Lisa as she discarded her shoes, wondering how much clothing she was going to remove. She sat on the chair, pulled off her tights, then unbuttoned her wrapper. She then stood up and let it fall to the floor. She picked it up and hung it beside my suit.

I thought about telling her to stop, but she was already making her way towards the bed with only her bra and knickers on.

"Don't get any ideas, Shug, I just don't want to get my wrapper creased, I'm on tomorrow," she said, as she lay down beside me. I turned myself towards the wall and she instinctively cuddled into me, putting her arm around me.

Fuck, watching her bouncing over the bed and snuggling up had given me a bit of a semi, and now my thoughts were turning to sex. I wondered if she would be up for it and if she was, would she mention it to Julie?

I decided to do the decent thing and go to sleep. I closed my eyes and tried not to think about Lisa, which was hard, having her wriggling about behind me.

I must have dozed off and was awakened by Julie's voice, "Well! This is cosy!" I heard her remark, not sure what she meant until I had a look at the position Lisa and I were in.

I was lying on my back, with my hand on her tit, and she had her leg across my waist and was cuddling my chest with her arm.

I quickly removed my hand then lifted Lisa's arm and leg from the top of me and manoeuvred myself out of bed. Lisa continued to sleep, unaware I'd moved.

"Hi, Julie, great to see you, and by the way, it's not what you think," I began to explain. "Shug, you've no idea what I think, and what you get up to is your business; I'm not your keeper," she told me, sounding really disappointed.

I give her a hug, thinking she would do the same, but she never responded, leaving her arms by her side. I explained exactly what happened and suggested she cut me a bit of slack.

She then hugged me back, apologising, saying she'd just had a bit of a shitty day and didn't mean to take it out on me.

I kissed her on the head and asked if we were cool and she kissed me back, telling me we were. All I could think was, 'Thank fuck! Because I really can't be arsed with any grief'.

Julie then gave Lisa a gentle push, rocking her back and forward until she came too. "Hi, Julie, howz things?" she asked her, as she opened her eyes.

"I'm okay, Lisa. But I would've felt better if I hadn't come into my room and saw you two on my bed," she told her. "Julie, we were just sleeping, honest. I just took my wrapper off to…..." Julie interrupted her.

"Relax, Lisa, I'm only messing about. I just thought we'd agreed we would wait until tonight to ravish him together!"

I never noticed that Julie had winked at Lisa before she spoke.

"You're right, Julie, we did - I was only warming him up," she told her, then they both burst out laughing.

I just shook my head and told them they were fuckin mental before I headed to the loo.

I stood in the toilet, wondering if they were taking the piss or if they actually meant it. I cast my mind back to my last visit and thought that they may well be up for it, considering what we got up to.

Thinking about it ended up giving me a bit of a hard-on, and it took me forever to get my pee out. Eventually, I emptied my bladder then headed back to Julie's room.

When I went in, they were both sitting on the bed, they had the cover tucked under their arms and in between their legs, and were kissing each other. Their legs and shoulders were in full view, and to me, it was obvious that they were naked.

I thought to myself 'Happy days, Shug! Game on!' They never even turned around to see who'd come in. I stripped off my jeans and top then made my way to the bed to join them, thinking I was onto a good thing.

Julie lifted her hand up, told me to stop where I was, then they both burst out laughing. I was a bit confused, to say the least, and asked her what was up?

"Apart from you?" she asked, pointing at my dick, making them laugh even more. "Nothing's up, Shug, we're fine, aren't we, Lisa?" "Sure are, Julie," she replied.

They nodded to each other then stood up. They both had their bra and pants on and had slipped their bra straps off their shoulders to make it look like they were in the buff. They were killing themselves laughing and I felt like a right prick.

"Okay, I get it," I told them, offering a wry smile, knowing I'd been well and truly stitched up. "Come on, Shug, admit it, you thought it was your birthday when you came in, didn't you?" I told her I certainly thought that my day had improved, that's for sure.

We then all had a bit of a cuddle and a laugh, and they were telling me it was just a bit of fun and hoped I would take it like that.

I told them we were all cool, then stuck my hand down the back of both their pants and gave their bums a bit of a squeeze, pulling them in towards me.

"Well, I think that's the least I deserve," I said, giving their bums a final feel. We then parted, without saying much, and started getting dressed.

Julie noticed I'd had my back done and commented, "Well, Shug, I guess there's no way back for you now then?" I asked her what she meant, forgetting all about my tattoo.

She pointed at my back, "I take it you've decided where your future lies?" "Yes, I thought it was time to get it done," I told her. "Does that mean you won't be moving down here then?" she asked.

"No, Julie, it doesn't mean that at all. If I get the job, I'll still be moving. Anyway, I'll fill you in later. How about we head to the pub for a few beers? I could murder a pint."

Lisa had put her wrapper back on and said to give her five minutes and then she'd be good to go. She then headed back to her room, leaving me and Julie looking at each other. "Come on, Julie, let's get ready," I told her, sitting down to put my boots on.

"Shug, I really don't understand? One minute, you're talking about wanting out, then you get the colours plastered all over your back in indelible ink!"

"Julie, it's complicated, please leave it and I'll tell you everything tomorrow, after my interview, okay?" I suggested.

Thankfully, at that point, Lisa burst back in. "Hey, hey, look who I found wandering the corridor." It was Calum and Becky. They followed her in, suggesting to us that they'd been ambushed.

We said our hello's then headed out. Walking from the nurses home to the pub, I spent most of the time listening, as they all spoke about nurses and patients and what had happened in the past couple of days at work, none of which interested me.

I was thinking about how Julie would react when I told her I was moving down to get involved in the new chapter, and more importantly, how she would take it when I told her Rooster would be coming as well.

Fuck! Then I remembered I hadn't even told her he was in hospital. We arrived at the pub and I asked Julie if I could talk to her before we went in. She told Lisa to get the drinks in and that we would only be a minute.

"What's up, Shug? You going to tell me what's going on?" she asked. "No, Julie, I need to tell you about Rooster, he's ..."

"Shug, I don't want to hear it, I'm not interested. Whatever he's done is his business," she interrupted. I jumped back in, "Julie, he's in hospital. I just thought you might want to know, that's all."

Fuck, she changed instantly to a funny grey colour, grabbing her stomach as she bent over a little, which struck me as a bit odd, considering she claimed she didn't give a fuck.

She quickly composed herself, straightened up, then demanded me to tell her what had happened. I tried to play it down a bit, telling her that he'd just fallen off his bike and that they were only keeping him in because he'd banged his head.

She then started asking me all sorts of questions about what had happened: How long he'd been in and when he was getting out. I told her what I thought she wanted to hear, but I don't think she believed a word.

"Listen, Shug, you obviously forgot I'm a nurse when you started bullshitting me with your made up shite, so cut the crap and tell me what the fuck's really going on with him."

I guessed I couldn't really make up anything else that would convince her he was okay so told her what the nurse had told me and that seemed to satisfy her. She then drew me a bit of a disapproving look and went inside.

I joined her and sat at the table beside her. She had a sip of her drink then turned, looked straight at me, and asked me what had caused him to fall off.

I told her we were both drunk and that he missed the corner and we'd ended up in a field. "You're a pair of fucking idiots and you need to grow up," she told me, then got up from her chair and headed to the toilet.

Lisa then asked me what was going on and I told her I'd no idea and that she'd need to ask Julie. She then got up and followed her into the loo. Becky went with her and Calum asked me what was going on.

"Beats me, man. One minute, they love you, the next, they fuckin hate you! I'll never understand them as long as I fuckin live," I told him, raising my glass and taking a healthy swig.

I got up, telling him I was going to get the drinks in, then went to the bar. I ordered the round and as I waited to get served, the bar manager approached me. "Hi, how are you doing?" he asked me, offering his outstretched hand. "I'm fine, how's yourself?" I replied, giving it a shake.

He then said: "I hope you don't mind me asking, but I noticed your colours have changed, have you now got another chapter down south now?"

"Yes, we have, and also a North chapter. So you may be seeing a bit more of me as I'm moving down here," I told him. "That's great, you'll all be welcome here anytime, and if you ever want the function suite, just let me know, it's on the house."

"Thanks, I might take you up on that," I told him. He picked up some glasses from the bar, nodded his head towards me, then left. I paid for the drinks, lifted them up, and thought about how observant he'd been. No one I was with had even noticed my colours, and there was this guy, that I'd only seen twice, who'd picked up on it.

By the time I went back to the table, everyone was back and they were all chatting away normally. I put the drinks on the table, sat down, and asked Julie how she was. She told me she was fine, apologised for going off on one then gave me a cuddle.

Fuck, I thought I was going to get a hard time! And here she was, apologising to me. I looked at Calum and shrugged my shoulders and he smiled and did the same back.

We had another couple of drinks and I suggested to Julie that I should head back as I didn't want to get too pissed (with the interview in the morning). She agreed and suggested we have one more then we would head.

It was my turn to get them in again so I toddled up to the bar. I was served by my new 'best friend' and he wouldn't take any money so I thanked him and laughed a bit to myself as I walked away.

My best guess was that he thought we were moving into this area and he wanted to keep me sweet. I really didn't give two fucks what he thought, but if he kept plying me with free drink then that was okay by me.

When Julie and I finished our drinks, I told everyone that we were leaving and this was met by the usual pleas of 'don't go', 'just one more', etc. I reminded them that I had to be up early and needed a clear head, but it seemed to fall on deaf ears.

We got up to leave and everyone else decided to come with us, suggesting a party in the room, but I told them it wasn't going to happen and that seemed to be enough for them to stay in the pub for another.

As Julie and I walked home, we chatted about the interview and Julie gave me a bit of background stuff on the hospital and offered a few pointers about things I should mention.

When we got back, I told Julie I was going straight to bed and to set her alarm to make sure I was up in plenty of time in the morning. I stripped down to my scants and jumped into bed.

Julie farted about for a bit, wiping off her makeup, combing her hair and doing all the shit women seem to need to do before they hit the sack.

I watched her as she did all this, wondering all the time what she would wear when she eventually decided to come to bed. She started taking her clothes off and removed everything except her bra and knickers before climbing in beside me.

We cuddled in together, spooning, with me at the back. I put my arm around her, placing my hand just under her boobs. The minute my dick touched her arse, I felt myself getting a hard-on and it didn't help when Julie started wriggling about, pressing herself against me.

At first, I thought she was trying to find her sleeping position, until she lifted my hand and placed it on her tit. I responded by giving it a bit of a squeeze, which made her push her arse even harder into my dick.

I knew she was up for a bit of a shag and was dying to turn her around and get into it, but I resisted, knowing I should really get some kip.

I whispered in her ear, telling her that, right now, I needed to sleep, but that tomorrow, after my interview, I was going to fuck her brains out.

She responded by telling me that just because she was up for it tonight didn't mean that she would still be up for it tomorrow.

"Hey, Shug, it's your choice, guess we'll just need to wait and see what tomorrow brings," she told me, then pushed her arse hard against my dick again.

'Fuck,' I thought to myself, 'What a cow she is, saying that. She knows I want to get a good night's kip, but she also knows there's no way I'm going to be able to resist her now!'

I turned her around until she was facing me and fiddled with her bra strap until it opened. I cupped her tits with my hands, giving both her nipples a tweak and told her she could be a real cockteaser when she wanted to be, which made her smile.

We started kissing, and within a matter of seconds, we were both naked and I was on top of her. I slipped my dick into her snatch and started moving slowly in and out of her.

Julie grabbed my arse with her hands, squeezing it tightly, then pulled her knees up to her chest and dug her heels into my back. She started bucking wildly underneath me, making me speed up my rhythm.

She was going at it like a woman possessed; it was as if she'd been celibate for years and just discovered how much she'd missed it. I asked her to slow the pace a bit, but she told me to shut the fuck up and keep going.

I did as I was asked, and within a matter of minutes, she'd shot her load, stopped bucking and was groaning and panting like she'd been at it for hours. I then slowed down, back to my original pace, and watched as she tried to composed herself.

Suddenly, I could feel my arse tingling and was sure she'd drawn blood. I wasn't getting anywhere near shooting my load so I stopped and lay beside her.

I asked if she was okay and she told me she was great. "Sorry about that, Shug, I just needed to come," she told me, still a bit out of breath.

"I think you've torn my arse cheeks to shreds," I said, laughing. Again, she apologised, looking a bit coy, then asked me if I wanted her to take a look, but I told her I was fine.

"What the fuck was that all about anyway, Julie?" "I'm not sure, Shug, I just had a real need to get fucked. Not sure where it came from, but when I got into bed and felt your cock rubbing on my arse, I knew I just needed to have it inside me."

I just smiled at her and told her I was glad to oblige, then reminded her that if she ever needed to do it again, I would be more than willing to help her out.

She gave me a playful slap, telling me not to be so cheeky, then cuddled in, suggesting we should go to sleep.

"Oh, so now you're satisfied and I've served my purpose, it's time to sleep? What about my needs? Don't they count?" I said, sarcastically.

"Eh, excuse me!" I'm not the one who needs to get up early tomorrow," she reminded me, then placed her hand on my now limp dick, giving it a good old squeeze.

"Well, you might be up for it, but he seems to be sleeping," she told me. "That's because he feels used and abused," I told her, "but I'm sure, in the right hands, he would wake up very quickly."

Pulling the covers back, she said: "Are you sure about that? He looks to me like he's done for the night." "Maybe he just needs a bit of encouragement?" I suggested, kissing her on the forehead.

Julie then slid down the bed a bit and took my dick in her mouth, expertly licking and sucking until it was back to its former glory. As she sucked, I could feel her teeth biting a bit which added to my pleasure.

I placed my hand on her head, trying to push her deeper onto my shaft, which she was happy to do. Within seconds, I was shooting my load down her throat.

She continued to suck and lick for a bit, until I was limp, then came back up beside me. I cuddled her into me and told her how much I'd enjoyed that. She responded by telling me she was glad too. We then kissed for a bit before drifting off to sleep.

I felt I'd only been sleeping for five minutes when the alarm rang. I switched it off and sat on the edge of the bed for a bit. I looked at Julie, who hadn't moved a muscle. As I watched her, I thought about Rooster and the need to let her know he was moving down here and wondered if, perhaps, I should have told her earlier.

I headed out for a quick shower, came back, got dressed and was sitting, staring out the window, having a smoke, before Julie even realised I was up.

Just as I was putting my jacket on, she began to stir and sat up. "Hi, Shug, what are you doing? Have you been yet or just going?" she asked me.

"Just going now, Julie," I told her. "Well, good luck, Shug. Just remember the stuff I told you and you'll be fine." I nodded, gave her a kiss, looked in the mirror, straightened my tie, then left.

As I walked towards the office block, I tried to recall the stuff Julie had suggested I mention, but all I could think about was Anna's husband and hoped to fuck he wasn't on the panel.

I went into the reception area and walked towards the glass partition. There was a guy sitting at a switchboard, with headphones on, who, when he saw me, held his hand up, gesturing for me to wait.

He was speaking to someone on the phone and after he pulled out a couple of cables and placed them in a different part of the switchboard, he slid open the partition and asked me what I wanted.

"I'm here for an interview," I told him, handing him my letter. He took it from me, had a quick glance at it, handed it back and told me to take a seat. He sharply closed the window and, again, started talking away on his headset.

I went and sat down, thinking to myself what an ignorant little cunt he was. Within a couple of minutes, an elderly lady came in and asked me if I was here for an interview. I told her I was and she asked me to follow her to the office.

As we walked along the corridor, she asked if I was Julie's friend and I told her I was. I asked her how she knew Julie and she told me that she'd cared for her mum and during that time they'd become friends.

Just then, she pointed to a door, knocked it and waited on a reply. We heard a female voice from behind the door telling us to enter. When we went in, the first person I saw was Anna's husband.

Fuck! He was the last cunt I wanted to be there. The female asked me to sit down and thanked the lady for bringing me along.

She was also an older woman, I guessed in her mid to late forties, and was as thin as a rake. She introduced herself as Mrs Boardman and told me she would be interviewing me, along with Mr Green. I smiled and nodded, not sure if I was supposed to say anything.

The interview lasted about fifteen minutes and consisted of some fairly simple questions like: Why I wanted the job? What I knew about the hospital and the kind of patients who were there?

At the end, she asked me if I had any questions. The only thing I asked her was when would I know the outcome.

I explained that I was staying locally with a friend until Monday and wondered if the decision would be made by then.

She told me that they were interviewing all day and would make their decision that night, after the final person had been seen. She then said that, if I wanted, I could call her in the morning and she would let me know if I'd been successful.

I got up, shook both their hands, thanked them for their time, then left. I went outside feeling confident. I thought I'd answered their questions pretty well and was happy in the knowledge that I only had to wait twenty-four hours to know their decision.

I slackened off my tie and made my way towards the nurses home. I played back the interview in my mind and couldn't believe how comfortable I'd felt with it, even with Mr Green trying to give me a hard time.

Everyone I knew talked about how they hated going for interviews, and how uncomfortable it made them feel. I, on the other hand, had really enjoyed the experience.

I got back to the home and headed to the canteen for something to eat. I got a couple of filled rolls for each of us and made my way back upstairs to Julie's room, expecting to see her up and about, waiting for me to return, but instead, I saw she was still lying in bed, snoring away.

I gave her a bit of a nudge and she eventually came too. I handed her two rolls and sat down on the chair. She sat up and asked me how it had gone and I told her I thought I'd done okay.

As I ate my rolls, I became aware that I was really tired and decided I would go back to bed when I was finished eating. Julie suggested we should go into the town for the day, find a decent pub, have some lunch, and make a day of it.

I told her I was happy to do that, but needed a kip first. She then agreed that she could do with another hour or so as well. Julie got up, told me she needed to pee, put her housecoat on then went off to the loo. As soon as she left, I stripped off and jumped into bed.

When she came back, she slipped off her housecoat and joined me. We then cuddled in together. The minute our bodies touched, I started to get hard. My thoughts of sleeping had now turned to thoughts of shagging.

I started rubbing and squeezing her bum, pushing it towards my dick. I then began kissing her. But when I went to explore her mouth with my tongue, she pulled away a bit.

"Shug, I thought you were tired? You said we were having a sleep," she reminded me. "I know, Julie, you're right," I told her, "but when you removed your housecoat and climbed into bed naked, I couldn't think about anything else other than fucking you."

I kissed her again and this time, she responded, so I knew she wanted the same as me. I got on top of her and gently slid my dick into her pussy. After a couple of strokes, we rolled onto our sides and I continued at the same pace. We were kissing passionately and I was gently caressing her breasts.

The next thing I know, Lisa, Becky and Calum are all standing beside the bed with their mouths open, staring at us. I turned round and asked them what the fuck they wanted.

Lisa then said: "Eh, sorry, we just came to see how you'd got on with your interview and the door was unlocked so I thought it would be okay to come in. We'll, eh ... We'll go and leave you to it," she told us.

By this time, Julie had sat up with the sheet wrapped around her and was looking really embarrassed. Whereas, I was fuckin fuming that they'd just barged in and spoiled my fun.

"Gonnae fuck off and give us a minute!" I roared at them. They all mumbled apologies as they made their way out. Lisa said, as she left, that they'd be in her room if we wanted to join them later.

As they closed the door, Julie jumped up and started ranting, "Fuck's sake, Shug, what a red neck, them catching us like that. I can't believe I never locked the door!"

"Julie, settle down. We've not done anything wrong - they barged in on us! If anything, it's them that should be embarrassed," I told her.

"That's not the fuckin point, Shug, and you know it. They just caught us shagging, for fuck's sake. I'll never be able to look them straight in the eye again. Fuck, I'm mortified."

"Julie, why are you freaking out so much? Are you forgetting the last time I was here? Fuck me, we all saw each other shagging; it was a fuckin orgy, for fuck's sake. Surely that was way much worse than this?" I suggested.

"That's what you think, Shug. I told them all that we weren't sleeping together and that what I did was a one-off that night, and now they know I've lied about it."

"So fuckin what, Julie? It's none of their fuckin business. And if they say anything, just tell them to go fuck themselves."

She just looked at me, shaking her head, then started getting dressed without saying another word. I followed suit. Within minutes, we were back sitting on the bed, fully clothed.

Julie looked really upset and I put my arm around her and told her to stop worrying, that everything would be okay.

She had tears in her eyes and looked really upset. I really didn't get why Julie was feeling like this, but I did my best to comfort her while she wept.

"Listen, I'll go and tell them to come back in and we can all head off up the town. I'm sure, by the time we get there, we'll all be laughing about it," I told her.

She jumped up and started ranting at me again. "That's fuckin typical of you, Shug, isn't it? Just sweep everything under the carpet, like it didn't happen, without a thought for anyone else's feelings. You really don't give a fuck about me, do you?"

"Whoa, Julie, hold it a fuckin minute, that's a bit harsh. Just because your fuckin friends barged in on us shagging doesn't make me the devil's fuckin spawn. Remember, it was you who left the fuckin door open in the first place, not me. And as for not giving a fuck about you, you have no fuckin idea how much I care for you," I roared back.

I finished tying my boots and grabbed my jacket, thinking I would fuck off to the local pub and get pished, leaving her and her friends to their fuckin tittle-tattle. But before I got to the door, she grabbed me and put her arms around me and started sobbing even harder.

'Fuck me, what now?' I thought to myself, as she began whispering apologies in my ear. I didn't know what to do, so I dropped my jacket, put my arms around her and told her I was sorry too, even though I had no idea why I was saying it.

After a few minutes, she started explaining that she'd been really emotional over the past week or so and that she thought it was because she'd developed strong feelings for me.

'Fuck me, I never saw that coming,' I thought, 'She was just using me to make herself feel better about Rooster'. Now I definitely had no idea what to say.

I just kept cuddling her and rubbing her back, trying to get my head around it. She stopped crying, wiped the tears away with her sleeve and suggested we should talk.

We both sat back down on the bed and Julie stared at me then began, "So what do you think, Shug? It's obvious we both feel the same about each other; do you reckon we could make a go of it?"

Holy shit, I didn't know where to look. I wanted to say we could, but then an image of Rooster popped into my head.

I don't know why, but I decided that now would be a good time to tell her about Rooster and the South chapter. "Julie, before I answer that, I need to tell you something, it's about the Bats, and it involves Rooster."

But before I could say any more, she interrupted, telling me she didn't want to hear it and that maybe she was being stupid, thinking we could be an item.

I then told her to shut up and listen, as she really would want to hear what I had to say, and to my surprise, she did as I asked.

I went through the whole thing, and as I was telling her, I could see her becoming more and more agitated.

I then said that she shouldn't worry, as he would be living about half an hour away, and suggested that the chances of her meeting him would be pretty slim. I finished off by telling her that I really would like to be in a relationship with her.

I wasn't sure which part of my conversation had made her the most agitated: the bit about Rooster coming or telling her I wanted to be with her, but whatever it was, she went off on another rant.

"Shug, why the fuck didn't you tell me all this shit when you arrived? Why wait until now? Is it because I told you how I felt about you or because you knew how fuckin upset I'd be? How the fuck could you even begin to imagine we could ever be in a relationship when he's living here? What are you going to say to him, 'Oh, Rooster, by the way, I'm just popping up to the hospital to shag your ex-bird, you know: the one that aborted your kid!'. Come on, Shug, get real, we both know that's not going to happen."

"Look, Julie, you need to calm it a bit. Think, if I get the job and move in here, we can be together. Rooster doesn't need to know about us right away; we can wait a while before we tell him."

"You think it's that simple, Shug: we just sneak around here, hoping no one notices. What about when he comes to visit you? Don't you think he'll want to see me? Are you going to lie through your teeth to him then, because I couldn't? Anyway, I thought you two were supposed to be 'best mates'. You know him, Shug, and you know it won't matter when you tell him, he'll never forgive you. I'm sorry, Shug, but this changes everything, there's no way we can get together now, and we both know it."

She then stood back from me and began pacing the floor a bit, still looking really edgy and I knew she was spot on. I don't know what the fuck I'd been thinking about, but she was right: if Rooster knew about us, he would go absolutely fuckin mental at me.

I grabbed hold of her and gave her a cuddle. I told her she was right and agreed that Rooster coming here had changed everything.

"I'm sorry, Julie, I know I should've told you when I arrived, but I was being selfish, I didn't want anything to fuck up my interview and I had a good idea this was how you would react so decided to wait until it was over."

Julie was sobbing a bit now, but told me she understood why I hadn't said anything and suggested, that if she was in my shoes, she would probably have done the same, but then she followed it up by saying that I was totally out of order by sleeping with her as I knew how she felt about me.

I just agreed with her, told her again I was sorry and said I knew it was wrong, but that I couldn't help myself.

She then laughed a bit, which lightened the mood slightly, so I thought it would be a good time to change the subject.

I kissed her on the forehead and suggested we should head out for some grub and a few beers, to which she nodded in agreement.

I told her I was going to the loo and asked her if she wanted me to give the others a shout when I was out. But she said it was up to me then made her way to the mirror to put on some slap.

I stood in the toilet, thinking about our conversation, and wondered how the fuck I was going to tell her Rooster was arriving the next day. I thought that telling her would just set her off again so decided it was best not to mention it.

I knocked on Lisa's door and tried the handle, but it was locked. I assumed that they'd all gone out and would probably be down the pub by now.

By the time I got back, Julie was ready to go and I saw she had changed her clothes. "Fuck, Julie, you look great, you don't half scrub up well," I told her. "Thanks, Shug, I thought I needed to give myself a bit of a shake."

Julie had a short summer dress on, which had a low neckline and showed off her assets to the full.

"I knocked at Lisa's door, but there was no answer so it looks like it's just the two of us today. You fancy the local for some food? Or do you still want to go into town?" I asked her.

"Shug, if you think I got dressed up to go down the pub then you're up a gum tree. You're taking me into town and we're going to eat at a posh restaurant. Oh, and by the way, you're paying."

"Okay, that suits me just fine," I told her. "Let's get going, we can phone a taxi from the reception. I'm guessing you won't want to get the bus in your glad rags!"

We made our way to the reception area and Julie went to the phone as I headed outside. It was a beautiful afternoon, the sun was high in the sky and I could feel it burning my face the minute I opened the door.

I sat down on the steps, lit up a fag, closed my eyes, and inhaled deeply. Within a matter of minutes, Julie was sitting beside me, telling me the taxi was on its way.

She asked me when I was planning to leave and I told her I would be going in the morning when I found out about the job.

I started to tell her that I'd arranged to meet some people from the South chapter, but was interrupted by the arrival of the taxi. We jumped in and I told the guy to take us into town.

As soon as we sat in it, Julie asked me if anyone else from home would be going to the meeting. I knew right away that she was talking about Rooster.

"Yes, there'll be about a dozen of us going. We've arranged to meet the guys from the club we're taking over."

"Will he be there?" she asked. "That'll depend on if he's out the hospital and able to ride. My guess is he won't be. But hey, you never know with Rooster."

"Well, if he is, make sure you don't mention us, okay? I don't want him knowing anything." "Fuck's sake, Julie, surely you don't think I'm so stupid that I would say anything to him about us, do you?" "No, I didn't think so, but I just wanted to be sure," she replied.

The driver then told us we were approaching the town and wanted to know where to stop. Julie gave him directions, and within five minutes, we stopped outside a restaurant.

I paid the guy then we got out. We stood at the door and Julie asked me what I thought of it. "Fuck me, Julie, looks a bit posh. Do you think I'll get in dressed like this?" I asked her. "Course you will, there's no dress code that I'm aware of, but maybe, after today, they'll make one," she said, laughing.

She grabbed my hand and pulled me in. When we entered, there was a guy standing at a lectern facing us. It had a sign on it saying: 'Please wait here to be seated'.

The guy asked us to wait a minute, as he was seeing to another customer, and excused himself. We stood about for a bit and, as I looked around the place, I was thinking to myself that I would rather be anywhere else, other than here.

Julie was looking at me, smiling and telling me how much she liked the look of place, but fuck, it didn't do anything for me. As far as I was concerned, it was full of pretentious pricks, trying their best to impress any cunt that would take them on.

I think that if I'd been with anyone else, other than Julie, I would've about turned and fucked off the minute I got in. She whispered to me again, telling me how great she thought the place was, and that everyone she knew, who'd been, had loved it.

Just then, the guy came back and apologised to us for keeping us waiting. He then picked up a couple of menus and asked us if we had a reservation.

"Eh, no, I don't. Do I look like a fuckin Indian?" I said, thinking I was being funny, but he ignored my attempt at humour then said: "Sorry, sir, what I meant was: Have you booked a table?" Julie then intervened, putting on a bit of a posh voice.

"No, sorry, we haven't booked. Do you have a table for two available, please?" He smiled at her and drew me a dirty look before speaking again.

"Certainly, madam. If you'd like to follow me, I'll show you to your table." He then pointed to a table at the window. When we got there, he pulled out the chair for Julie, and when she sat down, he slid it back in, lifted the napkin then placed it on her knee.

By the time he'd got round to me, I was already sitting and lifted my napkin, placing it on my lap before he started his pish patter on me.

He bumbled on about the wine list and the chef's special, all the time directing it at Julie, who seemed to be enjoying the attention. She smiled politely then thanked him.

"Can I get you a drink from the bar?" he asked us. "A pint of lager for myself and a glass of dry white wine for the lady would be good, that's of course if it's not too much trouble, thank you," I told him, in by best posh accent, smiling as I spoke.

"Certainly, sir, they'll be with you presently," he said, bowing slightly as he left the table.

Julie then leaned over to me and told me to stop taking the piss. "Fuck, Julie, I can't help it. He's a fuckin fud," I told her.

"I'll bet he was brought up in the slums, the same as the fuckin rest of us, and now he's acting like he's the big 'I am'. Listen to the way he's talking, for fuck's sake, it's not even a real accent!"

"Shug, can't you just leave it? Come on, let him do his thing, it's who he wants to be. We both know it's an act, but at the end of the day, he's only doing it for his job. I know it pisses you off, but please don't wind him up anymore, just let it go," she pleaded.

"Okay, Julie, fine, relax. For fuck's sake, I was only having a laugh. What's eating you anyway?" I asked her. "You know fine well what's eating me. And before you start, I don't want to discuss it."

Just then, one of the waiters arrived with the drinks and we changed the subject. I talked about my interview and Julie told me some more stuff about the hospital.

We had a nice meal and a couple of drinks, but I thought it was way too expensive and was glad when we left.

All the time I was there, I felt really uncomfortable, like I didn't fit in, it was like watching a war movie and seeing a cowboy chasing a tank on his horse - I felt like the cowboy.

I hailed down a cab, and as we headed back, I asked Julie if she wanted to go to the pub for a few, but she told me she'd rather go home and suggested I go myself.

I decided to give the pub a miss, thinking that we may end up shagging if she was in the mood. We got back into her room and I suggested we have a kip then go down the pub later.

"Shug, you don't really mean 'sleep', do you? I'm guessing what you really mean is you want us to fuck, don't you?" she told me.

"Well, actually, Julie, I meant both. I still feel really tired for some reason, and I thought if we had a sleep: afterwards, we could repeat this morning's exploits."

"Shit, Shug, you're fuckin unbelievable. After what you told me earlier, do you really think it would be that easy for me to just forget all about it and jump on your bones?" she moaned at me.

"Well, yes, Julie, actually I did. Just because he's moving down here doesn't mean we can't fuck. Our feelings for each other don't just fuckin disappear because of that."

"Shug, listen to yourself, you just don't get it, do you? No matter what you think of me, I don't do casual sex. The only reason I did it with you was because I stupidly thought we were both starting afresh. I thought that we were building a relationship, but oh no, you knew all the time that wasn't going to happen, but you just strung me along anyway, letting me think we had something. You know what, Shug? I'm really pissed about that. I actually feel sick about the whole thing and I think it's time for you to leave," she told me.

Fuck me, where did that come from? Talk about kicking a man when he's down! Well, she certainly knew how to do that.

"Come on, Julie, don't you think you're overreacting just a bit here. We've already been through it all, I thought we were sorted. And by the way, just for the record, I would never string you along, you should know that. How many fuckin times do I need to say I'm sorry? I knew how upset you'd be when I told you and was just trying to find the right time."

"Find the right time, Shug? The right time was way before you shagged me. The right time was before we went out gallivanting. The right time was the minute you fuckin arrived," she screamed at me.

By this time, I'd had enough, and let rip at her, "You know what, Julie? Fuck this shit. You're right, it is time for me to leave, there's no fuckin point in talking to you anymore. When you're acting like this, you're not listening to a fuckin word I say."

I grabbed my gear and headed out, slamming the door as I left. As I walked down the corridor, I could hear her shouting after me, but I never turned around. I went down the stairs and outside. I stuffed everything into my sleeping bag and tied it onto my bike. I jumped on, fired it into life, and sped off towards the back entrance.

I rode out the hospital and up the lane, towards the main road. I had no idea where to go so decided to go to the pub and think about it over a beer. Maybe my new 'best friend', the manager, would find me somewhere to crash?

I parked up and made my way to the bar. I ordered myself a beer and had a bit of a look around. Thankfully, I couldn't see any of Julie's friends. I asked the barmaid if the manager was about and she told me he wasn't, but that he would be in just before closing time. I looked at the clock, it was half past nine.

I thought if I sat there that long that I'd be well pished by the time he arrived. I asked her if she knew anywhere I could get a room for the night, but she said the only place I could get one was in the town.

I ordered another beer and made my way to an empty seat in the corner. It was surprisingly quiet for a Friday night, and most of the people who were in were ready to draw their pensions.

I'd been sitting for about fifteen minutes, mulling over my choices, when I saw Anna coming towards me. "Hi, Anna, how's tricks?" I asked her. "I'm okay, Shug, how are you?" she replied.

"Been better," I told her and asked her if I could get her a drink. "No thanks, Shug, I'm in with my friend, were just having a quick one before we head into town. When I saw you, I just wanted to say hello and congratulate you on getting the job."

"Fuck me, I got the job! That's great! I didn't know. Thanks for telling me. I was supposed to go in tomorrow and see them."

"Shit, Shug, you can't tell anybody I told you, my husband mentioned it earlier, I just thought you already knew. Please keep it to yourself?" she asked, almost pleading.

"Relax, Anna, I won't say anything. Look at me, I'm not exactly surrounded by people to tell, am I?" I told her.

She sat down and looked a bit uncomfortable so I reassured her again that I wouldn't say anything.

"It's not that, Shug. Since my man told me they'd given you the job, I've been really worried about what we did. I'm worried that it'll get out. Please tell me that you'll keep it to yourself?"

"Listen, Anna, you don't need to worry about it. I won't tell anyone and I'll make sure no one else does either. I promise. It'll be okay."

"Thanks, Shug, I really appreciate it. I better go now, my friend will be wondering where I've got to," she said, smiling as she got up.

I nodded and told her to enjoy her night, then watched her arse move from side to side as she made her way back to the bar. I began thinking about the job, and how really chuffed I was with myself for being able to get it, but very quickly my excitement turned to disappointment when I thought about Julie and the way I'd left her earlier in the evening.

Chapter 20

I started to wonder whether or not I would take the job now, half the reason I wanted it was to spend time with her and I wasn't sure if I could live in the nurses home now, knowing she was there and we weren't speaking.

I thought I should maybe go back and see her, to try and patch things up, but didn't want her to go off on one again. 'Fuck it, I'll just knock her door and tell her about the job, thank her for her help, and see what kind of reaction I get and take it from there,' I thought to myself.

I stood up, finished my drink, dumped my empty glasses on the bar and said goodbye to Anna and her friend before heading out. As I rode back to the nurses home, I actually had butterflies in my stomach, I guess falling out with Julie had affected me much more than I'd initially thought.

I parked my bike and made my way in. There seemed to be a bit of a party going on in the common room, which made it easy for me to slip past the warden and up the stairs.

I walked along the corridor and wondered if maybe Julie was at the party. I then thought I should've stuck my head in to see if she was there before coming upstairs.

I knocked at her door softly and listened to see if I could hear any movement, but the door opened almost immediately. "I told you I wasn't.... oh, it's you, what the fuck do you want?" she asked me, in a really aggressive tone.

I held my hands up, almost in a surrender pose, "I'm sorry to bother you, I just thought you should know that I got the job. I just wanted to thank you for your help as there's no way I would've got it without you," I told her. "I'm sorry if this is a bad time, I'll get out of your hair, I didn't mean to disturb you." I then about turned and started to make my way back along the corridor.

"Shug, wait, it's not you I'm mad with. Well, it is, but not for coming back. It's just I've had people constantly banging on my door, trying to get me to go to the party, and I keep telling them I can't be arsed. When you knocked the door I thought that it was someone coming to try again to get me to go. Do you want to come in?" she asked, leaving the door open as she disappeared.

I didn't need asking twice. I was straight in and had the door closed faster than you could say: 'Speedy González'. When I went in, I noticed she was sitting on the chair, staring out the window, in the dark. There was a half-empty bottle of vodka on the floor next to her and no glass.

"Look, Julie, about earlier, I'm really sorry for what I said and for fucking off in the huff," I told her, thinking it would smooth my way back into her good books.

"Whatever you say, Shug. I don't care about any of it now," she told me, sounding really low. She then picked up the vodka and had a swig from it. I went around beside her so I could see her and noticed she had tears rolling down her cheeks.

"Come on, Julie, this isn't like you. Why aren't you slapping me and giving me all sorts of abuse, telling me I'm an arsehole and shit?" I asked her.

"I told you, Shug, I really am past caring. However, if you've no place else to go, you can sleep on the floor. I'm early shift in the morning, so when you leave, drop the snib and just close the door over."

She then had another large swig from the bottle, got up, and went to bed. I wasn't sure what the fuck to do. I didn't know whether to leave or stay and try to talk to her.

I'd never seen her so flat, even when she was telling me about the abortion she still had a determination and a desire to move on, whereas now she sounded like she'd given up and it really worried me.

I knelt down beside her bed and asked her if we could talk. She replied without even turning around, "You can talk away all you want, Shug, but I've nothing to say."

"Come on, Julie, please turn around for a minute, I don't want to talk to the back of your head." She turned around and stared straight at me, looking really vacant. "What is it that you actually want, Shug?"

"I'm worried about you, Julie, you don't seem like yourself, I just want you to tell me what's up and what I can do to help."

"Look, Shug, I'm fine, okay? I just need to rest, I've had a really shit day. So if you really want to help then leave me alone and let me sleep," she told me as she turned back to face the wall.

I got up and sat on the chair, turning it a bit to face her, and lit up a fag. I watched her for a bit, wondering about her mood, it was like the lights were on, but nobody was home.

It was just so not her, she would normally argue the bit out and would always tell you what she thought, but this vacant stare and the vodka had me really worried.

When I'd left earlier, she was ranting and raving at me and that's what I expected her to be like when I came back. I wondered if she was having a bit of a mini-meltdown, she was actually reminding me of myself when Malky died.

I thought it best not to say anymore and get a bit of a kip then try again with her in the morning. I grabbed a cover and a pillow from the bottom of her wardrobe and crashed on the floor.

I positioned myself so that my head was under the alarm clock, just to make sure I heard it. When it went off, again, I thought I'd just closed my eyes. I sat up and switched it off. I looked at Julie and she never moved.

I gave her a shake and told her it was time to get up for her work. She turned around and sat on the edge of the bed and I asked her how she was feeling. "I'm fine, Shug, go back to sleep," she told me, as she got up.

I asked her if she wanted me to join her for breakfast, but she told me she didn't eat on her early shift and that she would get something in the ward.

She picked up a towel and her soap bag and went out. I lay down on the bed, trying to think of what I would say to her when she got back, but never came up with anything tangible.

When she came back in, I sat up and leaned my back against the wall. "Good shower?" I asked, 'Good fuckin shower? What kind of pish thing was that to say?' I thought to myself. "Fine," was all she said in reply. She then removed her towel and started to use it to dry her hair.

She was slightly bent over and I was staring at her bare arse and legs. I could also see one of her tits bobbing up and down as she rubbed her hair. Fuck, I couldn't believe it - I was starting to get a fuckin hard-on as I watched her.

They say a standing cock's got no conscience; well I'm testimony to that. I tried to focus on her head and asked her if it was okay for me to come and see her later.

"Please yourself, I won't be doing anything," she told me. She finished drying herself, placed the towel over the chair, then put on her bra and knickers before dressing in her nurse's wrapper. I tried a bit of conversation with her, but was greeted with only one-word answers.

When she was ready, she told me she was off and reminded me to lock the door when I left. I tried again to talk to her, but she just closed the door without giving me a reply.

I lay back down on the bed and tried to get some sleep, but I tossed and turned and couldn't get Julie out of my mind. I was really worried about her, to the point I wondered if I should talk to somebody about it.

I wondered if Lisa was working and thought about giving her door a knock. I looked at the clock and it was only just past seven.

I decided to go and get a roll and a cup of tea then I would make up my mind what to do. I was sitting in the canteen, eating, when I was approached by Mrs Boardman.

"Good morning, Ochil, this is a surprise, I didn't expect to see you here," she remarked. I looked up and smiled at her, "Good morning, Mrs Boardman," I replied. "Yes, I stayed over last night with a friend rather than go home," I told her, thinking she should have known I was here. I was sure I told her at the interview I was staying over.

"Do you mind if I join you?" she asked. "Yes, please do," I told her. "Give me a minute and I'll grab a coffee," she said as she headed to the serving area.

When she returned, she asked me how I thought my interview had gone and I said I thought it had gone okay, but that I didn't have anything to compare it to so wasn't really sure.

She then sipped at her coffee, for what seemed like an age, then put her cup down. "Ochil, I'm pleased to tell you that you've got the job."

"That's brilliant," I told her, trying my best to sound excited. "Thanks very much, I really appreciate it, I won't let you down. When can I start?"

"Well, Ochil, first you need to get a medical, and if that's okay then you can start straight away. I'll send you a letter out on Monday with all the details and we can take it from there."

I realised, at that point, that actually, I was well made up about it and had almost forgotten all about Julie.

I was now genuinely feeling excited about the prospect of working there and asked her if it was possible to get my medical on Monday, telling her I could stay until then. I suggested to her that I could also pick up my letter and it would save her posting it.

"I'm not sure I could organise it that quickly, but leave it with me. If you're staying here until Monday then come to my office at ten-thirty and I'll give you your letter and let you know if it's possible, but remember, don't be disappointed if I can't make it happen."

"No problem, I won't be," I told her, lying through my teeth. "I really appreciate you trying to do it so quickly, thanks very much."

"It's refreshing to see someone so keen to start, I'll do what I can, see you Monday," she said as she left, taking her coffee with her. I smiled to myself, thinking I was the dog's bollocks, then reality hit home.

I wondered what the fuck I was letting myself in for and had no idea where the fuck I would stay until then. I then turned my thoughts back to Julie and decided to go and give Lisa a shout. I finished my roll and made my way to her room.

I gave her door a knock and just as I was going to knock at it again, she opened it. She was wearing a long t-shirt and it didn't leave much to the imagination.

"Fuck, Shug, what do you want? It's the middle of the night," she asked, walking back to her bed. "Nice to see you too, Lisa," I replied. "And by the way, for your information, it's half past eight, hardly the middle of the night."

"I didn't get to bed until after three, so trust me, it IS the middle of the night. What do you want anyway?" she asked, pulling her covers back over her head. "I need to talk to you about Julie, I'm really worried about her, I think she's depressed or something," I told her.

She pulled the covers down under her chin and said: "Is this a fucking wind up, Shug? You're only in the hospital five minutes and you're already diagnosing conditions? Come on, get a grip, Julie's fine," she told me, closing her eyes.

"Listen, Lisa, I'm fuckin serious. She's really different, like she's not really there when you talk to her, I've never seen her like this before. You need to speak to her and see for yourself."

She sat up in bed, ran her hands through her hair and said: "Listen, Shug, I spoke to her last night and the only thing that's wrong with her is that she's pissed with you, so give her a bit of space and she'll come round. Now, if there's nothing else? I need to get back to sleep, I'm back shift today," she told me, snuggling back down under her covers.

I decided not to pursue it and thought it best to leave before I said anything I would regret. My parting words to her were "Okay, I'm off, but if she is depressed and does anything stupid, I'll hold you fully responsible." She just replied by saying, "Whatever." And I left feeling like I wanted to give her a good slap.

I went back to Julie's room, not sure what to do, but then remembered I was supposed to be meeting the Mutts' Prez at ten o'clock. Fuck, it was nine already and I hadn't even had a wash.

I quickly showered and got dressed. I glanced at the clock. Fuck, it was now half past nine! I got the address out of my pocket and memorised it before shoving it back in my jacket. I then made my way out to my bike.

I fired it up, headed out of the hospital and made my way to the city. I wasn't really sure where I was going so decided my best bet would be to speak to a taxi driver when I got there.

It took me about twenty minutes and as I approached the city, I saw the train station and drew into the taxi rank. I got directions and realised it was only minutes from where I was.

I rode straight down the main street, which was a hive of activity, with people rushing about everywhere, and suddenly thought I didn't want to be here.

I always kind of liked people, but I was never a big fan of crowds, it really made me feel pretty uncomfortable and was glad I was heading away from them.

I turned off the main street at the last junction, as directed by the taxi driver, and headed up a steep hill. At the top of the hill, I turned right into a small cul-de-sac and saw the house I was looking for. I stopped outside it and parked up. I took out a smoke, lit up and looked around.

I didn't know what I thought I was coming to, but this was the last thing I expected. I was in the middle of a street which had ten houses in it and looked, for all the world, like a street for retired old farts.

People were out in their gardens, pottering about, others were washing their cars and playing with what looked like their grandkids.

'Fuck me, what the fuck has Indie got us into here?' I wondered. I'd expected someone to have come out the house to greet me by now, but as no one had, I went and knocked on the door.

An old woman answered it and I asked her if I could speak to 'Gunner'. "Please don't call him that, I don't like it. His name is Robert and you'll get him in the garage round the back," she told me, then closed the door.

I thought she was a strange looking old dear, and way too old to be Gunner's mum, unless he was about forty odd. I went round the back and clocked the garage: it was huge, nearly half the size of the house, and it looked like you could park four cars in it and still have room to walk about.

As I got closer, I could hear an engine being revved up and it sounded like a bike. I opened the door and saw two guys: one sitting on a bike and the other was crouched down beside it, looking at the engine. The guy on the bike killed the engine and they both turned and looked at me.

"Hello, I'm Shug, I'm looking for Gunner," I said, walking towards them. The guy who was crouched down stood up. "That's me," he said, offering me his hand, which I shook. "Pleased to meet you, Shug, this is Titch, my little brother," he said, pointing to the guy on the bike.

I nodded in Titch's direction and he did the same back. Looking at them, you would never have taken them for brothers. Gunner was a big lad, taller than me, about twenty-five, with a shaved head, and I could see through his t-shirt that he was quite muscular.

Titch, on the other hand, was about seventeen. He was short and a fair bit overweight, he had frizzy hair, which grew out like an afro, and they didn't look alike in any way.

"Shug, Indie's asked me to show you around, point out where we hang, and where the other bikers meet and stuff. You want to go right now or do you fancy a roll and a cuppa?" he asked.

"Whatever suits you, man," I told him. "Okay, let's get something to eat first. Titch, go in and tell Gran to fire us up some rolls and we'll be in in a minute." "I'm going to do it and I want egg, I like egg Robert," Titch replied.

When he left, Gunner told me that his brother was a bit slow and had a few health problems, so if he was rude or anything, to just ignore it. I nodded and assured him I would.

We went inside and sat in the kitchen. The old woman, who I'd spoken to at the door, was already putting bacon, sausage and eggs onto rolls. Titch was trying to lift the roll with egg on it and his Gran hit him on the knuckles with her fish slice.

"Thomas, leave that alone and sit at the table," she told him in a stern voice. He said he was sorry, told her he was hungry then sat down and started crying.

Gunner put his arm around him and told him it was okay, and that his gran would give him the roll when it was ready.

"Okay, but I want egg, can I get egg, Robert? I like egg," he said again. "Yes, Titch, you'll get egg if you stop crying," Gunner told him, which seemed to do the trick.

His gran put two egg rolls in front of him, and after smothering them with tomato sauce, he munched away happy as Larry.

I wondered why Titch wasn't in hospital and was dying to ask Gunner where his parents were, but when his gran placed two rolls in front of me, I thanked her and began eating.

Gunner asked me about the Bats and how long I'd been with them. I gave him a bit of background, but nothing too heavy. I then asked him about the Mutts and he told me they'd been going for two years and had eighteen members and a couple of prospects, but that it was really just a bunch of mates who liked to ride and party.

He went on to explain that recently, some of the other bike gangs in the area had wanted to take them over and that this had caused a few arguments among the members.

"Some wanted to get patched over and others wanted to fight and try and take over the other clubs. Eventually, one of our guys who knew Stiff spoke to him for a bit of advice and him and Provo came to visit us. After we told them the script, they suggested that we should become Bats and create a new South chapter, then, with their help, we could take over the whole area. Provo said that he would oversee it, and within a couple of weeks would make sure that we were the only club wearing colours here. After they left, we had a meeting and unanimously agreed that was the way we wanted to go. But a couple of weeks later, we heard about Indie and Provo. I went to Provo's funeral with Rumba, he's my VP and the guy who was mates with Stiff. When we were there, we spoke to Indie and asked him if the Bats were still looking to patch over. He told me they were and that he would be in touch after he sorted out all his shit."

I asked him how he felt about no longer being President of his own club. He told me that he was cool with it as he would much rather be the SAA in a proper club than the President of a club that, compared to the Bats, were really just playing at it.

I digested what he said and began to think that he had no idea what he was getting into. I'm sure he thought that he would just continue to fart about, having a laugh, and that if they became Bats, all the rest of the clubs would leave them alone.

I knew what Indie was thinking and knew that his plan was to wipe out all the other gangs and anyone else who tried to stop him. I was sure he would put in place the same setup here as we had up the road.

"You do realise everything will completely change here when you become Bats?" I told him. "You do know what Indie's plans are for your club?" I asked.

"Yes, course I do, and we are all well up for it. Listen, were not stupid, we know there's going to be a fair bit of shit to do and that the next few weeks are going to be heavy, but we don't care, we all know the risks."

I decided not to say anymore as I didn't want to put him off and just told him I was glad that he was up for it and that I was looking forward to meeting everyone else.

"I've arranged for everybody to be at the pub for twelve so you'll see them all shortly," he told me. He then got up and gave Titch a bit of a clean-up as he had egg all over his face, then told him to go and sit with his gran, which he did without saying a word. He then said: "I'll just go and tell Gran we're off." I nodded, ate the last bit of my roll, then headed outside.

I started laughing a bit to myself, thinking about what Gunner had just said, 'I'll just go and tell Gran' I thought about how Indie would have reacted if he'd said that to him! Fuck, I reckoned he would've ripped him big time.

I'd just lit up a fag when he came back out. I offered him one, which he took, and I lit him up.

"Cheers, Shug, I'll just go and get my bike out and meet you round the front." I walked around to my bike and sat on it, facing the drive. I wasn't sure what kind of bike he had as I didn't get a look at it with him and Titch in my line of sight.

He pushed it out the garage then closed the door, fired it up and joined me at the front. He switched it off and continued to smoke his cigarette. "Nice bike, had it long?" I asked him.

"About nine months," he told me. "I see you've started chopping it," I said, pointing to the raised bars and king and queen seat. "Yeh, I plan to do a bit more to it, but haven't seen anything that I thought would improve it."

"I agree," I told him. "I like the z650, it's a cool shape the way it is." He smiled at me, obviously quite happy I liked his bike. "Let's go," he said, as he kicked his bike back into life.

"Where are we going, Gunner?" "I'll take you to the bypass," he told me, "then a ride through the town. I'll point out places I think you should know and I'll tell you about them when we get to the pub."

We rode off and within five minutes, were at the bypass. Gunner drew into the side of the road and I drew up alongside him.

"This is the bypass," he said, pointing to a newly constructed road. "It's only been open three months, the motorway used to stop at the north of the city then started again on the south side."

He then pointed to the left of the south side. "That area there is the 'Rippers' patch, they're our main rivals. We have the north side and they have the south. We're always clashing with them about who should have the centre of the city, but nothing is ever resolved. I think it's because we're pretty much equal in size. Okay, let's go, I'll take you through the city now," he told me. We rode slowly through the streets, Gunner pointing to places as we went.

He pointed to a few places, but I was intrigued when he pointed at a funeral parlour and made a mental note to ask him about it when we got to the pub.

We headed up a one-way street and he pulled in at the bottom of it. I guessed this was the pub they used as there were about a dozen bikes outside it. We parked up and he ushered me inside. The pub was very unassuming, there were no distinguishing features to it. We went into the bar, but there was no sign of his mates.

He continued to a door at the end of the bar and held it open for me. "Where are we going?" I asked him. "There's a room in the back we use. One of the guys Uncle owns the pub and he lets us use it. I think he's happier to give us a place to ourselves, rather than us hog the main bar, not everyone is biker friendly here, you'll find that out soon enough," he told me.

We went into the next room and I was pleasantly surprised. I was expecting a small dingy room, tucked away, with no windows and just a couple of tables and chairs. But it was pretty big and had large windows, a pool table, a dartboard, and a bandit. There was even a hatch which opened into the bar for getting served.

When Gunner opened the door, the place fell silent and all eyes were on me as we walked in. "Hey, guys, this is Shug, make him welcome," he told everyone, then said he was going to order us some drinks and made his way to the hatch.

Most of the guys mumbled my name and the rest nodded. At that point, I remembered what Indie had told me about first impressions and decided to go for it.

"Hi, guys, how's things? Are you all looking forward to the patch over? I hope there's a party arranged for afterwards, nothing like a good piss up to get to know everyone." No one said a thing, most of them carried on doing whatever the fuck they were doing before we'd come in.

I went to the hatch and asked Gunner if he'd got the beers in yet. "On their way, Shug," he told me then said: "Well, you certainly know how to make an entrance, I'll give you that."

"Not sure how it went down, though, never really got any feedback, but I'm sure it'll give them something to talk about for a while." The drinks then arrived and he handed one to me. He pointed to the seats where most of the guys were sitting and gestured for me to follow him over.

We sat down and the rest of the guys in the room all crowded around our table, bringing their chairs with them. Gunner then went round everyone, telling me their names. Each time, I nodded to them and they nodded back.

The first thing I noticed was that most of them were a bit older than me; I reckoned that the average age was around twenty-three.

After the introductions, I asked if anybody had any questions about the Bats and a guy called DD asked me when we were going to burst the Rippers. I told him that wasn't my call, but when Indie arrived with the new Prez, he should ask him. He then let rip at me.

"What's the fuckin point in asking you anything if you're just going to fuckin fob us off until the rest get here?" I wasn't really sure what to do about his aggression, but remembered again what Indie had said, so I went for it.

I stood up, pointing at him, "Listen here, arsehole, don't start all your fuckin aggressive pish with me. I can't give you a fuckin answer because it's not my fuckin call to make, okay? Now that's twice I've told you so get it into your thick fuckin skull because I won't be telling you a third time, got it?" I roared back at him, almost expecting to be fighting before I finished talking, but surprisingly, he held his hands up and accepted what I'd said.

I wasn't sure if he was scared of me or if he realised what the consequences would be when the rest of the guys came down, but he went from being a nutcase to a pussy quicker than I'd seen anyone do it. Even though I was well relieved, I also felt a bit disappointed.

If all it was going to take for this lot to roll over was a shouting match, I started to wonder if we may have bitten off a bit more than we could chew.

I sat back down and looked at Gunner. "This is some way to treat a fuckin guest, is it not?" I told him. "Sorry, man, DD's just mad because he got beaten up last week by three of them and wants revenge." I shouted over to DD and told him he'd have to wait until after today and assured him that we would sort it.

I shook my head and began to wonder how they dealt with their shit down here and actually felt a bit of sympathy for DD.

"Hey, guys, just thought I should give you all a heads up before the rest of the Bats arrive. If anyone feels the need to make any threats then they better be prepared to go all the way to back it up because the Bats don't think coming second is an option."

DD then spoke up saying, "Well, thank fuck for that, they sound like my kind of guys, I'll drink to that," before raising his glass and nodding in my direction.

He'd just put the glass to his mouth when the barman shouted over, "Hey, Gunner, there's a bunch of guys here saying they're friends of yours, you want me to let them in?"

"No, it's okay, Sam, I'll come and get them, thanks," he told him. Gunner got up and headed out. I went over to the other table where DD was sitting and asked him why he'd been behaving like an arsehole earlier, when clearly he wasn't one.

"Haha, I was just trying to see if it was true what people said about the Bats never backing down and I'm glad it is," he said, with a big smile on his face.

"I don't follow you, DD, what do you mean?" I asked him. "Well, what people say is that no Bat will ever back down, whatever the odds, and you proved that today. Fuck me, Shug, if we'd kicked off you would've got a proper pasting and you knew it, but you still stood up for the colours. Man, I can't wait to get my patch."

"Ha ha, got it, just wasn't sure what tale you were talking about. Fuck, there are so many rumours sometimes I forget the truth," I told him.

As we chatted, I noticed that most of the guys were listening intently to our conversation and I got the feeling that, all of a sudden, some of them weren't quite as up for the patch over as DD was.

Gunner came in with the guys and shouted over to the two prospects to pull some more tables over. I got up and greeted Indie and the guys. Then, as everyone was shaking hands and introducing themselves, Indie pulled me aside and asked me for a heads up.

"Well, Shug, what's the script then?" "Not quite sure," I told him. "All the guys seemed well up for it until five minutes ago, but now I'm not so sure. Had a bit of a run-in with one of them and now I think it's made some of the others a bit uncomfortable. If I was you, I'd tell them about what it's really like to be a Bat before I dished out any colours. My guess is that you'll spot the ones who don't want it straight away, I reckon you'll lose about five or six of them."

"Good stuff, Shug, I'll lay it on thick, well done, bro," he told me, before turning away to speak to Gunner.

I went and caught up with Flick and Cowboy. "Hey, Shug, ma man, how you doing? How'd the interview go? Did you get the job?" Cowboy asked me.

I told him I was fine and that I'd got the job, then asked him how Rooster was. He told me that he was out of hospital, but still not too great.

"Him and some of the guys were at Mark's kid's funeral this morning. He told me it was the worst thing he'd ever seen."

"Holy fuck, I forgot all about Mark's kid. I wish someone had let me know about it, Cowboy, I really wanted to go." "Listen, Shug, I knew you'd want to go, but we only found out about it this morning, an hour or so before it took place. Mark wanted it to be a small family thing and didn't tell anyone about it. I think him and his Mrs have split up. We heard he'd moved out of their flat and was staying with Scooter."

'Poor cunt' I thought to myself, 'he must be going through hell'. "Cowboy, you need to give me Scooter's address when we go back up the road, I need to go see him."

"No probs, a couple of the guys know where he lives so I'll get it for you when we're done here," he told me.

"Cheers, Cowboy, much appreciated," I replied. The next thing, Indie stood up and called for a bit of order and everyone who was standing grabbed a seat. Within seconds, the room was silent.

"Right, before I start, if anyone needs a refill or has anything to do then now's the time, you've got five minutes." He then sat back down with Gunner and Brutis.

The two prospects went to the bar and ordered drinks, a couple of the Mutts went for a piss and the rest sat in silence, watching us as we caught up and chatted away.

When everyone had sat back down, Indie brought the place to order again. "Right, guys, listen up, we're here because your club has agreed to a patch over and I have cuts for everyone, but before I give them out, I need to know you're worthy of it. I don't know any of you and will take you all at face value, but if any of you disrespect the patch in any way then you'll have me, and every other Bat who wears a patch, to deal with, and trust me, that won't be good for your health. Before we do the patch over you need to know a few things, firstly, when you become a Bat: it's for life, without exception, and it's not some weekend thing, riding with your mates, it's total commitment, which means the Bats always come first. If your mother dies and the Prez asks you to do something at the same time as her funeral then you would be expected to miss it, that's the kind of commitment required, so if you're not up for it then now's the time to fuck off. I'm sure you've thought a lot about it, but you need to be sure you want it. From our end, if you do commit, and you're not up to the mark, then we'll fuck you out, make no mistake about it. When you get your colours you can consider yourself full patch members, but as far as I'm concerned, you'll all be on probation. Consider it almost like a trial period, like you would do at a new job, with the Prez being your employer. Fuck it up and you're out, disrespect the patch in any way and you're out, there will be no second chances. What you do will determine if you walk away or leave in a box. I'm going to speak to your current Prez and your new Prez so you have fifteen minutes to decide where your future lies, coz when I come back, you'll be making a massive life changing decision. So right now, best you speak with some of my guys and get to know what's expected of you."

Indie then walked towards the door, with Brutis and Gunner close behind him. Most of the Mutts were crowding around the table, talking amongst themselves, and I made a point of chatting with the 'North' guys to try and get to know them a bit better.

I'd seen the four of them before, but the only one I'd spoken to was Scuba. He introduced me to the others and we chatted for a bit.

The main topics of conversation were about the guys sitting arguing with each other about whether or not to commit, and the bottom rockers. They were laughing about becoming a 'North' Bat, then, in less than a week, they'd changed their rocker to 'South'.

We tried to suss out who would bottle it and they reckoned, between themselves, that at least three of them would walk, but I was still sticking by my earlier prediction of five or six.

The door opened and Gunner came in. He went over and sat with the Mutts. We couldn't hear what he was saying, but got the gist of what it was about when four of the guys got up, threw their cuts on the floor, and left.

They continued to argue for another few minutes, then another one did the same with his cut and left. Gunner then went back out and returned with Brutis and Indie. I had a quick count round the room and clocked nine of us and thirteen Mutts, including the two prospects who, surprisingly, had stayed.

Indie opened the bag and placed the cut-offs on the table then gestured to Gunner to stand up. He handed the new cut with SAA on it to Brutis and asked Gunner to remove his old one, which he did.

Brutis asked Gunner to turn around then put the new cut on him, when he turned back around, Brutis shook his hand, gave him a manly hug and welcomed him to the brotherhood.

Indie then shook his hand, congratulated him and also gave him a bit of a hug. He then nodded to Brutis, telling him to present the cuts to the rest of the new members.

While Brutis was giving out the new cuts, Indie was busy removing the top rocker and emblem from two of them for the prospects. He then threw them to Brutis who told the prospects to come and get them.

After Brutis was done with the prospects, Indie stood up and raised his glass then said: "To the South chapter." Everybody then did the same, echoing his call. The guys were clinking their glasses together, hugging each other and cheering.

After a few minutes, Indie brought us to order and asked for a bit of hush. Everybody sat back down and looked at Indie, waiting for him to say something. As he talked, I noticed that the newbies were almost hanging on his every word.

He started off by congratulating everyone then went on to explain, that from now on, they would all need to eat, sleep and shite as Bats.

He gave them a few pointers about how they should behave, telling them that they had to make sure they followed the lead of Brutis and the rest of us, and told them they would be expected to do whatever Brutis wanted and do it without question.

"If anyone has a problem with any of that then they should remove their colours and fuck off now. I'm now going to speak with the officers. Anyone that's decided to stay should now get on their bikes and show their new brothers this miserable fuckin city of yours. Drive slowly, make plenty of noise, and let every cunt know the Black Bats have arrived," he told them.

A roar went up then we all started to leave. As I headed to the door, Indie shouted on me and all I could think was, 'What the fuck now?' "Shug, you stay, I want you here until Rooster's back, okay?"

Fuck, he didn't need to tell me twice. I don't know if it was the euphoria of everyone's excitement dragging me along or something else, but I was well made up that he'd asked me to stay.

Cowboy looked back, gesturing for me to get a move on, but I told him just to go as I was needed here. As the words came out, I laughed to myself, wishing I'd told him that 'I've got 'a bit of business to attend to' thing. I went back in and joined the guys at the table. I sat beside Gunner, who by now was looking a bit sheepish, I guessed that the penny had just dropped for him in terms of what he'd now got himself into.

"You okay, man?" I asked him. "Yeh, fine, Shug, just feel a bit like a rabbit in the headlights," he told me. I said I was the same when I joined, lying through my teeth, "Don't worry, everything'll be cool, you'll see," I said, trying to reassure him.

As we waited for the drinks to arrive, I started to wonder if Indie meant I was acting VP or SAA or if I was just making up the numbers until Rooster was well?

I didn't need to wonder for long. Within seconds of Indie starting, he told everybody that I was there as an extra officer until Rooster arrived and that Brutis would use Gunner as VP if he needed to.

He then asked Gunner to give him the lowdown on the Rippers, which he did. He then told him, that when the guys came back, we were all going to their bar to kick the living shit out of them.

Gunner started to suggest that going to their place wouldn't be a good idea, but Indie gave him a cold stare and told him he didn't care what he thought and that we WERE doing it, end of.

We then started to plan the attack. Indie got info from Gunner about the layout of the bar and where to park the bikes and stuff.

It turned out that the Rippers had a similar kind of setup to the Mutts. The plan was that Indie, Brutis and Gunner would go into their bar and one of them would kick open the fire door. We would then all bale in, tooled up, and set about them.

Indie then asked Gunner if they had any weapons. He said most of the guys had baseball bats and knives, but that they were probably at their houses.

"Right, come on, guys, everybody outside," he told us. By the time we all got out, almost on cue, the guys arrived back. When the noise of the engines had died down, Indie told them to go and get all the weapons they had and be back ASAP.

One of the guys asked why and Indie nearly ripped his fuckin head off. He grabbed hold of his jacket and pulled him towards his face, until they were almost touching noses, then reminded him about what he was told earlier regarding following orders, then suggested he say nothing else and get a fuckin move on.

I swear I thought the guy actually shat himself, he went a funny shade of grey and looked like he was temporarily paralysed. Even after Indie walked away, he was still in the same position until his mate gave him a bit of a dunt to bring him back to reality.

All the Mutts then left and Indie started talking to Brutis. "What in fuck's name have we let ourselves in for here? Fuckin city boys ... more like country fuckin bumpkins! I thought, living in the city, they would've been a bit sharper and much more aware than they actually are. Listen up, guys, we'll need to be on our guard tonight. If you get a chance, check out anyone who doesn't do the biz. Give me the wire and we'll make a fuckin example of them when it's over."

Cowboy then asked Indie what was going down so he gave them the heads up, which seemed to make them all happy. I still never got that thing when you were going to beat people up that you looked forward to it, I always felt a bit sick and really nervous that some kind of disaster would happen.

When the guys arrived back, Indie explained what was going to happen and told us all to ride two's up. "Any questions?" he asked.

DD then replied, "No questions, man, but I've only been a Bat five minutes and I'm already fuckin loving it. Come on, let's get the bastards," he roared.

We all doubled up and DD made a beeline for me and jumped on the back. "One baseball bat, one pickaxe handle, and two blades," he told me as we were leaving.

"Take your pick, Shug, I'm happy with anything to waste the pricks," he told me, smiling away. "A baseball bat will do for me, I've got my own knife," I told him. Within ten minutes, we arrived at a doctor's surgery and parked up behind the building. DD pointed across the road at the pub and told me the fire door was around the back.

We all made our way to the door and waited. Indie, Brutis and Gunner went into the pub by the main entrance then went straight through the bar and into the back room.

When they entered, all the Rippers stood up prepared to scrap, but Indie told them to cool it as they didn't want any trouble. Indie asked to speak to the Prez, who stood directly in front of him, demanding to know what they wanted. He told them that the Bats were taking over the city and offered them the opportunity to join up.

The Rippers' Prez told Indie he'd already refused the offer and had no interest in patching over. He then told him if he tried to come into his territory again then he had better bring an army because the Rippers were here for keeps.

Indie then told him he was disappointed with his decision and that he thought he wasn't seeing the big picture, but that he respected his decision. He then head-butted him and started to lay into him.

Brutis ran for the fire door and booted it open. Before any of the Rippers realised what was happening, we were all over them. Within ten minutes, it was a done deal, most of the Rippers were out cold and the ones who weren't had given up.

Indie ordered us to take their cuts, which we did without any resistance. He told Flick to take them outside and torch them. Indie grabbed the Rippers' Prez and slapped him a bit until he came too.

He grabbed him by the hair and neck and sat him up. "If we see anybody wearing a patch from now on - they're dead, got it?" he told him. The Prez just nodded then Indie gave him another punch in the face, rendering him unconscious again.

By the time we all went out, the colours were well and truly burning. I thought to myself 'Even if anyone was daft enough to wear colours again, they would need to get themselves new ones'.

We jumped on the bikes and headed back to the pub. There was hardly a bruise or a cut between us. All the Mutts were well pleased with their efforts and seemed to think that was it over.

Indie, however, wasn't thinking that way. Whenever he got back, he went straight to the phone and called the farm. He told the guys to haul their arses down here by nine the next day.

When he came back in, I asked him why he wanted the rest of the guys down and he told me it was because he was planning to start a war.

My thoughts turned to where we were all going to crash and I asked Gunner if he knew anywhere we could. He told me he'd arranged for us to sleep in the pub. I smiled at him and he knew exactly what I was thinking.

"Come on, Shug, you don't think he'll let us loose in his boozer all night, do you? He'll lock the hatch and the bar doors from the other side. He told me, that as long as I stayed with you, he was happy to let you all bunk down here."

He then said that he'd told Indie about the arrangements earlier and pointed to him, "I think he's now going to tell everybody that they'll be staying put tonight, including my guys, and I'm not sure how they'll take it," he told me, whispering.

I listened as Indie began. He told them that he'd called the guys up the road and that a squad of them would be arriving tomorrow morning and that everybody would be kipping in the pub.

When he'd finished, I looked around at the Mutts and could see by some of the reactions that a fair number of them were pretty pissed about it, but none of them dared say anything.

We had a few beers and got to know each other a bit better and it turned into a good night. The barman shouted Gunner over to tell him it was last orders and that he'd give us one more round before he locked up. So we ordered a rake of drink which kept us going until around 3a.m.

We all then crashed out, some in their sleeping bags, but most of us just crashed on the carpeted floor. The lucky ones grabbed the booths and slept there.

Indie had everybody up and organised by ten the following morning. He sent the prospects out to get some rolls and by the time the rest of the guys arrived, just before eleven, we were all outside, waiting to greet them.

Another twenty-two guys had arrived and I wondered why Indie had summoned them. It just seemed pointless after what we'd done the night before.

We all went back inside and Indie told us his plan. He wanted everybody to split up, in groups of five or six, and hit all the pubs and haunts where the Rippers would most likely be.

He told us, if we saw anyone wearing their colours, we had to beat them up, take their colours, then burn them just as we'd done the previous night. He made sure that most groups had a couple of Mutts in them, to show us where to go.

At Noon, we all left the pub, arranging to return there no later than 2p.m. My group consisted of Gunner, DD, Flick, Cowboy, and Freeko from up north. We had two places to go: one was a pub and the other was a tattoo shop. We hit the tattoo shop first and there was nothing doing. The guy who was doing a tattoo was one of the guys from the night before and he wasn't wearing colours.

He told Gunner that he was done with it and he had no interest in getting involved in any kind of turf war. He said that most of the guys felt the same and had also thrown in the towel.

We left and headed to the pub where we saw three guys, who Gunner identified as Rippers, and sat down beside them. One of them looked well beaten up and didn't have colours on. However, the other two did.

I guessed, because there wasn't a mark on them, that they hadn't been involved in the fight the night before. Gunner told them to remove their colours and give them to him, telling them the Rippers no longer existed.

Before they could say anything, he then offered them the opportunity to become Bats, telling them it was the only way they'd be allowed to keep wearing colours.

They both removed their patch and handed them to Gunner without saying a word. Gunner asked them again if they would like to become Bats and one guy said he would think about it, but the other two said that they weren't interested.

Gunner told the guy who was thinking about it to come to our pub before five if he wanted to join as after that he wouldn't have the choice. We got up, went outside, and set fire to the colours in full view of everyone in the pub. After a few minutes, we got on our bikes and headed back to the pub.

On the way, we noticed half a dozen guys wearing colours. They were sitting on a piece of grass where lots of shop workers were having lunch. I pointed to them then signalled for Gunner to stop. We about turned and drew up beside their bikes.

As we walked towards them, one of the guys spoke to DD. "Hey, DD, how's it goin, man? Haven't seen you for ages," he said, getting up and walking towards him.

"Doin great, Freddie, how's you?" DD replied. "Yeh, can't complain," he told him. They then shook hands and did the man hug bit before Freddie sat back down. DD looked at Gunner and gestured that he should do the talking and Gunner gave him a nod back, making him aware he was cool with it.

"Freddie, you and your mates are going to need to ditch the colours, man. We've patched over to the Black Bats and we're taking over the city so no one will be allowed to wear colours unless they're Bats. I know there are less than a dozen of you, and you keep yourselves to yourselves, but you either have to ditch them or patch over and join us."

"Fuck's sake, DD, come on, man, that's heavy shit. You know you won't get any aggro from us. We've been going for more than two years and never got involved with you or the Rippers. In fact, we've never had a beef with anyone in that time, so why the fuck do we need to ditch our colours now?" he asked.

Cowboy then butted in, "Because you do, okay? So make up your fuckin mind. Now, what's it to be, boys?" he asked them, in a really aggressive tone.

Freddie then got up, ready to have a go at Cowboy, but DD stood between them, making sure nothing happened. I grabbed Cowboy and pulled him back and DD told Freddie that they had until five to think about it.

"Listen, Freddie, you and your guys need to have a chat about what you want to do. If you decide you're up for it then come to our pub before five. If you don't show then we'll know you're not, and if that's the case, make sure you ditch the patches."

He then shook Freddie's hand again, nodded in the direction of the rest and we headed off. When we arrived back at the pub, some of the guys were already there, sitting outside, having a beer.

Jelly and Hotwire were sitting with Indie. Jelly asked us how we'd got on. Gunner sat down beside them and told him the script. The rest of us headed to the bar.

While we were waiting to be served, Flick asked DD if he thought Freddie and his troops would come on board. He told him he wasn't sure, but knew if they didn't, that they wouldn't give up their colours without a fight.

Flick then laughed, saying he hoped, for their sake, that they didn't want to fight. "Hey, Flick, you shouldn't laugh, they're all game as fuck and some of them can really handle themselves, don't underestimate them," DD told him.

"Listen, DD, if you're friends with them then you should jump back on your bike and go and convince them to join us or ditch their colours. Because, no matter how well they can handle themselves, they'll get wasted, mate, there's no doubt about that," Flick explained.

"You know what, Flick? I might just do that, bud. Right, cancel my beer," he told him, then headed off. As he left, Gunner joined us at the bar and asked where DD was going. Flick filled him in on the conversation and Gunner shook his head then said: "Fuck, I knew this would happen eventually."

He then started to explain to us, "DD and Freddie are stepbrothers. When Freddie was setting up his outfit, he wanted DD to join them as Prez, but he chose to stay with us and tried to get him and his guys to become Mutts. There was a bit of a fallout and they never spoke for about six months, until their mother died. Then, at the funeral, they sort of made up. They can both fight like fuck, and if Freddie doesn't come on board then there'll definitely be an almighty scrap."

Gunner then asked how they seemed with each other and I told him they were smiling and shaking hands like they were good mates. "Well, at least that's something," he told us, as he picked up his pint and made his way towards the door. We all followed him out without saying anymore and grabbed a seat in the sun.

By this time, everyone was back, except one group. Most of the guys had very little to report: a couple of the groups had seen guys with Ripper patches, but they'd handed over their colours without any fuss.

There were some other groups, like Freddie's, and they were all given the same option as he was. So now it was only a matter of waiting until five then Indie would let us know our next move.

We'd been sitting around, drinking and chatting, for about twenty minutes when the last group arrived. Again, their story was pretty much the same as the rest.

We'd been drinking for another half hour or so before DD arrived back. He parked up and got off his bike. As he was taking his helmet off, Gunner and another bloke he was sitting with made their way towards him.

They ushered him around the corner a bit and out of sight. I looked at Flick and Cowboy and we all shrugged our shoulders. About ten minutes later, the three of them reappeared, all smiles and chatty.

They went straight into the bar, smiling and nodding to everyone as they passed by, and it gave me that feeling you get in your gut when you know something isn't exactly what it seems.

"What the fuck do you think that's about?" I asked Cowboy. "Beats me, Shug, but something's definitely up, that's a fuckin certainty," he told me.

Indie obviously clocked it as well because he and Brutis headed in at the back of them and we guessed it wouldn't be long before we found out.

While they were inside, four guys arrived, looking to speak to Gunner. They were all on bikes, but none of them were wearing colours. Flick told them to grab a seat and someone would go and get him.

Being the nosey one, I told them I would go and get him, as I was dying to know what was going on inside. When I went in, I saw Indie pointing his finger at DD, with his other hand around his throat. The rest of the guys were standing watching.

Indie was talking to him through his teeth, but I couldn't really hear what he was saying. I made my way towards Gunner and told him about the guys outside. As I turned to leave, I heard Indie saying to DD, "So you can go and tell the fucking pricks that, okay?"

DD then replied: "Okay, man, I get the fuckin message, there's no need to go fuckin mental. I'll go and tell them that right now." Walking as slowly as I could, trying to listen to them, the last thing I heard was Indie saying: "Well get a fuckin move on then."

I'd just got back outside when Indie came to the door and shouted everybody back in. I clocked DD making his way out and I asked him if he was okay. He just mumbled something about Indie being a prick and I suggested to him he should keep those thoughts to himself. He just nodded and made his way to his bike before fucking off on it.

Gunner told the four guys to wait outside and he would come back and see them shortly. He was last to come in and closed the door over before grabbing a seat.

There must've been nearly fifty of us in the room and when Indie raised his hand, you could have heard a pin drop. "Seems like we have a bit of a problem, guys," he told us.

"Some of the Rippers, plus a whole bunch of the other diddy clubs, have given us an ultimatum. They've said, that if we don't leave by seven tonight, they're going to come and waste us."

At that point, there was a huge roar of laughter, mainly from the Central and North chapter guys, and shouts of 'Ooh, how scared are we'. Indie raised his hand, and again, everyone fell silent.

"I've sent someone out to pass on my counter proposal, which is: if they don't lose their colours by 5 p.m. tonight then every single one of them will end up in the hospital or the fuckin morgue. So best you get prepared to go to war, coz no cunt'll tell us what we can or can't do, especially those pricks."

He didn't say anything else, he just about turned and headed back outside. Within minutes, we'd all followed suit.

Gunner got hold of Indie just outside the door and pointed to the four guys waiting outside and explained that they wanted to join us.

Indie went over to them and told them that it wasn't a good time. "Guys, come back tomorrow at four and we'll sort you out then, okay?" They just nodded then made their way back to their bikes.

By the time they'd left, we were all back outside and I began to wonder what the fuck was going to happen now. I was hoping that DD would come back and tell us that he'd sorted things out and that they wanted to talk rather than fight, but I knew, in my heart of hearts, that was probably the most unlikely outcome.

We were all sitting chatting and digesting what Indie had told us, but, if truth be told, I wasn't really paying that much attention to any of it. All the time they chatted, I was clock watching and looking out for DD to show up.

After yet another look at the clock, I realised that DD had been away for over an hour. During that time, we had another half a dozen guys arrive, asking to join us. Gunner told them all the same as Indie had the first lot: to come back tomorrow at four.

Another fifteen minutes went by before DD came back and I was relieved when I saw he had no obvious signs of a kicking. Which, if I was honest, surprised me. He walked straight past us, looking directly at Indie and went inside.

Indie, Hotwire, Jelly, Gunner and Brutis then got up and followed him in. Brutis was last and closed the door behind him, making sure no one else followed.

"What the fuck do you think's going on now, Shug?" Cowboy asked me. "I've no fuckin idea, man, but I'm not sure I like it," I told him.

Flick then suggested that DD must have sorted it out. "My guess is that if he hadn't sorted it then he'd be well fucked. The fact he's back without a mark makes me think the rest of them have backed off."

I liked Flick's logic and told him I hoped to fuck he was right. Gunner then opened the door and told us all to go back in. DD then came out and made his way back to his bike.

"Fuck me, it's turning into musical fuckin chairs," Cowboy said, loud enough that most people, including Gunner, heard him. We got to the door and Gunner said to Cowboy: "Don't worry, dick, this'll be the last time you need to move, so stop your fuckin moaning and get fuckin in."

At that point, I thought Cowboy was going to blow a fuckin gasket. As he prepared to square up to Gunner, Flick and I grabbed hold of him and pulled him away.

Flick told him to leave it and suggested he should sort it out later. I looked at Gunner and told him he was well out of order and that he needed to apologise to Cowboy.

He then said: "Like that's going to happen. Listen, Shug, if Cowboy wants to make a big thing about it then I'm more than happy to pick it up later."

"Fuck's sake, Gunner, you've no idea what you're getting into here. Let me give you a piece of advice: Don't bite off more than you can chew, because, believe me, if you start anything, you'll lose," I told him.

"That remains to be seen, Shug. Let's just wait and see how it all pans out," he told me, smiling like a fuckin Cheshire cat. I just shook my head.

It took all the strength we had between us to get Cowboy away from him. We dragged him inside and sat down. I was still thinking about what Gunner said.

"What a fuckin prick he's turned out to be, guys. My first impression was that he was sound, but looking at the way he's behaving now, I think he's a fuckin arsehole who deserves a good slap." Cowboy then said, staring at him: "Don't you fuckin worry about that, Shug. Whenever this is over, he's gettin it."

Just then, Indie banged the table with a glass, looking for a bit of hush. He then started to give us an update. "Seems we have a bit of a standoff, guys. DD has been to see the Prez of the Rippers and a few of the guys from other clubs. They've decided to join forces and want to talk to us. I've sent him back to tell them I'm happy to meet them as long as none of them's wearing colours. If they don't agree then we'll go back to our original plan."

Somebody then shouted: "Indie, where are you planning to meet them?"

"I've told them to come here. I want them to see what we've got here and make sure that they know we have the same again up the road. I'm pretty sure that'll make them think a bit," he told us.

"If they actually decide to show their faces then we'll have the meet in this room. I want every one of you to hear what's said. So if you go outside, make sure you get your arses in here when they arrive."

"How do you think it's going to play out, Cowboy?" "Shug, I don't give a fuck about it. I'm going to see that cunt, Gunner, just now and kick his fuckin cunt in," he told me.

Flick suggested he leave it until after the meet, but Cowboy was having none of it. Gunner was standing with six ex-Mutts and Cowboy marched straight up to him with me and Flick in hot pursuit.

Indie was standing just to the side of Gunner and his crew, talking with Brutis, Jelly and Hotwire.

Cowboy squared up to Gunner, "Who the fuck do you think you are, talking to me like that, ya fuckin prick? I want a fuckin apology now, or we're boxing," he told him.

Gunner looked straight at him and said: "I think we should take this outside, cunt, because it looks like we're boxing, you're getting fuck all apology from me, ya dick."

By this time, Indie had clocked what was going on and looked like he was going to break it up. But before he could intervene, Cowboy head butted Gunner and grabbed hold of him. He then pulled him onto the floor, landing a few punches on him as they fell.

Indie and Hotwire then got in between them and split them up. Gunner was screaming at them to let him go and Cowboy was urging them to do the same.

At that point, Indie intervened, stood between them, and told them both to get a grip, "Right, you pair of cunts, listen up, and listen fuckin good. This shit ends now, you'll shake hands. When were done here, you can sort this out properly, okay? Until then, you'll respect each other as brothers, got it?"

He then stared at both of them until they nodded in agreement. "Now shake fuckin hands and let it go." He stood back and Cowboy offered his hand to Gunner, who was bleeding quite badly from his nose.

Gunner shook his hand and told Cowboy that he would respect Indie's wishes, but that he needed to know it wasn't over. Cowboy's reply was to tell him he was glad and that he looked forward to finishing it.

They shook hands and Indie pushed them away from each other, telling them that they better make sure if anything does kick off later, that they would still have each other's back. Neither of them said anything. Gunner went outside with his guys and the three of us went back to where we were sitting.

"Fuck's sake, Cowboy. Why couldn't you just leave it until later, man?" Flick asked him. "Would you have fuckin left it, Flick? I don't fuckin think so. So why the fuck would you expect me to?" he ripped at him.

"Whoa, man, calm your jets," I told him. "You need to let it go for now. Think about what Indie said, you can get him later. Come on, Cowboy, have a beer and try to chill a bit, buddy."

Flick changed the subject back to the matter in hand, "How do you think DD's getting on this time, Shug?"

"No idea, Flick, but I wish he'd hurry the fuck up and get back so we can find out what the fuck's going on. What do you reckon's going to happen, Cowboy?" I asked him, trying to involve him in the conversation.

"No fuckin idea, but I'm guessing we'll find out soon enough, there's DD back now."

I turned around and saw DD making his way towards Indie. As he approached him, all eyes were fixed on them both and the place fell silent in the hope of hearing something. We all watched as they chatted. The conversation probably only lasted for a couple of minutes, but to us, it felt like an eternity. So, when Indie asked for a bit of quiet again, you could hear a pin drop.

"Listen up, guys, it seems the meetings on, they're on their way and will be here shortly. Remember, I don't want anyone saying or doing anything until the meetings over, okay? When they've fucked off, that's when we'll talk."

He then sat back down and carried on chatting to Hotwire and Jelly. DD went to the bar and picked up a beer. He looked over to our table, nodded, and went outside.

Flick then said: "Shug, he gave you the nod there, man, go and see what's going on." I told him I was going to see him anyway and that he should take it easy.

I headed outside and saw DD was standing with Gunner and his mates. I went and joined them, just in time to hear him say that seven people were coming for the meet and that it was all the guys who ran the smaller clubs, along with the Rippers' Prez.

One of the guys asked what the deal was, but DD said he'd no idea because when they were talking, he'd been out of earshot. "I never heard what the plan was, but they'll be here any minute so we'll all know soon enough," he explained.

DD then asked Gunner what had happened to him, pointing to the swelling on his face. Gunner told him it was nothing and that he would be fixing it later. DD then said to count him in. Gunner just smiled and they raised their fists, knocking knuckles together.

I interrupted, asking DD if I could talk to him and he broke from the group. As we walked towards the car park, DD asked me what was up. "Nothing's up with me, man," I told him. "When you were leaving the pub, after talking to Indie, you nodded and I thought you wanted to speak to me."

DD laughed a bit and told me he was just nodding to acknowledge me so I apologised to him for the mix-up. DD then asked what had happened to Gunner and I told him that he'd had a bit of a spat with Cowboy and that Indie had stepped in and that they'd agreed to leave it until later.

Just as we were heading back in, we heard the roar of bikes. We turned to see about twenty-five of them heading towards us. "Didn't you say there was only seven people coming, DD?" I asked him.

"Hey, Shug, I can only repeat what they told me, and that's what I was asked to pass on."

As they entered the car park, I noticed that they all had their colours on and mentioned it to DD. "Why the fuck are they wearing colours, man, any idea?" "I've not got a fuckin clue, Shug, they never had them on when I was speaking with them earlier, looks like they've decided to fight to keep them."

DD walked over to Freddie and asked him what the fuck he was playing at by wearing colours. "Listen, DD, just come in with us and you'll hear why," he told him.

DD got hold of him and ushered him away from the rest of the guys to speak to him. "Look, Freddie, I gave you the heads up earlier. If you don't ditch the patch then you'll get well and truly fucked, bro. Take it from me, these cunts don't mess about," he told him.

"DD, don't worry about it, man, it'll be fine. Come in and listen to our proposal, I'm sure they'll accept it," he told him, putting his arm around him and walking him towards the pub. "Fuck, Fred, for your sake, I really hope to fuck you know what the fuck you're doing!" he told him.

When we went in, I grabbed the first available seat and kept my eyes firmly fixed on Indie. As the guys poured in, I could see the rage building up in his eyes.

Once everybody was in, Ludo, the Prez of the Rippers, who Indie had blootered earlier, approached him and began to speak. Almost immediately, Indie interrupted him, asking him what the fuck he was playing at by coming there wearing Colours.

"If you give me a minute, I'll explain," he told him. "You've got five minutes, then the colours are off, one way or another," Indie growled at him.

Ludo then started talking: "The way I see it, there are roughly seventy guys spread out all over the city who are all in different clubs. We all had our own areas and pretty much kept to them which meant we never really had much aggro with each other. But because you've come here and given us an ultimatum, we've now got together properly for the first time. We all had a good chat and we've decided that it's us who should be dishing out the ultimatums, not you. So here's our deal: We're happy to patch over as Bats as long as there are another two chapters in the city. We'll take the south side, Freddie will take central, and the Mutts can keep the north. It means you get your way, but we still operate as we are now. The guys who don't want to join us will change their clubs to MCC's."

Indie looked a bit shell-shocked and took a minute before he replied: "Well, well, well, you seem to have it all worked out then, haven't you? Just one little fuckin thing you haven't thought about, I'm guessing: What if I don't like your fuckin proposal, then what?" he asked him.

"Well, that's where I think we both have a problem. Because if you don't like it then we're going to pull all our resources and start a rival club. We'll keep what's ours and take back the north of the city from you. So the way I see it, plan 'B' won't be good for any of us, what do you reckon?"

"What do I reckon? Well, what I reckon is that you're either fuckin insane or you've all got a fuckin death wish. You must have grown one gigantic pair of fuckin balls since we last met, coming in here, full of your fuckin bravado shit, and still wearing the fuckin colours I told you to lose, then proposing this shit to me. Suppose you explain to me what the fuck I get out of this grand plan of yours?" Indie then demanded to know.

"What you get is the city. You'll have another three chapters under you and full control of Scotland, so in a nutshell, you get exactly what you wanted in the first place," he told him.

Indie then growled at him and roared: "Listen, you fuckin retard, I already have the fuckin city. And there's no way you and this fuckin lot will be able to take it back. Deep down, I'm pretty sure you all already fuckin know that. I'll tell you what, though, I like the fact that you're all prepared to fight for it, but the way I see it is that you don't have a fuckin hope in hell of winning. So if you don't join us as one club then the kicking you got earlier will seem like a little bitch slap. Right, here's the deal: I want to talk to you, and the six guys from the other chapters you mentioned, in private. Oh, and take those fuckin colours off before I rip them from your back."

Indie then pointed to Brutis, Jelly, Gunner and Hotwire, gesturing for them to go with him, which they did. Ludo then had a chat with Freddie, after which they both removed their colours and followed Indie out into the corridor, with the guys from the other clubs quickly behind them.

They all disappeared into a small room off the hall and closed the door. At that point, everybody else turned their attention to the guys that had come in with them.

I watched the group as they huddled together, chatting away, and I got the impression that most of them would rather've been anywhere else but here.

DD, and a couple of the other ex-Mutts, went over and had a chat with them, although I wasn't sure if he was trying to reassure them or just there playing devil's advocate. I, however, turned my attention to the guys I was sitting with.

"Hey, Cowboy, what do you reckon Indie's saying to them in there?" I asked him. "Not too sure about this one, Shug, but my guess is that he'll be giving them a final ultimatum. I think he wanted to do it in private, to make sure they didn't lose face in front of their own guys."

I asked him if he thought they would agree to his terms and he told me he wasn't sure, but hoped to fuck they did, because he knew what Indie would do if they didn't.

They'd barely been out ten minutes when they all returned. Brutis, Gunner, Jelly and Hotwire sat down at the table, facing everybody. Ludo, Freddie and the rest, went and joined their guys, and Indie stood in front of us, raising his hand and whistling to get everyone's attention, the place went silent immediately.

Indie then began: "Right, we've reached an agreement which is suitable to all parties, and here's how it's going to work: There'll be one Bats chapter here, which will be the South chapter: Brutis will be the President, Gunner the VP, Rooster the SAA, Ludo Treasurer and Freddie the Secretary. These positions will all be reviewed within the next three months."

At that point, Cowboy leaned over and whispered to me, "I would've loved to have been a fly on the wall during that conversation, don't you think?"

"Don't think any of us needed to be there, Cowboy, I'm sure we can all imagine how it went," I suggested. He just nodded in my direction then smiled at me without saying anything else.

Indie continued speaking, telling everybody that the officers were now going to meet to discuss the patch over details, and that everybody wearing colours, other than Bats, should now ditch them.

A lot of the guys were looking to Ludo and Freddie, waiting to see if they were happy about them removing their colours, and they assured them they should, so the rest of the guys followed their lead and placed them on the table.

Indie then summoned the officers back to the small room and told the rest of us to get ourselves into party mode.

That seemed to lift the seriousness out of the situation and I noticed, almost straight away, that there was a fair bit of relief all around the room.

The prospects went to the bar and began placing trays of drink on the tables, then one of them collected a fiver from everyone. "Looks like Indie got his way after all," Flick announced, not speaking to anyone in particular.

"Hey, come on, guys, was there ever any doubt he wouldn't?" Cowboy remarked. I then said that I thought it was touch and go for a while and that's why he'd taken them into the other room.

Flick then came back with a different take on it, "I reckon he took them into the room and told them that if they didn't agree to his plan then he would fuckin waste the lot of them." "Yep, that sounds about right," Cowboy agreed, raising his glass.

"Did you hear Indie when he said that Rooster would be SAA?" I asked Cowboy. "I did, and thought that a bit strange myself, Shug. Rooster will be well pissed when he finds out," he replied. "I know, I agree," I told him. "He was already having doubts about coming, but accepted it knowing he was going to be VP."

Flick then chucked in his tuppence worth. "Tell you what, guys, now that Ludo and Freddie are in the frame he might even end up with fuck all at the end of the three months. I reckon Indie might give it to one of them as a bit of a sweetener."

"No fuckin chance, Flick," Cowboy interrupted. "Think about it, man, how could he give it to one and not the other? Surely that would be worse than giving it to none of them. My guess is that Rooster will be fine."

"Yeh, I guess you're right, man, that makes a bit of sense," Flick agreed. I then chucked a spanner in the works with my suggestion.

"You know what, guys? I'm not sure Rooster will take it. I reckon he may tell Indie to stick it up his arse, you know what he's like when he gets his gander up." "Good shout, Shug, never thought about that," Cowboy agreed.

"Anyway, guys, it's been a cunt of a day, let's just put it to the back of our minds and focus on getting fuckin pished," I suggested. Both Cowboy and Flick raised their glasses, smiling as they clinked them together, nodding in agreement. I then made my way to the bar for some refills.

We'd scooped another two or three before Indie and the guys returned to the main hall. This time, however, Indie never said a word and made his way straight to the bar.

Brutis stood in the centre of the room, flanked by Gunner, Ludo and Freddie. As people started to notice their arrival, the place fell silent again, with all eyes on the four of them.

Brutis began by telling us that the patch over would now commence, starting with the officers. He handed over the new cut-offs to the three of them, shaking their hands and giving them a bit of a hug each time they put them on.

Brutis then stood back and let Gunner do the honours with the rest of the guys. After he gave them their new colours and shook hands with them, he passed them down the line, making sure they all shook hands with the other three.

When they'd received their new colours, Brutis then told us all to raise our glasses for a toast to our new brothers, which we did, cheering and whistling as loudly as we could.

When the cheering stopped, most people started shaking hands and doing the man hug thing. By now, with the help of copious amounts of alcohol, most of the guys were laughing and joking with each other, and it seemed that there was no longer any tension in the room.

I was still keeping my eye on Indie, who seemed to have deliberately faded into the background. He was now sitting on his own, at a table next to the bar, but watching everything that was going on.

I nodded to him and he gestured for me to go over, which I did. "Hi, man, how are you doing? Is everything okay?" I asked him. "Yeh, pretty good, Shug, glad we've got all this shit sorted out. Just to let you know, I've told everyone, that until Rooster comes down, you'll be the acting SAA." Fuck, I nearly choked on my pint. "Fuck, are you serious, man?" I asked him, spluttering as I spoke. "What the fuck do you think? Would I joke about something like that?" he replied.

"Sorry, I just thought that someone else from down here would be doing it, after all the shit today." "Listen, Shug, I need somebody I can trust, and I reckon you'll do okay, but hey, if you're not up for it then best you tell me now and I'll get Cowboy to do it."

"No, no way, man. I'm well up for it. You know I'll do my best, Indie, and I won't let you down, that's a fuckin promise," I told him.

"I know you won't, Shug, coz you know what'll happen if you do," he told me. I wasn't really sure how to respond to that, but thankfully, I didn't need to, because he held his hand out for me to shake and told me he trusted me and that he'd already let the rest of the officers know I would be doing it.

Fuck, even before he'd asked me, he'd told them I'd do it! I began to wonder if anyone had ever said no to him, and if they had, what was the outcome?

"Indie, can I ask you something about Rooster?" "Course you can, Shug. Fire away." "Well, I just wondered if you'd spoken to him about all this? … coz we're tight, and I'd never do anything to fuck up our friendship."

"Oh, is that right! So you don't think fucking his EX might affect your 'tightness'?" Fuck, you could've knocked me down with a feather at that point. I jumped right on the defensive, telling him I had no idea where he got his info from, but wherever it came from, it was a lot of shite.

"Shug, listen, I have eyes and ears everywhere, you know that, so don't ever question my info. You should know by now that I never use it unless I can back it up, so get off your fuckin high horse and wind your fuckin neck in. I don't give a fuck who does what with who, as long as it doesn't come back to the Bats in any way, it's fuck all to do with me, so just make sure it never is. As for Rooster: I've already spoken to him about the VP position and he's cool with it, so don't you worry about that."

"Indie, can I ask you how the fuck you found out about me and Julie? We were very careful and we thought no one knew about us."

"Shug, I didn't know anything about it, I just had my suspicions, and you've now confirmed I was right, but I won't mention it to anybody unless it causes bother between the two of you."

I couldn't fuckin believe what he'd just done to me, what a fuckin idiot I was! If only I'd called his fuckin bluff, what a fuckin prick I was - now he had something on me! All of a sudden, I felt like I'd just shafted myself, and I knew, eventually, I would rue the day.

"Oh, by the way, Shug, I only agreed to let Rooster come down here because he wanted a few months to try and get Julie back, just thought I should mention that. You should also know that I've already agreed, that when he comes back, he'll take over as SAA."

Fuck me, all the time when I thought I was playing them: they were actually playing me. I felt sick to my stomach and wanted to punch him right in the mouth, but knew that would be the worst thing I could ever do.

I decided I'd heard enough and reminded Indie that I needed to be at the hospital for ten the next morning and wanted to know if I should come back here or head back up the road?

"Why the fuck would you want to go up the road? You're here for at least the next three fuckin months," he told me. "Okay, I just thought, after our chat, that I was maybe better going back up the road?" I suggested.

"Like fuck you are, you'll stay here with Rooster and sort out all your shit before you go anywhere," he told me, smiling. I swear to God I actually thought he was loving seeing me squirm - the cunt!

"So where are we all staying for the next three months then?" I asked, changing the subject. "Gunner has rented a four-bedroomed pad just down the road from here. I'm sure there'll be plenty room for the lot of you to crash there," he told me.

"That's cool, I'm glad we're all crashing together," I told him. I then asked him if I could nip out and get a look at it. "Yeh, I'm sure you can, see Gunner and he'll give you directions and a key," he told me.

I asked him when he was heading up the road, and he told me that he'd be leaving first thing in the morning and wanted to know why I was so interested in his departure time. I told him it was because I was leaving about nine and wondered if he'd still be here when I got back, but he said he wasn't sure.

I got hold of Gunner and got the key off him for the house. I asked him for directions and he told me to go out onto the road, turn left, walk fifty yards, and it was the white house at the end of the road.

Fuck, I knew Indie said it was close to the pub, but I never thought for a minute it would be this close. I headed out and went for a nosey at it.

It was the only detached house in the street and had a fairly sizable garage behind it. I opened the front door and had a look around.

It was fully furnished and looked like someone actually lived there. I opened the fridge and noticed it was full of food; I checked the cupboards and they were also well stocked. The rooms all had ornaments and stuff lying around. The wardrobes, however, were void of any clothing, which was the only clue in the whole place that no one lived there.

I headed back to the pub and grabbed a seat beside Cowboy and Flick, who were demanding to know where I'd been and what Indie had wanted me for. I told them it was all about the SAA post and that I'd been to see our new digs. I then asked them what I'd missed and was told I'd missed absolutely nothing according to them.

They spent the next ten minutes spearing the arse off me about the SAA position. I told them what I thought they wanted to hear and, eventually, they seemed satisfied.

We had a few beers, but they were almost treating it like a celebration; I did my best to get them to keep it low key.

We cracked a few jokes, then after an hour or so, I told them I was heading to bed. "Thought we were all crashing here tonight, Shug?" Cowboy asked.

"Aye we were, but if I have a bed rather than a floor to kip on then it's the bed for me," I told him. Flick agreed and told me he would head with me, so Cowboy also decided to follow suit.

As we were walking out, Gunner shouted over to us, directing his comments mainly at Cowboy. "Is that the girlies heading home now? Can't you stand the pace, Cowboy? Is it time for your cocoa? Remember, your mummy won't be there to tuck you in, best you get your pals to do it for you!" He then started laughing and smiling, with his mates all joining in.

He hadn't even finished when Cowboy made a beeline for him, jumping on him and knocking him to the ground. As the two of them began to scrap, some of Gunner's mates were putting the boot in, so that was enough for me and Flick to wade in too. Cowboy was getting the better of Gunner and was on top of him, punching away at his face. His mates seemed a bit shocked that Flick and I had got involved, and after a few punches and kicks, they didn't want to know and backed off.

Indie and Hotwire, along with Freddie and Brutis, broke up Cowboy and Gunner. Then Indie told them he wanted to speak to them outside. The three of them went out and Hotwire and Jelly stood at the door, preventing anyone else from following.

Flick and I watched as they all went out and I think we were both wondering what Indie was going to do. "Do you think Indie is going to call a 'Bat Battle'?" Flick asked me. "I'm not sure, but I think, if he was, then he wouldn't have taken them outside," I told him.

"Yeh, I guess you're right, Shug, maybe Indie's going to give the two of them a bit of a licking." "That sounds more like it, Flick, Indie's not in the best of moods, so that might be his preferred option."

I noticed, at that point, that there was a distinct split in the group. It seemed all the original Bats were hanging with us, and the newbies were all with Gunner's mates.

Looking about, I noticed there were little pockets of discussion going on all over the place, relating to what was going to happen next. I really hoped that Indie could sort it without it ending in a mass brawl.

The door opened and the three of them came back in. Gunner and Cowboy went to the bar and Indie raised his hand for some hush.

"We had a bit of a problem with two brothers and it's now been sorted, if anything kicks off from now on, we'll settle it with a 'Bat Battle'. Anyone who doesn't know how that goes can ask around." Indie then went to the bar, picked up his beer and sat at a table with Gunner and Cowboy.

I watched them closely; they appeared to be genuinely happy in each other's company. "What the fuck went on outside, Shug?" Flick asked.

"Beats me, Flick, but whatever it was, it certainly worked. I can't fuckin believe it. Look at them, they're like best fuckin buds. Five fuckin minutes ago, they were going to fuckin kill each other! Come on, Flick, let's go and grab Cowboy and see what the fuck went down."

"Okay, I'll go for a piss then get him on the way back," he told me. While he was away, Freddie came over and sat beside me. "Hey, Shug, gonnae tell me how the fuck Indie managed that?"

"Freddie, I have no fuckin idea, mate. I know Indie can be very persuasive, but how the fuck he managed to get them to kiss and make up, to this extent, is beyond me. Tell you what, Freddie, I'll ask Cowboy and you ask Gunner, we can swap stories later." "It's a deal, Shug. Eh, by the way, do you think they'll tell us the same story?"

"Not sure, Fred, but it'll be interesting to find out." "Okay, man, I'll catch you later," he said, clinking his glass to mine as he left.

Just as he left the table, I saw Flick coming back into the hall and making his way towards Cowboy. They had a bit of a chat then Flick came back to the table on his own.

"Well? What's the script, Flick? What did he say? Why didn't he come over with you? What did Indie say to them?" I was almost demanding him to give me all the answers at once.

"Whoa, Shug, relax, man. One thing at a time, for fuck's sake. He says he's not coming over coz Gunner and him are spending the night getting to know each other. I asked him what happened outside and he told me that Indie made them realise they should be mates, not enemies."

"What a lot of pish that is, I'm going to see him and find out what the fuck really happened outside."

"Shug, if I was you, I wouldn't. You know he'll tell us later. Come on, man, just let it go tonight, eh? Let's have a few more before we split and we can quiz him tomorrow."

'Awe, fuck me,' I thought, 'five minutes ago, I was heading to bed, now I'm going to be stuck here for the rest of the night'.

While I made my way to the bar, I thought about what Flick had said and knew he was making sense, so decided to leave it. As I waited to be served, I looked around at everyone and it seemed to me that all the tension from earlier had reduced a little and people had started mixing again.

I noticed a guy setting up a disco in the corner as I walked back to the table. I was just putting the drinks down when about twenty or thirty girls came flooding in.

Flick rubbed his hands and said: "Shug, there's no way we're leaving now. Things have just got a little bit more interesting. I'm for a ride at something before the night is over."

"You go for it, big stuff. I'm going to drink these then head, I need to be up sharp tomorrow." Flick said his goodbyes to me then made a beeline to one of the girls and walked her to the bar to get her a drink.

Most of the guys were doing the same: laying down their markers on the chicks they planned to fuck. I couldn't be arsed with it and started to think about seeing Julie again. I wondered how she would be with me and couldn't decide if we'd be shagging or fighting.

I got up to leave, shook a few hands, and hugged a couple of the guys who were a bit worse for wear, then left. I headed back to the house, went in, chose a room, and sat on the bed. I set the alarm, took off my jacket and boots and crashed out. It had been one cunt of a long day, and I just hoped the next day would go more smoothly.

Chapter 21

When the alarm went off, I got up and gave myself a bit of a wash then headed to the kitchen for a cuppa. I stuck the kettle on and started to wonder why I was the only one who chose to crash there. I'd expected to get woken up by a rake of the guys coming in during the night, still in party mode.

I was totally bemused why they'd chosen to sleep on the hard floor in the pub, rather than the comfort of the house, but hey, that was their choice and it meant that I'd had a good night's sleep without anyone disturbing me.

I made myself a cup of tea, sat my arse on the couch, and glanced at the clock. I had about ten minutes before I needed to leave, which was just about enough time to have a smoke and finish my tea.

I walked back to the pub car park for my bike and noticed everything was calm. I guessed that it must have ended up a very late night and that everyone was still zonked.

I had a look in the window and my suspicions were confirmed, not a single soul was up and about.

I pushed my bike out onto the road and freewheeled down the hill a bit before I fired it up. I rode through the town and out onto the motorway, the sun was shining and, thankfully, there was no sign of rain.

I pushed on a bit, to make sure I'd be early enough to get changed at Julie's pad; I'd decided that it would be best not to let Mrs Boardman see me in my colours. I made good time and arrived with plenty to spare.

I turned into the hospital and slowly drove through the grounds. The hospital was very quiet, with hardly a soul about. I made my way to the nurses home and parked up. I headed inside, feeling pretty good. I was looking forward to seeing Julie and could almost taste the new chapter in my life which I thought was about to begin.

I skipped up the stairs, two at a time, and almost ran along the corridor. I knocked on Julie's door, but never got an answer. I guessed she must be doing an early shift, so nipped down to Lisa's room and gave her door a knock.

She opened the door and looked a right state: her hair was standing on end and her makeup was all over the place. "Well, someone's had a late night," I suggested to her. As I walked in, I started laughing, telling her that I wished I'd been there.

"Fuck me, Lisa, look at the state of you, you must've been the life and soul last night, considering the nick you're in," I commented, sarcastically. But she never replied, she just closed the door and stared straight at me.

"Shug, you better sit down, I'm guessing you've not heard about Julie?" she said, turning and making her way back to her bed. I followed her in, sat beside her on the bed and then almost demanded her to tell me what was up with Julie.

"Shug, there's no easy way to tell you this, but Julie took an overdose yesterday morning, she's in a critical condition. The doctors don't know if she'll survive; she's in a coma and on a ventilator to help her breathe."

I couldn't believe what I'd just heard. I knew she was feeling pretty low, but never in a million years did I think she was suicidal. "Fuck me, Lisa, what happened? Why did she do it? Does anybody know? Did she say anything to you? Did you notice anything was wrong? Did she leave a note?" I said, bombarding Lisa with question after question, again, demanding answers.

"I've no idea what happened or why she did it. The night before, we had a few drinks at mine and she left to take a phone call and never came back. We just thought she wanted an early night because she was early shift the next day. When she didn't turn up for work, the ward phoned the warden. When the warden got no answer, she opened the door and found her lying on the floor, unconscious, with a couple of empty pill bottles beside her. She was taken to the general hospital straightaway, in one of our ambulances, but she's still not regained consciousness." Fuck, I could feel the tears welling up inside as I began to speak.

"Holy shit, Lisa, what the fuck would make her do something like that? Have you any idea? Did she say anything odd to you? Do you know who called her?"

"I never found out who called her and there's nothing I can think of that would make her do anything like this."

"I bet it was that bastard, Rooster, on the phone! This'll be his fuckin fault, I'm sure of it. I'll have him when I get back, the fuckin prick," I screamed. I told Lisa I had to go and see Mrs Boardman, then I would head straight to the hospital to see Julie.

She tried to get me to stay and talk for a minute, suggesting that it might not have been him on the phone, but I was having none of it.

I left without saying anything else, listening to her shouts in the background, but I was way too focused on Rooster to hear, or even care, what she was saying.

I jumped on my bike and went to the admin block, parked up and went to Mrs Boardman's office. I knocked the door and she shouted for me to go in. I explained that I would need to go and why. She told me she knew about Julie and was expecting me to say that, and for me not to worry.

"When you have time, come back and see me, I'll keep everything on hold until then. I hope everything goes okay for Julie," she told me. I thanked her then left.

I made my way to the hospital and found out which ward she was in then headed there to see her. When I got there, I was told that she could only have two visitors and that both her parents were already there.

I suggested to the nurse that I just wanted to see her for a minute, and would happily wait outside until one of her parents came out. She seemed okay with that and pointed me towards her room.

I got to the door and looked in the small window: her parents were at either side of her bed, both holding her hands. Her father saw me and came to the door straight away. He closed it behind him and asked me who I was and what I was doing there.

I told him I was a friend and that I'd just found out about her being in hospital, and that I wanted to see her. He then asked me if my name was Rooster? When I told him I was called Shug, he seemed a bit less agitated.

"You can go in and see her just now, I'll take her mother for a coffee. Promise me you'll stay with her until we get back, I don't want her left on her own."

I assured him I would wait as long as he wanted me to, and he thanked me before going back in to get his wife.

They both left and I went in. I sat at Julie's bedside and clasped her hand with mine. She looked so peaceful … it brought back memories of when my mum was in hospital. I chatted away to her, telling her what I'd been up to, and hoped for some kind of response, which never came.

The nurses came in and took some readings. She then checked Julie for any responses then left. I'd been blethering away for about half an hour before her parents came back. When they came in, I got up to leave, but her father told me not to rush away.

He asked me if I could tell him why I thought she would try to take her own life? I told him I had no idea. He then ushered me outside and told me he wanted to speak to me without his wife hearing.

"Look, I have no idea why she would do this. I was with her for a couple of days, just before it happened, and she seemed perfectly fine to me," I told him.

"Well, it seems that someone called her, then she went to her room and that's when she did it. Do you have any idea who called her?" he asked. I told him I had an idea, but that if I found out, I'd let him know. He then became very animated, almost begging me to tell him who I thought it may have been, so I told him.

I was so mad that I blurted out my thoughts to him, but in hindsight, I know I shouldn't have.

"I think it might have been a guy called Rooster. Julie used to go out with him. They were together for over a year or so, but I can't imagine how he could upset her enough for her to do something like this. I've known him for years and I know he loved her to bits," I lied to him.

He then asked me how he could get in touch with him and I told him that he wasn't on the phone, but if he gave me his number, I would give it to Rooster when I went back home. He wrote it on a piece of paper, thanked me, shook my hand, then went back into the room.

I looked at the number as I walked out, unsure what to do with it. I got outside, sat on a bench, lit up a fag, and tried to weigh up my options.

I finally decided I would phone the farm and speak to Rooster, to try and get him to tell me what he'd said to her on the phone, then tell him what had happened.

I made my way to the call box in the corridor at the end of the ward and dialled the farm. Angel answered the phone and wanted me to update her on what was going on. I told her I needed to speak to Rooster first, then I'd give her an update.

Within a minute, Rooster was there. "Hi, man, what's up, Shug? Everything okay your end or are you missing me?" he sarcastically asked me. "Yeh, things are going well here," I lied. "Just need to ask you something, Rooster," "Go for it, Shug," he said. "Can you tell me why you phoned Julie yesterday?"

"What the fuck do you want to know that for? And who told you I phoned her? Are you with her just now? Listen, what we talked about has got fuck all to do with you, let me speak to her if she's there," he roared at me.

"Listen, Rooster, it's got everything to do with me, because whatever you said to her caused her to try and fuckin top herself! If she dies: I'm holding you fully fuckin responsible for it!" I roared back.

There was a minute or so of silence, followed by him telling me that this better not be a fuckin wind up, then me reassuring him it was fuck all wind-up then silence again.

"Where's Julie now?" he asked. "Where the fuck do you think she is?" I screamed at him. "She's in the fuckin hospital, in a fuckin coma. Where the fuck do you think she'd be? And by the way, when I get a hold of you, you'll be fuckin joining her!" I screamed at him.

"Hey, Shug, you better just calm your fuckin jets, right now. I know you're upset, but don't you ever fuckin threaten me like that again, or I'll punch your cunt in," he roared at me.

"Listen, I have no fuckin idea why Julie would do something like that, but it's got fuck all to do with what we spoke about, that's for sure. We never argued, and she was perfectly happy when she hung up the phone. I'm leaving right now and I'll be at the hospital within the hour. If you're still pissed with me then, we'll sort it out after I've seen her," he told me.

I then let rip again, roaring at him, "Don't bother your fuckin arse coming here, you're not fuckin wanted. And for the record, the next time I see you, I won't be responsible for my actions."

"And neither the fuck will I," he screamed back, before slamming down the phone. I slammed it down at my end as well then went back to the bench and sat down. I fuckin knew it was him, he was the only cunt who could've upset her enough for her to do something like that.

I lit up another fag and replayed the call in my head, the reality of what I'd said was now starting to sink in.

'Fuck, I've just called Rooster out! What a prick! How could I be so fuckin stupid? Nothing surer, I'm going to end up getting fuckin wasted. Here's Julie, lying in hospital, fighting for her life and Rooster, blazing mad, heading here to probably end up putting me in beside her! And just to top that, I've promised Indie I'd stay here with the new chapter as acting SAA. Fuck's sake, Shug, well done AGAIN! You certainly know how to make a cunt of things, that's for sure.'

While I'd been on the phone, Julie's father had been standing just outside the ward door, talking to a doctor, and had heard me ranting at Rooster. He then followed me out.

He sat down beside me and asked if everything was okay. I told him I was fine, but that he should be aware that Rooster was on his way to see Julie and would be here shortly. "I'll just go and call the cops," he told me as he stood up. "Whoa, hold it a fuckin minute, why would you want to do that?" I asked him.

"Well, I'm not having him coming in to see Julie and I certainly wouldn't be able to stop him, so it would be best if the police were here when he arrives. That way, they can deal with it."

"Look, you can't call the pigs. I'll speak to him when he arrives and sort it out. I'm sure I can make him see sense," I lied to him.

"Well, on your own head be it, but you need to know, if he does try to get in, I'll ring them and I'll let them know all about the phone call as well."

"Listen, I spoke to him about it and he said Julie was fine with him on the phone, so it must have been something else that caused it," I tried to reassure him. He wasn't convinced, but did say he would leave it just now and play it by ear when Rooster arrived.

I thanked him and told him I would catch up with him later. I headed to the car park, wondering what I should do for the next hour or so, and tried to figure out how I was going to approach him when he got there.

I sat down beside my bike and lit up yet another fag. I then closed my eyes and tried to clear my head a bit. I mulled over the phone call yet again and decided the best way to approach Rooster was to tell him I was sorry for threatening him. Hopefully, from there, we could have a chat - rather than an argument and a boxing match!

I'd been sitting for about half an hour or so when I heard his bike. I stood up, waving to him to come towards me. He saw me and drew up alongside my bike. He got off his bike and removed his helmet. Straightaway, I held my hand out, apologising to him for my rant, which thankfully, he accepted.

He asked me how she was and I told him she was still unconscious. I then explained to him what her father had said and suggested it would be wise not to barge in.

I told him he would be able to see her through the window, and that there was no point in going into the room and upsetting them when he couldn't talk to her anyway.

He decided he would settle for that and would wait until she came round before he went in. I felt pretty relieved that he'd agreed, I can tell you that. As we made our way to the ward, I asked him why he'd called her and he told me he just wanted to see how she was.

"I asked her how she was. Straight away, she started screaming at me, telling me that she knew I didn't care about her and to stop pretending that I did. I then told her I did care for her and that I was really sorry about how we'd parted. She then went on another rant about how it was all my fault and that the Bats had brainwashed me, and shit like that. I let her finish and told her I agreed with everything she'd said, then there was a period of silence. I then asked her if I could see her, as I had a lot of things I needed to explain. At that point, she seemed a bit more relaxed. We then agreed to meet next weekend at hers, and I told her I was really looking forward to it, and she said she would see me then, before hanging up. When I put the phone down, I was well chuffed that she'd agreed to see me. Then, next thing, I've got you on the phone, ranting like a madman, threatening me and telling me she was in hospital. I couldn't fuckin believe it."

I, again, apologised to him for going off on one and he told me just to forget it. We arrived at the ward and I pointed out the room she was in. Her mother and father were still sitting at her bedside. When Rooster saw her, the tears started rolling down his cheeks.

We stood for about fifteen minutes before I suggested we should split and come back the next day. Rooster just nodded then we made our way back to the bikes. "Are you heading back or do you want to head down and see the guys?" I asked him.

"Yeh, take me down to seen them. I've got a message I need to give to Indie, anyway," he told me.

We fired up the bikes and headed out onto the dual carriageway. I led, with Rooster close behind. Within twenty minutes, we'd arrived at the pub and parked up. There was a fair scattering of bikes in the car park so I guessed most of the guys were still inside.

When we went in, some of the guys were still crashed out. Others were having a beer, and some of them were stuffing their faces. First to clock us were Cowboy and Flick. They let out a roar, gesturing for us to go and join them, which we did.

Cowboy asked Rooster how he was and what the fuck he was doing there. Rooster told him he was there to pass on a message to Indie. Flick headed to the bar to get us a drink and Rooster told me he'd be back later, after he'd spoken to Indie.

When he left, Cowboy asked me what the fuck was going on and I gave him a quick version of events and finished just as Flick came back with the drinks. I asked them what I'd missed and they both burst out laughing.

"What the fuck's so funny?" I demanded to know. Cowboy told me that he and Flick had a bet that the minute I came in, I'd want to know what I'd missed, and right on cue, I'd done just that.

Rooster came back over to the table, lifted his beer and took a long drink. He'd hardly put his glass back down when Flick asked him what the message he'd gave to Indie was about and he told him he would find out in two minutes.

Indie then shouted for everybody to listen up. Within a matter of seconds, everybody was eagerly waiting in anticipation for him to start talking.

"Right, guys, we've got a bit of a problem. I've just had word from the North chapter that they've been hit again by the fuckin Cannibals. For all of you new guys who don't know about them, they're a shower of wankers who've sprung up recently, thinking they can wipe us out and take over our patches. We thought they'd already got the message, but obviously, they haven't. So I want every single Bat here, tooled up and ready to go, in thirty minutes. They've no fuckin idea what's coming to them, we're going to finish this once and for all." He then called on all the officers, including me and Rooster, to join him for a bit of a pow-wow.

The four of us kind of looked at each other for a minute then I asked Rooster what the fuck had happened. He told me it was a bit of a long story and he would fill me in later. As we joined Indie at the table, the rest of the guys were getting their shit together.

We all sat down at Indie's table and I was surprised when I looked around and saw the South chapter's officers there. For some reason, I thought they'd be excluded, but hey, the more the merrier.

Indie told us all that we'd be heading back to the farm to collect the rest of the guys before heading up north. His plan was to stop at the Bats clubhouse, check out the situation there, then head on to the Cannibals place and totally wipe them out.

Someone from the South chapter asked him what he meant by 'totally wiping them out' and I bet he wished to fuck he'd kept his mouth shut. Indie growled and stared straight at him then let rip.

"For your information, and for anybody else that isn't clear, what I meant when I said it was: they'll be getting totally wiped out and will never be able to call themselves a club again, okay? Is that clear enough for you?"

We all then went and got ready to leave. I got hold of Rooster and asked him about Julie and my job.

"Rooster, fuck's sake, man, we can't just leave Julie, we need to be here for her. I'm supposed to see the people at the hospital about my job tomorrow. Don't you think we should speak to Indie and see if he'll let us give it a miss?" I asked him.

"Fuck's sake, Shug, you still don't get it, do you? Indie would rip you to fuckin pieces if you even suggested it. Best you keep your mouth shut and prepare to leave. We can pick everything else up when we're done."

I couldn't believe it. Here I was again, with no choice, I just had to do what I was told and lump it. Fuck, this was tearing me apart. By now, everybody had arrived back and I could see by their faces that a lot of the South guys weren't particularly happy about going either, but, like me, they never uttered a word.

Indie then fired up his bike, raised his arm, pointed forward, and headed off. The rest of us? Well, we just rolled out behind him, most of us deep in thought, all heading for the farm. I had no idea what we were going to do, or how long it would take, but I sure as hell knew that this trip was going to herald yet another chapter in my life - that I was probably going to regret!

THE END

Printed by Amazon Italia Logistica S.r.l.
Torrazza Piemonte (TO), Italy